The Unwelcome Warlock

The Unwelcome Warlock

A LEGEND OF ETHSHAR

Lawrence Watt-Evans

WILDSIDE PRESS

THE UNWELCOME WARLOCK

Published by Wildside Press LLC.
www.wildsidebooks.com

Dedicated to
John Betancourt
for his help in keeping Ethshar alive

Chapter One

Hanner the Warlock looked at the tapestry without really seeing it; that constant nagging whisper was distracting him. He closed his eyes for a moment to clear his thoughts, but that only seemed to make it worse. He clenched his jaw, shook his head, and balled his hands into fists.

"Is this not what you had in mind, Chairman?"

The wizard's voice brought Hanner back to reality for a moment. He opened his eyes and forced himself to focus on the tapestry.

The silky fabric hardly seemed to be there at all; the image woven into the cloth was so detailed, so perfect, that he seemed to be looking through the tapestry into a world beyond, rather than at the material itself. In that world gentle golden sunlight washed across a green hillside strewn with wild flowers beneath a clear blue sky above. In the distance he could make out a cluster of handsome golden-tan buildings, though details were vague.

"Does it work?" he asked.

The wizard beside him glanced at the tapestry. "It does," Arvagan said. "My apprentice tested it before I sent for you. The tapestry that can return you to Ethshar is hanging in that house there, on the right." He pointed, but was careful to keep his finger well back from the cloth — the slightest contact would trigger the tapestry's magic and pull him into that other world.

"The tapestry that comes out in the attic of Warlock House?"

"Precisely."

"These tapestries will both work for warlocks?"

The wizard hesitated. "I *think* so," he said at last. "You understand, without a warlock's cooperation we have no way of testing it. Divinations are unreliable where warlocks are concerned. We know *some* tapestries work for warlocks — in fact, we've never found one that doesn't — and I don't see any reason these wouldn't, but magic is tricky."

That brief hesitation had been enough for the Calling to once again start to work on Hanner. He had turned his head away from the tapestry as if to listen to the wizard's reply, but then the motion had continued, and now he was staring over the wizard's left shoulder, to the north, toward Aldagmor.

He needed to go there, and soon. He needed to forget about all this Council business, forget about the wizards and their tapestries, forget about schemes to avoid the Calling. He needed to forget about Mavi and their children, and about his sisters and his friends, and about the other members of the Council of Warlocks, and just *go*. Whatever was up there in Aldagmor, it needed him, and he needed to go to it…

"Chairman?"

Hanner bit his lip. What he *needed*, he told himself as he forced himself back to reality, was a refuge where he couldn't hear the Calling and couldn't feel its constant pull.

That was what these tapestries were supposed to provide. That was what he had paid the Wizards' Guild the insane sum of eight thousand rounds of gold to obtain, a fortune that had completely wiped out his own assets, and half the Council's money as well.

Not that money would matter to him in Aldagmor...

"I'm sorry," he said. "What were you saying?"

"I was saying that we do not actually know whether this tapestry will do what you wanted. We don't understand your magic, any more than you understand ours, and we have no way of testing how those two magics will interact, other than sending a warlock through the tapestry. We know that warlocks have used *other* tapestries safely, but wizardry can be...erratic. We can't promise what *this* tapestry will do until a warlock tries it."

"You haven't tested that?"

"Chairman Hanner, you specifically forbade us from telling any other warlock anything about this project. That was part of our contract, and we have abided by it."

"Of course," Hanner said. "I didn't want to get anyone's hopes up. So you don't know whether I will be able to hear the Calling from that other world?"

Arvagan sighed. "Chairman, we have no idea what the Calling is. We don't know how it works, or whether it extends into the new universe we created for you — assuming we did create it, and not just find it; we don't really know *that*. We know that you can breathe the air there, and drink the water, and that my apprentice suffered no ill effects from doing so. We know he chewed on a blade of grass and wasn't poisoned. We know that the village in the tapestry was uninhabited when he got there, though we can't say with any certainty whether its builders, if it *was* built, might still be around somewhere. We know he says that he walked three or four miles around the area without finding any people, or any animals larger than a rabbit, or any edge to the world he was in. But that's about it as far as our knowledge goes. We don't know whether warlockry will operate there. We don't know whether there are natives dwelling somewhere in that world. We don't even know how long the day is there — he didn't stay long enough to determine that. Creating or finding new worlds is an unpredictable business, Chairman; we told you that when we first agreed to this."

"You did," Hanner admitted.

This had been a tremendous gamble, paying the wizards to open a way to another world, and there was only one way to find out whether it had worked, or whether he had thrown away an immense fortune for nothing. All he had to do was reach out and touch the tapestry, step into it, and he would be in that other world, that beautiful refuge.

He started to raise his hand, then stopped.

"Not here," he said. "I might not…"

He didn't finish the sentence; when he realized what he had been going to say, he forced himself to stop.

He had been about to say he couldn't use the tapestry because it might cut him off from the Calling, but that was what he had wanted; that was the whole *point*. This tapestry was intended to let warlocks escape from the doom that eventually befell them all.

Every warlock knew that the farther he was from Aldagmor, the weaker the Calling was — and the weaker his magic was, as well, but that was only a secondary consideration. That weakening had given Hanner the idea to find, or make, a place so distant from Aldagmor than the Call couldn't reach it at all.

The Calling touched every corner of the World; warlocks had established that. From sun-baked Semma in the southeast to frozen Kerroa in the northwest, there was no place in the World where a warlock was safe. So, obviously, the warlocks needed a refuge that wasn't in the World at all, and that meant they needed wizardry. The only three kinds of magic that could reach out of the World into other places were demonology, theurgy, and wizardry — herbalism, witchcraft, ritual dance, and the rest were limited to everyday reality.

The gods didn't recognize warlocks as human beings, and had trouble even acknowledging their existence, so theurgy wasn't going to help. The Nethervoid, where demons originated, wasn't anywhere anyone would ever want to go, and trusting demons was usually a stupid thing to do, so demonology was out, too. That left wizardry. Wizards had various spells that could reach other planes of existence. It wasn't clear whether these spells opened a path to places that had existed all along, or created new places out of nothing, but they could definitely provide access to other worlds. Hanner had even visited one, long ago, and found that warlockry did not work there, and that presumably the Calling did not reach it.

So here it was, the wizardry he had asked for — a Transporting Tapestry to another world that just might be the refuge the warlocks needed.

It looked lovely, but that didn't mean much. Arvagan's apprentice had survived a visit there, so it couldn't be *too* hostile, but would it really be a decent place to live? Would it be a safe home for his wife and children?

He grimaced. He was assuming that Mavi would want to accompany him, but he had not actually asked her yet. He knew she was worried about the Call, but worried enough to give up her life in Ethshar of the Spices, the city that had always been her home? It wasn't as if *she* was in any danger; he had invited her to become a warlock, to have that little adjustment made that would let her draw magical power from the Source, but she had never done it. She was content to leave the magic to him and the other warlocks while she attended to more mundane matters.

But she loved him and wanted to be with him, so of course she would want to come with him. She wouldn't need to stay; she could go back and forth at will, while he would need to remain in that other place once the Calling became too strong.

That assumed, of course, that it wasn't just as strong on the other side of the tapestry. He really would need to try it out someday, when the Call reached a dangerous level — maybe after he got back from Aldagmor…

He closed his eyes and clenched his teeth and held his breath.

He was *not* going to Aldagmor. He was not going to give in. The Call was obviously already dangerous. It was always there, every second, day and night, nagging at him, working insidiously to draw him away. Every time he used even the slightest bit of warlockry, or took a single step to the north, it grew a little stronger. Simply facing south was becoming difficult; his head kept turning involuntarily, and his neck was getting sore from his struggle to resist. He was leaking magic, he knew that; small objects tended to levitate around him without any conscious effort on his part. He *needed* a refuge.

And now, just in time, he might have one. All he had to do was reach out…

But the wizards didn't know, didn't *really* know, whether it was safe, or whether it would work. He should go home and discuss it with his wife before he did anything more. He should go home, to Warlock House, on High Street, just a mile north of this secret room on Wizard Street.

A mile *north*. A mile closer to Aldagmor. He shuddered at the thought, and at the same time he felt a deep longing.

It was very bad. He wasn't going to be able to hold out much longer. He couldn't sleep anymore; when he did, he dreamed of fire and of being cast down from the heavens and buried deep in the earth of Aldagmor, he dreamed of a need to go there and help, and he always awoke to find himself moving northward. He hadn't dared to sleep at all for the last two nights, and he had made do with brief naps for a sixnight before that.

He just had to reach out and touch the tapestry, but he couldn't lift his hand. He was so tired, so weary of fighting the Call — not physically, no powerful warlock's body ever tired, but mentally. If he gave in he could rest. He could fly, any warlock worthy of the name could fly, he could be in Aldagmor in no more than a day or two. He had been refusing to fly at all for about a month, so that he would not fly off to Aldagmor, but now that just seemed foolish. Why not get it over with?

"Tell my wife I love her," he said. "Tell her to wait for me in the attic of Warlock House. If this works, I'll meet her there and let her know. If it doesn't, well…"

"Should we tell her any details? About the tapestries?"

Hanner shook his head. "No," he said. "I'll tell her. She knows I was planning something, and I want to be the one to tell her what it was." He paused, then added, "If it works. For all we know, the Call will be even stronger in there."

"I suppose it might be," Arvagan admitted. "Though I don't see why it would be. Wherever that place is, it's not Aldagmor."

"But it could be *near* Aldagmor, somehow."

"I suppose."

Hanner turned to Arvagan. "You'll tell her?"

"The instant I see you enter the tapestry, I'll send word for her to go to meet you."

"Good. Good." He turned back to face that shining image of green fields and tried to step toward it, but his foot would not lift.

Inspiration struck. "Arvagan, would you do me a favor?"

"What sort of a favor?"

"Would you move the tapestry to the north wall? Or just turn it so it faces south?"

"Is it that bad, Chairman?"

"Yes, it is," Hanner said. "I didn't know… It took so long…"

"We told you when we started that it took a year or more to make a Transporting Tapestry."

"Yes, you did — but I hadn't realized how close I was to being Called. A year ago it was nothing, just a little murmur in my head; now it's…it's everything, it's constant, it's so *strong*."

Arvagan nodded. Then he reached up and pushed at the rod supporting the tapestry, being careful not to let his hand come too close to the fabric. Like the sail of a ship clearing the breakwater, the tapestry swung slowly around.

Hanner turned with it, and when it was due north, between him and Aldagmor, he found he could lift his arm and step forward, step northward. His finger touched the silky cloth.

And the secret room was gone, the wizard's house was gone, Wizard Street and the Wizards' Quarter had vanished, the entire city of Ethshar of the Spices was gone. He was standing on a gentle, grassy slope sprinkled with white and gold flowers.

He didn't notice.

A sun was shining warmly on his face, a sun that wasn't quite the same color as the one he had seen every day in Ethshar, and a soft wind was blowing against his right cheek. He didn't notice that, either.

Sky and sun and wind and grass and flowers, a sound of splashing somewhere in the distance, a cluster of strange buildings — Hanner ignored them all.

He was too busy listening to the silence in his head.

The Call was *gone*. The constant nagging, the murmuring voice in his head, the wordless muttering that he had somehow been able to draw magic from, was gone. There was nothing in his head but *him*.

He hadn't experienced such total mental freedom since the Night of Madness, seventeen years before. Even before he had consciously noticed it, he had lived with the constant whisper of magic for so long that its absence was overwhelming. Now he simply stood, listening for it, for several minutes.

At first he didn't show any reaction; the change was too sudden, too complete, to comprehend. Then the rush of relief swept over him, and his knees gave way, and he tumbled onto the grass, trembling with the impact of his release from bondage — and trembling with terror as well. His magic was gone, and it had been central to his existence for so long that he barely knew who he was without it.

He lay on the grass for several minutes and gradually began to notice his surroundings — the sun, the breeze, the grassy slope. He tried to stand up.

It didn't work.

He took a moment to absorb that, and to realize that he had become so accustomed to levitating any time he stood up that trying to rise using only his own muscles was difficult, surprisingly difficult. He had forgotten how to do it.

He had tried to spring directly to his feet — or really, since of late he had usually hung in the air with his feet an inch or so off the ground, "to his feet" wasn't quite right. He had tried to fling himself upright, but without magic it hadn't worked. Now he rolled onto his back and pushed himself up into a sitting position, then set his feet on the ground, one by one. Then he stood up, leaning forward and straightening his legs.

That time it worked.

He stood for a moment, taking in his surroundings and his situation.

He had no magic. Wherever he was, he wasn't a warlock here; probably nobody would be. All the little things he had done magically he either had to do with his own muscles or not at all.

He was dismayed to realize how many of them there were. He had been using warlockry to stand up, to walk — or rather, to fly; he realized now he hadn't actually *walked* in months, even when he told himself he wasn't flying and tried to stay close to the ground. He had been summoning things to his hand, rather than reaching out to take them. Magic had infiltrated every part of his life. Now that his head was clear, he could remember any number of ways he had used magic — walking, lifting, cooking, cleaning, heating, cooling, playing with his children, even making love to his wife. He had done it all without thinking. Even when he had begun to feel the Call, when his dreams had become nightmares and the whisper in his head had become a constant nagging, and he had tried to stop using warlockry because it made him more susceptible, he had unconsciously continued doing all those little, everyday magics. The power *wanted* to be used, so he had used it. Only now that he *couldn't* use it did he realize he had been doing so. He was standing here on a grassy hillside, and his legs were supporting his entire weight, his skin was unprotected from sun and wind, and it felt *strange*.

He thought he could get used to it, though. After all, he hadn't been born a warlock; he had grown to adulthood without any magic. Most people managed just fine without warlockry.

He sniffed the air and caught the scent of the sea, or something very like it. He walked cautiously down toward the cluster of buildings that he could not help thinking of as a village, though he had no idea whether that was really an accurate description.

As he drew near, he decided that they were indeed houses and did indeed comprise a village. They were built of some hard, golden-brown material — stone or brick or dried mud, he couldn't tell which. There were many small windows and a few arched doorways. Arvagan had said that the builders might not be human, but the proportions looked right for humans; Hanner didn't see anything particularly odd about the houses.

Beyond the village, the land continued to fall away, and he could see the ocean, or something very like it, spreading out in the distance. A tree-lined stream gurgled its way past the village, which accounted for the splashing he had heard, and the leaves rustled in the gentle breeze.

It was very pleasant, really. Arvagan had said that he couldn't guarantee anything about this place, that there might be hidden dangers, anything from insidious poisons to rampaging monsters to distorted time, but to Hanner it looked calm and inviting. The stream would presumably provide water, and the land looked fit for growing food; there might be fish in the sea, or even clams to be dug along the shore.

Or if appearances were deceiving, and that somehow proved impossible, if the tapestries continued to work as promised, he could still have food and even water brought in from Ethshar. Unless there were some nasty surprises awaiting him, he had his refuge — a place where warlocks could come to escape the Calling.

He wandered around for what felt like an hour or so, exploring the houses. They were largely unfurnished, as if their intended inhabitants had never arrived, never brought their belongings.

That was fine. That was *perfect*.

The air was sweet, the sun was warm, and there was no Call. It was everything Hanner had wanted.

In the one house, just as Arvagan had said, was the other tapestry, the one depicting the attic of Warlock House, the mansion that had once belonged to Hanner's uncle, Lord Faran. That bare, dim room looked dismal compared to the bright sunlit refuge, but Hanner did not hesitate; he knew his wife was waiting for him there. Mavi and the children had been worried about him; this refuge would be a relief for them all, even if none of the others ever set foot in it. Hanner walked up to the tapestry, and put a hand and a foot out to touch it, eager to tell Mavi the good news.

He knew the Calling would return, but he assumed it would take a few seconds to reach its old force. He thought he was ready for it.

Then he was in the attic, back home in Ethshar of the Spices, and he was wrong. There was no delay at all. The Call was instantaneously a deafening, irresistible screaming in his head, and he had had no time to prepare, no chance to brace himself. After an hour of freedom, his resistance was gone, and he could not restore it quickly enough. There was one final instant of clarity, one glimpse of Mavi waiting, a glimpse of her staring at him as he appeared out of thin air, and then there was no room in his mind for any thought but the desperate need to get to Aldagmor as fast as he could, by any method he could. Nothing could be permitted to stand in his way, and with a wave of his hand he shattered the sloping ceiling, splitting the rafters and tearing wood and tile to shreds as he soared out into the sky. He could not spare so much as a second to tell his wife goodbye before flying northward.

He did not hear Mavi call his name, did not hear her burst into tears as he vanished. He did not see Arvagan's apprentice rush up the attic stairs to her side, to catch her before she collapsed.

By the time the apprentice brought Mavi to Arvagan's shop, Hanner was thirty leagues from the city. By the time word went out to the Council of Warlocks, Hanner was in Aldagmor. He could not tell them what had happened. He could not tell them that the refuge was a success, and only failed because he had been caught off-guard by the sudden instantaneous return of a Calling he had only barely been able to resist *before* he stepped through the tapestry. No one knew how very, very close he had been to giving in before he touched the fabric and was transported to that other reality.

All they knew was that Hanner, Chairman of the Council, had stepped through the Transporting Tapestry still able to fight the Call, and upon emerging had instantly flown off to Aldagmor.

There were some who theorized that the Call was somehow stronger on the other side of the tapestry, some who thought the magic of the tapestry itself somehow added to the Call's power, some who really didn't care about the details, but the Council as a whole agreed: The Chairman's attempt at creating a safe haven for high-level warlocks had failed.

The tapestry was rolled up and stored securely away — after all, it was bought and paid for, and belonged jointly to the Council and Hanner's widow Mavi, and perhaps someday some new spell or divination would allow them to use it safely. A new Chairman was elected.

And the Calling, that inexplicable melange of nightmares and compulsions, continued to snatch away any warlock who grew too powerful.

Chapter Two

The cold air rushed past Sensella's face, drying her eyes and chilling her skin, but was not enough to distract her from her ferocious *need* to reach Aldagmor — or rather, a specific place in Aldagmor; she knew she was probably somewhere in Aldagmor now, but she still had a league or two to go. Nothing else mattered — not the cold, not the dark, not the family she had left behind. She knew her children and grandchildren would be upset that she was gone, that she had flown off in the middle of the night, but that wasn't as important as getting to the thing in Aldagmor, to whatever it was that was calling her. Her magic didn't matter, other than in helping her get there; if it were to suddenly vanish and she survived the fall, she knew she would just get to her feet and walk, or better yet, run, to answer the Call.

She had left before dawn, flown the day through, and now the sun had been below the horizon for more than an hour, but she would not be traveling much longer. Dark forests rolled past beneath her feet as she flew through the night sky, stars twinkled overhead, and she knew she was getting close. That was so important, so urgent, that she was barely aware of her surroundings —

Until the sky above her lit up in a blaze of light and color that flashed in an instant from red through orange to yellow, and then turned impossibly white, lighting the World so brightly that everything was washed out, every shadow banished.

And while the Call did not stop, it was suddenly overwhelmed by a wave of reassurance, of comfort. The Calling was wordless, but put into words it would say more or less, "Come to me." This new message, equally wordless and far more powerful, answered, "*We have come.*"

But it wasn't speaking to *her*.

Sensella slowed in her flight, and blinked, trying to understand what was happening.

The landscape ahead was lit with that strange, intensely white light that leached the color from everything. It was fading somewhat, not as bright as it had been, but it was still more than enough to see. There was a valley, there were forested mountains on the far side. It was uninhabited wilderness — no roads, no houses, no farms.

But in the middle of the valley was a mound, a strange dark mound directly ahead of her; Sensella could not make it out clearly. It was not overgrown with trees or grasses, like a natural hill, nor was it bare stone or earth. It was made up of hundreds or thousands of objects piled one upon another, but in the eerie whiteness Sensella could not judge their size, or discern their colors.

The source of that unnatural light hung directly above the mound, and was descending slowly toward it.

The Calling, she realized, came from the mound. *This* was what she had come to Aldagmor to find. This was the source of the warlocks' magic. She could feel the power surging through her. Until just a moment before she had been unaware of it, unable to use it for anything but flying closer, but now the spell was — not broken, but countered, by that gigantic *thing* that was slowly sinking down from the heavens.

She looked up, trying to see through the glare, and her brain refused to resolve what her eyes saw into a comprehensible shape. There was *something* coming down from the sky, something the size of a small city, something that glowed as brightly as the sun, but in a different spectrum, and Sensella could not make herself see it. She thought it was more or less round, and at least twice as wide as it was tall, but beyond that she could not make sense of it.

That overwhelming message of reassurance came from the thing in the sky, just as the Call's demand for aid came from the mound — or from something beneath the mound. The thing in the sky had come in response to the Call, just as she had herself; she knew it. She could not have explained how she knew it, any more than she could have said exactly what the Calling had been whispering to her all these years, but she did know it, completely and irrefutably.

Sensella had slowed in her flight, but not stopped; she was still approaching the mound, and now, as her eyes adjusted to the glare and her mind to the alienness of what she was seeing, she realized what the objects composing the mound were.

They were people. Hundreds of people, packed face-down into an immense pile. Most of them were dressed in black — warlock black.

Shocked, she stopped in mid-air. She hung about sixty feet off the ground, staring at that great heap of humanity.

She could not hear anything. The Call and the Response made no actual sound, but they drowned out everything else all the same, filling the part of her brain that might otherwise have reacted to what her ears detected. She could smell nothing but the cool night air of the forested hills of Aldagmor. She could see the mound, but the strange light made it hard to know exactly what she was seeing, and she could not tell whether the people stacked up before her were breathing, whether they were alive or dead. Certainly, they weren't *moving*.

The idea that she was looking at a gigantic pile of corpses horrified her, and she reached out with her magic, with that awareness of location and movement that was a part of a warlock's supernatural abilities. She tried to sense the people she saw, to tell whether they were dead or alive.

She couldn't. Something stopped her perceptions.

It wasn't just that they were dead; warlockry could sense a dead body perfectly well. No, something was blocking her magic.

She looked up at the glowing thing. It was still descending. If it didn't stop, it would land upon that mound and crush all those people.

"No!" she shouted. She moved forward again, descending, and landed running. It was only when her feet hit the dew-covered knee-high grass that she realized she was barefoot; she had risen from her bed in the middle of the night, and had been drawn away by the Calling in her nightgown, without shoes or a coat.

That didn't matter, though. She had to get to that mound. She had to help. Somewhere deep in her mind, she knew that she was confusing different urges, that she was combining the Call's demand to come to this place with her desire to help those poor helpless people, but right now it didn't matter; they both drove her toward that mound.

To her surprise, she reached it before the descending monstrosity did — she had misjudged either the thing's speed, or its size. She stopped just short of the mound, despite the relentless Calling that still tugged at her; she forced herself to stop, to look at the situation. The Response had drowned out enough of the Call to let her think, to allow her to remember that no Called warlock had ever returned, and she looked at the great pile in front of her and guessed that if she touched it she would be pulled in, never to escape. She was inches away from the motionless back of a gray-haired man in a black tunic, she saw, and to one side of him stood a white-haired woman, and beyond that a black-haired man; to the other side were more, wearing the black garb of warlocks, or assorted nightclothes, or in some cases nothing at all.

Looking between the shoulders of this front layer, she could see more people, jammed together skin to skin, and stacked atop the people at ground level were others, standing or kneeling on shoulders and heads, leaning forward. The entire mound seemed to be a great mass of people, piled together too tightly to move or breathe, all utterly still, completely unmoving. She heard no movement, no breathing, no heartbeats — yet they did not *look* dead. Her warlock perception could not detect anything at all; it was as if the World ended a step in front of her. The surrounding hills and forests, the grass beneath her feet, the air around her and the earth upon which she stood were all their normal, natural selves, composed of a myriad of tiny particles and subtle forces moving and interacting in ways that she, as a warlock, could sense but not explain, but the pile of people in front of her was just...*blank*.

She let her gaze move up, past the head of the man in front of her, past the woman sprawled above him, to where the stars and moons should have been, to where the mysterious, incomprehensible *thing* was instead. If that monstrosity did come down to crush the mound, she realized, she wouldn't be able to get out from underneath it in time; it filled the entire sky above her, a gently-glowing immensity she still could not bring into focus.

But then the descent stopped, and something protruded from the hovering mass, reaching down toward the mound of people. Something shimmered, and something moved, and she sensed thumping and rustling — sensed it more than heard it, though she realized that her hearing was beginning to adjust to the overwhelming presence of the Response. She stepped back — and even as she did, she marveled that she *could* step back, away from the source of the Calling.

She knew she should be terrified, should be *mad* with terror, being here and seeing these things — that gigantic thing in the sky, the huge pile of what could only be Called warlocks that were neither alive nor dead, these displays of magic completely outside human understanding — but somehow she was not. The Response, even though it was very clearly not directed at anything human, was so reassuring that it calmed her and let her watch everything with a certain detachment.

Then the first body rolled down the mound and thumped onto the ground a few feet away.

She started, and turned to find a middle-aged man lying on his back in the grass, looking dazed. She turned to help him. "Are you all right?" she asked, as she reached for his hand.

His gaze was fixed on the thing in the sky, and he did not take her hand. She was unsure he had even heard her. "What *is* that?" he asked.

"I don't know," she said. "Can you sit up?"

He finally turned his head enough to see her, and her outstretched hand. "Am I dead?" he asked.

"I don't think so," Sensella replied. "But if you don't move, that may not last."

"But I —"

He was interrupted by the thump of another body hitting the ground.

"Come *on*," Sensella said. "I don't think we should stay here!"

He finally took her hand and allowed her to help him to his feet, just as an elderly woman fell to the ground a dozen feet away.

"What's going on?" the man demanded. "Where are we?"

"We're in Aldagmor," Sensella told him. "But I don't know what's happening."

"That thing," the man said. "Who is it talking to?"

Sensella glanced up. "Then you hear it, too?"

"Of course I do! How could I not? It's deafening!" He turned and looked at the mound. "And...the Calling? I answered the Call?"

"So did I," Sensella said. "I think they all did."

"Was I in there?" The expression on his face worried Sensella; it seemed not so much the apprehension or revulsion she would have expected, but eager longing.

More people were tumbling down the sides of the mound, falling onto the grass; a few cried out in pain and surprise as they hit the ground. Then one of them, a woman Sensella thought looked about thirty, caught herself halfway down and flew to one side.

As if that reminded the others that they were warlocks, several people took to the air; suddenly curious, Sensella did the same, lifting herself up, leaving the confused man behind.

Her magic worked as well as ever — better, in fact. She shot upward with astonishing ease and had to catch herself before she slammed into the underside of the gigantic glowing object.

Once airborne, she had a clearer view of what was going on. A long, thin, grayish-white projection of some sort, vaguely tubular, was reaching down from the hovering thing and pushing down into the mound of people, pulling some of them out and heaving them aside, where they tumbled down to the ground — or if they reacted in time, caught themselves before they fell that far. Some of them, Sensella saw, then flung themselves back against the mound, trying to get back into it. She couldn't tell whether any of them succeeded.

Most of them, though, were able to resist the Calling, as Sensella could, now that the Response had come. They were flying about the scene in a cloud of warlocks, like gnats around a lantern, looking at the mound and at the thing blotting out the sky.

"*It* was Called, too!" someone exclaimed, pointing up.

"Listen to it," someone else replied. "That's what was being Called all along! Whatever's down there didn't want *us*, it wanted *that*!"

"We just got caught up by accident?"

"But what *is* it?"

Dozens of people were talking at once now, in a dozen languages, and Sensella could no longer follow it all. She ignored the other warlocks and tried to understand what was happening.

The pile, she knew, was made up of warlocks who had answered the Call, and the only reason she had not plunged right into it and become part of it, trapped in whatever spell held it together, was that the Response, as she thought of it — the voiceless message of comfort that came from that gargantuan flying thing that had come down out of the sky — had drowned out the Calling and let her think again.

The Calling came from *beneath* the pile of warlocks, she was sure, and whatever was down there was protected by a spell of some kind, a spell that had frozen the warlocks when they got too close, a spell that had made them imperceptible to her own magic. It was probably a defensive spell, a magical barrier, guarding the Call's source until the thing it was Calling came for it.

But now the Response *had* come, more than thirty years after the Calling began, and it was digging through the trapped warlocks to get at whatever was down there.

It had been Calling warlocks for all those years; that was a *lot* of warlocks. Thousands of them, surely! Already, dozens of people were flying around, and most of the mound was still untouched.

But it couldn't be *all* the Called warlocks, could it? Could there be people who had been trapped in there since the Night of Madness, back in 5202? That was thirty-four years ago! Sensella herself had been a baker's apprentice, fifteen years old, the night she woke up screaming, hanging in mid-air above her bed, suddenly aware of every motion in the room around her, her mind filled with images of fire and falling. Hundreds of people, maybe thousands, had vanished that night — they had flown off to Aldagmor, never to return. Ever since then any warlock who grew careless, who used too much magic and made himself too receptive to the Calling, had eventually been drawn away — just as she had herself, less than a day ago.

"Aunt Kallia?"

Sensella turned to see a man she judged to be in his late thirties staring at a young woman. Both were flying above the mound, and their almost random flight had brought them near one another, and near Sensella as well.

The woman turned to look at the man. "Do I know you?" she asked.

"I'm Chanden! Your nephew Chanden! Luralla's son!"

The woman blinked at him. "But Chanden's just a boy!"

"I was on the Night of Madness, when you vanished, but that was more than twenty years ago."

"Thirty-four," Sensella interjected.

The young woman looked confused. "I don't understand," she said.

"Thirty-four?" Chanden turned to Sensella. "How do you know?"

"I wasn't in there," Sensella said, pointing down at the pile of humanity. "I was just arriving when...when *that* appeared." She pointed up.

"So — so it's 5236? I'm eight years in the future?"

"It's 5236, yes. Were you in there for eight years?"

"I...I suppose I was." He looked down. "It doesn't *feel* like it. I was...I answered the Call, and I flew here, and I saw that, and I didn't understand what it was, but I knew I had to get in there, so I flew down to it, and then — then I was thrown back out, and that thing was up there saying everything was all right now, and…" His voice trailed off.

"If it was 5228 when you came, then it's been eight years."

"It didn't even feel like eight *minutes*."

"Magic," Sensella told him. "*Strong* magic."

He looked up. "Yes," he said. "It must be."

"Your aunt," Sensella asked. "She disappeared on the Night of Madness?"

"Yes."

"And that's her? She's out now?"

"Yes! It flung her out just now. I saw it, and I recognized her, but she doesn't know me…"

"It's dug down to the first warlocks, then?"

Chanden turned. "Oh. I guess it has, yes."

Sensella was not sure why, but that troubled her. The Response, whatever it was, must be almost down to the source of the Call. She looked down and was suddenly aware that she was standing on nothing, perhaps a hundred feet up.

She had done that dozens, maybe hundreds of times since the Night of Madness. She had flown for miles without feeling any worry, but now it troubled her. She swooped down, eager to get back on solid ground. She landed perhaps fifty feet from the mound and turned — just as the next big change came.

The first had been when the flying thing had appeared out of nowhere and she had felt the Response; the second had been when it started burrowing down into the mound, flinging warlocks aside.

And the third was when the spell holding the immense mound of people together suddenly stopped.

The change was abrupt, completely unheralded — one instant the pile of people was motionless, undetectable to warlock senses, magically frozen in time, and the next instant they were awake and aware of their surroundings, aware of being trapped in a gigantic three-dimensional mob. They were writhing and screaming, spilling outward in all directions, trying to get out before they were smothered or crushed.

"It's all right!" Sensella shouted, using her magic to snatch the nearest person out of the seething mass. "You're safe! Just use your magic!" She pulled a second person free, and a third, dropping them unceremoniously on the grass a few yards away from the suddenly-expanding ball of screaming, crying warlocks.

The mound collapsed and vanished, and still people came spilling out, flying, running, walking, jumping, or crawling. The mound was gone, and in its place was a pit, and the pit was jammed full of people.

Sensella was not the only one helping; dozens of other warlocks were calling reassurances and pulling panicky people to safety. The crowd surrounding the pit extended for a hundred yards in every direction and was still expanding, and hundreds or even thousands of warlocks were flying above, as well.

Sensella looked up at the swarm of warlocks with an inexplicable sense of foreboding. She didn't know why, but she was absolutely certain this was a bad time to be flying. "Get down!" she called. "It's not safe up there!"

Still more people were clambering or flying out of the pit. Sensella could not see it through the crowd anymore, but she could sense it magically now, and she knew it was deep, very deep — the people at the bottom *needed* their magic to get out.

Thank the gods that only warlocks heard the Call; every one here *had* the magic they needed to escape.

Some of them, though, might not know it — if they had been among the very first, drawn away on the Night of Madness, they might have no idea how to control their power, how to use their warlockry to do anything other than answer the Call. Sensella was no longer close enough to be heard, or to reach anyone in the pit with her own magic when there was so much other power seething in the air, but she could sense that others were helping. The pit was mostly empty now.

Then the fourth change came.

The Calling stopped. With staggering abruptness, the constant demand, the need to come to this place that had filled every head, was simply gone.

And with that, the warlocks' magic vanished.

Chapter Three

Hanner awoke suddenly to find himself trapped in a mass of humanity, pressed in on all sides by other people. Instinctively, he pushed out with his magic, trying to clear himself a little breathing room, only to find himself pushed *in* on every side by magic as strong as his own.

He could still hear the Calling, summoning him forward, but the people ahead of him were packed too tightly to move. Maybe if he went around, he thought — around, or over. He tried to move himself upward, and was able burst free. He was still in the midst of a crowd, but no longer in danger of being crushed.

The Call wanted him to come to it, but there was something else, something new, coming from somewhere overhead, something that let him know the Call was already answered. He tried to make sense of that.When he looked up, he could see only a swarm of flying warlocks against a glowing background, a background that he could not see properly even when there was no one in the way.

What was going *on*?

He was vaguely aware of screaming, of human voices calling on all sides.

What *was* going on? He tried to remember how he had gotten here, wherever "here" was. He had been in Arvagan's shop; he had looked over the tapestry he had ordered, and then he had stepped through it into the refuge, and the Calling had stopped. He had looked around, taken a leisurely stroll on legs he hadn't used properly for years, and then he had stepped back out, into the attic of Warlock House —

And the Calling had caught him off-guard, and he had flown away to Aldagmor. He had a vague memory of soaring over the city wall and out past the trade villages and farm markets, past farms and across the Great River, over more farms, and grassland, and forest, and hills, and then he had come swooping down, and there had been something ahead of him, but he didn't bother to look, and…and here he was.

What *happened*?

In all the hours he had spent trying to imagine what the source of the Calling might be, he had never pictured being packed in a great mass of people, like seeds in a pod. Had the *people* somehow generated the magical summons? But that didn't match the images everyone had seen on the Night of Madness, or in their dreams once they began to feel the Call.

He needed to get clear, to see what was happening. Ordinarily he would have gone up, but that great glowing thing that filled the sky worried him. Instead, he veered sideways.

That glowing thing — was *that* the source of the Calling, the source of warlockry?

No, he could sense that it wasn't. The Calling came from below; the answer to it came from the glowing thing. He flew sideways, slipping through narrow gaps in the tangle of limbs around him, looking for clear air.

And then the Call stopped, and his magic disappeared, and he found himself falling. He stretched out his arms to catch himself, and collided with a woman, but she was falling, too; he bounced from her to someone else, and then to other people, but they were *all* falling, they had *all* lost their magic.

He landed heavily on a pile of bodies, and someone else immediately landed on top of him, knocking the breath from his lungs. Hanner flung up his hands to shield his head.

The Calling was gone, just as it had been in the refuge the wizards had made for him. Could something have transported them all into another world?

People were still screaming, and he could feel the people around him writhing and struggling to get free of the immense heap of fallen bodies, but the volume of sound was less now — Hanner no longer heard or felt the thump of more people landing atop him.

But then there was a *new* sound, and a vibration, a shaking, like nothing he had ever felt before. He tried to turn, to see what was happening, and someone slid aside just in time to give him a view of the sky, and of that huge glowing thing that hung above them all. Thus he saw the *other* thing as it rose up from below, pulled up out of the ground by its airborne companion.

He recognized it. He had seen it in his dreams, and especially in his nightmares, for years, though he could never have described it or put a name to it. This was the thing that had fallen out of the sky on the Night of Madness, the thing that had plunged, fiery and screaming, down into the earth, blasting a great pit into the heart of Aldagmor. The pit had fallen in on it, the fire had damaged it, and it had been trapped there.

It had called for help. It had sent out a magical shout that kept repeating endlessly. Hanner knew that — he had been Called, and now that the Calling had stopped and he could think clearly again, he understood what he had heard. It had never been clear so long as he was able to resist its pull, but once he had come here and heard it clearly, close up, he understood, even though the message had not been in words, nor even really in human concepts. He was able to interpret it, translate it into images and ideas he understood; they might not be *exactly* right, but they were close.

The thing had called for help, and because it was not from the World, not from this entire universe, it had needed to call so very loudly that its call resonated in certain human minds. Some of those humans had immediately obeyed, their will overwhelmed by the demand that whoever heard the Call must come and help; others had been able to take the sheer *power* of the Call and shape it with their own will, using it to perform magic.

But the more they had used that power, the more they had become attuned to it, until at last they received the message and had to obey.

The message wasn't *meant* for humans, though, and humans could do nothing to help the trapped thing. Instead, they ran into the defenses it had set up to protect itself while it waited. The thing had not wanted to stay awake down there, trapped, frightened, and alone, until rescue came; it had cast a protective spell, put itself into a timeless, dreamless sleep, and anything that came too close to it was trapped in the same spell, frozen into unconsciousness and immobility.

Now help had finally come, the help it had been calling for all along. The protective spell was broken, and the signal the trapped creature had been sending had stopped.

What's more, it was no longer trapped; its rescuer had pulled it free, scattering the warlocks that had covered it in all directions. As Hanner watched, the thing that had been the source of all warlockry was pulled up to join its rescuer, and then both of them rose, ascending and accelerating, until they dwindled amid the stars.

Behind them, strewn across this valley in southeastern Aldagmor, they left thousands of people who had once been warlocks.

Hanner watched the two monstrous things vanish, then realized he was kneeling on somebody. His first instinctive response was to try to fly, to get off whoever it was, but of course he couldn't — the Call had ended, and the source of warlockry was gone.

The warlocks remained, though, and Hanner could hear them calling, groaning, and crying on all sides. He turned, and tried to see where he was, where the shortest route to the ground might be.

"This way!" someone called — a woman, not a voice he recognized. "There's room over here!"

Hanner scrambled in the direction of the voice, mumbling, "Excuse me, I'm sorry, please, I'm sorry," as he clambered over the bodies of his fallen comrades, many of whom were now trying to free themselves, as well.

So far every body he had put a hand or foot or knee on had felt warm and alive, but Hanner was beginning to realize that some people must have died, must have dashed their brains out or broken their necks when they hit the ground, or been smothered or crushed by the people on top of them. There were hundreds of people here; he couldn't tell how many, really, but from what he saw and heard it had to be at *least* hundreds.

There might be more deaths to come, as well. As he moved out of the press of bodies he could feel the night air, and it was cold, cold enough, Hanner thought, for unprotected people to die of exposure.

They were somewhere in Aldagmor, in a valley in the mountains of Sardiron; how cold did it get here? What time of year was it? He had been Called in early summer, and this was definitely not early summer. He looked up, but all he could tell from that was that it was night. The greater moon was a half-circle in the western sky, but other than providing a little light that didn't help.

He couldn't really see much of anything in the dimness; his eyes had not yet adjusted after the glowing thing's departure. He was crawling on all fours, finding his way by feel more than by sight, and his left hand finally came down not on cloth or flesh, but on cold, damp grass — not the soft grass of a lawn, but the rough, scratchy grass of the wilderness. He pulled himself onto it, then got to his feet and looked around.

He was surrounded by shadowy forms — people were standing, or kneeling, or crawling on all sides. He wished he could hold up his hand and make light, as he had so often in the past, but his magic was gone. It had vanished with the Calling, and the source had flown away, gone forever. The World had once again changed suddenly, without warning, just as it had on the Night of Madness, when warlockry had first come into being, and just as it had then, the change had brought chaos.

Someone needed to take charge here. If no one brought some order out of this chaos, more people would die needlessly.

"*Hai!*" he shouted. "I am Hanner, Chairman of the Council of Warlocks! If you're unhurt, please get to clear ground and stand up, and then help those who aren't so fortunate!" He glanced around. "Does anyone have a tinderbox, by any chance, or some other way to make a light?"

This was greeted by a chorus of questions. "Hanner?"

"Who?"

"*Lord* Hanner?"

Hanner grimaced; at least some of them recognized his name.

Someone behind him, a woman, shouted, "Listen to him! If you can give us light, do it! If you can't, help spread everyone out — there are still people in danger of being crushed!" Hanner thought it was the same woman who had called out a few moments earlier directing people. He looked about, trying to spot her, and at the same time he tried to direct people away from the central pit, out to safer, more open areas.

"This way!" he called.

Then, at last, a light flared up. For an instant Hanner wondered why it had taken so long, but then he realized — these were *warlocks. Powerful* warlocks, strong enough to be Called. Up until a few minutes ago, they hadn't needed flint and steel to make fire; they had magic that could set an entire house ablaze in an instant.

That realization left him wondering why anyone *did* have a tinder-box; he peered toward the light.

The man holding a torch was no one Hanner recognized; he was not dressed in traditional warlock black, but in the yellow tunic and red kilt of a guardsman. Hanner briefly wondered whether the Hegemony had sent guardsmen to Aldagmor, but then dismissed the idea — Aldagmor was one of the Baronies of Sardiron, outside the Hegemony entirely, and any guards sent here who got this close would have been Called.

But there was one obvious explanation — this man must have been Called on the Night of Madness, seventeen years ago!

But…was it seventeen years? Or was it more? Hanner knew that he had been Called in Longdays of 5219, but he didn't know how long he had been trapped by that protective spell. Certainly, not all of these people had arrived in a few sixnights, and Hanner had not been on the outside of the great mass of trapped warlocks. He might have been there for a year or more!

That soldier had probably been here since 5202. No other explanation made sense.

"You!" Hanner called. "Bring that light over here!"

The guardsman looked uncertain, but he came, holding the torch high. "What's going on?" he demanded. "Who are you?"

Calling himself Chairman of the Council probably wouldn't mean anything to this man; if Hanner was right, he had been in Aldagmor since before the Council was created. Still, Hanner thought he knew a name the man *would* recognize and respect. "I'm Lord Faran's nephew," he said. "I'll explain the rest later — I'm sure there are a lot of people here who don't understand. For now, we just need to make sure everyone's safe."

"Lord Faran? From Ethshar of the Spices?"

That caught Hanner off-guard. "Yes, from Ethshar of the Spices," he said. "Where are *you* from?"

"Ethshar of the Rocks."

"Ah. Well, we're in Aldagmor, in the Baronies of Sardiron, right now, so I don't think it matters which of the three Ethshars we're from. Here, see if you can get more torches lit without setting the grass on fire — it's cold and dark, and some of these people may be in trouble. We need light, and we can probably use the heat, too."

"Yes, my lord," the soldier said, raising a hand in acknowledgment. He turned toward the heart of the crowd.

Hanner, on the other hand, was still heading away from the center, to make room, to get some breathing space, and to see if he could find a better vantage point. He was also looking for the woman who had been shouting. The more level-headed helpers he could find, the better. As he moved he pushed people in various directions, trying to get them spread out, and kept calling instructions.

"Chairman Hanner!" someone called, and there she was, the woman who had been shouting. She was a little on the short side and appeared to be at least fifty; her hair was graying and her face lined. He felt a twinge of jealousy; *he* hadn't made it to fifty before being Called, but only into his late thirties, despite trying to avoid doing any strong magic.

He hadn't been very successful at avoiding it. His position as chairman had required him to use magic sometimes, and his own natural tendency toward sloth had contributed as well — it was so much *easier* to fly than to walk, or to use magic rather than arms and legs to lift and carry. A warlock spark was so much more convenient than flint and steel, and making the air glow worked better than a lantern. Especially when his children were young and constantly demanding attention, warlockry had just been so handy that he had used it constantly, even though he *knew* he was inviting the Calling.

He had thought the Calling meant death. He smiled wryly. It seemed they had all been wrong about that part.

In fact, remembering the soldier and looking around, he wondered just how many warlocks had actually died in all those years. Not many, he guessed. Warlocks didn't die of old age; they were always Called first. They generally didn't die of disease or injury, either; their magic could be used to heal. A few had managed to get themselves killed, by other magicians or by assassins, but most had been Called and vanished into the mysterious depths of Aldagmor.

"*Hai*," he said. "Who are you?"

"My name is Sensella of Morningside," the woman replied. "I was Called about a day and a half ago."

"I'm sure we all think it's just been a day or two —" Hanner began.

"*No*, Chairman," Sensella said, interrupting him. "I never reached the…the…that pile. I got here the same time that big glowing thing did. I wasn't caught in the guarding spell the way everyone else was."

"Oh? Then I'll want to talk to you, but for now I think we need to concentrate on everyone's safety. We need to get them out of that…where the thing…"

"Out of the pit," Sensella said. "I agree. What can I do to help?"

Hanner turned to look and assess the situation. Things seemed to be more under control now; he no longer heard actual screams, though there were still shouting voices, and someone was crying somewhere.

"We'll need fires to keep everyone warm," Hanner said. "Shelter, and water, and food. Are there any farms nearby?"

Sensella looked at him with an expression he hoped to never see again, as if he had not merely failed her, but had failed her so stupidly it amounted to betrayal. "Chairman, we're in *Aldagmor*," she said. "No one has lived within miles of this place for thirty years!"

"*Thirty?*"

"More, really. Thirty-four. You were Called a long time ago."

A sudden realization burst upon him. "But my *wife…*"

Hanner was interrupted by a sudden blaze of light. As he turned he thought at first that that fool soldier had started a grass fire, but then he saw just how bright the light was, and that it was coming from somewhere high up, and he thought that perhaps that glowing thing had returned.

Then he saw the black-robed man hanging in mid-air, glowing like a bit of the sun, and his mouth fell open.

"I don't understand," Sensella said from beside him. "I thought the magic was all gone!"

"*Our* magic *is* gone," Hanner said. "This is something else."

"A wizard, maybe?"

Before Hanner could reply the glowing man spoke, and his voice was magically amplified until it was as loud as thunder.

"I am the Emperor Vond," the apparition said, his words rolling across the crowd and echoing from the surrounding hills. "I am the absolute master of the southernmost part of the Small Kingdoms, and as you can see, I alone, out of us all, am still a warlock. It is by my magic that I built my empire, and by my magic that I rule. I am going to return to my realm now, and I wish to return in a manner befitting my station — with an honor guard. Any of you who swear fealty to me will accompany me to my empire, where you will be given positions of authority under my rule. If you wish to join me, simply raise your hands above your head!"

"By all the gods," Hanner said. "Who *is* that? What's he talking about?"

"Don't raise your hands," Sensella said. "I'll explain later."

Hanner had no good reason to trust Sensella, but he had no reason to trust this Vond, either; he kept his hands by his sides.

Hundreds of others, though, were less restrained, and as each pair of hands rose, the owner of those hands rose as well, soaring up into the sky to hover a dozen feet below the self-proclaimed emperor.

Others shouted questions or protests in a variety of languages, but Vond ignored them; he simply lifted his new followers skyward, one by one.

After about eighty or ninety, by Hanner's estimate, they began to rise less steadily, and not as quickly; he guessed that this Vond was reaching the limits of his power. Not long after, people stopped rising at all; the remaining raised hands were ignored.

"Farewell," Vond said, his voice booming out in a thoroughly unnatural fashion.

And then he, and his hundred or so volunteers, flew away southward, leaving Hanner, Sensella, and thousands of others in the cold darkness of Aldagmor.

Chapter Four

Kelder of Radish Street had gone to bed early after a long day moving furniture, but he had been asleep for less than an hour when he was awakened by a loud thump. His head jerked up and his eyes sprang open.

The room was dark; he rolled out of bed, found the shutters by feel, and opened them, letting in what little light the surrounding city and the greater moon provided. So far as he could see in that dim glow, nothing looked out of place; he was alone in his attic room, just as he should be, and the furnishings seemed undisturbed.

Then he heard a scraping, and what he thought might have been a moan, and realized that the sound came from above. Someone, or something, was on the roof.

He turned to the window, pushed the shutters back, and opened the casement. He leaned out and looked up, but the eaves extended out too far for him to see anything above. Cautiously, he climbed up on the windowsill, hooked his left arm around the window frame, and leaned out further, craning his neck to see over the eaves.

"Help," someone said weakly, and the sound guided his eyes.

A woman was lying on the roof; she was wearing black, and her long, black hair hung over much of her face, rendering her almost invisible in the darkness.

"What's going on?" Kelder called.

"I don't know," the woman answered, her voice thin and unsteady. "I fell."

Kelder glanced around, confirming what he already knew — old Tarissa's boarding house was the tallest structure on the block. There wasn't anywhere this person could have fallen from other than the sky.

That meant magic was involved. The black clothes probably meant she was either a warlock or a demonologist, but witches or wizards sometimes wore dark colors, too.

"Are you hurt?" Kelder asked.

"I think so," the woman answered.

"Can you move?"

There was another scraping, and she inhaled sharply. "It hurts when I try," she said. "I think something's broken."

Then she wasn't a warlock; even if for some reason her magic had not protected her from the fall, a warlock could mend broken bones. For that matter, Kelder had heard that witches could block pain and do some healing, so she probably wasn't a witch, either. He didn't see a flying carpet or any other devices, but if she was a wizard, a failing levitation spell might explain her presence. Still, it didn't seem the most likely possibility. "Are you a demonologist?" he called, looking around for anything that might be flying near. "Did a demon drop you here?" He did not want to climb out there and find some horror from the Nethervoid waiting.

"No. I'm a warlock," she said.

"But..." Kelder was confused. "But then how... Why can't you move? Why can't you heal yourself?"

"I don't know!" she said miserably. "I was flying, and then I wasn't — it was as if my magic just disappeared."

Kelder had never heard of anything like that. Magic didn't just disappear unless a magician wanted it to. Oh, there were stories about places where wizardry didn't work — there were rumors that the overlord's palace in Ethshar of the Sands was such a place, ever since that madwoman Tabaea, the self-proclaimed empress, had died there — but warlockry wasn't like that. The only places it might not work were out at the edges of the World, too far from the source in Aldagmor. Here in Ethshar of the Spices, it worked just fine.

He looked at the injured woman, lying helpless on the roof tiles, and then looked down at the street four stories below. There was no way to get her in through his window safely, not if she was really hurt, and there was no door or trap opening onto the roof.

"I'll go get help," he said. "Is there some other warlock I should ask to come get you?"

"Maybe. Where am I?"

"You're on the roof of a boarding house on Old Market Street, in Hempfield."

"Hempfield? I don't know anyone in Hempfield."

"That's unfortunate. Let me see if I can find someone. I'll be back as quickly as I can."

She made a noise that he didn't think was intended to be words, and he carefully lowered himself back into his room. Then he paused to think.

The obvious solution would be to find a ladder and get a couple of people up there to carry her down, but Kelder didn't know anyone with a ladder long enough. No, they needed a magician.

Hempfield was not exactly the Wizards' Quarter. There were three herbalists in the neighborhood, if one defined "neighborhood" broadly, and a few blocks to the north lived a witch of dubious reputation by the name of Kyrina of Newmarket, but the nearest warlock Kelder knew of was a journeyman calling himself Berakon the Black, who had a place on Locksmith Alley in Allston. Kelder was not at all sure Berakon could even fly — he had located his shop in Locksmith Alley because he earned most of his living working with locks and other small hardware — but he was a warlock and only about a dozen blocks away.

Kelder pulled on his tunic and boots, grabbed a jacket, and headed out the door.

He called a brief explanation to the landlady on his way, but did not take the time for more. The sooner he found help for that poor woman, the better.

Ten minutes later he was at Berakon's tiny shop — or really, his stall; it was a single room, barely wider than its double doors and perhaps ten feet deep. Kelder had wandered past it several times and looked it over, so he was familiar with its appearance. He knew he had the right place.

But it was closed. The doors were shut and secured by a large brass padlock.

Kelder frowned. Locksmiths usually worked late, since people found themselves locked out at all hours, but Berakon's stall was definitely closed. He hurried to the much larger but non-magical locksmith's shop next door.

A bell jingled as he opened the door, and the proprietor looked up from a disassembled mechanism.

"Where's the warlock?" Kelder asked. "There's an emergency."

"He closed up a few minutes ago," the locksmith said. "Said he wasn't feeling well. He asked if I knew a good healer witch."

Kelder blinked. That didn't make sense. "A *warlock* not feeling well?"

The locksmith grimaced. "I know, but that's what he *said*."

Kelder shook his head. "What did you tell him?"

"I sent him to Alasha of the Long Nose, up on Superstition Street."

Superstition Street was another four long blocks to the south, toward the Arena. Kelder was not eager to range that far from home.

"Thank you," he said. "Do you know of any other warlocks around here?"

"Around here?" The locksmith shook his head. "No." He hesitated, then asked, "What's going on? Why do you need a warlock?"

"One fell out of the sky and is stuck on my roof," Kelder said. "She says her magic stopped working. I thought another warlock could get her down and maybe figure out what was wrong."

The shopkeeper studied him for a moment, then said, "Berakon borrowed a padlock."

Kelder had been trying to decide whether to head for Superstition Street, or back to the boarding house, or maybe to Warlock Street in the Wizards' Quarter, so he had not really been listening.

"What?" he said.

"Berakon borrowed a padlock," the locksmith repeated.

"I'm sorry, I don't see..." Kelder let the question trail off.

"He never *needed* a padlock before," the locksmith explained. "If he went out, he used his magic to weld the doors shut, and then undid it when he got back. I didn't think he really needed to lock it at all, because who would be stupid enough to steal from a warlock? But he did it anyway, every time. Until tonight, when he asked me if I knew where he could find a witch, and then borrowed that lock from me."

Kelder stared at him.

"You think they *both* lost their magic," he said. He tried to think how that could happen. Might there be some contagious disease that stole a warlock's magic? He had never heard of such a thing, but that didn't mean it couldn't happen.

"Maybe," the locksmith said. "Maybe they did. And maybe it's not just the two of them. I mean, warlockry just appeared out of nowhere on the Night of Madness, didn't it? That's what my mother told me. I was just a baby, so I don't remember it myself."

"I wasn't even born," Kelder said, "but yes, that's what I always heard."

"Well, maybe tonight it just *stopped*, as suddenly as it started."

Kelder started to protest, then hesitated.

Why not? Maybe it *had* just stopped.

If so, then there wasn't any point in looking for other warlocks. He needed some other way to get that poor woman off the roof. What other magic might work?

Well, wizards had various ways to fly or otherwise reach inaccessible places, but wizardry was *expensive*. A demonologist could probably get her down, but they were dangerous. Kelder wasn't about to hire a demonologist without a much better reason than this. He had no idea whether a theurgist, or a witch, or a sorcerer, or some other sort of magician could do anything to help.

Maybe he had been hasty in deciding magic was called for in the first place. He had never seen a ladder tall enough to reach that high from the ground, but couldn't it be set on the roof next door?

"Thank you," he said. He dropped a copper bit on the counter, then turned to go.

Rander the house-carpenter had some good ladders. Maybe he could help.

Lador the Black was leaning over the girl's sickbed, systematically sweeping the poisons from her blood, when suddenly he could no longer sense anything beneath her skin at all. He could still see her face, her brow slick with perspiration, and the soft green blanket tucked up to her chin. He could hear her labored breathing, smell the foul odor of illness, but everything below the surface had vanished.

His head felt strange, almost empty. All the things he normally perceived that ordinary people could not were gone — including that nasty, insistent murmuring that he knew would someday have drawn him away to Aldagmor. His hand, which he had been holding over her chest for dramatic effect, was no longer glowing; the only light came from the oil lamp on the shelf over the bed.

He blinked and straightened up, confused.

"Something's wrong," he said.

"What?" the girl's mother asked. "What is it?"

"I don't know," Lador said.

"Is she worsening?"

Lador shook his head. "No," he said. "No, something's wrong with *me*." He looked down at the girl, who seemed to be breathing a *little* easier. "She's no worse. I think I helped her a bit. But…something is *wrong*. I can't do any more. I'm sorry; you'll need to find someone else."

"But you said you could cure her!"

"I thought I could," Lador said. "I've seen this kind of fever before, and I've cured it, but this time…" He frowned. "I'll return your fee, of course."

"But what about Larsi?"

"You'll need to find another magician," he said. "Perhaps a witch would do better."

As he spoke, he had been trying several little experiments — trying to extinguish the lamp, trying to move the blanket, trying to lift himself off the floor, trying to warm his hand.

None of them had worked. His magic was gone. All of it. It had simply ceased to exist.

He was no longer a warlock.

That raised a thousand questions — was his magic gone forever? Would it return in a few minutes, a few hours, a few years? Were other warlocks affected? Did this mean he would never be Called?

That last question brought another — if there was a way to get his magic back, did he *want* to?

Thira the Warlock had been sitting in her kitchen, trying to decide whether wine made the nagging in her head better or worse, and wondering whether *oushka* might make it stop, or might overcome her resistance entirely. She had been dreading the night ahead; if she slept she knew she would have nightmares, and she knew she might wake up in mid-air on her way to Aldagmor, but if she *didn't* sleep, she would weaken as she grew wearier, and might doze off and find herself as badly off as if she had just gone to bed. Maybe worse.

She had been toying with a carving knife, wondering whether suicide might be preferable to the Calling, and wondering whether suicide was even *possible* for a warlock, when the Call stopped.

It was like a physical blow; she rocked back in her chair, her eyes wide, and the knife fell from her hand and clattered on the floor. She fell half an inch onto her chair as the magic that she had been unconsciously using vanished.

The kitchen was suddenly all there was. The whispering, the barely-glimpsed images in her head, the awareness of the composition of everything around her, had all disappeared. Only the real, solid, everyday world remained. The hard seat of her chair, the lingering scent of garlic left from supper, the lamplight reflecting from the brightly-glazed bowls on the shelf, were all newly intense because everything she had sensed through her magic was no longer distracting her.

"*Oh*," she gasped.

She sat for several minutes simply taking in the silence, the *clarity*. Then she finally allowed herself to think about what it might mean.

It meant she was no longer a warlock; she found that out quickly enough. Everything she attempted failed. Her magic was completely, utterly gone.

That assumed, of course, that this was real. For the last sixnight, she had often been unsure what was real and what was not, as the voices and images in her head crowded out her natural senses. Could this be some new, different illusion? Perhaps this was all just her imagination, and she was actually flying to Aldagmor even now, only *thinking* she was still safe in her own kitchen. After all, she had never heard of a warlock who had gone past the nightmare threshold to the very brink of being Called suddenly recovering like this.

She rapped her knuckles on the table. It certainly *felt* real, and the sound was clear and distinct.

But if it was real, *why*?

This was beyond her understanding. She wanted to talk to someone, someone who might be able to explain this.

The only place she could think of where she thought she might find answers was Warlock House, on High Street in the New City. She had only been there once, when she completed her apprenticeship and formally joined the Council, but of course she remembered where it was.

She stood up and found herself slightly unsteady on her feet without magic to support her; she caught herself on the table, regained her balance, and smiled.

"It must be real," she murmured. "Why would I imagine *that*?"

She wondered what the people at Warlock House would have to say about this. Had it ever happened before? Might there be dozens of ex-warlocks living in secret in the city?

Moving slowly and carefully, she turned and headed for the door.

Little Sammel focused all his attention on the coin, as he had a dozen times that day, but something felt wrong. He could not sense it — he could *see* it, but could not *feel* it, and the coin refused to move. The power seemed to have failed him.

"Something's wrong, Master," he said.

His master did not reply immediately, and the apprentice turned to see whether the elder warlock was angry, or merely distracted.

He did not appear to be either one; he looked *frightened*.

But that was silly; what could frighten a powerful warlock like Dabran the Pale?

"Master?" Sammel asked, uncertainly.

"Sammel," Dabran said, his own voice unsteady. "Do you feel it?"

"Feel what, Master?"

"The...the *quiet*."

"I don't feel *anything*, Master. I can't...my magic seems to be gone."

A crooked smile appeared on Dabran's face.

"Mine is, too, apprentice," he said. "Mine is, too."

Over and over, in shops and homes, streets and skies, all through the Hegemony of the Three Ethshars and in a dozen other lands, similar scenes played out. A few warlocks died when their magic failed; so did a few of their customers, and a handful of bystanders. A few more people were injured. Some former warlocks bemoaned their loss of power; others delighted in knowing they were free of the Call. Some thought they were alone and tried to conceal their vulnerability; others gathered to compare notes on what might have happened.

In the Baronies of Sardiron warlocks were almost unknown; that realm was too close to Aldagmor for comfort, the Calling too strong. In the more northerly Small Kingdoms, warlocks were scarce because they were not welcome; in the southernmost Small Kingdoms, warlocks were nonexistent, by edict of the Wizards' Guild, which had banned them from the area in 5224. Word was therefore slow to spread in those regions.

In most of the towns and cities of the World, though, it was well known by morning that there were no more warlocks, and no more Call.

What was not yet widely known was why.

Chapter Five

Hanner looked out at the torchlit thousands of people sitting huddled on the grass, stretching out hundreds of yards in every direction, most of them shivering from the cold — as yet, no one had gathered fuel for proper campfires.

"Water is probably the most urgent need," he said, "but if we don't get some sort of shelter, some of the older people may freeze."

"It's too bad there isn't any snow," Sensella said. "We could use that for water *and* shelter."

"We can't stay here, either," Hanner added. "There's no food."

"That's true." She looked around at the dark surrounding hills. "There were farms here once, I believe."

"There were," a young man said from just behind her elbow, speaking Ethsharitic with a thick Sardironese accent. "My family's farm was just over there." He pointed. "We grew wheat and beans, mostly."

Hanner said, "You're from Aldagmor?"

"Yes," the young man said. "I'm Rayel Roggit's son."

"It must be a shock, waking up to find your home gone," Hanner said.

Rayel shuddered. "My home, and more than *thirty years*, gone in the blink of an eye! I was in bed, and I had this strange nightmare, and I thought I heard something like thunder but I wasn't sure because I was still asleep, and then the next thing I know I'm jammed in among my family and my neighbors down at the bottom of a pit in the dark, and everyone's screaming and crying and we can't breathe, and when we get out — those of us who did; I'm pretty sure my brother died in there — we find *this*."

"I'm sorry about your brother," Sensella said.

Rayel shook his head. "It doesn't seem real. He *can't* be dead, but I didn't see him get out."

Hanner nodded, then said, "If you're from around here, then you must know where we can find water."

"We had a well, but I think it must have fallen in years ago. There's a stream half a mile that way, though." He pointed to the southeast.

"Thank you." He had already sent people out looking for water, so he did not rush to send more. It wasn't as if they had buckets in which to fetch it back; the closest thing to a bucket he had found so far was a soldier's helmet. There were about a dozen guardsmen, and half of them still had their helmets; he had sent that half-dozen out with the water-seekers.

It could have been worse. Most of the throng spoke Ethsharitic, and most of the rest spoke Sardironese, so they could communicate fairly well. Hanner thought it was fortunate, in a way, that the thing, whatever it was, had been trapped in Aldagmor, where the population of the surrounding area for a dozen leagues in every direction spoke only those two languages. If it had landed in the linguistic chaos of the Small Kingdoms, no one would have been able to organize this mob. As it was, the more varied areas were far enough away that they had produced few warlocks.

Also, there were few children to worry about, and those few generally had parents with them — almost the entire population of Aldagmor as of the Night of Madness had been in that pit, but outside the immediate area the Calling had mostly drawn adults. A few older children had been caught, but only a few.

There were a good many older people, but most were in excellent health — thanks to their magical healing, warlocks were not subject to the sort of accumulated damage that most people acquired over the years. As with children, there were a few drawn here on the Night of Madness; they had never consciously been warlocks, and had therefore never had a chance to heal themselves of time's wounds.

For the most part, though, the throng of former warlocks was disproportionately made up of unusually fit adults in their middle years.

Even so, Hanner and Sensella had agreed that once the sun was up, they all needed to get moving, to get out of this isolated valley and back to civilization. Even if they had tools, even if they had time to raise crops before they starved, this place couldn't support so many people. They needed to find food for all these thousands of hungry mouths.

What was happening out there in the rest of the World? It seemed certain that warlockry had vanished everywhere — but that left the mystery of Emperor Vond. Some of the later arrivals had given Hanner a very brief account of who Vond was, but no one had a good explanation of why he had been so extraordinarily powerful, why he had been able to conquer a dozen of the Small Kingdoms, and why he apparently still had his magic. Was it really warlockry, or something else?

Hanner knew that on the Night of Madness other sorts of magicians had become warlocks; he had known some of them personally. Even as powerful a wizard as Manrin the Mage, a Guildmaster, had been affected. Hanner wished old Manrin were here, but Manrin hadn't been Called; he had been executed by the Wizards' Guild for breaking Guild rules.

So maybe Vond had some other sort of magic, and had warlockry on top of it, and even with warlockry gone he had still had the other sort — but what sort was it? Did anyone else have it?

Did anyone else *here* have *any* magic? A witch or a wizard might be very handy right now.

"*Hai!*" he called. "Is anyone here a magician other than a warlock? Are there any wizards or witches or sorcerers, or people who used to be?"

No one responded immediately, but the question was passed on through the crowd, and a few minutes later a handful of people made their way to Hanner's side. To his surprise, he recognized one of them, though she was older than he remembered. "Alladia of Shiphaven?"

"Yes, Chairman." She was staring at him, and he realized he was probably staring, as well. "You do know that you were Called ten years before I was, don't you?"

"I do now," he said. "And…you were a witch?"

"No, a priestess," she said.

"That's right, I'm sorry. It's been a long time."

"It has," she agreed. "So long that I don't know if I can remember a single invocation properly. I don't know if I still have any of the talent at all."

"Could you try?" Hanner asked. "Is there a god who will feed the hungry, or provide warmth, or water?"

"Of course. Piskor the Generous can provide food and water — though perhaps not for *this* large a multitude. Tarma or Konned could keep us warm." She frowned. "I don't remember how to summon Konned at all. Piskor — I think I remember part of it. It has the standard opening for her class of deity, and ends with *awir ligo*…No, *awir thigo lan takkoz wesfir yu.* But I'm not sure of the rest."

"Do your best," Hanner said. "Maybe you can find other theurgists."

"I'm a theurgist." A man Hanner did not recognize stepped forward. "I haven't been…I mean, I came here on that first night. I don't have my scrolls or anything, but I remember my spells."

"Good! Then the two of you can work on that. Anyone else?"

"I'm a witch," a man said, struggling to get the words out. Hanner had not noticed immediately in the dim, flaring torchlight, but now he saw that the man was exhausted, his face drawn, unsteady on his feet. "I've been trying to heal some of the injured."

"And you're killing yourself in the process, aren't you?" Hanner asked.

The man turned up an empty palm. "I had to try. There are…there are more of us, and I was resting, so when your call came —"

"Thank you," Hanner said. "Healing is probably the best thing for you witches to do, but please, don't do too much. I know witchcraft drains your strength. Please, sit down, rest." He gestured, and two nearby men helped the witch to seat himself on the trampled grass. Then Hanner raised his voice. "Who else?"

"I am Thand the Wizard," someone answered. He wore a nightshirt, and shivered as if he was freezing in the cold night air. "But I came here straight from my bed; I don't have any of the ingredients I would need for my spells."

"I have my...my dagger," a woman in a green wizard's robe said, "because I was out late that night, but I didn't bring anything else. If we can find the right plants or stones, we might be able to work a few simple spells."

"But I don't have my book," Thand said. "Even *with* the ingredients, I can't do much without it."

"I was a wizard before I was a warlock," an old man said, "but I had to forsake wizardry and leave the Guild. I don't think wizardry is going to do us much good here. None of us have our books of spells, and only those who were Called immediately on the Night of Madness can do any magic at all."

"I'm a demonologist," a woman volunteered, "but if you think I'm going to summon a demon here, without any wards or safeguards, without my books and contracts, you're mad."

"A demon probably wouldn't help much in any case," Hanner said.

"I'm a dancer," another woman said, glancing about uncertainly, "but we'd need at least eight people, and I'm not sure what we could do."

Hanner could not think of anything to say to her; he had never been sure ritual dances really worked at all. "Anyone else?"

Others spoke up, but the results were not encouraging.

No one who had learned warlockry as an apprentice knew any other magic, of course, and of those who had become warlocks on the Night of Madness, most had given up their other magic long ago, and completely enough that they could no longer use it at all, even now that warlockry was no longer blocking it.

Those who had been Called on the Night of Madness included representatives of every sort of magic Hanner had ever heard of, but most were fairly useless. Wizards could do almost nothing without their books and tools, though a few could assist in lighting fires.

The witches were all attending to the injured or frightened, and undoubtedly doing considerable good, but did not have the power for anything dramatic.

None of the sorcerers had any useful talismans with them. Most had come directly from their beds and had no talismans at all. A fellow named Senesson of Lordiran had a tiny glass box that glowed like a miniature lantern, and Karitha of Seacorner had a sorcerous weapon that she said could kill a man at twenty paces, but there was no sorcery to provide food or water or shelter.

The herbalists had brought no herbs with them, save for one who found a single bundle of a leaf that would cause gentle sleep in his belt-pouch, and of course their gardens were far away and probably long gone. They could not hope to find anything useful in the dark, but once the sun rose, they might manage something.

As always, the scientists and prestidigitators were no help.

None of the demonologists would attempt anything without the safe-guards they had had at home. The ritual dancers seemed more coopera-tive, but did not immediately agree on what should be done, or how to do it, and at least two of them did not think anything could be done until the sun came up.

The theurgists seemed like the best prospect for providing real help; four or five of them had gathered to summon Piskor, Tarma, and a water-god named Tivei.

None of the magicians could explain Vond's magic.

"I think it's something in Lumeth of the Towers," Sensella volun-teered.

Startled, Hanner turned. "What?"

"I think it's something in Lumeth," she repeated.

"Why?" Hanner asked.

"Several years ago, after you were Called, the Wizards' Guild banned all warlocks from Lumeth of the Towers, and everywhere else in a twen-ty-league radius, and it apparently had something to do with the Empire of Vond."

"The Wizards' Guild? Why?"

She turned up both palms. "No one knows; they wouldn't say. But practicing warlockry anywhere within twenty leagues of Lumeth is pun-ishable by death. They made a big dramatic announcement — a bunch of wizards went all over the southern Small Kingdoms issuing edicts."

"When was this?"

Sensella had to think for a moment. "5224, maybe? About then. I was living in Ethshar of the Sands, so I didn't hear about it right away, but I think it was 5224."

That was five years in the future, as far as Hanner could remember, but he knew it was really a dozen years ago. "But...why?"

Sensella shook her head. "No one knows. Well, no one except the wizards, and you know how they are about keeping secrets."

Hanner turned to look at the miserable handful of wizards who had come to Aldagmor in their robes and nightshirts. They had all been here since 5202. Even if he could somehow get past the Guild's secrecy rules, none of them would know anything about events in 5224.

If warlockry had been forbidden in the southern part of the Small Kingdoms, there wouldn't be anyone here who had been Called from that area after 5224. It seemed as if it was destined to stay a mystery, at least for the present.

However it worked, wherever it came from, Vond's magic would be no use.

Hanner looked at the sky. The eastern horizon was brightening now. Dawn was almost upon them; that might help. He turned to see how the theurgists were doing, just in time to see a blaze of light. He felt a sudden pressure on his face and in his ears, and blinked. When his eyes opened again a woman was standing before him, a beautiful woman in a green gown and golden crown, thick black hair tumbling down her back, surrounded by a golden glow so intense Hanner could see nothing through it except the woman.

Or rather, the goddess, for there could be little doubt that this was one of the deities the theurgists had wanted to summon. From Hanner's point of view, though, she was not over near the theurgists, but standing right in front of him, scarcely out of arm's reach, looking directly at him and speaking directly to him.

You will have food for three days, she said, speaking without sound. *The water of the stream will be pure and clean. Because humanity must rely on itself and not upon gods, this is all I will give you until a year has passed. And before that year has passed, you will repay this by giving comfort to one who needs it — a blanket to one who has none, a roof to one who needs it for a night, or a meal to one who has not eaten that day.*

Then she was gone, and an excited babble ran through the throng. As he listened, Hanner realized that every person there had seen the goddess as standing before him or her, and addressing him or her directly. And as he looked around, Hanner saw that a cloth-wrapped bundle lay in front of every person in the crowd, including himself. He knelt down and unwrapped his.

The brown stick-things inside were unlike anything he had ever seen before, but when he took a wary nibble of one, he found it tasted sweet and perhaps a little nutty, and had a consistency something like a syrup-covered biscuit. He took a larger bite, chewing carefully. Then he swallowed, and called to the theurgists, "Well done!"

Alladia waved an acknowledgment.

"Well, at least we won't starve," Sensella said from behind his right shoulder.

"Not for three days, anyway," Hanner agreed. "But we're still stranded out here in the hills of Aldagmor, and if there were ever any roads around here, they've had thirty years to fade away."

"We can find our way by the sun," Sensella said. "If we head south, we'll reach civilization eventually."

"I'm not worried about the direction so much as the terrain," Hanner said. "What if we need to cross rivers, or climb mountains?"

"Then we'll wade, or swim, or climb. Hanner, we all thought we were doomed. We thought the Calling was a death sentence, but here we are alive! We have a second chance. We may have to struggle to get there, but we can all go home again, to *stay*."

Hanner looked around at the mobs of people.

"Then what?" he said. "There are *thousands* of people here! And I'm sure many of them don't have homes to return to. You said it's been more than thirty years since the Night of Madness. Even those of us who came later can't go back to our old lives; we made our living off our magic, and now that's gone."

"We'll manage," Sensella replied. "We have our lives back. Yes, we have problems to overcome, but we have our lives back."

"Not all of us. I don't know how many people were crushed to death in that pit, but —"

"Yes, *they're* dead," she agreed, a trifle impatiently. "But *we* aren't. I'll see my children and grandchildren again. Don't you have any family back home?"

Hanner swallowed. "My wife. Mavi. We have three children — but it's been seventeen years. They must be grown by now. They must think I deserted them."

"I'm sure they understand about the Calling," Sensella said.

"Maybe." He looked around at the crowds. Most of the former warlocks were eating the divinely-provided food. Guardsmen had returned from the stream and were distributing drinking water in their helmets. The skies had brightened enough that they no longer needed torches for light. "What if we followed the stream south?" he asked. "Then we'd have drinking water for the journey, and it must empty into either the Great River or the sea eventually."

"Good idea," Sensella agreed.

Hanner looked east, where the sun was peeking above the horizon. "We should make a start soon. Walking will help people keep warm." He remembered the dozens of injured the witches were tending. "The stronger men can help carry anyone who's too badly hurt to walk."

"You think all of us should stay together? I don't think the Sardironese or the Srigmorans will want to go south."

"I'm not going to force anyone," Hanner said. "I couldn't if I wanted to. If they want to go north or west, let them, but *I* intend to head south, and I expect most of the others will, too."

Sensella did not argue further.

Hanner raised his arms and shouted, "*Hai!* Everyone! We have food and water now, but we can't stay here! We need to get back to civilization. I'm going to follow that stream south, toward Ethshar."

"What about the priests?" someone called. "They're still chanting!"

Alladia heard this, and hurried toward Hanner. "They're still trying to summon Tarma," she said. "Give them another few minutes."

"I want to finish eating," someone called.

"I'm too tired, I need to rest a little more."

"It's still too cold!"

"Let the sun get above the trees, so we can see."

Hanner grimaced. "Fine!" he shouted. "Fine! Half an hour, and then we go."

That seemed to meet with general acceptance, and Hanner settled to the ground, cross-legged, to wait.

As he sat, he wondered what had become of Mavi. Was she still living in Warlock House, the mansion that had once belonged to Hanner's uncle Faran? Probably not; after all, she wasn't a warlock. He had owned the house, and she was his heir, but the Council of Warlocks might not recognize that.

Perhaps the Council had acknowledged her ownership and paid her rent. Hanner hoped so. He had not left her wealthy; so much of his money had gone toward that ridiculous tapestry and its useless refuge that Mavi would have been far from rich after his departure. He hoped she had been all right. He had a sudden, horrible image of her and their children camping in the Hundred-Foot Field and shuddered.

But surely his sisters would have looked after her, if only for the sake of their nieces and nephew. Mavi might be living in the overlord's palace, as a guest of Lady Alris, Hanner's youngest sister. Mavi and the children *should* be all right.

But he wanted to get back to them and be sure. Sitting on the trampled grass was not getting him any closer to seeing them.

Finally, he looked at the sun, well above the horizon, and decided he had waited long enough. He got to his feet and was just about to call for attention when someone screamed behind him.

He turned, startled.

Then there were more screams, and fingers pointing at the western sky. Hanner heard the word that was being screamed, and his blood went cold even before he saw what those fingers were pointing at.

It was unmistakable, and he added his own bellow to the screams.

"Dragon!" he cried. "It's a dragon!"

Chapter Six

Lord Sterren, Regent of the Vondish Empire, was taking a morning stroll on the battlements of Semma Castle, looking out toward the Imperial Palace, when a movement in the northern sky, far beyond the palace, caught his eye. He raised a hand to shade his eyes and peered into the distance.

There were several flying objects out there, dark shapes against the blue sky — more than several; scores, maybe hundreds. They were too far away to make out details, and the lack of a background made it impossible to judge their precise size or distance, but they did not move like birds and were not proportioned like birds.

There were too many to be dragons — or rather, if they were dragons, the whole World had gone mad. Which was not impossible, but it seemed unlikely, and they didn't look like dragons.

They looked like people. In fact, they were coming rapidly nearer and looking more and more like people with every second.

Flying people meant magicians, and not just any sort of magician — herbalists and ritual dancers couldn't fly, so far as Sterren had ever heard. Demonologists only flew when carried by demons, and besides, Sterren doubted there were that many demonologists in all the Small Kingdoms. There were a few other unlikely possibilities, but the odds were good that these were either wizards or warlocks. Or both.

Either one would be bad news. Both would be *very* bad news.

Warlocks were banned from the Vondish Empire. A delegation from the Wizards' Guild had made that *very* clear twelve years ago. If these flying people were warlocks, their presence in the Empire amounted to a declaration of war between themselves and the Guild. Sterren really, *really* didn't want to be anywhere near a war between a hundred warlocks and the Wizards' Guild. He had seen a war fought with magic when he first came to Semma — in fact, he had been the one who brought the magicians into it. That had been a very small-scale affair, fought by some of the least-powerful magicians available, and it had still been frightening. He had then seen Vond build the empire, which had been awe-inspiring. Both of those conflicts had only had magic on one side, and they had been quite ugly enough. A war of warlocks against wizards would be *very* bad.

If these were not warlocks, but wizards, then the question was, why would they be coming *here*, to the southern edge of the World? Why would they be *flying*, and by themselves, rather than on carpets or the other aerial vehicles wizards generally favored? Why would there be so *many* of them? When that Guildmaster, Ithinia of the Isle, had delivered the Guild's ultimatum, half a dozen wizards with their feet on the ground had been more than enough to cow the entire empire.

But then a thought struck him; flying people meant magic, yes, but they didn't *all* have to be magicians. Many of them might just be passengers, carried along by the magicians. That might not be so bad, then. Perhaps these people had offended a wizard somewhere and were being sent into exile here in Vond.

Somehow, Sterren doubted the situation was that benign, but it *might* be. His luck had often been excellent. Really, with few exceptions, he had been fortunate ever since he tricked Vond himself into making himself susceptible to the Calling. Yes, the Imperial Council had insisted on naming him regent and had refused to let him leave and go back home to Ethshar, but he had long ago gotten used to his position. He was happily married, with five healthy children; the empire was doing well and had managed to avoid getting into any border wars for more than a decade.

He very much feared, though, that his good fortune was coming to an end. He turned to the stairs and shouted down to his guard, "Send word to convene the Council, and put the entire garrison on alert!" He looked back over his shoulder at that cloud of people and added, "And see what magicians are in the castle — I want to see whoever's available in the throne room immediately!"

Then he trotted down the stairs, bound for the Imperial Palace, still trying to guess who these aerial travelers might be.

If it had been just *one* man, there would have been an obvious, if nightmarish, possibility. There was a reason Sterren's title was regent, rather than emperor. There was a reason he didn't live in the Imperial Palace. Officially, the Vondish Empire still belonged to the Great Vond, the warlock who had been Called to Aldagmor almost fifteen years ago; Sterren and the Council were just looking after it until he returned. That was generally considered a polite fiction — but maybe it wasn't. No warlock had ever come back from Aldagmor, but Vond had done a good many things no one else had ever done. He had found a way to draw warlock-like magic from a source in Lumeth, as well as the one in Aldagmor, and had used the magic to build his empire. There had never been another warlock like him.

If *one* warlock had appeared in the sky, Sterren would have thought it might be Vond.

He shuddered at the very idea. Vond had never really intended to be cruel or destructive — indeed, he had for the most part been a beneficent tyrant and had significantly improved the lives of the common people of the eighteen kingdoms he conquered — but he had a temper. A *bad* temper. Sterren still remembered the sight of poor Ildirin's mangled corpse

— Ildirin, the butcher who Vond had brought from Ksinallion to be one of his palace servants, had spilled wine on his master, and the warlock had smashed the unfortunate man against a stone wall, then crushed his skull, all without touching him.

And worst of all, Vond had then carried on the discussion as if nothing untoward had happened.

Vond also had grandiose ambitions. He had built the Imperial Palace by magically reshaping the bedrock, deliberately making it larger and grander than Semma Castle, but that was the least of it; he had lit the night sky for miles around, he had turned up a chunk of the earth itself to make a barrier at the edge of the World, he had done any number of spectacular feats, merely to show that he could.

Only when he realized that he was still susceptible to the Calling, despite drawing his power from a different source, had he stopped looking for bigger and bigger ways to display his magnificence. Instead, he had huddled in his palace, trying to use no magic at all, until one night he had flown off to the north, never to be seen again.

Vond had known Sterren betrayed him, but had done nothing about it, because Sterren was the closest thing to a friend he had, and the only other person in the empire's capital of Semma who understood anything about warlockry. He had needed Sterren. But if he came back...

But this wasn't just one warlock; there were dozens of people flying.

The possibility that they were *all* warlocks who had somehow learned to use the Lumeth source occurred to Sterren, and he almost fell down the stairs at the mere thought. *One* such warlock had reshaped the Small Kingdoms; what might scores of them do?

But how could anyone else have tapped into the Lumeth source? No, that didn't seem very likely. The Wizards' Guild wouldn't allow it.

He paused on the third floor of the castle to catch his breath, call a few more orders, and take a look out a north-facing window.

The flying people had arrived more quickly than he had expected; they were already settling to the ground in Palace Square, while the capital's inhabitants made way and stared in astonishment.

One of them, though, was not descending with the others; he was hanging in the air above the great doors of the Imperial Palace. He was tall, thin, and pale, and wore a black robe embroidered with gold. Sterren felt his throat tighten and his stomach knot. It had been fifteen years, but he remembered a robe like that.

That had been what Vond wore.

Sterren reached out and opened the casement just as the apparition began to speak, and even though he was at least half a mile away, Sterren could hear every word — the warlock was using magic to amplify his voice.

"People of Semma!" the flying man said. "I, the Great Vond, have returned! I have come back from a far realm to resume rule over my empire! Let the word be spread from Quonshar to Ksinallion that I am here!"

"Oh, this is bad," Sterren said. Vond was back, and judging by his words, as egotistical as ever. But how was this possible? He had been *Called*, and no warlock ever returned from the Calling.

Or at least, none had until now.

Sterren turned away from the window and found two of his personal guards standing in the passage. "You, Bragen," he said. "Go find Lar Samber's son. Whether he likes it or not, he's about to come out of retirement; I need to talk to him as soon as possible. Do whatever it takes to get him to come; he probably won't want to. Threaten him if you need to."

Bragen bowed. "Yes, my lord." He turned and hurried away.

Sterren looked at the other guard. "Noril, go find Princess Shirrin and as many of my children as you can, and tell them to get out of the castle and away from Semma as quickly as possible. Go with them. Head for Akalla. If they can get to Ethshar, so much the better. Travel anonymously — you understand?"

Noril hesitated. "I…I think so, my lord."

"Don't just *think* so! That's Emperor Vond out there, and if he loses his temper and doesn't like what we've done with the place since he left, this whole city may be a hole in the ground by tomorrow, and I don't want my family here if that happens."

Noril bowed hastily. "Yes, my lord." Then he, too, turned and hurried away.

Sterren forgot about his dignity as regent and ran for the stairs; he had to get to Palace Square at once. It was certain that Vond would want to see him, and keeping the warlock waiting was never a good idea.

Fifteen minutes later he trotted out into the plaza to find Vond waiting for him, hanging a foot or so off the ground. A mob of strangers and townspeople lined the sides of the square, but had left a wide berth around the warlock.

Most of the strangers, Sterren saw, wore black clothes — that probably meant they were more warlocks.

That was very, very bad.

Sterren was unsure just how best to greet the emperor, and decided not to go to either extreme; he stopped perhaps eight feet away and bowed, but did not kneel or otherwise abase himself. "Your Majesty," he said.

Vond stared at him for a long moment, then said, "Sterren? Is that you?"

Sterren straightened up and looked Vond in the eye. "Of course it's me," he said.

"You've changed."

"It's been fifteen years — and I notice, your Majesty, that you *haven't* changed. Frankly, that comes as something of a surprise."

Vond smiled crookedly. "You didn't expect me to come back at all, Sterren — you know it, and I know it. You don't need to pretend."

"I wasn't pretending, your Majesty. You're quite right, I didn't expect you to come back. How did you manage it? Who are these people you brought with you?" He gestured at the surrounding strangers.

"They're warlocks," Vond said. "Or at least, they used to be." He smiled unpleasantly.

"*Used* to be?" Sterren asked. "I take it there's been some drastic change in...well, in something?"

"Oh, yes, there certainly has." The smile broadened to a grin. "The Calling has ended, Sterren. *Ended*."

That raised a great many questions, but Sterren settled on one to start with. "Ended? Permanently?"

"Oh, I think so, yes. The thing that was doing the calling, that was the source of warlockry, that fell out of the sky on the Night of Madness? That thing? It's gone. It went home."

Sterren considered that for half a second, then asked, "You don't expect it to return for a visit, then?"

"No, I really don't."

"It hadn't acquired a liking for Aldagmor?"

"Not at all."

Sterren stepped closer and lowered his voice to a whisper. "So there isn't anything magical in Aldagmor anymore? The only warlocks who can still work magic are the ones who use the source in Lumeth, instead?"

Vond nodded.

"Did you teach these people to use it?" Sterren gestured at the observers.

"No," Vond said. "Not yet. I might, in time."

"Or they might hear the buzz for themselves, the way you did."

Vond's smile vanished, and he looked around, suddenly uncertain. He clearly hadn't thought of that possibility.

"But what you actually mean," Sterren said hastily, to distract the emperor before he could do anything regrettable, "is that you are now the only warlock in the World."

The smile reappeared. "Exactly! I am almost as powerful as I was before, and now I have no need to worry about the Calling. There's nothing to stop me from expanding my empire further. I could unite *all* the Small Kingdoms!"

That was more or less what Sterren had feared, but something else Vond had said caught his attention. "*Almost* as powerful?"

"Almost, yes. I was drawing on *both* sources before, even when I didn't know it, and now there is only one. In Aldagmor I found out I wasn't as strong as before — these people are all I could carry, where I used to be able to move the World itself. My power increased as I flew south, though. I expect I will soon be stronger than ever."

"It was most likely because of the distance, your Majesty; Aldagmor is a long way from Lumeth."

"Do you think that's it?" Vond glanced around again. "You're probably right. I hadn't thought of that."

"You said these were all you could carry? Then there were more who survived the Calling?"

"What? Oh, yes, of course. Thousands of them; probably every warlock who was ever Called. We were all trapped in the thing's protective spells — that's why I haven't aged. Has it really been fifteen years?"

"Yes, your Majesty, it has."

"I see there are new buildings everywhere, and my palace is showing some wear." He stared critically at the huge double doors; Sterren knew their finish was noticeably more weathered than it had been when Vond left. Giving them a fresh coat of varnish had never made it into the imperial budget.

That wasn't important now, though. Sterren asked, "Your Majesty, what happened to the others?"

"What? The other Called warlocks? Oh, they're probably still in Aldagmor." He waved dismissively. "They aren't my problem."

"May I ask, then, why you brought *these* people?"

Vond turned back to face Sterren. "I told them they were my honor guard, and I would give them important positions in the empire," he said, "but the truth is, I wanted some company — people who speak good Ethsharitic, and who can understand what it's like being a warlock. Being an emperor was sort of lonely sometimes." His expression turned thoughtful. "I suppose my harem is gone?"

"Long ago, your Majesty."

"Well, I have plenty of time to find a new one. For now, though — well, I see you're still here, and my palace is still here. What about the empire?"

"Still intact, your Majesty. Your overthrow of the old nobility was thorough enough that no one saw any point in restoring them. The Imperial Council has been administering the empire in your name ever since you left."

"The Council?" Vond glanced around, as if looking for the other councillors, but found none. "What about you? Are you still chancellor?"

Sterren had been dreading this question. He was unsure just how Vond would react to the situation, but he was very, very glad that he had refused the title of emperor. "The Council named me regent, your Majesty, but I let the Council handle as much of the government as possible."

"Regent?" Vond considered that. "That sounds sensible. So you were ruling in my place?"

Sterren suppressed a sigh of relief. "That's right. Just until you came back."

"And none of the eighteen kingdoms have gotten away?"

"None."

"Have you conquered any more?"

"No, your Majesty. We thought this was plenty to handle."

"Well, you'll have more soon." Vond gestured expansively. "I think Lumeth of the Towers will be next, since that's where my power comes from."

Sterren hesitated for an instant, debating the necessity of delivering bad news, then said, "Ah, your Majesty — there's a problem with that."

Vond frowned. "What sort of a problem?"

"We...we made a treaty with the Wizards' Guild," Sterren said.

"The Wizards' Guild?" Vond looked puzzled. "What do *they* have to do with anything way out here?"

"It seems they have interests in Lumeth, your Majesty," Sterren said. "Twelve years ago they banned all warlocks from Lumeth, and the empire, and Shassala, and Kalithon, and Gajamor, and Calimor, and Yaroia, and Zenda, and maybe a couple of others I'm forgetting. In fact, your return may be a violation of their ban all by itself."

Vond's frown deepened, and he glared at Sterren. "What, you *agreed* to this?"

"They guaranteed our borders, Vond," Sterren explained. "We were on the verge of war with several of our neighbors. You weren't here, and our other magicians are...well, not very impressive. The Guild was not in a mood to compromise on the ban on warlockry, and honestly, we didn't really want any *other* warlocks here, and we didn't think you would be back. They forced peace on the whole region. It seemed like a good deal."

"Not to *me*."

"You weren't here!"

"I am now," Vond growled. "I'm back, and I intend to stay, whether the Wizards' Guild likes it or not. I *will* take Lumeth for my empire, and whatever else I like." He raised a hand dramatically. "I may just take Ethshar itself! After all, I grew up there, and maybe I'd like to go *home*."

As he finished his speech the warlock blinked, as if surprised by his own words, and Sterren began, "I don't think —"

"You don't have to think!" Vond waved a hand at Sterren, and the regent found himself flung roughly backward through the air. Fortunately for him, if not for the others involved, he hit the line of people surrounding the plaza, rather than anything particularly hard and unyielding.

"I am the only warlock in the World," Vond announced, rising into the air and amplifying his voice again, "and the most powerful magician in history! I will do as I please, and the Wizards' Guild can't stop me!"

Sterren disentangled himself from the people he had struck, but was in no great hurry to get back on his feet, or to confront Vond further. He knew, though, that every part of that latest announcement was wrong. There was at least one other warlock who could draw on the Lumeth source, specifically Sterren himself. There had been several magicians over the centuries who could probably match Vond's raw power, from Fendel the Great to the late, unlamented Empress Tabaea. And if it came down to open warfare, the Wizards' Guild almost certainly *could* stop Vond.

The question was, how much of the World would be destroyed in the process?

Chapter Seven

Hanner stared at the approaching dragon, trying to think what he should do. He had never seen a full-grown, flying dragon before, only the hatchlings kept as pets by the more ostentatious among Ethshar's ruling elite, and the half-grown juveniles displayed in the Arena. *Those* dragons were always killed before they reached adulthood. The only adult dragons he had ever heard of were out in the wilderness, far from all human habitation.

But then, they were in eastern Aldagmor, which had been uninhabitable by humans for the past thirty-odd years — this *was* out in the wilderness. Why *wouldn't* there be dragons here?

This one was still coming, and Hanner began to realize that this wasn't just any dragon, it was a *huge* dragon, easily a hundred feet long. Its wings and flanks were a rich emerald green, and its throat and belly were golden yellow, and it was so big that its wings seemed to fill half the sky.

And as it drew closer, he could see that there was something on its back, at the base of its neck. Hanner blinked.

Meanwhile, all around him people were screaming and running. Some were bright enough to scatter into the surrounding forests and hills, but most were simply fleeing directly away from the dragon, running more or less due east.

Hanner was not going to do that. The dragon could overtake anyone it tried to, he was sure, so there was no point in running. If it intended to eat someone, it could pick whomever it wanted.

But if it wasn't just looking for a snack and planning to grab the first person it could, then perhaps it could be reasoned with. Hanner had always heard that some of the larger dragons could talk; maybe he could talk to this one. If all it wanted was a meal — well, it wasn't a pleasant idea, but Hanner knew there were dead bodies in the pit, people who had been crushed or smothered before they could climb out. He would have greatly preferred to give all those poor people a proper funeral and burn the bodies, but feeding them to a dragon was certainly better than letting it eat living people.

A dragon this size couldn't be stupid, or it wouldn't have lived long enough to get so large. It surely couldn't make a habit of eating people, or it would have drawn the attention of dragon-hunters.

At least, that was what Hanner tried to tell himself.

And that thing at the base of its neck…Hanner realized that it was a person, a man seated in a sort of saddle. Hanner blinked again, and shouted, "*Hai!*" He waved his arms over his head.

The dragon wheeled and turned upward, craning its long neck to look down at Hanner; it looked around, and found clear ground nearby — all the other former warlocks in that area who were capable of it had fled, leaving a space large enough for the beast to land without stepping on anyone. It settled gracefully to the ground, and the wind of its arrival forced Hanner back two or three steps. It folded its wings, then swung its immense head around to look at Hanner with slit-pupiled golden eyes the size of cartwheels.

The man riding on its back leaned over to look at Hanner, as well, and Hanner looked back, seeing a handsome, black-haired young man dressed in fine leathers.

But it was the dragon, and not the rider, who spoke.

"Our compliments, sirrah, and are you, perchance, in a position to speak for all, and to explain your presence here?"

Its voice was deep and rumbling, as if a thunderstorm had spoken, and on top of that it spoke Ethsharitic with a curious accent, a little like one Hanner had occasionally heard from very old people when he was a boy in the overlord's palace. It took a moment for Hanner to make sense of its words.

His comprehension was not aided by the constant awareness that he was standing a few feet away from a mouth that could swallow him in a single gulp. Hanner's instinctive terror was tempered by the realization that the creature seemed more interested in talking to him than in eating him, but he was still terrified.

It did not help that he realized he could smell the dragon; he was that close to the great beast. Its odor was not quite like anything he had ever smelled before, but reminded him of dust, blood, and hot metal.

"As much as anyone is, yes," he said at last.

"Pray you, then, speak, and expound to us how you come to be standing untroubled not a hundred yards from the Warlock Stone — if indeed, the Stone remains."

The stone the dragon spoke of could only be the source of the Calling. "It doesn't," Hanner said. "It's gone, back where it came from."

"And was that then the great disturbance that we saw from afar a few hours gone, in the depths of night?"

Hanner had reached his limit in making sense of the creature's questions. "I…what?"

"May I, Aldagon?" the man in the saddle called.

"And you would," the dragon replied, turning to look at its passenger.

The black-haired young man smiled, and slid from his place on the monster's back. He dropped a few yards to the ground, but managed to stay on his feet, and came walking up to Hanner, hand extended.

They shook, and the young man in leather said, "I'm Dumery of the Dragon, and this is Aldagon, She Who Is Great Among Dragons. Aldagmor is named for her."

This seemed to Hanner to be an extravagant and unlikely claim, but he was hardly in a position to argue about it, and after all, these were unlikely circumstances. "I'm Hanner," he said. "Formerly Hanner the Warlock, formerly Chairman of the Council of Warlocks."

Dumery nodded thoughtfully, and looked around. "*Formerly* a warlock," he said. "I didn't know that was possible. Interesting. I saw hundreds of other people here before they all hid from Aldagon; were *they* all warlocks?"

"Yes," Hanner said. "They used to be."

"So the Warlock Stone is gone, and…what? It released you? You had all been Called?"

That was close enough to what had actually happened that Hanner just nodded. "Yes," he said again.

"There were a *lot* of you."

"Yes," Hanner said, and this time he thought a little more explanation was called for. "It was everyone who was ever Called, ever since the Night of Madness. We were caught in the…the Warlock Stone's protective spells."

Dumery let out a low whistle. "*All* of you? But there must have been *thousands*!"

"Yes," Hanner said again, hoping he didn't sound stupid, saying the same thing over and over.

"What will you all *eat*?"

"That's a very good question," Hanner said. "We have some theurgists, and they were able to summon Piskor the Generous. She gave us those bundles — see?" He gestured toward the one at his feet, and then at the hundreds that had been dropped by people fleeing Aldagon's approach.

"That doesn't look like enough to last very long," Dumery said.

Hanner turned up an empty palm. "Three days, the goddess said."

"Then what?"

"We were hoping we could reach civilization by then."

"'Twould be a vigorous walk, to reach a city so soon," Aldagon rumbled.

Hanner started, and looked from Dumery to the dragon, then back. "How… You were *riding* it."

"Her," Dumery corrected him. "Yes, I was."

Hanner gave the dragon a sidelong glance, not wanting to say anything that could possibly offend it — or rather, her. "Have you… Is she…"

"Is she tame?" Dumery grinned. "No. Far from it. But we're business partners."

"Partners?" He looked back and forth from the dragon to the man, but could read nothing from either's expression. "Is that…is that sort of thing common? I was caught in that spell for seventeen years, so I don't know what the World is like now, but — partners?"

Dumery smiled. "No, it's not common. I think Aldagon and I are the only such partnership since the Great War. We've been working together for about ten years now." He turned his smile toward Aldagon. "I think we've both been pleased with how it's worked out," he said.

"Aye, I am not displeased," Aldagon said. "Though certes, I am kept from my repose more than e'er I was these four centuries past. Dumery would work me to skin and bone, did I allow."

"Oh, you were bored silly until we met, and you know it," Dumery said, reaching up to slap Aldagon's jaw — the only part of the dragon he could reach from where he stood.

"Said I not, I am not displeased?"

Hanner closed his eyes for a moment to gather his wits.

As far as he was concerned, a day or two ago he had been trying to fight off the Calling while Arvagan finished up the Transporting Tapestry he had ordered. He had been home in Ethshar of the Spices, living with his wife and children in his late uncle's mansion on High Street, and everything had been fairly normal.

Now he was standing in the mud of Aldagmor, a hundred yards from the pit where the Calling had originated, talking to a dragon. He had seen and heard a goddess. He had seen and heard the Response that had carried the Warlock Stone back into the sky. He was seventeen years in the future.

That was all a little difficult to absorb.

"But see you, friend Hanner," Aldagon said, interrupting his thoughts, "while I would do you no harm, you and your compatriots are in lands that have known no human habitation in many a year, and lands that I and mine had thought our own. I had thought these lands to be forbidden to your kind, and like to remain so. My home lies not far hence, chosen that none should trouble me there, and likewise I should trouble none with my presence, yet here you are, in your thousands. Do you, then, intend to dwell in this place henceforth?"

"What?" Hanner looked up, startled. "Oh, no, we aren't staying — at least, most of us aren't. I told you, we want to get back to civilization." He looked around, and saw several people watching, but they were all keeping their distance; no one wanted to approach the dragon. "Some of these people *did* live here, before the Night of Madness, but I don't know whether any of them want to rebuild."

"I suspect they could be persuaded not to," Dumery said. "No offense, Aldagon, but most humans are unlikely to want dragons as neighbors."

Aldagon looked as if she was about to reply, but then stopped, cocked her head to one side, and said nothing.

Dumery laughed. "She's too polite to say the feeling is mutual," he said. "But it is, and I really think you people do need to get out of the area as soon as possible."

"We were planning to," Hanner said. He pointed. "We were going to follow that stream south."

"You're heading for Ethshar, rather than Sardiron?" Dumery asked.

"*I* am. Many of us are. I can't speak for everyone."

"It's probably wise," Dumery said with a nod. "Heading northwest, toward Sardiron, would take you directly through Aldagon's territory, and there are other dragons there who are…well, they're much younger, too young to talk, but still big enough to eat people."

"Oh," Hanner said.

"It's a long walk to Ethshar, though."

"Then we should get started," Hanner said. "We were getting ready when you, ah…interrupted —"

"You mean, when Aldagon scared everyone into running off in a hundred different directions?"

Hanner smiled wryly. "Yes."

"Well, then," Dumery suggested, "perhaps we can guide you, or carry a message somewhere, to make up for our little intrusion."

Hanner blinked. "Could you?" he said. "That would be appreciated. That would be *very* appreciated."

"We'll also make sure the other dragons don't bother you," Dumery added.

"Aye," Aldagon said. "I've no desire for bad blood betwixt our peoples."

"That's…that's very kind of you," Hanner said. He was still having some difficulty in accepting the fact that he was holding a civil conversation with a hundred-foot dragon.

"'Tis naught but sense," Aldagon replied. "Come, then, and call your folk together. Gather yourselves up, make ready, and be off with you, and Dumery and I shall do what we can to ease your path."

Slightly stunned, Hanner said, "Thank you." But then he remembered some details of the former warlocks' situation. "We have injured people," he said quickly. "I was expecting to arrange for them to be carried, but is there anything you could do to help? And some of us died — I don't know how many."

Dumery and the dragon looked at one another.

"Hmm," Dumery said. "I don't see how we can help with the injured, and you'd need a necromancer to help with the dead."

"Oh, I know there's nothing we —"

"A thought strikes me, but I know not if your folk might reckon it unseemly," Aldagon said, interrupting him. "Is't not your custom to burn the dead, that their souls may be freed of flesh and might travel unhindered to heaven?"

"Yes," Hanner said, "but we don't have time to gather the firewood for a proper pyre for so many. We need to go, get moving while we still have some food left."

"You have no need of wood when you have a dragon to hand," Aldagon said.

Hanner blinked again. "Oh," he said. He considered that for a moment. Being eaten by a dragon would be undignified, to say the least, but to have dragonfire for one's funeral pyre seemed almost ennobling.

But it wasn't necessarily his decision to make. "I think that might be a good idea," he said, "but I'll want to discuss it with the others."

"Certes," Aldagon said.

"About the injured," Dumery said. "I know several wizards in the three Ethshars — would you like me to talk to them, and see if they can send help?"

"But how…?"

"Aldagon will fly me to Ethshar of the Spices," Dumery explained. "It won't take more than a day or so."

"That would be wonderful," Hanner said, immensely relieved. If someone in Ethshar knew they were out here, someone might send aid.

"They'll probably want to know what's happening here anyway," Dumery said. "In fact, I wouldn't be surprised if we're being watched by a hundred scrying spells right now."

Hanner started to ask why, then stopped. The answer was obvious. Warlockry had vanished a few hours ago, and that would have been noticed throughout the Hegemony by now — not *all* the warlocks were among the Called. "You're right," he said. "But I'd feel better if you carried that message anyway."

"Then we'll do it," Dumery said. "We'll leave at once. Those of you who feel up to it should ready the dead; Aldagon will burn the bodies as soon as we return, if that's what you want. Even in this cold, you shouldn't leave them for long."

"Agreed," Hanner said. He glanced at Aldagon.

"If I may," she said. "I will carry Dumery to the gates of Azrad's Ethshar, that he may speak to the wizards of the city, that they may send what aid they can. Then I shall return, and incinerate the bodies prepared for me in this place. In exchange for my services in these matters, you — *all* of you — will hie hence forthwith, and return no more. You will depart to the south and east, as you choose, but none will go to the north or west, for those lands are home to my kin. Is this our complete understanding, friend Hanner?"

"It is," Hanner said.

"You accept these terms, and speak for all present?"

"I accept these terms, but I can't speak for everyone. I'll do everything I can to persuade everyone to accept them, but there may be some uncooperative idiots."

"And such there be, you will bear no malice for any actions I take upon them, to secure my home?"

"I think you've been more than fair," Hanner said.

"Then let us away, Dumery, to Azrad's Ethshar."

"Right," Dumery said, with a look around. Hanner's gaze followed the dragon-rider's, and he saw that scores, or hundreds, of human eyes were watching — apparently when Hanner was not immediately roasted or devoured, some of the others found the nerve to stop running and observe.

Then Aldagon bent her head low, and Dumery clambered up her flank, pulling himself up the saddle-band and onto her neck. A moment later he was back in the saddle, and Aldagon crouched.

"Get back!" Dumery shouted, and Hanner stepped back — but not far enough; when Aldagon leapt upward, wings flapping, the wind of her rise knocked Hanner entirely off his feet and sent him sprawling on the cold ground.

Embarrassed, he got slowly back to his feet, and turned to watch the gigantic dragon flying south. She was already half a mile away, the morning sun gleaming from her scales as she dwindled into the distance.

Chapter Eight

Five members of the Imperial Council sat around the table, listening to Lord Sterren explain the situation as best he could. Not all of them found the regent's explanations entirely convincing.

"I thought warlocks *never* came back from the Calling," Lady Kalira said. "In fact, I thought *you* told me that."

"They never have before," Sterren said. "But apparently everything changed last night, just as it did on the Night of Madness, but in reverse."

"That's really the Great Vond?" Lord Goluz asked. He was the youngest member of the Council, and had never met Vond before. He had been a mere merchant's apprentice when the Empire was created.

"It's really Vond," Sterren replied.

"Can he hear us in here?" Lady Arris asked.

"I don't think so," Sterren said. "Warlocks do have enhanced senses, but I don't *think* hearing is one of them."

"What does it matter if he *can* hear us?" Prince Ferral asked. "We aren't saying anything terrible. Even if we were, it's not as if we could do anything to stop him from doing whatever he pleases."

"I wasn't planning to say anything treasonous," Arris replied nervously. "I just wanted to know."

"Where is he now, do you think?" Goluz asked.

"He was talking to some of those people he brought with him," Lady Kalira said.

"Out in the plaza," Sterren confirmed.

"I wish Algarven was here," Goluz muttered.

Sterren sympathized; Algarven was one of the steadiest, most sensible voices on the Council. Unfortunately, he was off inspecting the ports, to help the Council decide whether to expand the facilities in Quonshar, or put more resources into the harbor in Akalla of the Diamond, or whether there was a third option worth considering. Quonshar was closest to the empire's border, and to Ethshar, while Akalla was closest to the imperial capital of Semma. The best natural port, though, was probably Kalshar, which lay between the others.

"But he *isn't* here," Sterren said. "Neither is Lady Tanna. There are just the six of us gathered here."

The councillors exchanged glances.

"Why *are* we meeting, really?" Ferral asked. "The Emperor is back, he's reclaimed his position, and we can't do anything but accept it and go on administering the empire."

"That's probably true," Sterren admitted. "I thought it might be a good idea to make sure we all understood the situation, that's all. You seem to have a solid grasp of the realities, your Highness, but perhaps not everyone here was as quick to realize our position."

"*I* wasn't," Goluz proclaimed.

"Vond is probably going to want to talk to us at some point, to hear what we've been doing since he left," Sterren continued. "I didn't want anyone to be caught off-guard. We need to answer his questions honestly; don't try to lie about anything." He hesitated, then added, "Except, of course, your loyalty to him. Whether you really *are* loyal or not is irrelevant; never give him any reason to doubt you. Let him think you're an incompetent and he'll probably just accept it, but say even a word of defiance and he might squash you."

Lady Kalira glanced in the direction of where poor Ildirin had been smashed against a wall fifteen years before, and shuddered. Ildirin had not been defiant. He had not even been seriously incompetent; merely unlucky.

"If any of you do come up with any schemes to overthrow the emperor, I would strongly suggest you don't tell the rest of us," Sterren said. "If you succeed, then I'm sure we'll accept it, but I do not want to see this entire council destroyed if a plot goes wrong and we're all implicated. That would be very bad for the empire, as well as for us."

This time it was not just Kalira who shuddered.

"Please notice, though, that I'm not telling you that you shouldn't try to remove Vond," Sterren said.

"You think seven plots are more likely to result in one that succeeds than a single big conspiracy is," Ferral said.

"I am not going to comment on that," Sterren said, nodding.

"You don't think multiple conspiracies might get in each other's way?" Kalira asked.

Sterren turned up an empty palm. "Who knows?"

"The Wizards' Guild banned warlocks from the empire," Lady Arris said.

"They did," Sterren agreed. "I expect they will attempt to enforce that eventually, but it may take some time, and I don't know how effective they'll be."

"Or how much damage they'll do in the process," Ferral said. "The stories about that lunatic magician calling herself Empress Tabaea in Ethshar of the Sands aren't encouraging."

"The Cult of Demerchan might be interested to know Vond is back," Kalira suggested.

"They might be," Sterren agreed.

"Fellow councillors," Goluz said, glancing around, "I am concerned by what I am hearing here. Don't any of you think Vond's return might be a *good* thing? After all, he built this palace in a matter of days, and built roads, and used his magic in a dozen beneficial ways."

Kalira and Sterren exchanged glances. "He may do more useful things," Sterren acknowledged. "I don't think he actually wants to hurt anyone. His rule *may* do more good than harm. But he isn't strong on self-control, and he has the power to do a huge amount of damage very quickly. I don't think any of us are about to assassinate him tonight, by any means; I think most of us will want to wait and see how matters develop. But if they develop badly, it would not hurt to have a few ideas of how to improve the situation."

"As Lady Arris said," Kalira added, "the Wizards' Guild banned warlocks from the empire. I do not like the idea of being caught in a battle between Vond and the Guild."

"But if that battle happens, shouldn't we side with Vond, rather than the Guild?" Goluz asked. "He's our emperor!"

Sterren grimaced. "You're free to decide for yourself," he said, "but I don't *ever* want to be on the side fighting the Wizards' Guild."

"If I *do* decide to assassinate the emperor," Lord Vorash said, speaking for the first time, "I will be careful not to mention it to *you*, Lord Goluz."

That provoked nervous laughter for a few of the councillors — though not, Sterren noticed, from Lord Goluz.

"I think we've said quite enough," Prince Ferral announced, pushing back his chair. "I'm going to go attend to my own business now. If the emperor wishes to speak to me, I will be at his disposal."

Lady Arris rose as well, and then the others, and a moment later Sterren was alone in the room.

He sat for a moment, thinking.

Maybe Lord Goluz was right. Maybe having the only warlock in the World as their ruler would be a good thing. Maybe he would build roads and dredge harbors and heal the sick. Certainly, he would enforce the peace within the empire.

But almost the first thing he had said upon returning was that he intended to conquer a neighboring kingdom. He had asked after his harem. He had admitted abandoning thousands of former warlocks in the wilderness of Aldagmor, and made no mention of doing anything to help them.

Those weren't the words of a thoughtful and effective ruler.

Sterren sighed, and got to his feet.

He found Lar Samber's son waiting for him outside the council chamber door. The man was showing his age; his hair was white, and he moved stiffly as he rose to greet his employer. His weight had varied over the years, and at the moment he was stout, verging on fat. His weight seemed to be slowing him down, where it never had before. Sterren felt a twinge of guilt at summoning him; Lar had been more or less retired for the past few years.

"Regent," Lar said in Ethsharitic. "You sent for me."

"I'm not a regent anymore," Sterren said in Semmat. Ethsharitic was the official language of the empire, while Semmat was the local tongue; Sterren knew both well. Vond did not; he was only fluent in Ethsharitic. The council meeting had been conducted entirely in Ethsharitic, since not all the councillors spoke Semmat, but now Sterren switched to the language the emperor did not understand. "Vond has reclaimed his throne. I suppose I might be chancellor again, though."

"I stand corrected," Lar said in Semmat. "You *did* send for me, though."

Sterren sighed again, and nodded. "I did," he said. "As I'm sure you know, Vond is back. He says the Calling has stopped, and he's the only warlock left."

"Is *that* what happened? There were rumors."

Sterren smiled wryly. *He* hadn't heard any rumors yet, but of course Lar had. Retired or not, he had spent most of his adult life as a spy, and he still seemed to know everything that went on anywhere in Semma. "Yes," he said. "That does appear to be the case."

"That's an interesting situation," Lar remarked.

"Indeed. I'd like to know what Guildmaster Ithinia thinks of it," Sterren replied.

"Ithinia? If I may, my lord, why her, in particular?"

"Because I don't know of a wizard who stands higher in the Guild than she does — I'm sure there are some, but the Guild does not choose to identify them to outsiders. Besides, Ithinia did seem to take quite an interest in imperial affairs when she visited us twelve years ago."

"Ah," Lar said.

"I think she should also be informed that apparently there are thousands of former warlocks who have been turned loose in Aldagmor, and may be stranded there."

"Are there?" Lar asked, raising an eyebrow.

"So I'm told."

"I'll see that the news reaches her," Lar said. "Though by the time I can get word to her, she may well already know all about it."

"I know, but I think we should make the gesture."

Lar nodded. "Of course."

"I'm also curious about whether the Sisterhood has an opinion on Vond's return."

Lar nodded. "Anyone else?"

"The Brotherhood, while we're at it. The Council of Warlocks, if it still exists. The three overlords of the Hegemony. The Cult of Demerchan. Anyone you can think of."

"Oh — is that how it stands?"

"I'm afraid so. But Ithinia first, I think."

Lar bowed stiffly. "As you say."

"Leave as soon as you can."

"Yes, my lord." He turned, and walked away, toward the nearest door out of the palace. He didn't run, as if he were in a hurry, or march, like a man obeying orders, or creep, as if he didn't want to be seen; he simply walked, like someone who was headed somewhere but wasn't in a great rush. No one would give him a second glance.

Sterren watched in admiration for a second or two, then hurried down the corridor to the entry hall. Dozens of people were there, milling about or talking in small groups; about half of them were strangers, mostly dressed in black, from the group Vond had brought back with him from Aldagmor. The others were mostly palace staff and imperial officials of one sort or another, with a few confused-looking guards mixed in.

Sterren spotted one of the Council's messengers and beckoned her aside. She glanced about, then joined him by the wall.

"Yes, my lord?" she asked in Ethsharitic.

"Where's the emperor?" he asked in Semmat.

She replied in the same tongue, "He and the chamberlain are upstairs, seeing to the accommodations. His old apartments were long ago put to other uses."

"I know," Sterren said. "I gave the orders for that myself. So he's inspecting the palace?"

She nodded.

"Has he said anything about the people he brought with him?" Sterren jerked his head toward a clump of black-clad strangers.

"We are to treat them as honored guests."

"That's all?"

"I'm just a messenger, my lord."

"Thank you." Sterren patted her on the shoulder, then turned and smiled at one of the strangers.

He smiled warily back, and Sterren strode over to him.

"Welcome to the Vondish Empire!" Sterren said in Ethsharitic, raising a hand in greeting. "I am Lord Sterren."

"My name is Korl of Cliffgate," the stranger replied, in an accent that seemed to indicate an origin in Ethshar of the Rocks.

"I'm pleased to meet you," Sterren said. "I understand you are a warlock?"

"Well, I *was*," Korl said.

"Yes, I understand the power you drew upon is gone."

Korl shuddered. "Yes," he said.

Sterren got the very definite impression that Korl did not care to discuss whatever it was that had departed Aldagmor, and he had no problem with that; he was more interested in matters closer to home. "How did you come to know the emperor?" he asked.

"I *don't* know him," Korl replied. "I mean, I'd heard of him — I was Called a few years after he conquered all those…well, after he conquered *here*, I guess. But I never met him."

"Oh? Then if you don't mind my asking, how do you come to be here?"

"Well, we'd just been freed, and the…the Source had left, and Vond flew up and called for volunteers to come with him, and I raised my hands because I was cold and scared and we were stranded out there in the wilderness at night, with no food or water or magic, and he said he would bring us here and give us important positions. It seemed better than starving or freezing in Aldagmor, or being there if that thing came back."

"I see," Sterren said. "Very sensible."

"Maybe," Korl said, looking around uneasily. "I'm not sure. No one here was expecting us, and we haven't gotten any food yet, though they did find us wine and water. No one seems to know where we're to sleep, or what's to become of us. Vond hasn't said what he wants us for. And I have this horrible headache, as if my skull were buzzing. I'd think it was an after-effect of losing my magic, but it didn't feel like that in Aldagmor."

"Ah, yes," Sterren said. "I've heard of that. It's a local effect. It's said that that was why there were no warlocks here until Vond came — the headaches. They never stop; they just get worse and worse."

"Really?" Korl looked around. "But then how does Vond stand it? Why does he still have magic at all?"

Sterren feigned surprise. "He hasn't told you?"

"No. I thought that maybe he would teach the rest of us how we could be warlocks again, but he hasn't said a word about it."

"Ah, I suppose he wants to keep the secret for himself," Sterren said. "As it happens, he was working for me when he found it — that's why he kept me around, and how I became a lord here. I don't suppose there are a hundred people in the empire who know about it."

"*What* secret?"

Sterren looked around, as if to be sure no one else was listening, then leaned forward. "The headaches were making him utterly miserable, you see, and finally he said something very foolish — he said he would give his soul to make them stop. And apparently he was in the wrong place, or phrased something just right, because a demon heard him, and appeared, and made a bargain with him — in exchange for his soul, Vond would be given enough magical power to shut out the headaches."

"A demon?"

Sterren nodded. "I can't say its name; I don't want to attract its attention."

"I thought demons wouldn't touch warlocks."

That was news to Sterren, but he didn't let that slow him down. "This one would," it said. "Maybe it was because we're so far from Aldagmor here that Vond barely *was* a warlock anymore."

Korl did not seem to think much of that theory. "Go on."

"The deal didn't work out quite the way either of them expected," Sterren said. "Apparently it takes a *lot* of power to shut out the headaches, so much so that Vond was able to use it to build this empire. And Vond thought that having his soul promised to the demon would mean that the Calling couldn't get him, but it didn't work out that way. He was Called anyway." Sterren glanced around. "You know, I hate to suggest it of my own liege lord, but I wonder whether he might have brought you people here to see if he could swap your souls to the demon in place of his own, now that he's safe from the Calling."

Korl threw an uneasy glance over his shoulder. "So he's not a warlock any more? He's a demonologist? All his magic is demonic?"

"What else could it be? There isn't any more warlockry, and you know warlocks can't be wizards or theurgists, and a witch would never have the sort of power he does. I mean, he's wearing a black robe — not exactly hiding it, is he?"

Korl frowned. "I thought...I don't know, I thought maybe it was another kind of warlockry."

Sterren snorted. "Really, how likely is *that*? Isn't it strange enough having *one* of those things arrive on the Night of Madness and snatch away thousands of people, and now you're suggesting there was a *second* one that only affected *one* person? And that one person just happened to already be an Aldagmor warlock?"

"Well, I..." Korl frowned. "That does sound unlikely."

"It's a demon. A big one. Sometimes you can glimpse it in the desert east of here, a big shadow with glowing eyes."

Korl bit his lower lip so that his beard bristled.

"I'm afraid you'll just have to put up with the headaches," Sterren said. "At least, if you value your soul."

"What causes the headaches, though?"

Sterren turned up an empty palm. "Who knows? An old curse, maybe? A wizard's spell gone wrong? Some left-over magic from the Great War? Or maybe it's the demon itself, trying to lure victims."

Korl's eyes shifted nervously.

"So will you be staying here in the capital, do you think, or might this position the emperor promised you be somewhere else?"

"I don't know," Korl said. "I don't know much about the Vondish Empire."

"Oh, well, there are eighteen provinces," Sterren said. "Eight of them lie along the South Coast, and the rest are inland. We're in Semma, the capital; you landed in Imperial Plaza, the heart of New Semma, and across the valley is the Old Town, where the regent's castle is. We speak twenty different languages in the empire, I'm afraid, but Ethsharitic is the official imperial tongue." He smiled. "There are eighteen provinces *now*, but his Imperial Majesty has already said that he wants to add a nineteenth, Lumeth of the Towers."

"Oh? Where is that?"

"A few leagues northwest of here, in the foothills of the central mountains. Vond never conquered it in his first reign because it was under the protection of the Wizards' Guild, but apparently he feels that he's now powerful enough to defy them."

Korl, already a little pale, went white. "The Wizards' Guild?"

"I'm afraid so — but I'm sure they'll be too busy elsewhere to involve themselves."

"Of course."

Sterren frowned. "You don't look well; the headaches must be getting to you. Should I see if I can find a witch? Vond never found their healing very useful, but it might be better than nothing."

"No, that's…that's…I'll be fine. Thank you." Korl turned away.

Sterren let him go, then stepped back to the wall and found the messenger still there.

"Did you hear that?" he asked her in Semmat.

"No, my lord."

He gave her a glance, unsure whether to believe her, but her face did not give much away.

"I think some of our guests may be departing the capital soon," he said. "Perhaps the empire itself."

"Yes, my lord?"

"I think we should accommodate them," he said. "Are you available to carry a message?"

"Of course, my lord."

"Then I want you to head for the coast at once, and visit all the eight ports, from Akalla to Quonshar, and tell the harbor masters that any former warlock who wishes to leave the empire is to be provided with free passage to Ethshar of the Spices as quickly as possible. I will pay any expenses out of my own funds; invoices can be sent to the castle, and will be given the very highest priority."

"Free passage for all former warlocks, from any port in the empire?"

"Exactly. Paid by the Regent's exchequer. And your own fee, as well — I believe two rounds of silver would cover it?"

She blinked. "Very generously, my lord."

"If you reach all eight ports before the first warlocks arrive, you'll get *three* rounds. Now go."

"Yes, my lord!" She turned and hurried away.

Sterren watched her go, then turned to see Korl whispering intensely to three other members of Vond's new entourage.

Sterren didn't know whether Vond had any intention of teaching other warlocks to use the same source he did; quite possibly the emperor would prefer keeping the power to himself over sharing it. Still, if some of these people were getting headaches, they might eventually tap into the Lumeth-based power on their own, just as Vond had. One power-mad warlock was bad enough; Sterren considered anything that would scare the others away before they managed the transition to be a good thing.

Now, if only he could find a way to restrain Vond himself!

Chapter Nine

The dream was completely unlike any Hanner had dreamt in years; there were no inhuman whispers, no images of flames, no sensation of falling, no desperate irrational urges. Instead he found himself standing in a wizard's workshop, face to face with a stranger, and every detail was clear and comprehensible. Still, Hanner was fairly certain it was indeed a dream. While he supposed he might have been magically snatched away while he slept and brought here, something about it did not have quite the solidity and definition of real life, and he knew well that wizards could communicate in dreams.

"Chairman Hanner?" the stranger said, his tone deferential.

"Yes?" Hanner replied cautiously.

"I'm Rothiel of Wizard Street. Guildmaster Ithinia asked me to contact you."

"Ithinia? Is she still…" He didn't finish the question; he realized it was foolish. Ithinia had been the senior member of the Wizards' Guild in Ethshar of the Spices from before the Night of Madness until Hanner was Called, and since she had already been a couple of centuries old then, there was no reason to think she wouldn't remain the senior member for the rest of Hanner's life. He had only been gone seventeen years; that was nothing to a wizard of her ability.

"The Guildmaster sends her greetings. She says she remembers you fondly."

"I'm flattered."

"I am speaking to you in your dreams by means of a spell —"

"The Greater Spell of Invaded Dreams," Hanner interrupted. "I was a student of magic before I became a warlock. I was responsible for keeping an eye on the various magicians for Azrad VI."

That was not entirely accurate; he had been sent to study and oversee the magicians of Ethshar by his uncle, Lord Faran, not by the overlord himself. Faran had nominally been working for Azrad, though, so it seemed close enough to the truth for now.

"Oh," Rothiel said. "Then you understand —"

"I understand that if anything wakes me up, this conversation will end abruptly and may be difficult to restore, so please tell me whatever Ithinia wanted you to tell me."

"Yes, of course." Rothiel was visible flustered, but continued quickly. "Well, firstly, Dumery of the Dragon delivered news of your situation to several wizards in Ethshar of the Spices, and it was passed on to the Guildmaster. We will be sending assistance fairly soon."

"Good!"

"However, matters here are somewhat chaotic. As you probably realize, warlockry vanished not just in Aldagmor, but throughout the World, last night, resulting in a great deal of confusion. Other magicians are being called upon to fill in everywhere that warlocks suddenly couldn't. There were several injuries and even a few deaths when the warlocks' magic failed." He waved toward a window that hadn't been there before, and Hanner looked out to see warlocks plummeting onto rooftops and fires bursting out here and there throughout the city. "We are still gathering information about the damage. Your party is not necessarily our highest priority. Can you give us any details about what you need?"

"Everything," Hanner said. "Food, water, shelter, clothing, transportation."

Rothiel nodded. "How many of you are there?"

"Our best estimate is somewhere between fifteen and twenty thousand, not counting the dead."

Rothiel appeared to be momentarily stunned.

"Fifteen *thousand*?" he said at last.

"At least."

"Dumery said there were thousands, but we didn't…I mean, we…"

"Fifteen to twenty thousand," Hanner repeated. "That's the survivors. We counted four hundred and eighty-six dead, but we may have missed some. We couldn't get an exact count on the living."

"You…I understood your group to be warlocks who somehow survived the Calling."

"That's right," Hanner said, starting to become annoyed. "We *all* survived the Calling. It turns out that the Calling itself was *never* fatal. The deaths here all occurred after it ended, when some of us were crushed, or fell out of the sky. Most of the dead were people who had been in Aldagmor on the Night of Madness — they were crushed to death, or smothered, as they were at the bottom of the pile when we woke up. We've dealt with the dead as best we could, and now we're all trying to go home — at least, those of us who still *have* homes; it seems dragons have claimed eastern Aldagmor for themselves, so the survivors from that area are homeless."

"But fifteen thousand —"

"Wizard," Hanner said, trying not to lose his temper, "*every single person who was ever Called*, from the Night of Madness right up to the last few days, just woke up in the wilderness where the Warlock Stone used to be. Our theurgists managed to get us a three-day supply of food, but none of them can get us back to civilization — our best priestess, Alladia of Shiphaven, says that Asham the Gate-Keeper could do it, but she can't remember how to invoke him, and none of the others were ever at her level. We're getting water from the streams running down out of the mountains, but even that isn't going to be enough for all of us. We are in desperate straits. Dumery and his dragon chased us out of the immediate area where we woke up, but there are so many of us that by the time we had laid out the dead for cremation, and made arrangements to transport the injured, we were scarcely able to cover two leagues before we had to stop for the night — and even that left most of us with aching feet; we aren't accustomed to walking. We are bound for Ethshar of the Spices because it's the closest of the great cities; we cannot head toward Sardiron because the dragons' nesting ground is in the way. There are no roads out here. We have no one who knows the route with any certainty. We think there are wild beasts in the area — not just dragons, but other creatures that have taken advantage of Aldagmor's depopulation. There may be other dangers, as well; we don't know. Some of us are fairly sure we have homes and families waiting, while others have been gone for ten or twenty or thirty years and have no idea what the World is like now, or whether anyone remembers us. If the Wizards' Guild can help us, we will be grateful for whatever aid you provide."

"Of course." Rothiel was recovering quickly from his surprise. "My apologies, Chairman; I admit we thought Dumery must have been exaggerating, but clearly he was not. We will see what can be done. We'll put out the word that all Called warlocks are returning; some of you may indeed be hearing from friends and relatives soon."

"*Thank* you!" Hanner said, greatly relieved.

"Is there anyone you would like us to speak to on your own behalf?"

"Oh," Hanner said. The question had caught him off-guard.

"The current Chairman of the Council of Warlocks for Ethshar of the Spices is Zallin of the Mismatched Eyes; would you like us to inform him that you're alive?"

Hanner started; he remembered Zallin of the Mismatched Eyes. That annoying youngster was now *chairman*? He had been only a year or two out of his apprenticeship, and very fond of stupid jokes, when Hanner last saw him; Hanner could almost still hear his irritating bray of a laugh.

"No, I don't care about him," Hanner said. "But if you could find my wife, Mavi of Newmarket — is she safe? Is she well?"

"I'll see what I can find out."

"And our children — we have three children. They must be grown by now."

"I will make inquiries."

Hanner had already made a few inquiries of his own, asking warlocks who had been Called after him, but no one seemed very sure what had become of his family. That worried him.

Most of the warlocks he had known who were Called before him had turned out to be alive and unhurt; he had found Rudhira of Camptown, and Varrin the Weaver, and Desset of Eastwark, and most of the others who he had gathered on the Night of Madness. He had found other warlocks he had known through his seventeen years as Chairman of the Council of Warlocks. He had talked to several warlocks who had been Called after him, from Goran the Tall, who appeared to have flown north just a few days after Hanner himself, to Sensella of Morningside, who never did quite reach the Source.

But he hadn't found anyone who knew what had happened to Mavi, or to Faran, Arris, and Hala.

"Is there anything else, Chairman?"

"Ithinia might want to know this, if she doesn't already — Emperor Vond is still alive and still able to work magic."

"Emperor Vond?"

"Yes. He was after my time, but from what the others have told me, surely you've heard of him?"

"I don't understand," Rothiel said. "I know the name, but wasn't the Great Vond a warlock who was Called fifteen years ago?"

"Yes, he was," Hanner said. "Or so I am told; I never met him, so far as I recall, and as I said, he didn't build his empire until after I was gone."

"But warlocks can't do magic any more, can they?"

"Most of us, no, or we wouldn't be here, but apparently Vond can. I thought Ithinia should be told."

"How is that possible?"

Hanner glared at the wizard. "How should *I* know? *I* can't do magic anymore! You're a wizard; you figure it out."

"Is Vond with your group, then?"

"No. He flew off yesterday morning. He took eighty or ninety volunteers with him to reclaim his empire, which I'm told is somewhere in the Small Kingdoms."

"Volunteers?" Rothiel's expression was a mix of fear and bafflement. "Can *they* still do magic?"

"No. Or at least, they couldn't when they left; for all I know, Vond may have taught them by now."

"This is very disturbing news. Can *any* of the other warlocks with you use any magic?"

"We have about half a dozen theurgists, maybe a score of witches, and a few others, including a handful of wizards and former wizards, but if you mean can anyone else still use warlockry, none that I know of. Someone might be hiding it, I suppose, but I don't know why anyone would."

"Theurgists and witches?" The fear had passed, but Rothiel's confusion was more obvious than ever. "I thought you were all warlocks."

"We were," Hanner said. "How old are you?"

"I don't see —"

"How old are you?"

"I don't see what it has to do with anything, but I'm thirty-one."

"Thank you; that's about what I would have guessed, but one can never be sure with wizards. Then you don't remember the Night of Madness, but you must have heard about it."

"Yes, of course."

"Then you know that in that one night, thousands of people went off to Aldagmor, never to be seen again."

"Well, yes, but —"

"And you must have heard that it seemed to strike almost at random."

"Yes."

"If you choose three or four thousand people at random from the population of the Hegemony of the Three Ethshars, how many of them do you think will be magicians?"

"Oh." Understanding spread across Rothiel's face.

"Now do you see? Most of our magicians were Called on the Night of Madness, snatched away in the middle of the night, without their supplies. A few who became warlocks that night without being Called immediately went on to give up their other magic and live for a time as warlocks, but now that they've lost their warlockry, their old magic has returned — though as you might guess, they're badly out of practice."

"I think I see."

"We seem to have more witches than one might expect," Hanner remarked, "but witchcraft and warlockry always seemed to have some similarities, so that's probably why."

"A large part of your group, then, is people who disappeared on the Night of Madness, almost thirty-five years ago?"

"Yes. I'm sure they were all thought to be long since dead. No one expects to just go home after all this time and pick up where they left off."

"Haven't many of them died of old age?"

"Oh, didn't I explain that?" Hanner smiled. "No. The protective spells on the Warlock Stone preserved us all perfectly. We didn't age a day, whether we were caught there for thirty-four minutes or thirty-four years."

"The spell was strong enough to preserve *all* the warlocks who were ever Called?"

"This was the *source* of all warlockry, wizard. It had all the power it would ever need for anything it wanted to do."

"Of course. I see. So there are fifteen thousand of you, and most of you disappeared years ago and are now returning unchanged to families that thought you long dead. You understand that this may...complicated."

Hanner glared. "I am not an idiot, Rothiel."

"Yes, but this is... This is not what we expected."

"It's not what *I* expected when I was Called, either, but here we are."

Rothiel nodded. "I will speak to Ithinia, and I hope we will be able to assist you soon."

"Thank you."

"Good night, Hanner, and good luck."

With that, the wizard's workshop suddenly crumbled away, leaving Hanner standing on trampled grass back in Aldagmor, surrounded by sleeping warlocks.

Then that, too, dissolved, and he was alone in lightless emptiness — clearly, the dream the wizard had sent had ended, but his sleeping mind was not yet ready to let go. He shouted, but there was no one to hear him, and his voice seemed small and faint in the void.

And then he woke up, his back stiff, a blade of grass tickling one ear. He was cold and damp, lying on cold, damp ground. He was looking at white fabric, though it seemed rather dim. He shivered, then rolled from his side to his back and looked up at a gray sky; clouds had rolled in during the night, and it was not much after dawn. He sat up.

Sleeping bodies stretched out in every direction, though less so to the south; he had been near the front of the throng. That white fabric was the back of Rudhira's tunic; she was still wearing the white tunic and green skirt she had worn when she flew off to Aldagmor, all those years ago — clothes she had borrowed from the wardrobe Lord Faran had kept for his mistresses. She had left one green shoe behind on the streets of Ethshar, and somewhere she had lost the other, leaving her feet bare. Her long red hair trailed across the muddy grass.

Finding her among the crowd in Aldagmor had been a shock for Hanner; despite Sensella's warnings and his conversation with Rayel, it had not been until he saw Rudhira that the effects of the time-stopping protective spells around the Warlock Stone really hit home. Rudhira was the same lovely young woman she had been when she flew away, just a few days after the Night of Madness; if anything, she was prettier than he had remembered.

She hadn't recognized him. He had aged seventeen years, and she, not at all. She had been a few years older than he when they first met in Witch Alley; now she was at least a decade younger.

She had been a streetwalker before the Night of Madness; then, for a few days, she had been the most powerful warlock in Ethshar of the Spices.

What would she be now?

Rothiel had said their situation was complicated, and Hanner was well aware that he was right. Twenty thousand former warlocks were about to start arriving in the towns and villages and cities of the Hegemony of the Three Ethshars, and the Baronies of Sardiron, and the other realms of the World. Some of them might have friends and family eager to welcome them back, but most would not. Some would have other trades to pursue now that they could no longer be warlocks, but others would not; someone who had apprenticed to a warlock at age twelve, had studied and practiced nothing but magic, and had earned a living for his or her entire adult life with that magic, did not have a great many career choices open to him. The younger people could still learn new trades, but what was a man of forty or fifty supposed to do? A man of that age could not join the city guard, which was the last resort for a youth who never found an apprenticeship or other job.

Hanner very much feared that many of his companions here might wind up sleeping in the Hundred-Foot Field, begging for scraps.

It was possible, though unlikely, that *he* would wind up doing that. After all, he had never been apprenticed to a trade; before becoming a warlock he had worked for his Uncle Faran, who was long dead. He had inherited some money and property when Lord Faran died, but he had more of less turned the mansion over to the Council of Warlocks, and he might not be able to reclaim it — it was a long-established principle that Called warlocks were legally dead. His money was almost certainly long gone. Even before his Calling, he had spent most of his fortune on magic of one sort or another — especially those blasted Transporting Tapestries.

He knew now what had happened to him, how his experiment with the tapestries had gone wrong. He had simply been unprepared for the impact of the sudden return of the Calling after the mental silence in that refuge. His mind had had no time to adjust, no chance to restore the barriers he had built up and then let fall.

He did not know, though, what had become of the tapestry that led to the refuge. Sensella had never heard of it, nor had any of the four or five other people he had spoken to who had been Called from Ethshar of the Spices after his own departure. It ought to be worth something, he thought. Whoever possessed that tapestry controlled access to a minia-ture world; surely, that was valuable to someone.

Mavi might have it, he thought. Or Zallin, though it had been Hanner's property, not the Council's. Or maybe it had been lost, or destroyed.

And what *would* become of Warlock House? The Council no lon-ger had any reason to exist, so perhaps Hanner could reclaim the house, since he had never formally relinquished ownership.

Besides, he had connections. Surely, Mavi was still alive, and his children, and there was no reason to think they would be poor. His two sisters and their families were wealthy and successful, and surely they would have seen to it that Mavi and Faran and Arris and Hala were safe and comfortable. They should be glad to see him return, as well. Oh, it was possible that ruin and doom had somehow befallen them all, but it was vanishingly unlikely. He had no reason to worry too much about his own future; he would be fine.

But what about all these other people? Hanner looked out at the crowd; some of them were beginning to stir, to sit or stand. What would become of them all? He pulled his black tunic tight across his chest, shivering.

He looked down at the sleeping Rudhira. What would become of *her*? Would she go back to Camptown, and a life of warming soldiers' beds? What would happen when she got too old to interest them?

Hanner had never really thought about that before; what *did* happen to old whores? He had never had much contact with any — well, any other than Rudhira. He knew some of them wound up as beggars, sleep-ing in the Hundred-Foot Field, but surely not all of them. Maybe some of them married soldiers, or found other work.

But there were plenty of people here whose prospects weren't even *that* good. Some of them might end up not just as beggars, but as slaves — there probably wasn't enough room in the Hundred-Foot Field for *all* of them, and slavers were free to take any homeless person they found elsewhere in the city.

Maybe the people who had gone with Vond had been the smart ones; in fact, maybe they should *all* think about heading for the Small King-doms...

"Hanner," someone said. He started, and turned to find Sensella standing a few yards away, looking at him.

"Yes?"

"Should we start waking them up?"

Hanner considered that, then spread his hands. "No," he said. "Let them rest while they can. We're going to have a long day."

Sensella nodded. "Do you have any idea how far it is to Ethshar?"

"Fifty leagues, maybe? Sixty? But I hope we won't be walking that far; I've heard from the wizards."

"What?"

"I heard from the wizards. In a dream."

Sensella looked confused and unconvinced.

"It's called the Spell of Invaded Dreams," Hanner explained. "They can appear to you while you sleep. Someone named Rothiel of Wizard Street spoke to me."

"I never heard of him. Are you sure it wasn't just an *ordinary* dream?"

Hanner hesitated.

Up until she asked, he had never doubted the dream's authenticity, but now that he thought about it, he had no actual *proof* that it had been magical in origin. The proof would come when Guildmaster Ithinia sent the promised aid.

"Well," he said, "we'll just have to wait and see."

Chapter Ten

Ithinia of the Isle slumped in the wicker chair, drumming her fingers on its woven arm as she considered the reports she had just received. She had the latest accounts from the wizards she had assigned to investigate various matters, from her agents in the city guard and the overlord's palace, from the network of spies the Guild maintained throughout the city and the Small Kingdoms, and from the witches and theurgists she had consulted. They all confirmed the simple, obvious truth.

The source of the warlocks' magic was gone.

She supposed she should have expected this. That thing in Aldagmor had been calling for something for more than thirty years; was it really such a shock that it had finally been answered?

But who would have expected it to be so *sudden*?

Most of the mess wasn't really significant. Ethshar had gotten along without warlocks for centuries, and it could get along without them again. Having a bunch of suddenly-powerless magicians around was a nuisance, but most of them would probably find places for themselves eventually. The ones who hadn't yet been Called should be no problem at all.

That huge mob working its way south from Aldagmor, on the other hand, was more awkward. By wizardly standards most of them were young, and thanks to their now-vanished magic most of them were disgustingly healthy, so they should manage well enough, but Ethshar's economy hadn't had to absorb so many people all at once since the end of the Great War, and there would inevitably be some disruption.

She sighed. There would undoubtedly be some unfortunate results — more crime, more beggars, more slaves taken. A few decades, though, and it would all be out of the way. Wizards as old and powerful as Ithinia tended to take the long view.

Besides, if this sudden flood of people was *too* inconvenient, some of them could be removed. There were any number of spells that could trim excess population. Killing them would be ugly, and should be avoided if at all possible, but petrifying most of them until the situation improved wouldn't be so very terrible; many of them were *already* decades out of their own time, and a few more years would scarcely matter. If anyone could perform Llarimuir's Mass Transmogrification, they could be turned to trees or some other relatively inert creature; that might be preferable to petrifaction. Ithinia didn't know the spell herself, but there were wizards far more powerful than she.

Those former warlocks in Aldagmor could be handled.

Vond, on the other hand, might be real trouble. According to every source that mentioned him, he still had his ability to draw warlock-like power from the towers in Lumeth. Details, unfortunately, were scarce; scrying spells directed at him had failed. This might be because no one knew his true name, and divinations directed at an individual were never reliable without that, or it might be that his new magic blocked wizardry just as much as true warlockry had. Certainly, every manifestation of his power to date had behaved exactly like warlockry.

Ithinia blinked as she considered that. The towers were sorcerous in nature — an ancient high sorcery that was long lost, not the feeble sort of thing modern sorcerers could do. Did that mean the Warlock Stone had been sorcerous in nature?

But everyone knew that warlockry was somehow related to witch-craft; then was witchcraft related to sorcery? It certainly didn't appear to be.

She shook her head. This was not the time to ponder some grand theory of unified magic. She needed to decide what to do about Vond. He was reported to be on his way back to his empire, if he had not already reached it. The Wizards' Guild could not simply ignore him if he had indeed returned to Semma; they had issued an edict that no warlocks were permitted within twenty leagues of Lumeth, and they could not allow Vond to defy that edict. The Guild did not assert its authority in such matters very often, but when it did, it had to be absolutely ruthless, giving not the slightest hint of weakness.

They would probably need to kill Vond. If it came to that, it had to be done quickly and effectively. That affair with Tabaea and her enchanted dagger had not done the Guild's reputation any good at all, and they could not afford a repetition. If they did decide to kill Vond, it needed to work cleanly on the first attempt, and it needed to be very clear that this was the Guild enforcing its ultimatum.

The problem was, of course, that wizardry didn't work properly on warlocks. Every warlock, no matter how feeble, was effectively guarded by powerful protective spells simply by being a warlock.

But that had only really been tested on *ordinary* warlocks; it was not clear whether it would hold true with Vond. He might be just as well protected as any other warlock, or he might be completely unguarded, or he might be *totally* immune to wizardry — no one knew, and there was no safe way to test it without his cooperation.

Somehow, Ithinia doubted that the Great Vond, self-proclaimed emperor, would agree to help wizards test his vulnerabilities. The question then became, what spell could be absolutely certain to kill Vond on the first attempt?

The Seething Death had worked on Tabaea, but it had done significant damage in the process, and stopping it had required the use of forbidden magic; Ithinia had no desire to see anything like that used against Vond.

The Call of Celestial Debris might work, but it would probably flatten half of Semma in the process. Since it involved purely physical projectiles, Vond's magic shouldn't interfere with the spell itself.

But on second thought, Ithinia realized, if he saw the meteors coming, he was probably powerful enough to deflect them. That wouldn't do.

The Devouring Earth wouldn't work; Vond could fly. He wouldn't fall when the ground opened beneath him.

The Spell of the Smoke Noose would probably just evaporate when it hit his magical barriers, and from what Vond had done during his first reign it was possible he no longer needed to breathe, so even if it *didn't* collapse, it might not kill him.

Zil's Dehydration, Fendel's Assassin, the Rune of the Implacable Stalker, the Spell of Ghastly Dissolution, the Cold Death, the White Curse — any of them *might* work, but none of them were *certain*...

"Mistress?"

She started at the sound of her manservant's voice, and sat up. "Yes, Obdur?"

Obdur was standing in the door of the solarium; he bowed. "Chairman Zallin of the Council of Warlocks insists on speaking to you."

"Zallin? Whatever for?"

"He did not say."

A thought struck her. "Did he call *himself* Chairman of the Council of Warlocks? Or did you just remember him by that title?"

"*He* did, mistress."

Ithinia gave a small snort. *What* Council of Warlocks? Except for Vond and Sterren, there *weren't* any more warlocks — well, unless Vond had been making more.

Which was another reason to deal with Vond *quickly* — he *could* make more Lumeth-based warlocks. That was known. From what she had heard of him Ithinia doubted he really wanted to share his power, but he *could*, and if he wasn't disposed of promptly, he might.

But Zallin probably didn't know anything about Vond.

"I will meet him in the parlor momentarily, Obdur."

Obdur bowed. "Yes, mistress." He turned and slipped out of the room.

Ithinia sighed and got to her feet. Zallin didn't really have any business here; he hadn't been invited, and he no longer represented anyone the Guild needed to treat with respect. If he wanted to buy a spell, he could go to the Wizards' Quarter like anyone else.

Maybe he was coming to formally renounce his role and disband the Council of Warlocks; after all, it had been created to appease the Hegemony and the Wizards' Guild, and it had been Ithinia and the Guild that had forced the overlord to accept it. It would be appropriate for an announcement of the Council's dissolution to come to her, as the city's senior Guildmaster, and also to the overlord or his representative. The overlord who had first accepted the Council's existence was dead, of course, but his son now reigned as Azrad VII — though perhaps not for very much longer, given his age. Ithinia's best sources said that Azrad was taking a cautious attitude toward the disappearance of warlockry, waiting to be sure there weren't any nasty surprises involved.

The resignation of the Chairman of the Council might be a surprise, but it wouldn't be a nasty one. She had the impression that the overlord and his court weren't particularly fond of Zallin.

She guessed that if that was indeed Zallin's errand, the only reason he had come here first was that it was more or less on the way from Warlock House to the palace.

Remembering what Zallin was like, she doubted that he was coming to renounce anything. Poor Hanner, the first Chairman, might have done that, but Zallin? No.

"Poor Hanner?" But Hanner was coming back, wasn't he? Rothiel had spoken to him with the Spell of Invaded Dreams, and confirmed that he was alive and well, at least for the moment. Strange, to think she might see him again. She hadn't known many Called warlocks, so she had not really been thinking of them as individuals, but she remembered Hanner. He had been a well-meaning sort, usually not very assertive, but able to show real backbone when pressed. For the most part, she had found him very agreeable. When he was Called, she had thought of him as dead — but the dead didn't come back. Well, not unless necromancy was involved, and she had never done much of that.

She took her time walking up the passage to the parlor, straightening her robe as she went; as usual, she was dressed in a white robe, this one relatively simple and trimmed with blue and yellow.

She hoped Zallin had come to formally dissolve the Council, but she doubted it. More likely he was here to plead for her help — perhaps he had taken on some job he could no longer perform, and wanted her to do it for him. That was much more typical of Zallin of the Mismatched Eyes than any sort of formality.

She took a deep breath and swept into the parlor.

Zallin was there, standing in the center of the room, smiling crookedly at her — a nervous smile, not the smirk he displayed when he was pleased with himself. He wore the traditional black tunic and breeches of a warlock, with no sign of office. The most distinctive thing about him was his eyes — the left one a very ordinary brown, the right a peculiar shade of pale blue.

"Zallin of the Mismatched Eyes," she said. "Why have you intruded upon my privacy?"

He hastily bowed, and when his head came back up he said, "Guildmaster, I'm sorry to trouble you, but I'm here on a matter of some urgency."

"Urgent for *you*, perhaps."

"Oh, I believe this concerns *everyone*, Guildmaster. Are you aware that warlocks throughout the city have *lost their magic*?"

She stared at him, trying to keep her face impassive; it would not do to laugh. "I have been informed of this, yes," she said.

"Well...do you know what caused it?"

Ithinia considered carefully before answering.

She knew that warlocks did not do divinations. They could not hear thoughts, as witches did, or foresee the future. They could not ask questions of the gods. They could not buy secrets from demons. They could use none of the dozens of spells that wizards used to investigate mysteries. They claimed to be able to see into the structure of everything around them, all the particles and flows of energy that made up the World, but only within a limited radius. Information was not where their talents lay. Still, it was hard to believe that this man was as ignorant of the situation as he appeared to be.

"The source of your magic, which fell from the sky on the Night of Madness, has departed from the World," she said. "Something came to its aid, and took it back into the sky, to whatever universe they both came from."

His mouth fell open, but no words emerged. She watched calmly as he attempted to gather his wits.

"It's...it's *gone*?" he said at last. "It's not just Ethshar of the Spices?"

"It's gone," she confirmed.

"Can you bring it back?"

It was her turn to stand in stunned silence, though she managed to keep her jaw from hanging. Finally, she said simply, "No."

"Are you sure? I came to you because I thought perhaps the Guild had found a way to block it from the city, and I was going to plead for you to remove the spell — but you say it's really *gone*?"

"It's really gone."

"The Wizards' Guild didn't have anything to do with it?"

She suppressed her annoyance. "Why would the Wizards' Guild want to interfere with warlocks, Zallin?"

"I don't know! I was going to ask what we had done to offend you."

"Why did you think it was our doing at all?"

"Because who else has magic powerful enough to do such a thing? The gods can't even *see* us, let alone harm us, and while demons might have the power, who could afford to pay them enough? I suppose it *might* have been demons, but wizards seemed much more likely."

"You assumed it must be some rival school of magic? Why?"

"Well, who else would want to harm us?"

Ithinia suppressed a grimace. "Zallin, are you sure you would call it harm?" she said. "You do realize that this means an end to the Calling, as well as warlockry?"

He waved that aside. "The Calling — if we're careful, that's not a problem. I can survive a few nightmares. But without our magic, how are we to live?"

"Learn an honest trade. Expand the Hegemony's borders, perhaps — I'm told there is still good land in the northeast that a hard worker can clear and farm. Now that the Calling is gone, there's no need to avoid the region just south of Aldagmor."

"Farm?" Zallin's expression implied that she had just said something obscene.

"Or take up carpentry, or smithing," she suggested.

He shook his head violently. "No," he said. "I'm a *warlock*, not a tradesman! Please, Guildmaster, isn't there anything you can do? Isn't there some way to lure back the source?"

"I do not know of any, nor would I use it if I did," Ithinia replied.

"But Ithinia, think of the city! What will people *do* with no warlocks? Who will dredge the harbor? Who will repair streets and walls? Who will heal the sick?"

She turned up an empty palm. "Ethshar managed well enough before the Night of Madness. I'm sure we can manage again now that the madness is gone."

"Warlockry isn't madness!"

She sighed. "No," she admitted, "it wasn't. But it's gone, and it's not coming back."

"Can't you find some other source, then?" he pleaded. "Is there no great wizardry you might perform that would restore our power?"

"Zallin, a sixnight ago you would have claimed that warlockry deserved to be considered the equal of any other school of magic; do you really think one wizard can restore it?"

"I don't know!" he wailed. "I don't understand wizardry, but you people have always claimed to be able to perform miracles, to create entire worlds with some of your spells — how do I know you can't provide a new power source for us?"

She met his gaze and said, "I cannot create a new source of power for warlocks." She did *not* say she could not *provide* one; she was all too aware that one already existed, in Lumeth of the Towers. "Zallin, have you noticed that I have not called you chairman?"

"I…no. I don't understand."

"There are no more warlocks in Ethshar, Zallin. There *is* no more Council of Warlocks for you to chair. Accept it."

He straightened and threw back his shoulders. "I do *not* accept that, Guildmaster! I will *never* accept it!"

"You should. But even if you refuse to acknowledge that the Council is no more, it is unclear whether you are still its chairman."

"What?" He looked shocked.

"Zallin, the departure of the Source did not merely put an end to warlockry; before it left, it released all the warlocks it had Called. *All* of them, back to the Night of Madness, magically preserved just as they were when they reached Aldagmor. It's estimated to be at least fifteen thousand people, and most of them are on their way here right now."

"What? I don't understand."

"All the Called warlocks are *coming back*, Zallin. And that includes Hanner, the original Chairman of the Council of Warlocks. If I were to recognize *anyone* as chairman, it would be Hanner, not you."

"But he's… They aren't *dead*?"

"They aren't dead. Oh, a few were killed in the confusion, but most of them are alive and well."

"But that…but…"

Ithinia could almost see him trying to grasp that, and trying to decide whether it was good or bad. Obviously, he knew he should think it was a good thing that thousands of his elders had not died, as he had always assumed, but at the same time, he *liked* being the city's senior warlock, and did not want to be shoved aside.

And if she remembered correctly, he and Hanner had never much liked each other.

After a moment, he reached a conclusion.

"You can't restore my magic?"

"I cannot."

"Can any wizard?"

"Not that I know of, but we're a secretive lot. I can't say for certain that there is no spell that would serve your purpose, only that if there is, I never heard of it."

"Then I am sorry to have troubled you, Guildmaster." He bowed. "I will be going."

"As you please," she said with a nod. She stepped aside, and heard Obdur opening the front door as she did. She watched as Zallin marched out, clearly trying to look haughty, but only managing petulant.

Obdur closed the door behind him, and Ithinia stared at it for a moment.

There was a man who would be very happy indeed if Vond did start training warlocks to use the power of the Lumeth towers. She would have to make sure that he would never have the opportunity to ask Vond's assistance.

"Obdur," she said, "go fetch the gargoyles; I have messages to send."

Chapter Eleven

Someone had been killed and partially eaten during the night. Several people insisted it must have been a dragon, probably one of Aldagon's spawn, but after looking at the remains, Hanner didn't believe it.

"Look at the tracks," he said, trying to ignore the fact that he could see his own breath and could barely keep from shivering. He didn't want to think about the cold and what it might do. "Those don't look like dragon's claws to me. There are no scorch marks, and no one saw any light or heard anything; wouldn't a dragon use fire?"

"They don't *all* breathe fire," someone said.

If true, that was news to Hanner, but he wasn't about to admit it. "But the tracks! No dragon would leave tracks like that."

No one could argue with that; the tracks were like nothing any of them had ever seen before, diagonal grooves very closely spaced that looked nothing at all like the talon-marks a dragon would leave.

The dead man — no one seemed to know him — had been sleeping well away from his nearest neighbors; he had probably just wanted a little peace and quiet, away from the noise and smell of so many people. That had apparently been his undoing. His isolation meant, though, that the ground where he had died had not been trampled by a hundred feet; the marks in the soft ground were unusually clear.

Clear, but very strange indeed.

"It's probably a mizagar," someone murmured, not far from Hanner's right shoulder. He turned to see a woman a little older than himself staring down at the muddy mess.

"A what?"

"A mizagar," the woman repeated. Hanner didn't recognize her, and her attire suggested that she had been Called on the Night of Madness — she wore a green flannel nightgown that was unfashionable even when Hanner was a boy.

"What's a mizagar?" he asked.

The woman looked around nervously. "They're…an old story," she said. She spoke Ethsharitic with a strong Sardironese accent. "My grandfather told me about them when I was a little girl. They're supposed to be leftovers from the Great War, creatures that the Northerners turned loose in areas where they didn't want to bother putting soldiers or magicians. They're as big as a horse in the body, but with short, thick legs and much larger heads. Their hide is leathery and hairless and completely black, so black they're practically invisible at night, and they move low to the ground, to make them even harder to spot and so they can move more silently. They're very, very fast. Humans are their preferred food, but they can live on other things for as long as necessary. They don't breed, but they don't age, either — if there's one around here, it's more than two hundred years old. They won't go near houses, because the Northerners didn't want them to attack outposts, but no one in Aldagmor would ever sleep out in the fields or woods for fear of them."

"You're from Aldagmor?"

She nodded.

"I know her," Rayel Roggit's son volunteered. "This is Fanria the Clever; she lived a mile east of us."

Hanner said, "Fanria?" He had never heard the name Fanria before, but he supposed Ethshar and Sardiron might have different naming customs.

"Yes," she said. "I'm Fanria."

"You think these things might be around here?"

"We're out in the wilderness here," she said. "Even before that thing fell out of the sky, no one lived here. It's just the sort of place the old stories say they live."

"Do they ever attack by daylight?"

She glanced around uneasily, and saw Rayel smiling encouragingly at her. "I only know my grandfather's stories," she said.

"Well, what did your grandfather say about that?"

"He said…they wouldn't bother a large group by daylight, but if anyone wandered off alone, a hungry mizagar might try to pick him off. And at night — well, I think this was done by a mizagar." She gestured toward the bloody remains and churned-up mud.

Hanner nodded. "Then we won't give them any more targets; from now on, everyone stays together, and we'll post guards at night."

"We should burn the body," Sensella said.

"I'll leave that to the magicians," Hanner said. "The rest of us should get moving. The sooner we get to civilization, away from dragons and mizagars and whatever else is out here, the better."

There was a muttered chorus of agreement, and much of the crowd began turning southward, picking up any belongings they might have put down and starting to walk.

Of course, most of them *had* no belongings other than the clothes they wore and the magical provisions Piskor had given them. Still, Hanner thought as he watched them, at least they were alive. While several people were limping, or shivering, the mizagar's victim had been the night's only known fatality. It could have been far worse.

Hanner turned south himself just as the shouting started.

"Look! Look!" someone cried.

"We're saved!"

"Run!"

"The wizards have come!"

"They're here to rescue us!"

"They'll kill us all!"

Hanner's gaze followed some of the pointing fingers, and saw the dark little shape in the southern sky, drawing rapidly nearer. It took him a moment to identify it, and he marveled at how sharp some people's eyes must be, to have recognized it so quickly. It was a flying carpet, and three people were seated on it. The wizards had found them.

"They won't hurt us!" Hanner shouted. "They sent me a dream last night; they're here to help!"

His words did not carry well over the general racket, but apparently the people saying they should run were a small minority; most of the crowd was cheering and waving.

The carpet descended until it hung a dozen feet above the ground, above the heads of the milling throng, about a hundred yards southwest of Hanner's own location; several of the people beneath it were stretching their arms upward, trying to touch it. Some of them were even leaping up toward it, though so far as Hanner could tell none of the outstretched fingers managed to reach the carpet.

One of the people on the carpet was speaking, but his voice was completely lost in the noise of the crowd. Hanner grimaced; warlocks could vibrate the air to make their voices louder, and could therefore be heard over *anything*, no matter how loud, but these wizards apparently did not have an equivalent spell, and of course there *were* no more warlocks, except for Vond.

"Quiet!" Hanner bellowed. "We want to hear the wizards!"

Beside him Rudhira was up on her toes, trying to see through the crowd; she was not tall enough to peer over all those shoulders. Once upon a time, Hanner recalled, she would have been able to fly straight over everyone's heads to the wizards' carpet, or for that matter, straight to the city; she had briefly been the most powerful warlock in Ethshar of the Spices. Now, though, she was just a tired, frustrated woman in a green skirt and embroidered tunic, trying to follow what was happening around her.

The wizard was still talking, waving his arms, but no one seemed to be listening. Hands were still stretching up toward the carpet, and people were squeezing closer together, trying to get at the wizards.

That could be dangerous, Hanner realized. People could be crushed.

"*Hai!*" he shouted. "Give them room!"

No one paid any attention, but a moment later the wizards seemed to see the danger for themselves; the carpet rose up a few feet, then swept forward, over the heads of the former warlocks.

Someone screamed.

"Don't leave us!" someone else shrieked.

Several panicky voices joined in.

"Calm down!" Hanner shouted, arms raised. "Calm down! Let them talk!"

No one paid attention; the wizards were looking at one another uncertainly, and the carpet seemed to be drifting gradually higher, and moving slowly northeast — toward Hanner.

Hanner frowned, and reached out to grab Rayel's shoulder. He turned, found Sensella, and grabbed her, as well.

Rudhira was looking up at him for guidance.

"Shut up!" Hanner shouted. "You two, all of you who can hear me, tell everyone to be quiet, so we can hear what the wizards have to say." He pushed Rayel to one side, and Sensella to the other. "Quiet! Listen!"

Rayel got the idea quickly, and began grabbing shoulders, turning people to face him, and hushing them, a finger to their lips. Sensella saw what Rayel was doing and turned to Hanner, who nodded; then she, too, began forcing herself in front of people and trying to silence them.

"Stand still! Face the wizards!" Hanner called, and this time his voice was somewhat more audible over the din — his neighborhood was gradually growing quieter.

As he had hoped, the wizards noticed; one of them pointed at the little cluster of people standing silently, as if waiting. The carpet veered and swooped, and a moment later it was hanging almost directly over the bloody remains of the mizagar's victim, about fifteen feet up.

The watching crowd gradually quieted.

Hanner grimaced, wondering whether the wizards had noticed the body.

"Is someone in charge here?" the tallest wizard called, when the crowd's noise had died away enough for him to be heard. He wore a deep purple robe trimmed with gold.

Hanner had not yet decided whether to respond when Rayel pointed at him and said, "He is!"

The wizard leaned forward and peered down at Hanner. "Are you?"

"As much as anyone," Hanner called back. "I'm Hanner, formerly Chairman of the Council of Warlocks."

"Ah! I've heard of you," the wizard replied. "I'm Molvarn of Crookwall. I am here as a representative of the Wizards' Guild, and on behalf of Azrad the Seventh, Overlord of Ethshar of the Spices, Triumvir of the

Hegemony of the Three Ethshars, Commander of the Holy Navies and Defender of the Gods."

Hanner bowed at the overlord's name.

The wizard looked out over the throng; there were still hundreds of raised voices and waving hands, though most of the crowd had quieted and the nearest portion was entirely silent. "I understand you people need help."

"Yes," Hanner said.

"You were headed for Ethshar of the Spices?"

"Yes."

"The overlord does not feel that the city has the facilities to accept so large a group of refugees," Molvarn said. Then he continued quickly, before anyone could protest, "But we are here to offer you other choices." He held his hands to his mouth and bellowed at the top of his lungs, "Is anyone here from Ethshar of the Sands?"

A few tentative voices replied, and a few hands rose uncertainly.

"If you could gather over here, please?" Molvarn called, gesturing to his left.

Slowly, with much muttering, people began to move through the crowd toward the indicated spot.

"And anyone from Ethshar of the Rocks?"

Again, a few hands were raised. Molvarn gestured to his right. "Over here, please?"

"Pass the word!" Hanner called. "There must be hundreds of people who didn't hear — pass the word!"

"Thank you, Chairman," Molvarn said with a nod. "Now, all of you over here — we are going to be providing transportation to the Grandgate barracks in Ethshar of the Sands. The magic is on its way, about an hour behind me. I don't know just how fast we will be able to move people through, it may take some time, but we can transport everyone from that city; the spell has unlimited capacity. We're going to start with the more recent arrivals, since you'll still probably have friends and family who can help you once you're home. We're also going to ask those of you who do still have homes to help your less fortunate fellows — some of you were trapped in Aldagmor for more than thirty years, and not only are your homes and families long gone, there may not be anyone left who remembers you ever existed. I know that's hard, that it's not what you want to hear, but it's the simple truth. I don't see anything to be gained from misleading you."

That elicited unhappy murmurs, but no open protest.

Molvarn gestured toward the sea of people milling about, too far away to hear. "Please tell your compatriots as they arrive." Then he turned to the other side and announced, "If you heard what I just told the others, we have about the same news for you — there's a spell on the way, an enchanted tapestry, that will transport you to a small shop in Ethshar of the Rocks, on Wizard Street where it passes between Center City and Highside. More recent arrivals should go first, to find their families, and we hope you'll be able to arrange to help some of the people who were here longer."

"Pass the word!" Hanner repeated.

Molvarn turned back toward the main crowd. "I'm sure some of you're wondering why we don't have magic ready to take you to Ethshar of the Spices. We're working on it. Unfortunately, most of the existing magic we wizards use to visit Ethshar of the Spices is not suitable for this group. Please be patient. Now, my companions would like to speak." He slid back on the carpet and rotated it slightly, bringing one of the other two passengers to the front.

This was a woman in a long maroon coat over a white tunic and maroon skirt; Hanner had at first taken the coat for a wizard's robe, but now he saw that it was not. She cleared her throat, and started to speak.

Hanner could barely hear her, and quickly shouted, "Louder!"

She paused, frowned, and tried again. Listening required an effort, but Hanner could make out her words now.

"Lord Azrad has conferred with Lord Ederd and Lord Wulran, and sent word to the Council of Barons in Sardiron. Many of you undoubtedly came from farms or villages, and of course, if you still have families to return to, you are free to do so. Most of you, though, either worked as warlocks and have no land or trade to return to, or left so long ago that you were presumed dead, and any holdings you may have once had are gone. You need new lands." She spread her arms and gestured at their surroundings. "*This* land is unclaimed. It lies almost ten leagues east of Sardiron's borders, and well north of the Hegemony's inhabited areas. This was a battlefield of the Great War that changed hands many times, far from the major trade routes, so it had not been settled by the Night of Madness, and after that — well, it was uninhabitable, until now. We are about sixteen leagues from the outermost villages of the Hegemony. There are no roads, no houses, nothing but wilderness — but it's good land, with enough water, and moderate summers. Yes, the winters can be hard, but they aren't as fierce as in Sardiron or Tazmor or Srigmor. Lord Azrad, with the provisional consent of Lord Ederd and Lord Wulran, is offering all this land, from this point south and west to the borders of Sardiron and the edge of existing farms, to anyone who cares to claim and work it. He assures you that roads will be built, and that supplies to survive the winter and make a start will be brought in. He suggests that raising beef cattle would be profitable; you already know that the lands north of here are home to dragons, and strange as it may sound, those dragons will buy your cattle, through human agents. I will be in charge of settling anyone who wants to work these lands; a group of advisors is on the way to assist me."

"I don't want to stay in Ethshar!" Fanria protested. "I'm Sardironese!"

Hanner was unsure whether the woman on the carpet heard Fanria or not, but the third rider, a man in a green wizard's robe, was straightening up and cupping his hands to his mouth.

"*Ie ban Bergen fin Aldran!*" he shouted.

Fanria had turned to Hanner to voice her objections, but now she whirled to face the man on the carpet.

"*Ie shtarfur Rada Garafai al yez, be kardin bar Kor Azrad!*"

"Is that Sardironese?" Hanner asked.

"He says he's speaking on behalf of the Council of Barons, but only provisionally; it was Lord Azrad who actually sent him," Fanria replied.

That seemed to be a lot to fit into the one sentence, but Hanner had always heard that Sardironese was more efficient than Ethsharitic. Northerners didn't like to keep their mouths open any more than they had to; it let in the cold air.

"His name is Bergen Aldran's son," Rayel added.

No one had specifically said it was Sardironese, but the translations from the two Aldagmorites left little doubt.

The green-robed wizard launched into a speech now, and Hanner made no attempt to follow it. He knew some Trader's Tongue and a few words apiece of three of the dead languages wizards sometimes used in their spells, but found Sardironese completely incomprehensible. The scholars said it had originally been a blend of Ethsharitic military slang of three hundred years ago and one of the languages spoken in the old Northern Empire, but to Hanner it was gibberish. He waited patiently while Bergen spoke and the Sardironese in the crowd listened intently.

At last the speech ended.

"What did he say?" Hanner asked Rayel.

"He said…" Rayel paused, obviously trying to switch from thinking in his native tongue to thinking in Ethsharitic. Then he continued, "He said the Council of Barons is still debating the situation, but the Wizards' Guild stands ready to transport us to Sardiron of the Waters, once permission is granted. If we don't want to go to the capital, the Guild is also talking to the Baron of Aldagmor about sending some of us to his keep, just the other side of the dragons' territory. He says the Baron — well, it's the grandson of the man who was the last baron *I* knew about, and he's very different. The old baron was obsessed with mining; he thought the hills must be full of gold. The new baron is more interested in trade. There isn't much farmland available, but we can probably find work. It's all still pretty vague."

"Still, they're trying," Hanner said.

"Yes, they are," Rayel agreed. "But it's…it's very confusing."

"It is," Hanner acknowledged.

It was confusing — but it was encouraging, as well. The Wizards' Guild and Azrad VII had responded with gratifying speed, and seemed to have been surprisingly thorough. Old Azrad the Sedentary, the current overlord's father, would never have been this effective, especially not after Lord Faran's death.

So everyone from Ethshar of the Sands or Ethshar of the Rocks would be sent home, and anyone who wanted to settle down on new land as a farmer would be welcome to do so, and arrangements were being made to send all the Sardironese home. That would take care of thousands of the former warlocks; Hanner didn't have any real idea of the exact numbers, but thousands.

But it wouldn't be all of them. It wouldn't help *him*.

He hoped the wizards and the overlords would get to the rest of the former warlocks soon, before the weather turned any worse.

Chapter Twelve

"You know," Vond said, as he looked down at his capital, "there really isn't any reason to stay here."

"This has been the heart of the empire for fifteen years, your Majesty," Sterren protested. "Moving the entire government would be —"

"I don't want to move the *government*," Vond interrupted. "I'm talking about *me*."

"Oh," Sterren said. He turned up a palm. "Well, you can do as you please, of course."

"I only stayed here because of the Calling," Vond said, rotating slowly to take in the view. The two men were hanging in mid-air, perhaps sixty yards up. "I only let you hire me and bring me here in the first place because of the Calling. I was trying to get as far from Aldagmor as I could. I only stopped conquering kingdoms because I could hear it again when we got to Lumeth."

"I remember."

"The Calling isn't there anymore. I could go home to Ethshar."

"After all these years, your Majesty; it's probably not quite as you remember it."

"Neither is Semma."

That was obviously true, so Sterren did not bother to argue.

"I'm the only warlock left," Vond continued. "I'm the most powerful magician in the World. I should live in the most powerful city in the World, not way out here near the edge."

Sterren resisted the temptation to correct Vond, and point out that Sterren himself was also still a warlock, albeit a very feeble one. He also found himself in a dilemma; he would be very happy to see Vond go away, but at the same time, he dreaded to think how much damage the warlock might do in Ethshar of the Spices. That one great city probably held more people than Vond's entire empire.

"You would be avoiding conflict with the Wizards' Guild," he said at last, unsure whether Vond would consider that a benefit or a challenge.

Vond was staring off to the north, not really listening. Sterren suddenly began worrying that the warlock would get distracted and let him fall. He glanced down between his feet at the plaza far below; the fountain at the center was splashing merrily, and people were going about their business, only occasionally glancing up at their emperor and his chancellor. "Your Majesty?"

"What? Oh, yes. The wizards. I'm not really concerned with them. They haven't tried to enforce their edict yet, have they? I think they've thought better of defying me."

"It's only been a couple of days, Vond."

"That's true." He frowned, and turned back to Sterren. "Do you think they'll try something?"

"I'm afraid I do, your Majesty."

"Maybe I should go take a good look at those towers. From what you all have told me, that seems to be what they were most concerned about."

"That might provoke the wizards, your Majesty."

"What if it does?" He turned up an empty palm. "That doesn't concern me."

"I think you may underestimate them, your Majesty."

"Oh, I don't think so," Vond said. "I was there the day they ordered the city guard to leave the warlocks alone, you know."

Sterren, who was too young to remember the Night of Madness, was not sure what Vond was talking about; he said, "Oh?"

"I was a boy of eleven, starting to think seriously what trade I would apprentice myself to, and I was walking down Merchant Street when I heard the commotion and went to see what was happening. Azrad the Sedentary had sent a bunch of soldiers to escort some warlocks out of the city — he wanted to exile them all. I was just in time to see the earth rise up between the soldiers and the warlocks, and split open to reveal half a dozen wizards, with their robes and staves, who ordered the guardsmen to go back to the palace and tell old Azrad to leave the warlocks alone. They said warlocks were their equals."

"Did they?"

"They did. And that was back at the very beginning, before anyone even knew what warlocks could do. Do you know what *I* think?"

"No, your Majesty."

"*I* think they knew, even then, that warlocks were more than a match for wizards. We don't need books and spells, no spider's blood or hair of an unborn child, no magic daggers or fancy chants; whatever we want to happen simply happens. I think they wanted to ingratiate themselves, so that *we* would not return and drive *them* out of the city. That was why I apprenticed myself to a warlock a sixnight after my twelfth birthday. Magic that didn't need books and ritual, magic that wasn't weak like witchcraft, or dependent on the whims of gods or demons — I wanted that."

"I see."

"*I'm* not afraid of the wizards; they're afraid of *me*. The Calling was the only thing that kept warlocks in check, and now it's gone, but I'm still here."

"Obviously." Sterren glanced uneasily down, between his dangling feet. "However, there is only one of you, and there are hundreds of wizards."

Vond waved a hand dismissively. "Most of them can barely light a fire, while I can do *this*."

A huge band of red flame appeared out of nowhere, writhing around the two men like a serpent; Sterren heard muffled shrieks from below.

"Some can do considerably more," Sterren pointed out. "There's the Tower of Flame in Eknissamor; a wizard made that."

Vond grimaced. "Well, yes — we flew near that on the way here. It's fairly spectacular. Some of the wizards can indeed do more than light fires; that earthquake on High Street was also very impressive. But I think much of it is just pretense, just for show."

Sterren felt his gut tighten at that. "Why do you say that?" he asked.

"Because if they were really as powerful as they pretend, wouldn't they rule the World? Why would they allow the overlords to rule the Hegemony, rather than doing it themselves? And all those silly little kings and councils in the Small Kingdoms — why put up with that nonsense? *I* didn't; why would the wizards, if they really had the power they claim?"

"I don't know," Sterren admitted, hoping he didn't sound desperate and wishing he could think of a better answer.

He suspected that the truth was that wizards didn't *want* to rule the World, any more than Sterren had wanted to rule Vond's empire after the warlock was Called. He was certain, though, that Vond wouldn't believe that for a minute; his mind didn't work that way.

"So, you see?" Vond said, spreading his arms. "I'm not worried about the wizards. But I don't want to stay here. It's pleasant enough now, but I remember what this place is like in the summer. I can keep cool if I want to, no matter how hot and dry it gets, but why should I? And people would be asking me to do things for them, saving crops and the like, and that's dull. You know, it's a curious thing — without the Aldagmor Source, using my magic isn't as much fun as before. There was something about that whisper that made it *exciting*, and the Lumeth source doesn't do that. I don't *mind* using magic, obviously, but I don't have any great *urge* to do so."

"I hadn't known there was a difference."

"Oh, yes. Besides, I did most of what I wanted to do before I was Called. I built the palace, I built the roads — you see them?" He pointed; Sterren looked down at the network of stone-paved highways radiating out from Semma and nodded. Those roads had been essential in keeping the empire intact and making its economy work. "That's all done, and from now on it would be dealing with people, and they're all either boring peasants or unpleasant aristocrats obsessed with genealogy. There's no Arena here, no Games Street, no street performers or streetwalkers."

Sterren knew perfectly well that there were gamblers and whores and various performers if one knew where to look, especially now that Semma was the capital of a thriving empire rather than a tiny, poverty-stricken kingdom, but he didn't see any point in telling Vond that.

Vond waved a hand. "And all those different languages! I want to hear good Ethsharitic around me."

"What do you propose, your Majesty?"

"What I *propose*, Sterren, is that I'm going to go home. But I'm going to make a tour of it; I'll stop in Lumeth and investigate at the towers, then get a good look at the Tower of Flame by night — I rushed past it before. There was something strange on the eastern slope of the mountains north of that, too. Then I'll go on back to Ethshar and find myself a home — maybe a mansion in the New City. Maybe I'll live in Warlock House, on High Street! After all, I'm the only warlock left."

"What about the empire?"

"You and the Council seem to have done a fine job of running it. I'll let you go on doing it."

"I'm honored that you think so, your Majesty."

"Oh, stop it. You aren't one of these idiot Semmans. Don't pretend you're my humble obedient lapdog. You aren't honored."

Sterren turned up a palm. "Pleased, then. Yes, I thought we did a pretty good job, but that doesn't mean *you* thought so."

"The empire was still here when I got back, and it looks peaceful and prosperous. That's more than I expected. I thought it would all fall apart in a month without me here to keep everyone in line."

"Oh. Well, we did the best we could."

"And you did well. So I don't need to stay here."

Sterren hesitated, then asked, "So do you intend to abdicate?"

"What?" Vond had been looking off to the north again; now he turned and stared at Sterren. "No, of course not," he said. "Why would I do that?"

"Well, if you don't intend to stay here and rule the empire…"

"It's still *my* empire, though! It's gotten along fine without me for fifteen years; it can do so for a few more. I'll probably come back eventually, when I get bored. Maybe I'll conquer all the Small Kingdoms, and reunite Old Ethshar. Or conquer the entire World."

"So you won't be naming an heir to rule after you're gone?"

"No, of course not. I don't need one. You do know warlocks don't die of old age, don't you? At least, not if we're any good. We can heal ourselves."

In fact, Sterren had not known anything of the sort; as long as the Calling had existed, old age hadn't been an issue. "Oh," he said.

"No, I'm keeping the empire," Vond said. "And I'm not naming an heir. But I think I *should* name a regent, to take care of things while I'm gone. I don't want to let your fifteen years of work go for nothing."

"Oh," Sterren said again.

"It should be easier this time," Vond continued. "After all, if anyone starts a rebellion or a war, the regent can just send me a message, and I'll come take care of it."

"I see," Sterren said. He noticed that Vond referred to "the regent," rather than saying "you," and braced himself — was he going to be dismissed, told that he'd done his job and was free to go?

Or was he going to be killed for what he had done to hurry Vond's Calling, fifteen years ago?

"That's why I brought you up here to talk," Vond said. Sterren had a vision of being allowed to plunge sixty yards to the pavement below, and took a deep breath. "I wanted to make sure we weren't interrupted."

"Your Majesty?"

"Would you like to come with me to Ethshar? You're from the city, too — aren't you sick of being stuck out here in the corner of the World, surrounded by shepherds and farmers and inbred princelings?"

"I — I'm not sure I understand."

"I'd want you to handle things for me, all those annoying everyday things that I'd rather not bother with. You wouldn't be chancellor anymore, you'd be, oh, chief of staff, I suppose."

Sterren tried to think quickly; he didn't want to make a mistake. The wrong choice could get him killed, and probably a good many other people, as well. If he stayed in Semma there would be no one to keep Vond from running amok should he lose his temper, no one who could try to talk him into behaving in a civilized fashion — but there was no certainty that *he* could keep Vond's temper in check, and that he wouldn't wind up like Ildirin, his brains splattered on a stone wall somewhere.

His family and friends were all in Semma now; he had lived here almost his entire adult life. If Vond did go off to Ethshar without him and went berserk, the Wizards' Guild or some other magician would probably be able to dispose of the renegade warlock, while Sterren lived in quiet retirement with his wife and children.

It occurred to him that Vond did not know that Sterren had a wife and children; the emperor hadn't bothered to ask, and Sterren was not about to volunteer the information. He *certainly* wasn't going to volunteer the fact that he had sent his family into exile the moment he realized Vond was returning. He had no desire to anger the warlock.

"I'm flattered, your Majesty, but…" he began.

"If you stay here, of course, I'd expect you to continue as regent," Vond said. "If you come with me, perhaps you can suggest your replacement."

That eliminated the possibility of a quiet retirement. Sterren had been thinking he and Shirrin and the kids might find themselves a comfortable place in Inshar or Wunth, or maybe go all the way to Ethshar of the Sands, away from both Vond and his empire, but it seemed his choice was between being regent or being chief of staff, with no option to leave the whole mess behind.

He had been trying to leave all of his obligations here behind ever since Lady Kalira had found him playing dice in a tavern, and informed him that he was the hereditary warlord of Semma. No matter what he did, he had always wound up back here, saddled with responsibilities he didn't want.

Of course, once Vond was gone, and Sterren was married to a Semman princess, and the treaty with the Wizards' Guild had prevented any more border wars, it hadn't been so bad.

But Vond was back, the treaty had been violated, and he had sent Shirrin away. He was back where he started.

And a possibility occurred to him.

When he went back to Ethshar to recruit magicians, all those years ago, he had intended to slip away and lose himself in the city. Lady Kalira had anticipated that and prevented it.

Lady Kalira, whatever her other failings, was smarter than Vond.

Merely slipping away probably wouldn't work; there were ways to find people, and if those weren't available Vond might simply tear the city apart looking for him. But if he could convince Vond there was a reason not to pursue him, he might manage to escape once and for all. Perhaps he could fake his own death.

Once he was free, he could find Shirrin — he'd ordered Noril to try to get her and the children to Ethshar, so she might be there waiting for him. They could settle down quietly somewhere. They wouldn't be drawing a salary from the imperial treasury anymore, but Sterren was sure he could find a way to get by. Cheating at dice, perhaps. After all, he was one of two warlocks left in the World, and the only one no one knew about.

"I think Lady Kalira would make an excellent regent," he said. "Or really, any of the older members of the Imperial Council."

"Then you'll come with me?"

"I think it's a fine idea," he said. "But I'll need to pack, and give some final instructions."

"Of course," Vond said. Without warning, the two of them began to descend slowly. "Shall I come back for you tomorrow afternoon? I'll take the time to look around a little, see how the empire is doing. You can tell everyone what's happening; I'd rather not do it myself."

"As you please, your Majesty, but are you sure you don't want to make the announcement yourself? You don't want anyone thinking it was my idea to lure you away from your beloved subjects."

"I don't want to see anyone celebrating my departure, either," Vond said. "I'd hate to ruin my day with the necessity of killing a bunch of people for disloyalty."

"Ah," Sterren said. "Yes, I can see that. Tomorrow, then, an hour or so past noon?"

"Or thereabouts. I expect you'll be ready and waiting near the palace door."

Sterren glanced down at the approaching ground, and the crowd that had cleared a broad swath of pavement beside the fountain, ready for their master's landing.

"That would be fine," he said. "I'll be ready."

"Good," Vond said. "I'd hate to have to kill *you*."

Then Sterren's feet touched stone, and he staggered slightly. When he straightened up again, Vond was soaring upward, then curving to the east before dwindling rapidly to a mere speck, vanishing in the distance.

Chapter Thirteen

Hanner's feet hurt, and he was horribly cold, chilled through and through, as he sat on the bare ground; there wasn't enough fuel handy to keep more than a few fires going, and the young, the old, and the injured were given priority in crowding around those few — even, gruesomely, the pyre of that poor half-eaten person, whoever he was. The theurgists never had managed to contact Tarma or Konned, the witches were still busy with healing and calming, and the wizards had devoted their efforts to planning and transportation, rather than warmth.

Hanner wished the wizards had brought out a few better theurgists, as well as tapestries and bureaucrats; the handful of theurgists who had been Called warlocks had not accomplished anything at all after their initial success with Piskor the Generous. Not only would Tarma or Konned have been useful, but Alladia said that Asham the Gate-Keeper could get everyone home quickly. Unfortunately, it would take a really top-level theurgist to invoke him. If the wizards had found a theurgist like that, it would have been lovely. They hadn't, so most of the throng of former warlocks was still here, sitting and waiting, cold and hungry. Rudhira was huddled against Hanner, shivering; that pretty white tunic of hers was not warm enough for this weather.

It wasn't very white any more, either, after this stay in the wilderness.

Still, everyone was doing what they could, and progress was being made. Hundreds of people had been sent safely off to Ethshar of the Rocks and Ethshar of the Sands; the magical tapestries were hanging from sturdy frames, and a half-dozen apprentices were checking names, dates, and addresses before allowing anyone to touch them. Sensella of Morningside, having been the very last arrival from Ethshar of the Sands, had been one of the very first to go.

It was startling, watching the tapestries in action. A person would give his or her name to the apprentices, who would write it down. He would give his last address, so that the apprentices could check it against their maps and make sure the person actually knew the city he claimed to live in, and then the date of his Calling. One of the apprentices would then ask a question or two about the news of the day for that time, to make sure the earlier warlocks weren't trying to sneak in ahead of their proper place.

When the apprentices were satisfied, they would move aside, and the applicant would step forward and touch the tapestry.

And then the applicant was simply gone — there was no transition, no flash, no bang, no fade or flicker or whoosh or whisper, the person just wasn't there anymore. The eye didn't want to accept it; it was almost easier to believe the person had never been there at all. The heavily-trampled ground in front of the tapestry was as empty as ever.

Whereupon the apprentices would let the next one through, and the scene would repeat.

Hanner hoped very much that the wizards were telling the truth, and that those people had indeed been transported instantaneously to the right places. He knew that Transporting Tapestries were real, obviously, since he had commissioned a pair of his own, but he had no proof that these two were really taking people to their alleged destinations; the rooms depicted on them could have been anywhere. He couldn't think of any reason the wizards would lie about it, but you never knew, with wizards.

If they were going to lie, though, they would probably have claimed one of the tapestries led to Ethshar of the Spices, since there were more people who wanted to go there than to either of the others. As yet, no third tapestry had arrived, any more than had Asham the Gate-Keeper.

Someone was making another announcement in Sardironese, but Hanner had stopped listening to those. The Council of Barons kept sending out decrees, and then changing their minds an hour or two later. Rayel and Fanria had gone to join several of the other Sardironese in the group clustered around the wizard relaying the news.

The Baron of Aldagmor was definitely willing to accept refugees, whether the rest of the Council did or not, but no one had a tapestry to anywhere in his domain — at least, no one would admit to having one available to lend; Hanner suspected there were a few stashed away somewhere that their owners preferred not to display. In the absence of a tapestry plans were being made to use flying carpets, or some other magical method, or even just a wagon train to get some of the crowd safely past the dragons to his keep.

Hanner turned his head and craned his neck, peering off to the southwest; that was the direction most of the would-be settlers had gone. An entire carpet of bureaucrats, wooden stakes, strips of colored cloth to use as markers, and pre-prepared, half-written deeds had arrived an hour ago, to assist in claiming land, and that maroon-clad woman had led the bureaucrats and a couple of hundred former warlocks off to start choosing homesteads. Hanner would have preferred it if the wizards had sent a carpet loaded with food, blankets, or firewood, rather than property markers, but no one had asked him.

He had to admit, though, that the Wizards' Guild and the overlord's bureaucrats had done an impressive job of organizing a rescue effort. There was still plenty more to be done, but they had made a very effective start.

He picked up one of his last brown sticks of divine nourishment. Piskor had said she was providing a three-day supply, but most people — those who hadn't simply lost theirs — had eaten them all by the end of the second day. Rudhira, on the other hand, had hoarded hers, perhaps because her past life had accustomed her to going hungry. Hanner didn't know how many she still had out of her original dozen, but he was fairly certain it was more than his own supply. He was down to three more sticks, despite being very careful, and the wizards had yet to bring in more food.

The Called wizards and witches, Hanner remembered, hadn't received any food in the first place; the goddess apparently hadn't considered them worthy. A few people had shared their supply with the magicians; Hanner had given one stick to one of the witches who had been healing the injured, but only one. Thousands of other people had received Piskor's gift, so he had seen no need to shoulder more than his share of the burden.

He wished he had something he could drink, to wash the brown stuff down. The stream the horde had been following had been reduced to a muddy trickle by the attention of thousands of hands, cloths, and improvised receptacles, but the wizards had not yet brought water, either. Two of the witches were purifying water for the injured, but soon a lot of other people would be getting thirsty.

Just then a low rumble sounded; Hanner looked up, expecting to see an approaching storm, but the sky was mostly clear, with only a few scattered, fluffy clouds.

The rumble increased, and the ground began to shake; around him, Hanner heard people screaming and shouting questions.

Then the earth humped up about forty feet away, rising up in a mound; people tumbled down the new slopes and quickly scattered, desperate to get away. Hanner sprang to his feet, startling poor Rudhira, just as the mound split open and fell away to either side, revealing a young man holding a large sack. He stepped forward, and another man seemed to rise out of the ground behind him.

Hanner realized he had seen this spell, or one very like it, once before, long ago, when the leaders of the Wizards' Guild had intervened between the overlord's guards and Hanner's collection of warlocks. This time, though, the people rising up out of the ground were not wizards in formal robes, carrying staves and ultimata; instead they were tradesmen in brown or tan, and all of them were carrying bags and bundles.

There were a *lot* of them; they seemed to be emerging in an endless stream from an opening in the earth itself.

"Beer!" one of them called, lowering a bundle from his shoulders to the ground. The bundle clinked with the unmistakable sound of bottles. "Good dark beer from the breweries in the Old Merchants' Quarter, three bits a pint. I've got Shipmaster's Brown, Felris Stout, and Old City Ale!"

"Good white bread, two bits a loaf!" called another, lowering his own pack.

Well, Hanner thought, there was the food and drink he had hoped for. Unless things had changed during his long absence, though, those prices were outrageous — a single bit should buy a loaf *and* a pint. And most of the people here had no money; they had been Called out of their beds, or from the privacy of their homes.

But Hanner had his purse, he realized. He had given it no thought at all since he first awoke atop the Source, but the pouch still hung on his belt, just as it had when he had entered Arvagan's shop to inspect his new tapestry. He reached down, tucked his gift from Piskor back into its wrapper, and dug into his purse. He groped to make sure he wasn't missing anything, then pulled out every coin in it. There weren't many; he had two bits in silver, and a handful of coppers.

More tradesmen were still appearing, carrying wine, blankets, vegetables, cheese, and candles, and some of the weary warlocks were gathering around them, coins in hand.

"*Hai!*" Hanner shouted. "Don't forget, not everyone has money! Share what you can!"

A few people glanced at him, but he saw no sign his words were having any real effect. He laid a reassuring hand on Rudhira's shoulder, then strode forward — or tried to; it was really more of a limp, thanks to his blistered feet. He pushed through to the man with the sack of bread. "Is there a quantity discount?" he demanded, holding out a silver bit.

The man paused, eyed the coin, then looked Hanner in the eye and smiled. "Six for five?" he suggested.

"Seven. You know these prices are ridiculous."

"It's what the market will bear, friend, but fair enough, seven loaves for the silver." He started counting them out with one hand while the other accepted Hanner's coin. He handed the bread to Hanner, then turned to the next customer.

Clutching his armful of bread, Hanner pushed his way back through the growing crowd around the vendors to where several tired-looking people were sitting disconsolately on the ground. "You aren't buying," he said.

"No money," one of the women answered.

Hanner nodded. "Here," he said, handing her a loaf. "Share it out." Then he marched on to the next group.

Five more loaves went to strangers; he gave the last to Rudhira, who hesitated, then passed it on.

When he had distributed all his purchases he turned back to the sellers, and was pleased to see that his actions had apparently shamed some of his comrades into following his example — bread was being shared, wineskins and beer bottles passed from hand to hand. He fished out his other silver bit and started pushing his way back.

There was a wizard among the salesmen now, in a honey-brown robe and old-fashioned pointed hat, and Hanner realized he looked familiar, but it took a moment to place him. It wasn't Molvarn or Arvagan...

Rothiel, that was it. The one who had come to him in his dreams. He hadn't been wearing a hat in the dream.

Just as Hanner recognized him, Rothiel spotted Hanner. "Chairman Hanner!" he called. "I've been looking for you!" He raised a hand and beckoned.

Hanner blinked in surprise. "You have?"

"Yes, yes! Come here!"

Hanner hesitated, glancing back over his shoulder at Rudhira. He beckoned to her, as Rothiel had to him; he felt responsible for her, and she seemed so small and helpless — though he knew, from her brief time as a warlock, that given half a chance she was anything *but* helpless.

She rose, and slipped quickly through the crowd to his side; then the two of them made their way past the merchants to the wizard's side.

From here, for the first time, Hanner could see that the brewers and bakers and vintners and greengrocers were coming up a stone stairway that had appeared from nowhere, and which seemed to lead endlessly downward into the earth. A steady stream of merchants was making their way up this stair, while those who had sold everything they had brought were gathering alongside it, waiting idly, chatting quietly amongst themselves.

Rothiel was standing a little to one side of the topmost step, and as each tradesmen completed his business, Rothiel would direct him to join the waiting group. The wizard glanced down at the crowded steps, then at Hanner and Rudhira.

"I hope this pleases you," Rothiel said. "We debated inviting butchers and fishmongers, but we weren't sure you would have any way to cook anything."

"It's fine," Hanner said, "except that most of these people have no money; they were Called out of their beds."

Rothiel turned up an empty palm. "Alas, there are limits to our generosity."

"The best thing you could do is get them all back to civilization, where they can find their families, or work for their keep."

"Indeed, we have every intention of doing that. We finally realized the absurdity of flying carpets back empty after bringing staff and supplies out here, and from now on, every carpet will take passengers back. You've seen how we are sending people home to Ethshar of the Rocks and Ethshar of the Sands, and we have a tapestry ready for Sardiron of the Waters if the Council of Barons can ever make up its collective mind."

"But nothing for Ethshar of the Spices?"

"I realize how unlikely it sounds, but in fact, we do not have a single suitable tapestry available."

"It seems you could use this magical stairway to take people to Ethshar, rather than bringing supplies here — or does it only work in one direction?"

"Oh, it works both ways, once it's open, but it can't be kept open indefinitely, and we thought bringing food and blankets was the better use, for now."

Hanner did not think he agreed, but rather than argue he said, "Our theurgists tell me that Asham the Gate-Keeper could get everyone safely home; none of our people can invoke him."

"Asham the Gate-Keeper? Oh, now, *that's* interesting! We didn't know about that one. We've been speaking to some theurgists, but either we chose the wrong ones or asked the wrong questions. I'll see about that as soon as we get back." He glanced down. "Oh, good, that's the last of them."

Hanner glanced down as well, and saw the line of people climbing the stairs was coming to an end; a woman with an absurdly large sack on her shoulders was the last of them. "Then what?" he asked.

"Then we will send these people back," Rothiel said, gesturing at the waiting merchants. "And the others when they've sold their goods. Then you and I will go back to the city, and Hallin's Transporting Fissure will be permitted to close."

"But what about all these others..." Hanner started to wave at the waiting crowds, then stopped. "Wait. You and I?"

"Yes, you and I. Guildmaster Ithinia wants to talk to you. Directly, not in a dream."

"But what about these others?"

"I *promise* you, Chairman, we will get them to safety as soon as we can. As soon as they've finished sending people to the western cities, those apprentices who are guarding the tapestries will start sorting the others, and loading them onto flying carpets, or preparing them to use another of these fissures. And if this god Asham can truly help, we'll see about summoning him. For now, though, we want *you*."

"Why?"

"Ithinia trusts you."

That dumbfounded Hanner. He knew Ithinia, of course; they had dealt with one another several times over the seventeen years he chaired the Council of Warlocks. He had never been sure she really trusted *anyone*, and while they had been reasonably comfortable with one another, he had never considered her a friend. While he remembered speaking to her about a month ago, he knew that for her it had been seventeen years; that she would want to see him again after so long, out of all the Called warlocks, baffled him.

But then, he didn't suppose she would have much contact with warlocks in the normal course of events.

"I'm not sure I should leave," Hanner said at last. "I feel responsible for these people."

Rothiel, who had been watching the last merchants climb the steps, said, "Excuse me, Chairman." He stepped up and put a hand on the last woman's back, urging her forward, then turned to the group waiting to the side. "Go on, please," he called. "One at a time! Walk briskly, but don't run, and don't slip, just the way you did in the other direction. You, you go first."

The merchants obeyed, and began marching back down into the ground, while the later arrivals hawked their merchandise.

The crowd of buyers had thinned; there were still plenty of Called warlocks in need of food and the other commodities on offer, but apparently either no one else had money, or they preferred to wait until they could get to civilization. Still, the later peddlers were doing a brisk trade, while their earlier brethren made their way one by one back into the magical fissure.

Once he had the proceedings moving smoothly, Rothiel turned his attention back to Hanner. "You shouldn't feel responsible," he said. "Unless you had an apprentice or two, *you* didn't turn anyone into a warlock, and you certainly didn't lure them all out to the middle of nowhere and strand them there with winter coming on. You aren't any more responsible than anyone else here. It seems to me you've already done more than your share."

"Nonetheless, I wouldn't feel right, abandoning them."

Rothiel glanced out at the throng. "Chairman Hanner," he said, "let me put it this way. You are no longer a magician. Do you *really* want to antagonize the most senior master of the Wizards' Guild in Ethshar of the Spices?"

"Um," Hanner said.

"Do you really want her to reconsider her plans to help all these people, which were based largely on *your* cooperation, when I spoke to you in your dream?"

"I don't," Hanner said.

"Then when these merchants are done, and the last of them starts down these stairs, you will follow him — or her, as the case may be. I will be right behind you, and the fissure will close behind us when we emerge back in Eastgate Market, but further assistance will be sent as soon as practical, possibly including theurgists who can invoke this gate-keeper you mentioned. Agreed?"

"*Eastgate* Market?"

"It has the least normal traffic of any market in the city, so using it caused the least disruption."

That made sense; in fact, his surprise had been because Eastgate Market saw so little use that he had almost forgotten it was there. It was still the best place to get fresh shellfish, as well as oranges and dates in season, but other than that it could not compete with the city's other markets. "I see," he said.

"Then you'll come?"

Hanner looked around, saw Rudhira listening at his side, and said, "Only if she comes with us."

Rothiel looked at the slender redhead. "And who is this?"

Rudhira did not answer, but looked up at Hanner expectantly.

"Rudhira of Camptown," Hanner said. "A very old friend I haven't seen in a long time."

"Called before you?"

"Years before me. Is that a problem?"

"You're taking responsibility for her? I don't want her to wind up in the Hundred-Foot Field."

"I can take care of myself," Rudhira said, before Hanner could speak.

"If she doesn't go, neither do I," Hanner said.

He knew this was irrational; Rudhira really *could* take care of herself, and it wasn't as if the two of them had ever been very close. They had only known each other for a few days — but they had been very *important* days, from the Night of Madness to Rudhira's Calling, and then from the moment they awoke in Aldagmor to now.

It occurred to Hanner that while he hoped Mavi was alive and well and would welcome him back, she would probably not appreciate having him show up with a streetwalker at his side. Mavi was not particularly prone to jealousy, but she was his wife.

But he had stated his position, and he was not going to back down. Rothiel was right in saying that he wasn't responsible for all the thousands of the Called, but he could at least take responsibility for *one* of them.

"All right," Rothiel said. "You can bring her along. If anyone objects, *you* can explain it."

"That's fine, then," Hanner said. That settled, he stepped aside to make more room for the peddlers.

He was startled to feel the touch of Rudhira's hand on his shoulder. He looked down at her.

"Thank you," she said.

Uncomfortable, he murmured an inaudible reply.

Almost half an hour later the last candle was sold, the last peddler's pack folded, and the last merchant had started down the steps. Rothiel gestured for Hanner to follow.

He hesitated, then gestured for Rudhira to precede him. She smiled, and obeyed.

He followed her, and heard Rothiel call a few final instructions to nearby apprentices before the wizard, too, started down the steps.

Hanner took a final look around as his head reached ground level, then took the next step down into the earth, in the narrow space between two stone walls, with nothing to see ahead of him but the brightly-colored top of Rudhira's head.

Chapter Fourteen

Sterren grew steadily more nervous as he waited in the plaza, between the doors of the imperial palace and the fountain in the center of the square. Vond had said he would be here an hour after noon, and by Sterren's reckoning it was now half an hour beyond that. The little crowd Sterren had gathered was growing restless.

"Lord Sterren," Lady Kalira said, "is there a problem?" She still spoke Ethsharitic with a slight accent, even after all these years.

"I don't know," Sterren replied. "He said he would be here."

"I think I've changed my mind," said one of the former warlocks. "I'll find another way to Ethshar."

"That's your choice," Sterren told her. "I don't even know whether the emperor would take you, but I thought it wouldn't hurt to ask."

"It *might* hurt, though," another of the "honor guard" said. "I've heard stories about his temper. He might think we're getting above ourselves."

"But he said we would have positions of authority!"

"He said we'd have them *here*, not in Ethshar."

Several of them began speaking at once, and Sterren stepped away.

Lady Kalira followed him, and whispered, "Do you still think he's coming?"

"I don't know," Sterren said. "Honestly, he said he would."

"The wizards may have trapped or killed him."

"I thought of that," Sterren admitted. "If they did, wouldn't they tell us?"

"They might not bother." She glanced back at the arguing warlocks. "Could something else have happened to him? Maybe there is something even worse that happens to warlocks, something that the Calling had protected him from."

Sterren grimaced; that possibility had never occurred to him, and while he didn't think it was likely, it was not a pleasant idea. After all, he was technically a warlock himself. "I don't know," he said. "*Nobody* knows much about how warlock magic works, and they know even less about Vond's version."

"If he never comes back, you're still regent."

"No, *you* are!" Sterren protested. "He appointed you regent last night!"

"He didn't tell *me* that; I have only your word for it."

"Are you doubting my word, then?"

"As a matter of fact, Lord Sterren, I often doubt your word. In this case I think you were probably telling the truth — but I also think I will deny I ever said that. I'm not interested in this sort of responsibility; I don't *want* to be regent."

"I *never* wanted to be regent. That was the council's idea."

"That's why you were good at it!"

"I did as little as I could; that was good?"

"That was *excellent*. The secret of good government is to let people go on about their own business. Oh, there are times you must act, but unless your people are asking for your help, usually it's best to do nothing."

"Not everyone would agree."

"No, but ask your overlords back in Ethshar some time. I think they would."

Sterren had never paid much attention to government in his youth, back in Ethshar, but he suspected Kalira was right. "Well, then it shouldn't be hard for you to be regent," he said. "You've just told me the secret of good government; all you need to do is apply that knowledge."

She glared at him.

"Can you suggest anyone better?" Sterren asked. "There might still be time to change Vond's mind."

"Lord Algarven, perhaps?"

"How old is he? And I don't think Vond likes him."

"Those are not the most important qualifications."

Sterren turned up an empty palm. "I suggested you. If you want to argue with the Great Vond about it, I won't stop you."

"*If* he comes back, maybe I will."

"As you please." Sterren glanced past Lady Kalira at the cluster of Called warlocks; he had gathered twenty-six of them, but there were no longer that many. Some of them had clearly decided they didn't want to ask about being carried to Ethshar after all.

He had only been able to find about thirty of the eighty or more who had originally accompanied Vond; the rest had presumably either believed the rumors about Vond's power being demonic, or had been so beset by headaches they fled, or had simply gone about their own business. A few of the thirty had said they were happy staying on as guests of the empire, leaving the twenty-six who had been waiting on the plaza with Sterren.

Some of them admitted to having headaches; others reported a nagging buzz or hum; others claimed not to perceive anything out of the ordinary. Sterren guessed that even though they were all warlocks, there were variations in their brains that affected how they reacted to the Lumeth source — if they reacted at all.

So far, none showed any signs of being able to exploit the Lumeth source to power magic, as Vond did. That was good. Sterren had made sure that they all knew the Wizards' Guild had forbidden warlocks to enter the empire, or several of the other southern kingdoms, which he hoped would temper any interest in regaining their magic.

He wondered what the Wizards' Guild would do about Vond — or what they *had done* about Vond, if that was why he was so late. If Vond was dead, would his subjects blame Sterren? Would they consider him a traitor?

Or would they celebrate? Yes, Vond had created the empire, overthrown the old kings and removed the worst of the old aristocracy, built the palace, built the roads, and brought peace to the region, but he had also killed anyone who got in his way, gathered a harem, and generally treated the empire as his personal playground. Sterren had not been able to get a good feel, as yet, for how Vond's return was received.

And how would the Wizards' Guild look at Sterren? As regent he had agreed to keep warlocks out, but he had welcomed Vond back; the wizards might not appreciate that.

Sterren looked up to the east again, then blinked. At first he thought he might be imagining it, but no — that black shape in the distance was Vond, approaching quickly. He let out his breath.

"There he is," he told Kalira, pointing.

"What?" She turned, startled. "Oh, yes!"

"Are you going to ask him to choose someone else?"

Kalira hesitated, then shook her head. "No," she said. "Maybe after I see how it goes." She squared her shoulders and stood up straight, awaiting her emperor.

A moment later Vond swooped down to hang a foot or so above the plaza, facing Sterren. He was smiling cheerfully as he approached, but once he stopped, his expression turned serious. "Are you ready?" he demanded.

Sterren gestured at his baggage — two large bundles and a trunk. "I am, your Majesty."

"Good! Then let us..." Vond began. Then he stopped.

Sterren had felt himself tugged upward, but he used his own feeble magic to resist, to pull himself back down, keeping his toes, if not his entire feet, on the ground. He had no doubt at all that Vond could easily overcome his opposition, but this would at least get the emperor's attention.

"Was there something else?" Vond asked.

"Two things, your Majesty," Sterren replied. "First, would you please confirm Lady Kalira as the new regent, if such is your pleasure?"

Vond glanced at the woman in question, then turned his gaze back to Sterren. "And the second?"

"Second, some of the people you brought from Aldagmor would like to accompany us to Ethshar." He gestured at the waiting Called. "I understand they do not feel comfortable here."

"Ah," Vond said, looking over the former warlocks thoughtfully. They were a worried and tired-looking group, about evenly split between male and female, all watching Sterren and the emperor nervously. "Headaches, ringing in the ear, perhaps? That sort of thing?"

"Exactly, your Majesty."

"Then by all means, they should come with us! Well done, Sterren, thinking of that."

"And the regency?" Sterren prodded gently.

"Yes!" Vond rose a foot or so and amplified his voice, so that the entire square echoed with his words. "Lady Kalira, I hereby name you regent, and appoint you to administer the empire in my absence! Rule wisely until I return!"

Lady Kalira curtsied deeply in response, and by the time she rose once more to her feet, Sterren and the former warlocks — Sterren counted nineteen, nine men and ten women — were rising upward into the air.

Some of them were muttering or calling questions, which Vond totally ignored. He had his attention focused to the northwest, toward Ethshar of the Spices.

Sterren watched the plaza fall away, then turned to the south to see Semma Castle receding as he was pulled upward and northward. Within a few seconds of Vond's final word, Sterren and the others were passing over the red tile roof of the imperial palace, leaving behind the marble walls and tile roofs of New Semma, and the half-timber and thatch of Old Town.

Once they were well clear of the buildings, Sterren glanced back and down, and saw that his luggage was following them.

The former warlocks, of course, had no luggage; they still had only what they had brought with them when they were Called. They did not look very happy, which struck Sterren as slightly odd — they were being given a free ride back to Ethshar, after all. Shouldn't they be pleased?

Vond, unlike the others, seemed quite cheerful. He was smiling, and his movements were calm and easy.

Wind whipped at Sterren's hair and whistled in his ears, so he had to shout to be heard. "You seem to be in a good mood," he said to Vond. "Are you so pleased to see the last of the town you built?"

Vond turned his smile on Sterren. "I had a pleasant night," he said. "And I'm looking forward to seeing Ethshar again — it's been almost a year!" Then he blinked, and said, "Or fifteen years, from your point of view."

Sterren nodded, and did not try speaking again; it wasn't worth the effort to be heard over the wind.

By now they were sailing over mile upon mile of small farms and scattered villages; the fields were mostly brown, the harvest in. The names of the months were not even remotely accurate this far south, but even so, by this late in Newfrost most of the crops had been brought in.

Sterren felt a certain pride at the landscape below. Sixteen years ago, when he first came to Semma, this land had been far less productive, the population far smaller. The roads Vond had built had something to do with that, but as regent Sterren had made sure that the roads were maintained and extended, irrigation canals built, and the peasants allowed to work the land as they chose, undisturbed by wars or the sometimes ruinous whims of the nobility.

There was no way to tell when they left the province of Semma and entered Ksinallion; the once-fortified border was gone without a trace. Again, when they passed from Ksinallion into Thanoria, Sterren was only aware of the distinction from years of studying the empire's maps and learning the relevant landmarks.

But then the roads and canals stopped, and the farms grew smaller, less even, and less prosperous, and Sterren knew they had left the empire and passed into Lumeth of the Towers.

He shivered at the realization. They were now breaking the treaty with the Wizards' Guild, defying the Guild's edict. Long ago, Ithinia of the Isle had calmly told him that if he ever set foot in Lumeth, he would be killed. She had also told him that wards had been set all along the border to alert the Guild if the empire tried to invade any of its neighbors, or vice versa.

He hoped that those wards did not extend this far up, and that flying over Lumeth, not under his own power, would not have the same result as setting his feet on the ground; all the same, he knew he would feel much safer once they were beyond Lumeth, and beyond Eknissamor — Eknissamor was the most northerly of the kingdoms where warlockry was forbidden. Once they had passed that point, they would no longer be in violation of the Guild's rules.

He glanced back at the emperor's "honor guard," and suddenly realized that most of them were in pain — several were clutching at their temples, and at least one had started screaming; Sterren had not recognized the sound as anything but more wind at first.

He silently cursed his own stupidity in not foreseeing this. "Your Majesty!" he shouted. "Your Majesty! *Vond*!"

"Hm?" The warlock turned to see Sterren pointing at their suffering companions.

Abruptly, their forward motion stopped, and the entire party hung motionless in mid-air, a at least hundred yards up.

"What's happening?" Vond asked.

Sterren pointed north and made a gesture that he hoped indicated a tower.

"Oh?" Vond said. "*Oh!*"

Suddenly they were moving again, but to the southwest, rather than northwest, and descending. A moment later they began landing in an empty field that Sterren judged to be just inside the empire's border. Most of the former warlocks stumbled, and about half of them fell, upon touching ground; Vond had not been particularly gentle about bringing them down, and while they had all flown before they were accustomed to being in control of their own motion, not being dragged about by someone else's magic.

"Wait here," Vond told them. Then he and Sterren shot upward.

The sudden motion was frightening, and Sterren's stomach did not take it well, but he managed to keep his lunch down.

"They're feeling it, aren't they?" Vond demanded, once he was sure he and Sterren were well out of earshot. "The hum. The power."

"I think so, yes," Sterren said. "After all, they were all powerful enough to be Called, just as you were."

"I can't take them any closer, then."

"They might adjust to it, as you did; then you wouldn't be the only warlock."

Vond shook his head. "I don't want that. I don't know these people, not really. I don't know whether I can trust them with this magic."

Sterren glanced down at the others, scattered on a farmer's field. Several were still holding their heads and appeared to be moaning. "Then you mustn't take them any further into Lumeth."

"But I wanted to see the towers!"

"The Wizards' Guild doesn't want us anywhere near the towers."

"To Hell with the Wizards' Guild! I'm going back to Ethshar, and that should be good enough for them. If I want to do a little sightseeing along the way, I don't see how that hurts them, and I don't care if it does!"

"It hurts *them*, though," Sterren said, pointing down at the nineteen Called warlocks.

"Then maybe I'll just leave them here."

"*Strand* them out here in the middle of nowhere?"

Vond hesitated. "Blast it. It was *your* idea to bring them; why didn't you realize this would happen?"

"I didn't know what route you were going to take!" Sterren protested. "You didn't give us time to discuss it."

He knew, though, that he *should* have expected it; he had known that the warlocks could sense the energy Vond was using, and found it uncomfortable.

Vond frowned. "Fine. I'll take them to the nearest port and let them take a ship, and when that's done, you and I will go take a look at the towers, and the Pillar of Flame, and then we'll go to Ethshar."

"As your Majesty pleases."

Vond looked around. "Where *is* the nearest port?"

Sterren looked out across the landscape, trying to match it to the maps of the empire, and finally said, "Akalla of the Diamond. That way."

"Good," Vond said. He looked down, and the former warlocks were suddenly snatched upward, and a moment later the entire party was flying southwest at high speed — much too fast for further conversation.

An hour later nineteen terrified, exhausted, miserable people were unceremoniously dumped on a pier in Akalla, and the emperor's voice boomed from overhead.

"Send them to Ethshar!" he said. "Put them on the next ship, at my expense!"

Sterren watched for a moment as people scurried about, rushing to please the warlock emperor. Then he was swept away northward again, toward Lumeth of the Towers.

Chapter Fifteen

Hanner emerged from the magical staircase in the middle of Eastgate Market and looked around at a city that was simultaneously familiar and strange. He had not been in Eastgate Market in a year or more — or rather, for at least eighteen years. It had changed.

Oh, the gate itself was still there, standing tall between the mismatched towers, and the city wall stretching away to either side was much the same. The Hundred-Foot Field, just inside the wall, was still an expanse of tents, improvised shelters, cook-fires, beggars, and garbage. The guards still wore the familiar red and gold uniforms, and lounged by the gate and under the red-and-gold pennants that separated the Field from the market. The market itself was hard-packed brown earth, and smelled of fish and the ocean. Dozens of merchants were still hawking clams, oysters, and crabs from stalls, tents, and tables; one or two displayed a few sorry boxes of dates, oranges, or other fruit.

But none of them were merchants Hanner recognized, and the layout of the stalls was different. The old Eastgate Inn that had occupied the center of the north side of the market, just west of the Field, since the end of the Great War was gone, and the open-sided pavilion that stood in its place did not look new; its timbers were darkened from exposure to the weather, and the signboard proclaiming it to be the Eastgate Labor Exchange was faded. The ornamental gateway that had stood beside the inn at the entrance to East Wall Street was still there, but had been repainted with an entirely different color scheme — Hanner remembered it as blue and white, but now it was red, blue, and gold.

The stonemason's shop between the gate and Lighthouse Street was now an ironmonger's shop, and its stone walls, which had always been unadorned, now boasted elaborate wrought-iron trim.

The block of shops at the west end of the square looked much the same; Hanner thought one or two might have changed tenants, but that happened frequently. On the south side the tunnel-like entrance to a warren of small shops around an irregular courtyard was gone, replaced by a weaver's workshop displaying a lovely array of bright fabrics.

Rudhira had stopped dead a few feet ahead of him, and Hanner realized that the changes must be even greater and more shocking for her than they were for him — she had not been here for thirty-four years. She probably remembered the old brewery that had stood on the south side, and had the ornamental gate even been built yet that far back?

Then he realized that she wasn't staring at the buildings; she was staring at the ground. Puzzled, he took a step forward and peered over her shoulder.

"Hanner," she said, "what is *that*?"

Hanner looked down at the green, big-eared, vaguely frog-like creature that was grinning up at them, the top of its head roughly even with Rudhira's kneecaps.

"I have no idea," he said.

"It's a spriggan," Rothiel said from behind them.

"What's a spriggan?" Hanner asked.

"*That* is," Rothiel unhelpfully explained. Then he continued, "A spell went wrong several years back, somewhere in the Small Kingdoms, and started producing these things. It took years before anyone managed to stop it, and there wasn't any way to reverse it and dispose of the ones that had already gotten loose, so there are thousands of these things running around now. They won't hurt you, but they do get into things and make a mess sometimes. They're attracted by magic, so there are probably dozens of them around here right now, drawn by Hallin's Fissure."

The green thing nodded vigorously. "*Lots* of spriggans!" it said, in a squeaky voice.

"It talks!" Rudhira gasped.

"Oh, yes. They talk," Rothiel agreed. "I'm a little surprised you didn't see any in Aldagmor."

"Pretty hair," the spriggan said, staring up at Rudhira, still grinning idiotically.

"They like bright colors, too," Rothiel said. "But if you don't mind, we need to get you to Ithinia. You can observe how the city's changed later." He turned, and called, "Move away from the fissure, please!"

The spriggan's attention suddenly shifted; it dashed between Rudhira's legs, dodged around Hanner, and ran for the magical staircase. "Magic!" it squeaked.

"Oh, blood," the wizard said. "Grab it, someone!"

Two people dived for the creature, whacking their heads together in the process; Hanner winced at the sound of impact. It was someone else entirely, a girl in a blue tunic, who actually managed to capture the spriggan and hold it up.

Rothiel did not spare the time or effort to congratulate her on her feat; he was concentrating on the fissure, staring at it intently, both his hands raised in a sort of warding gesture.

Then the ground began shaking; everyone in the market stepped back, and the spriggan squealed excitedly.

Hanner watched with interest as the ground seemed to rise up and flow together, then sink back to its natural level, flattening out and leaving no trace of the stair that had been there a moment before. The trembling subsided, and the packed earth of the market was back to normal, with no sign it had ever been disturbed.

Several of the watchers, mostly merchants who had sold their goods to the Called warlocks in Aldagmor, applauded. The spriggan suddenly squirmed free from the girl's grip and ran to dance on the empty place where the fissure had been. The two who had dived for it — a boy in his teens and a middle-aged man — sat up, rubbing their heads and glaring at one another.

Rothiel let out a relieved sigh. "There," he said, letting his hands fall. "Now, as I was saying, let's get you to Ithinia."

Hanner did not argue, but followed as the wizard led them west on East Street. He glanced back over his shoulder at the spriggan — or rather, the spriggans; three of them were now chasing one another through the marketplace crowds.

Rudhira followed the two men; Hanner considered saying something, suggesting she set about finding herself a place of her own rather than tagging along to a meeting that would probably be a waste of her time, but then decided her presence would do no harm, and it was none of his concern if she wanted to come.

It was a little over two miles to Ithinia's house on Lower Street; the route took them through the middle of the Eastgate district into southern Hempfield, to the tiny patch of open land called Old High Street Market. In the summer, as Hanner remembered it, flowers bloomed in the triangle of raised beds, surrounded by street musicians, jugglers, and hawkers selling candy and trinkets, but the flowers were done for the year, and either the weather now was cold enough to deter them, or things had changed during his absence — the place was deserted save for an old man huddled against a wall, and a brown-striped cat prowling the flowerbeds, looking for mice.

Hanner had expected to stay on East Street, but Rothiel led them up the left-hand fork, onto Old High Street and into Allston.

Old High Street merged into High Street at roughly the halfway point of their journey, and it occurred to Hanner that if he simply stayed on this road he would soon be home, at Warlock House, once Uncle Faran's mansion.

But Mavi and the children probably wouldn't be there to welcome him. It was hard to believe it had really been seventeen years; to Hanner it had only been a couple of days since he left Mavi and the children at Warlock House while he went to see his new magical tapestry. He hoped she was all right; none of the wizards had yet told him anything about her circumstances.

He knew that time had really passed, and the city had changed. He had seen Eastgate Market, and as he followed Rothiel through Allston he could see differences here, as well. The late afternoon shadows were lengthening, obscuring some of the details, but Hanner was fairly certain there were new tiles on some roofs, different paint here and there, shrines added or removed, and so on.

Even so, this was familiar ground. To reach Warlock House he needed merely stay on High Street — but that wasn't what he did; instead he followed Rothiel as the wizard turned right on Arena Street and followed it two blocks down the hill, toward the overlord's palace, before turning left onto Lower Street.

This neighborhood was not Allston, of course; they had left that district behind. This side of Arena Street was the New City — or at least, it had still been called that seventeen years ago. Perhaps the name had finally been changed by now, since the area had not actually been new for more than two hundred years.

The houses here appeared exactly as Hanner remembered them; whatever changes might have overtaken other parts of the city, Lower Street seemed untouched. So far as he could tell in the orange glow of the setting sun, Ithinia's gray stone house, second from the corner on the north side of the street, was just as it had always been.

One of the gargoyles on the cornice slowly turned its head to watch their approach, and Hanner tried to remember — was that one Glitter? No, Glitter's niche was in back, overlooking the garden; Hanner thought this one was called Fang. He waved cheerfully to the stony monster.

A spriggan he had not previously noticed jumped up on the gargoyle's shoulder and waved back, reminding Hanner that he was indeed in this strange new future.

The gargoyle flapped a gray wing and sent the spriggan flying, but the little creature caught itself on the cornice, hanging on by just a few fingers, then squealed and swung itself back up behind the gargoyle's leg, whereupon Hanner lost sight of it.

Then Rothiel was knocking on Ithinia's door, so Hanner lowered his gaze, squared his shoulders, and prepared to greet the Guildmaster. Rudhira was standing at his side, and he considered saying something to help her ready herself, but then the door opened and there was Ithinia, in a white robe trimmed with golden-brown fur.

"Hanner!" she said. "Come in, come in; I'm pleased to see you after so long!"

Hanner bowed. "I'm honored, Guildmaster," he said. "May I present my friend, Rudhira of Camptown?"

Ithinia cocked her head. "I believe I remember you," she said. "Long ago — in 5202, I suppose. In the harbor."

Rudhira met Ithinia's gaze. She clearly knew what the wizard was referring to, and Hanner remembered the incident, as well. Rudhira had picked up what had seemed like half the water in the harbor, to test the strength of her magic. "Yes," she said. "That was me."

"You were Called soon after?" Ithinia asked, her tone conversational.

"A few days, yes."

"It was an impressive demonstration of what warlockry could do."

"Yes, it was." Her gaze did not waver; Hanner hoped that her boldness would not annoy the Guildmaster. They no longer had their own magic to protect them, should the wizard decide they were not showing the proper respect.

Ithinia considered the little redhead for a moment longer, then smiled and said, "Come in, both of you; you must be exhausted." She stepped aside to let them enter.

"Thank you," Hanner said, hurrying past her and into the parlor.

It had been refurbished since he last saw it — he was surprised at first, then remembered that it had been seventeen years. A small marble-topped table was familiar, but everything else was new. The predominant colors were red and gold, where the furnishings had been mostly white the last time Hanner visited. There was a faint odor of cinnamon, though Hanner could see no source for it.

Rudhira settled into a red velvet armchair without waiting to be invited; Hanner hesitated, and was still standing when Ithinia swept into the room and said, "Please, sit down. Make yourselves comfortable."

Rudhira smiled at Hanner as he took a seat on a matching armchair.

"Guildmaster," Rothiel said from the door.

Ithinia turned. "Yes?"

"Hanner suggests that the god Asham the Gate-Keeper might be able to send the other warlocks home. If I may, I'd like to see if I can find a theurgist who's familiar with this deity."

Ithinia said, "Asham?" Then she let out a wordless noise of dismay. "Of course, Asham! I must be getting old, to have not remembered sooner. The Sanctuary of the Priests of Asham is on Priest Street, north side, midway between Arena and Magician Street. It's a very difficult summoning, so you may need to bargain."

"Priest, between Arena and Magician? Thank you, Guildmaster!" The brown-clad wizard bowed, and hurried out.

That left Hanner and Rudhira alone with the woman generally believed to be the most powerful wizard in Ethshar of the Spices, and Hanner had no idea why they were there. He waited until Ithinia had closed the door and returned to the parlor, but then got straight to the point.

"Why did you want to see me, Guildmaster?"

Ithinia produced an expression that was not quite a smile, though it came close. "Would you like something to eat, before we get to business?" she asked. "A drink, perhaps? I had Obdur brew a pot of tea — it's Luvannion leaf, the early harvest."

"Tea would be lovely," Hanner admitted; he had had nothing but water to drink, and not much of that, since being Called.

"And honey cakes? Sadra baked them this afternoon."

Rudhira perked up. "Honey cakes?"

Ithinia smiled. She turned and called over her shoulder, "Obdur! Tea and cakes for our guests!"

"At once, Mistress!" a voice replied, though Hanner and Rudhira could not see the speaker.

Ithinia then sank into the last of the three velvet armchairs, straightened her robe, and said, "I want to reinstate you as Chairman of the Council of Warlocks."

Hanner considered that for a moment. It made no sense that he could see. He asked, "*What* Council? What warlocks?"

"Vond," Rudhira said, before Ithinia could reply.

The wizard nodded. "There's Vond, yes," she said, "but we don't expect Hanner to deal with the emperor all by himself; that would be too much to ask of a man with no magic. No, we want him to deal with Zallin, and to help all the Called readjust to their altered circumstances."

"Zallin?" Hanner asked. "Zallin of the Mismatched Eyes?"

"Yes, that Zallin. He was the last Chairman of the Council."

"So I had heard," Hanner said. "But again — what Council? What warlocks?"

"I'm afraid that Zallin has decided not to accept his fate," Ithinia said. "He is determined to find a way to restore his magic, and thereby retain his position as chairman. I don't think he's the only warlock who is unhappy with the sudden change in his situation."

"I'm sure he isn't," Hanner said, "but I don't see why that's any concern of mine, or of the Wizards' Guild."

"Vond," Rudhira said again. "If he still has his magic, so can others."

"You're a very astute young woman," Ithinia said. "That's exactly right. And there's no Calling to restrain him, or anyone like him, now."

"You think Zallin is going to find out how Vond kept his magic, and get his own magic back?" Hanner asked.

"We're afraid he might try, yes," Ithinia said. "We want you to do everything you can to discourage him, and anyone else who has the same idea."

"Why me?"

"Because you are Chairman Hanner," the wizard said. "Every warlock in the city who remembers you respects you. You created the Council and prevented Azrad the Sedentary from declaring war on all warlocks. You guaranteed that the Council would keep order among warlocks, and see that they obeyed the law, and you ran the Council effectively and fairly for seventeen years. From what I've heard, you also became the leader of all the Called, and took charge of getting them safely out of Aldagmor."

"I didn't...I was just one of several people!" Hanner protested. "Sensella of Morningside, and Rayel Roggit's son, and Alladia of Shiphaven..."

"Morningside? She's from Ethshar of the Sands? Is that where she is now?"

"Well...yes," Hanner admitted.

"Then she'll be no help *here*. And the others?"

"Rayel's from Aldagmor," Hanner conceded. "But Alladia..."

"She's a theurgist," Rudhira interrupted. Hanner turned to glare at her.

"You were the first chairman," Ithinia said, before Hanner could argue further. "And you were a lord, and a student of magic, before that. You're perfect for what we want."

"I still don't understand what that *is*," Hanner protested.

"We want you to do everything you can to prevent anyone from seeking out Emperor Vond in hopes of getting back their magic. We want you to be a calming voice, a voice of authority, a fatherly friend helping former warlocks find places for themselves now that their magic is gone. We want you to serve as a go-between between the Called and the Wizards' Guild."

"I suppose I could *try*," Hanner said, doubtfully.

"We'll pay you for your services," Ithinia said.

"How much?" Rudhira asked.

"Enough," the wizard snapped.

Rudhira frowned, and slumped back in her chair.

Ithinia looked at her, then back at Hanner. "There's something else," she said. "I would have preferred to keep this between the two of us, but I won't insist; would you rather have Rudhira hear it, or not?"

Hanner glanced at Rudhira. He did not want sole responsibility for anything.

"I'd rather have her here," he said.

"As you please," Ithinia said. "The other detail is this — if any other warlock *does* succeed in regaining his magic, we'll kill him." She glanced at Rudhira. "Or her."

Hanner snorted. "Then what do you need *me* for? Just tell them that!"

Ithinia shook her head. "People can be stubborn," she said. "If we say we'll kill anyone who tries it, some will take that as a challenge, and we do not *want* to kill *anyone*. We would prefer you talk them out of it without bringing the Guild into the discussion. We don't want to appear as if the Guild is exceeding its authority. We don't want the overlord to think we are usurping *his* authority."

"But you *are*."

"Yes, but we don't want to be blatant about it." The not-quite-a-smile hardened.

Hanner grimaced. "So you want me to be the pretty frosting on a poisoned cake."

"More or less, yes."

It was at that point that Obdur appeared in the doorway with a large tray holding a teapot, three cups, and a huge platter stacked high with honey cakes. Business was put aside as the tea was poured and a few of the cakes distributed.

When Obdur had retreated, and Hanner had downed three cups of tea and four of the little cakes, Ithinia said, "There's something else I wanted to tell you."

Hanner looked up from licking crumbs off his fingers. "Oh?"

"Yes," Ithinia said. "We found your wife."

Hanner jumped up, scattering crumbs and crockery in all directions. "Where is she? Is she all right?"

"She's fine," Ithinia said. "She's fine, and all three of your children are fine."

"Where are they?"

"I can give you her address. She's living on Mustard Street, in Spice-town." Ithinia looked at Hanner sadly and finished, "With her husband."

Chapter Sixteen

Except for their size, the towers did not look like much. Vond and Sterren flew three circles around them, and Sterren really did not see anything very interesting. They were just towers, tall, unadorned cylinders, made of some unfamiliar gray substance that appeared to be midway between stone and metal. One of them was broken off on a rough diagonal about two-thirds of the way up, and the exposed surface revealed an incomprehensible jumble of mysterious stuff — crystal shards that glittered gold in the light of the setting sun, curving yellowish-white things that might have been bones, pipes made of a dozen different substances, colored cables, and so on, some of it partially melted. Other than that, the towers were featureless.

Going by what the break exposed, they were almost solid, with no stairs, ladders, or other way to ascend the interior; certainly they had no windows, and the tops of the two intact ones were rounded and smooth, not intended for anyone to stand on.

They made Sterren nervous.

"Can you feel it?" Vond asked, his voice amplified to a thunderous roar. "Feel the power!"

That, Sterren realized, was what was making him nervous — he *could* feel the power, and he had spent the last fifteen years suppressing any hint of magical ability he might have. Vond had altered Sterren's brain so that he could draw energy from these towers, just as Vond himself did, but Sterren had deliberately refused to do so. He did not *want* to be a warlock. Oh, he *had* wanted to, a long time ago, when as a boy of twelve he had tried to apprentice himself to a warlock, but he had long since decided that he had been very fortunate to have failed that apprenticeship by showing no talent for warlockry. He had not wanted to ever be Called. And once the Wizards' Guild banned warlocks from the region, he had not wanted to anger the Guild. Before that he had sometimes allowed himself just enough magic to win at dice more than was natural, but after Ithinia delivered the Guild's ultimatum he had forsworn even that.

But here, flying maybe fifty feet from the towers that gave Lumeth of the Towers its name, he could feel power in the air around him. He could feel it flowing through his body, and his head almost seemed to be vibrating with it.

Vond clearly enjoyed this, but Sterren emphatically did not. "Can we go now?" he asked.

Vond gave him an angry glare, then took another long look at the towers. He swept up close and reached out one hand to touch the sleek gray side of the nearest one.

There was a sudden crack, like the sound of a tree limb snapping, and a green flash, and Sterren felt himself falling. He flailed wildly, reaching out, trying to find something to catch, to hold himself up.

Then he stopped in mid-air; Vond had caught him. He had fallen perhaps sixty feet — and so had Vond, Sterren realized.

Or no, Vond had fallen perhaps fifty. Where before the two men had been flying at the same altitude, Sterren was now several feet below his companion, and Sterren's luggage hung unsupported still lower.

"It would seem there are protective spells on them," Vond said. "Probably wizardry, from the feel of it."

"Oh," Sterren said, looking down at the hundred-foot drop beneath him.

"It's a good thing we're warlocks," Vond continued. "That blast would have killed most people. My magic protected us."

"Oh," Sterren said again.

Vond frowned. "That was quite a powerful spell," he said.

"Are you sure it was a spell, and not the towers themselves?" Sterren called up.

"No," Vond admitted. "There's something…something *very strange* about these towers. They're magical, and of course we already assumed that, but it's very *strange* magic. And the stuff they're made of — it isn't anything I've ever seen before. It's got magic all through it, but I can't tell what *kind* of magic."

"Your Majesty," Sterren called, "as your chief advisor, I suggest we stay well away from these things."

"But this is where my power comes from!"

"They cause headaches in normal warlocks, one of them just tried to kill us, and the wizards claim to have put a variety of wards and safe-guards around them."

"Did they?" Vond glanced down at him, then up at the towers. "That might explain the green flash."

"Yes, your Majesty, it might."

Vond stared at the towers a moment longer, considering, then turned up an empty palm. "We can always come back later," he said.

Then the two of them were swooping off to the northwest, Sterren's baggage trailing behind, moving so quickly that for a moment Sterren had trouble breathing.

He glanced back at the towers, standing tall and straight, their west sides bright and the east sides black with shadow. Whatever they were, he was glad to be moving away. Being close to those towers was inexplicably disturbing.

He was also very glad Vond had not landed. He did not want his feet to touch Lumethan soil.

The sun was on the horizon and sinking fast; the detour to deliver the Called to Akalla had delayed their flight. Sterren wondered how far Vond intended to go tonight. As a warlock he was tireless, of course, and could generate his own light if necessary, so they might travel the entire distance to Ethshar, but he rather hoped they would not; *Vond* might not tire, but *he* did. He was not exerting himself in any way to stay airborne, but the journey was tiring nonetheless; the constant wind was wearing, the cold air sucked the warmth from his flesh, and he could not keep from tensing. He knew, intellectually, that he was securely supported by Vond's magic, but some deep animal part of his brain did not accept that. It was convinced he was falling, and kept bracing for the inevitable impact, which became exhausting after a time.

Sterren was fairly certain that the towers were near Lumeth's northern border; they were certainly a league or so northwest of the capital. He would be glad to be out of the forbidden area, and he thought Vond probably intended to fly at least that far before going to ground.

Indeed, the sun was still a red sliver on the western horizon when they came in sight of a castle perched atop a mountain, somewhat to the west of their route. Until now they had been passing over larger and larger hills, and this peak ahead and to the left was the first that was definitely, inarguably, a mountain, rather than a hill.

The first, but by no means the last; as they neared it Sterren could see a line of mountains extending northward, growing ever higher. He knew enough geography to know that this castle was Calimor, at the southern tip of the Southern Mountains, the range that ran down the center of the Small Kingdoms from Sevmor to — well, to here, to Calimor.

They were traveling below the height of the peaks and on the eastern side of the ridge, so that the mountains appeared as great dark shapes with the sun's fading glow outlining them in red and gold. Calimor Castle was likewise a silhouette, one that passed and fell quickly behind as Vond flew steadily north-northwest.

They flew over a deep valley walled with rocky cliffs, a valley running east and west and separating the half-dozen most southerly mountains from the rest of the range. Sterren was fairly sure that marked the boundary between Calimor and Eknissamor; those cliffs made it impossible to cross directly from one nation to the other without using magic. To the east a kingdom called Yaroia extended from the foothills out onto the plain, and there were roads from Yaroia to both Calimor and Eknissamor, while to the west were similar routes through Gajamor, one of the largest of the Small Kingdoms. Up in the mountains, though, there was no non-magical way across that rift.

Calimor was a very small country, and it was only moments before Vond and Sterren were across the border valley and into Eknissamor. The mountains to the west grew steadily higher, blocking more and more of the sunset and subsequent twilight; the foothills to the east were larger, as well. There was no broad, fertile plain here, as there was back in southern Lumeth or in Thanoria; there were rocky uplands where sheep grazed between stony outcroppings.

Then, as full night should have been falling, Sterren noticed a glow in the sky — but not to due east, as the sunrise should be, nor due west, where the sun had set; it was to the northeast. A few minutes later they came in sight of the source.

"The Tower of Flame," Sterren said.

It was a column of bright orange flame roaring upward into the night sky, easily a hundred and fifty feet high; as they neared it the mountain air lost its chill, and when they stopped about fifty yards away Sterren could feel its warmth on his face, as if he were standing right beside an ordinary fire.

This was no ordinary fire, though; quite aside from its size, it was burning on solid rock, with no visible fuel. The pillar of flame rose from a patch of bare stone perhaps a dozen yards down from the summit of a good-sized mountain — good-sized, but not particularly steep; the long-ago wizard who lit the fire could have reached the site on foot, without any magical assistance.

The entire peak was bare stone. They were well above the timberline, and had left the grazing sheep behind; nothing of any size lived this far up. This was the central ridge of the Southern Mountains, not far from the highest peaks.

Those highest mountains were faintly visible in the darkness to the northwest, where they formed a virtually impassable barrier between Ansumor to the west and Swezmor to the east; Vond and Sterren were close enough that the mountains would have been plainly visible in daylight, towering over them. Even by night, they could be made out as black shapes, darker than the sky and untroubled by stars.

Here in northern Eknissamor the peaks were lower, and the slopes were still gentle enough to be climbed without any magic or special equipment, and according to legend some wizard, long ago, had stopped here for the night. He or she had used a trivial little spell to light a camp-fire on the eastern slope of a mountain.

The spell had gone spectacularly wrong, though, and the immense fire was still burning, centuries later. The dozen sticks of firewood the wizard had brought had been consumed in the first few seconds, and the magical flame had been burning without fuel ever since.

It was famous. People came from far away to see it — as Vond and Sterren were seeing it now. There were roads leading down to the capital towns of Eknissamor in the east, Ansumor in the west, and Luvannion to the southwest, and sometimes those roads were almost crowded.

Sightseers generally did not come here this time of year, though; the risk of being caught in a winter storm was too great. Spring was a much safer season for a visit. Visitors would come up in tens and twenties and set up camp around the Tower of Flame, observing it throughout the day, so they could see it against the daylit sky, could compare it to sunrise and sunset, and could see how it lit up the night sky.

There were few signs of those camps, though; the guides generally tried to keep the area clean, and of course, there were no ashes or scorch-marks from campfires — why bother to build any lesser fire when *that* was available? Cooking one's dinner in it was part of the experience, and required nothing but the food and a very long stick.

Vond and Sterren hung in the air, staring at the flames and feeling the heat wash over them.

"It's impressive," Sterren said.

"It is," Vond agreed.

After a long moment of silence, Vond added, "It takes a lot of energy to do that. It's been burning for a century?"

"Eight hundred years," Sterren said.

"That long?"

"So they say."

"A wizard did it?"

"Yes."

Vond fell silent again, but eventually said, "I'm not afraid of the Wizards' Guild."

Sterren resisted the impulse to glance at his companion or show any sign of surprise or concern. Vond's comment hardly followed directly from anything they had said, but its roots were plain enough. "So I understand," Sterren said.

"I'm not afraid of them," Vond repeated, "but they *do* have some powerful magic. They did that." He pointed toward the flame.

"Yes," Sterren said.

"I don't think they could kill me as easily as they think, but there's no reason to anger them if I don't need to."

"Of course not."

"They banned warlocks from the empire?"

"Yes, your Majesty."

"Including me?"

Sterren hesitated. "I do not recall whether you were mentioned specifically," he said. "After all, you had been Called; we didn't think your return would be an issue."

Vond nodded. "I could fight them — but why should I? I only went to Semma in the first place to avoid the Calling; I never wanted to stay there, not if I had a choice. If the Guild doesn't want me there, why should I argue?"

"I don't know," Sterren said helplessly.

"They don't frighten me, and I don't believe they're anywhere near as powerful as they pretend to be, but what's the point of antagonizing them?" He was staring at the Tower of Flame as he spoke, and Sterren thought there was something odd in his tone, as if he were trying to convince himself of something.

The question didn't seem to need an answer, so Sterren said nothing.

"Sterren, do you have a warlock's sight?" Vond asked.

"Do…" Sterren hesitated, trying to guess what answer Vond wanted to hear, but could not decide what would be safest. He settled for the truth. "I'm not sure," he said. "Not really."

Vond glanced at him. "What do you mean?"

Sterren felt trapped, but he still saw no reason not to be honest. "I don't see all the little bits of everything, the way some warlocks say they do, but sometimes I can…I don't know how to describe it. I can tell how something is moving, and where the strains are."

Vond nodded. "That's how it starts," he said. "But you can't see heat?"

"Not any more than anyone else. If the air ripples, I can see that."

"No, that's the air. I meant the heat itself."

"No, I can't see that."

"You've been a warlock for fifteen years, and you haven't learned to see energy?"

"I never *tried* to," Sterren protested. "I never *wanted* to. I didn't want to be Called."

Vond glanced at him curiously. "You didn't want to be a warlock?"

"Why would I? I was your regent! Who needed dangerous magic on top of that?"

"So you're a coward?"

Sterren's head jerked back, but then he relaxed. There was no reason to let Vond's words upset him. No one had dared to call him a coward in a very long time, but when one looked at it realistically, there was some truth in the accusation.

"Pretty much, yes," he said.

"*I'm* not. I'm not afraid of anything."

Sterren remembered Vond cowering in his palace, trying desperately to resist the Calling; if Sterren was any judge, the warlock emperor had been *terrified*. But if he chose to forget or ignore that, Sterren was not inclined to argue, because Sterren *was* a coward, by some measures. He was afraid of a great many things. He tried not to let that interfere with doing what needed to be done, and he might try to hide it from others, but he wasn't going to pretend to himself that he wasn't scared by Vond, and by the Wizards' Guild, and by any number of other things.

To Vond, those miserable nights of fighting Aldagmor's pull had been just a few days ago. He was probably still at the stage of being embarrassed by his own fear, and trying to deny it. In a few years he might admit that yes, he had been frightened, but right now, Sterren thought, Vond was trying to demonstrate, to himself as much as to anyone else, that he was a brave man, and that the Calling had not reduced him to a whimpering child.

"Of course not; why should you be?" Sterren said. "You're the Great Vond."

"Exactly!" Vond was staring at the Tower of Flame again. "Do you know why I asked whether you could see energy?"

"No."

"Because I wanted to talk to you about that fire."

Sterren looked past Vond's legs at the flames. "What about it?"

"It's not really flame, in the usual sense," Vond said. "It's...it's something else, something I've never seen anywhere else."

"Well, yes," Sterren said. "It's magic."

"Yes, I know *that*," Vond said. "But I've never seen magic quite like it. I've never seen anything magical that was so *big* before. Usually when I watch wizardry in action it's all sort of vague — I can't focus on it. It's as if it's not really all there, or as if I'm seeing it through a dirty window. But this thing has a *pattern* to it; there are streaks of...of unreality, woven together with something that looks and feels like fire, but...the actual fire isn't *there* anymore. We're seeing a fire that burned a long time ago, trapped in magic and reflected over and over."

"Really?" Sterren stared at the flame, but all he saw was flame.

"Yes. And I think I see how I could break it."

"What?"

"I think I see how I could break the pattern. I could put it out."

Sterren stared up at Vond's back, then back at the tower. "Legend has it that various wizards tried to put it out, off and on for seventy or eighty years, and never managed it," he said.

"They were wizards. I'm a warlock."

Sterren nodded. "So you are," he said.

"I'm very tempted to do it, just to see if I really can," Vond said.

"That would be a disappointment to the local guides who bring visitors up here to see it," Sterren said.

"Oh? I suppose it would. I hadn't thought about them. I was wondering, though, whether it would upset the Wizards' Guild if I snuffed their little candle."

"You could really just…snuff it out?"

Vond hesitated. "Well, actually," he said, "I'm not sure. I know I could break the pattern that holds it together, but I'm not sure where all that…that *stuff*, that magic, would go. It might just disappear."

Sterren did not like the sound of that. "Might?"

"Or it might explode," Vond said.

Sterren considered that for a moment, then said, "I'd rather not be here when you try it, then."

"Good point," Vond said. "And there are those guides you mentioned. But I might want to try it someday."

"If you're worried about annoying the Guild, you could just *ask* them if they mind. For all I know, they'd be glad to get rid of it."

"That's very true." Vond contemplated the burning pillar for a moment longer, then raised an empty palm and turned away to the west. "It can wait, then. On to Ethshar!"

"On to Ethshar," Sterren echoed, without much enthusiasm.

But as they flew on, and the Tower of Flame receded behind them, it struck him that being Called had mellowed Vond a little. At the height of his power, when he was paving highways and erecting his palace and reshaping various bits of landscape, he would have tested his theory and blown out the flame immediately, without worrying about the Guild or the guides or Sterren. His caution was a good sign.

But he was still insanely dangerous, and Sterren was looking forward to getting as far away from him as possible once they reached Ethshar.

Chapter Seventeen

The house on Mustard Street was unremarkable. It stood three stories tall on the west side of the street, half a block north of Inlet Street. It was about twenty feet wide, with a central door flanked by shuttered windows; candlelight leaked through the slats. The eaves above him were carved, though the night was too dark for Hanner to see what they represented; the doorposts, which were more visible, were carved to resemble trees wrapped in flowering vines. There were no shrines, signs, or other displays in sight.

Hanner stared at the house for a moment. He glanced back at Rudhira, who had accompanied him from Ithinia's house, then stepped forward, squared his shoulders, and knocked.

He heard muffled voices inside, and waited, and a moment later the door opened a crack. "Yes?" a familiar female voice asked. A burning candle appeared in the opening, held up to illuminate the caller's face.

Before Hanner could reply, that familiar voice said, *"Hanner?"*

The candle dropped and went out, and Hanner heard thumping as the person who had held it stumbled back against the wall of the entryway.

"Mavi?" he called. "Mavi of Newmarket?"

"Mavi?" another man's voice called from inside the house.

Hanner stepped back. He was unsure what was happening in there, but he did not think barging in would improve the situation. There was more thumping, and some rattling, and Mavi's voice said something Hanner couldn't catch.

That voice was different. When she had spoken previously, Hanner had not been sure that it was Mavi; the voice had been familiar, but had not carried that instant recognition that it always had before. It had changed in his absence.

Once again, he forced himself to remember that he had been gone for seventeen years, even though it felt like less than a sixnight. His sudden reappearance had obviously come as a shock. He waited on the step, giving his wife time to recover.

He heard that man's voice again, and then the door was flung open and light spilled out into the street, silhouetting a tall man's figure. A woman was peering over the man's right shoulder, and holding a candle aloft.

Hanner blinked. Mavi had *changed*. Oh, there could be no question that the woman holding the candle was his wife, but her hair was shorter and streaked with gray, her face was wider and lined with age, and her expression as she stared at him wasn't her usual calm half-smile, but a look verging on horror.

"Who are you?" the man in the doorway demanded.

"Hanner," Hanner replied. "Formerly Hanner the Warlock, now just Hanner. Who are *you*?"

"My name is Terrin Adar's son," he replied. "What do you mean, *formerly* Hanner the Warlock? What are you doing here?"

"I'm looking for my…for Mavi of Newmarket."

"Why? What do you want with my wife?"

Hanner stopped breathing.

He had not wanted to believe what Ithinia had said, that Mavi had remarried, but here her new husband was, standing before him.

After all, Hanner had been gone for seventeen years, and it had been settled long ago that Called warlocks were legally dead. He could hardly expect a wonderful woman like Mavi to remain a lonely widow.

And there she was, staring at him over her new husband's shoulder, not saying anything, her face seventeen years older than he remembered it.

Hanner let out his breath. "I was her first husband," he said. "The father of her children."

"No, you aren't *that* Hanner," Terrin said, frowning. "He was Called years ago."

"Yes, I was," Hanner agreed. "But now I'm back. The Source is gone, and all the Called warlocks are coming home."

"It's really Hanner," Mavi said from behind Terrin. She raised the candle for a better view. "It really *is* him. He hasn't aged a day."

"About three days, actually," Hanner said. "Three very long days. Or maybe four or five, if you count the time it took me to reach Aldagmor — part of it is a bit hazy."

Terrin threw his wife a glance, then turned his attention back to Hanner. "I heard rumors, but I didn't believe them," he said. "I knew something was wrong with the warlocks, but I didn't know the Called were coming back."

"The source of all the warlocks' power…*went away*," Hanner said, waving a hand. "That means no more warlocks, and it released everyone it had Called. It hadn't killed us, just trapped us, and it let us go. So here I am." Then he remembered his companion. "Here *we* are," he said, gesturing to take in Rudhira.

"Who is that?" Mavi asked, craning to see.

"Rudhira of Camptown," Rudhira answered. "We've met, but you might not remember — it's been more than thirty years, for you."

"Rudhira? But you were Called *ages* ago! And you don't look any older!"

"The Warlock Stone was protected by a preserving spell," Hanner said. "Anyone caught in it didn't age; for me, the last seventeen years didn't happen. For Rudhira, it's thirty-four; last she knew we hadn't even formed the Council of Warlocks, and Azrad the Sedentary was still the overlord."

"This isn't real," Mavi moaned. "It *can't* be. You're some shape-shifting demon, come to torment me, or some wizard's illusion."

"I hadn't intended to *torment* you at all," Hanner protested. "I thought you'd be happy to see me."

"After *seventeen years*? Hanner, I waited for two years, just in case you found a way to escape the Calling, or in case that refuge of yours did something, but I had to get on with my life. I met Terrin when he did some work on the house, and...and you were *dead*, we thought."

"I understand," Hanner said. "I'm not angry at all; seriously, I do understand. You had every right to remarry; in fact, I'm glad you weren't alone all those years. But I'm back now."

"But I'm *married*."

"You're married to *both* of us, Mavi."

"I'm not interested in sharing, warlock," Terrin growled.

Hanner stared at him. "It wouldn't be my preference, either," he said. "But here we are."

"No, no," Mavi said. She glanced at Rudhira. "No, I'm sorry, Hanner, but I can't pretend the last seventeen years didn't happen. Besides, even before you flew away, you were...we were...." She swallowed, then continued, "You were *distracted*. I never saw you."

"I was trying to resist the Calling," Hanner said, trying to keep calm.

"You were pulling away from me," Mavi said. "And I let you go. And...now I'm seventeen years older, and you aren't. It's...it's not right, Hanner. You can't just reappear and reclaim me. Our marriage ended seventeen years ago, and now Terrin is my husband."

Hanner bit his lip, fighting back tears. "You don't want me back?"

"No, I don't." There was an edge of hysteria to her voice that had a perversely calming effect on Hanner's own raw nerves.

For a long moment, no one spoke. Then Hanner said, "What about the children?"

"They're still your children," Mavi said. "They're grown now, of course."

"What's happened to them?"

Mavi and Terrin exchanged glances. "Faran owns an antiquities shop in the Old City," Mavi said. "He and Sadra have four little girls. Arris has a bakery in Fishertown; she's married to Thurin the Ferryman. They have a boy, Hanner Thurin's son."

"They named him for me?" Hanner said, absurdly surprised and pleased.

"Yes, they did. He's nine."

"What about Hala?"

Mavi managed an uncertain smile. "We apprenticed her to her Aunt Alris."

"Alris?" Hanner blinked in surprise. "Isn't Alris a little... No, I suppose she isn't, anymore." He had been going to suggest she was too young to be taking an apprentice, since the only reason for someone in her position to do so would be to train her own successor, but he had once again forgotten the difference those lost years would make.

"Who is Alris?" Rudhira asked.

"*Lady* Alris," Mavi said. "Hanner's sister. She's the overlord's Lady of the Household; she oversees the palace staff."

"And Lady Hala is her assistant," Terrin said proudly. "The palace servants are terrified of her."

Hanner tried to take this in, but it was too much, too fast. His wife had rejected him, his children were grown, and he had half a dozen grandchildren he had never met. His daughter was working for his sister in the overlord's palace? Last Hanner had seen of her she wasn't yet big enough for long skirts, and spent half her time running shrieking through or around Warlock House, playing fanciful games with her friends and siblings.

And this stranger who had taken his wife — Hanner could hear the pride in his stepdaughter, in Hanner's daughter, in his voice.

"Hanner?" Rudhira asked. "Are you all right?"

Hanner realized he had been standing motionless on the step, trembling silently, for several seconds.

"I'm fine," he said. "I...I'll be fine."

I faced down a hundred-foot dragon a couple of days ago, Hanner told himself. *I can face this.*

"Yes, well," Terrin said. "I think you should go now."

"But...go where? I was hoping..." He stopped. He had hoped to stay with Mavi, but that obviously wasn't going to happen; this was Terrin's house, not his.

"Lady Alris could probably find you a room in the palace," Terrin suggested.

"Or you could stay with Nerra," Mavi said. "She and Emner have that big house, and Emner the Younger and Kelder have both moved out now."

These were both reasonable suggestions on their face, but the idea of wading through palace bureaucracy at this hour, or walking all the way to his brother-in-law's mansion on Extravagance Street in the New Merchants' Quarter, was more than Hanner could cope with. The events of the last several days all seemed to be catching up with him at once, overwhelming and exhausting him.

"Or Warlock House," Terrin said. "Even if you aren't really a warlock anymore."

"They still have some of your things in storage there," Mavi added. "I'm sure they can find a bed for you and Rudhira." She did not look at the redhead.

"Beds," Rudhira corrected. "Not *a* bed; beds."

Mavi gave Rudhira only the briefest glance. "That's your business, not mine," she said.

Hanner grimaced; that comment told him that Mavi was serious about not wanting him back. He started to turn away, then stopped. "I'll want directions to our children's homes," he said. "When would be a good time to come by for that?"

Mavi glanced at Terrin. "Any time," she said.

"Any time during the day," Terrin corrected her.

Hanner nodded. "Thank you," he said. Then he did turn away.

They had walked the two long blocks to the left onto North Street before Rudhira said, "I'm sorry, Hanner."

"It's been seventeen years," he said.

They were crossing Moat Street when he said, "I should have waited until tomorrow. I should have just gone to Warlock House in the first place, and then gone to see her in the morning, when we weren't so tired."

"It might have been better," Rudhira agreed.

"I'm not *used* to being tired!" Hanner said angrily. "I never was when I was a warlock."

"I was only a warlock for a few days," Rudhira said. "I didn't have time to adjust."

At that, Hanner lowered his head, ashamed of himself. Yes, he had been flung seventeen years into the future, he had lost his wife, he had missed seeing his children grow up and his grandchildren's births, but he still had family, and probably friends, and if Mavi was right and he still had belongings stored at Warlock House, he wasn't destitute. Whatever happened now, he had had seventeen years as a powerful magician.

Rudhira had nothing. She had never had anything, except for a six-night or so when she was the most powerful warlock in the World. She had lost twice the time Hanner had, thirty-four years; most of the people she had known were probably dead.

They turned right onto Old Merchant Avenue and started up the hill toward High Street. The lamps were lit, but most of the shops were closed for the night, and the few pedestrians they saw were hurrying home.

Hanner hoped that they *could* find beds at Warlock House; he did not like the idea of looking for somewhere else. Lady Nerra and her husband lived not *that* far from here, really, but they might well be sound asleep by the time Hanner and Rudhira could get there. And while Lady Alris could undoubtedly find space for them somewhere in the palace eventually, getting past the guards to talk to her at this hour might be impossible.

If worse came to worst, there was always the Hundred-Foot Field, but Hanner *really* didn't like that idea.

Old Merchant Avenue did eventually connect to High Street, but there was a shorter route, taking West Lower Street diagonally over to Merchant Street and then turning up Coronet Street. That brought them to the iron-fenced dooryard on High Street, and a few more steps carried them around the corner, across a brick pavement that had not been there when last Hanner saw the place, and through the wrought-iron gate to the front door of Warlock House.

The gate was open, and the lanterns on either side of the front door were lit; that was a promising sign. Apparently Warlock House was still in use, even if there were no more warlocks. Hanner stepped up and knocked.

As he did, he glanced at the brass door-handle, and saw that it was scratched and gouged.

The last time he had been here, which seemed as if it was no more than a sixnight ago, he had used his magic to open the latch; that was the standard method. Since only warlocks and their guests were permitted inside, there had been no need for locks or keys that ordinary people could use.

But then warlockry had abruptly ceased to function. That must have been awkward for whoever was here at the time, but presumably someone had managed to get the door open somehow, damaging the handle in the process.

Hanner looked up at the lanterns on either side of the door, and saw that they held oil lamps. Sometimes those had been lit with magic — some bored warlock would keep them glowing — but now the light came from ordinary burning oil.

Then the door swung open, and Hanner found himself face to face with Zallin of the Mismatched Eyes.

The two men stared at each other for a moment as Hanner took in Zallin's face. When last they met Zallin had been more youth than man, with pimples on his brow and an embarrassingly sparse attempt at a beard, but now, in his late thirties, his features had matured, his skin had cleared up, and his beard had filled in. But there could be no question of his identity; his eyes still did not match. The left was brown, and the right a blue so pale it was almost silver.

"*Hai*!" Zallin said. "Do I know you?"

"Hello, Zallin," Hanner said. "It's been several years, but you don't recognize me?"

Zallin stared for a moment, then stepped back in surprise. "Chairman Hanner?"

"This is Rudhira of Camptown," Hanner said, gesturing toward his companion. "I don't believe you've met. Rudhira, this is Zallin of the Mismatched Eyes. I'm told he was my most recent successor as Chairman of the Council of Warlocks."

"You've come back?" Zallin asked. His tone mingled surprise and outrage.

Hanner frowned. "I would think that was obvious."

"Ithinia said you would, but I didn't really…well, not so *soon*."

"Zallin, may we come in?" Hanner asked wearily. "We need somewhere to sleep tonight."

Zallin hesitated, then sighed. "Of course," he said, opening the door wide. "Come on in. Which room would you like?"

"Which are available?" Hanner asked, stepping into the entrance hall.

"All but mine," Zallin said. "Everyone else left when their magic failed." He hesitated again, then added, "I have the master bedroom. I suppose it was yours, originally."

It had been Hanner's for seventeen years, but for sixteen of those he had shared it with Mavi. Right now, he thought he would do just as well in one of the others, where he would not be quite so strongly reminded of her absence.

Hanner looked around at the entry. One of his successors had done some redecorating, he saw; Uncle Faran's old-fashioned white-and-gold wallpaper had been replaced with an intricate pattern in black and gold on cream, and the gilt was gone from the white pilasters and the doors. The fine wood wainscoting was intact, though, and the dark wood of the stairs and balusters was freshly polished. The old red stair-carpet had been replaced with a red-and-gold one.

The parlor to the left was dark, but Hanner didn't care. He was tired and ready for bed.

"Come on," he told Rudhira, heading for the stairs.

"Hanner, we need to talk," Zallin protested.

"In the morning," Hanner said without stopping.

"But…"

"*In the morning*," Hanner repeated.

It took a conscious effort at the head of the stairs to turn and head for the nearest of the ten guest rooms, rather than marching straight ahead into the master's chamber, but Hanner managed it.

At the first door he paused. The door stood slightly ajar, and no light came from within. Lamps were burning in the entryway and stairwell, but not in the passage or chamber. He started to say something, then decided not to bother. He didn't have the energy to make any more arguments or demands; he just pushed the door open.

Whoever last vacated this chamber had not bothered to make the bed. Except for cooks, Warlock House had not had ordinary servants in decades; warlocks had generally enjoyed using their magic to attend to all their needs. That meant there were no housemaids to attend to such details. Other than the rumpled sheets, though, the room was reasonably tidy.

"Rudhira," Hanner said. "This one is yours."

Rudhira seemed somewhat startled, but then she nodded. "All right," she said.

"I'll take the next one," Hanner said.

"As you please, then," Rudhira said.

Zallin had followed them up the stairs, and he stood and watched as Rudhira stepped into her room and closed the door behind her. She had not bothered to strike a light; apparently she had no problem maneuvering in the dark.

Hanner was not quite so agile, and managed to bump his shin on a night-stand before falling gratefully into the great soft featherbed in the next room. He pulled off his battered and muddy boots, but did not bother to undress; the room was warmer than the chilly outside air, but still somewhat cool.

He called a good night to Zallin and Rudhira, though he doubted they could hear him. Then he rolled over and was instantly asleep.

Chapter Eighteen

Sterren had fallen asleep hours ago; Vond might have a warlock's supernatural endurance, but Sterren had carefully avoided ever acquiring any such talents. By the time they left the Southern Mountains behind, flying westward across the night-shrouded forests of Ansumor, he was having difficulty keeping his eyes open, and somewhere past a castle — Sterren had not been sure whether it was Yorbethon or Lumeth of the Forest — he had dozed off.

Now, though, he jerked awake at the sound of Vond's voice, and found himself in mid-air above sandy beaches. To his left, sand and scrubby plant-life extended as far as he could see, with a few houses and shacks scattered across the dunes; to his right open sea glittered in the morning sun that was shining on his back.

Directly ahead was the city wall of Ethshar of the Spices. The wall extended a hundred yards out into the sea, and ended in the Seacorner Lighthouse; a watchtower stood on the beach, and he could see the top of another watchtower in the harbor beyond. Behind that farthest tower was a tangle of masts and spars — that, Sterren realized, would be the ships berthed at the wharves of Seacorner and Newmarket. A little farther inland the city wall was broken by the mismatched towers of Eastgate. He and Vond were going to pass over the wall between the gate and the beach.

"I've been gone for fifteen years," Vond said. "You haven't. Where would you suggest we find lodging?"

"A good morning to you, too," Sterren said. "I haven't been back to Ethshar since you were Called, either."

"You must have heard some news, though."

"Well, yes, but I generally didn't concern myself with locating the best inns in Seacorner."

"We don't need to stay in Seacorner. I was thinking we might find a place in Warlock Street. I shared a shop there once." With that, they veered southward, away from the water.

"I'm sure your shop is long gone," Sterren said. "In fact, I suspect all of Warlock Street is in disarray right now."

"Oh — yes, I suppose it would be," Vond agreed, slowing.

"If you want to find more former warlocks, like the ones you left in Akalla, that would probably be the place to look."

Vond shook his head. "No," he said. "I want somewhere comfortable to stay, but someplace that will reflect my status as the only remaining warlock in the World."

"The most powerful, anyway," Sterren said, shaking his head to clear it. He was still only half awake. Then he realized what he had said, and almost bit his tongue; he did *not* want to remind Vond that he, too, was a warlock, albeit an incredibly feeble one.

"Yes, the most powerful warlock in the World," Vond said thoughtfully. "Which should make me Chairman of the Council, shouldn't it?"

"I don't know," Sterren said. "Is that how it worked?"

"I don't really know, either," Vond admitted. "But really, if I declare myself Chairman, who's going to argue with me? Where are any other warlocks who might claim the title?"

"I don't know," Sterren said. "Where *are* they?"

"Warlock House," Vond said. "At the corner of Coronet and High Street."

"What?"

"I mentioned it before. I think I may claim it as my new home. That's where the Chairman of the Council lives. It was Karannin of Zobaya when I left Ethshar, and before that it was Lord Hanner, who founded the Council."

"I never heard of them," Sterren admitted.

"You weren't supposed to. The Council was warlock business, not intended for outsiders. Oh, the other magicians knew about it, and the city magistrates, but they didn't exactly hang out a signboard."

"I knew there was a council," Sterren protested. "I just didn't know who the chairman was."

"You weren't really a warlock."

Sterren couldn't argue with that, and in any case, he was distracted by the sight of the city wall passing beneath their feet. There was a guardsman on the ramparts, watching them; the fellow did not look particularly alarmed.

Sterren wondered whether everyone in Ethshar knew that warlockry had, except for Vond and himself, vanished from the World. If so, then that soldier probably assumed they were wizards, levitating themselves with one of the various spells that would allow a person to fly.

Except from what Sterren knew of wizardry, which was admittedly not much, there were no spells that provided the speed and control of a warlock's flight — well, other than the spells that required a vehicle of some sort, such as a flying carpet. The levitation spells Sterren knew anything about were mostly slow and awkward, allowing the user to drift on the wind or walk on air, rather than soaring like a warlock.

But the soldier on the rampart might not know that, and there might be spells Sterren had never heard of. At any rate, the guard did nothing to stop Vond and Sterren from flying into the city, nor to warn anyone of their arrival.

Once the two of them were past the wall they were above a maze of streets, rooftops, and courtyards, and Sterren could make little sense of it. From the location of the lighthouse and the watchtowers he knew they were over Seacorner, but beyond that he was lost. He had grown up in the Old Merchants' Quarter, on the far side of the city, but more importantly, he had never looked at the streets from above before, and he hadn't seen Ethshar at all for more than fifteen years. He could see a clear area ahead that was too big, and too open to the streets, to be a courtyard, and knew it must therefore be a market square, but was it Newmarket or Hempfield? Or possibly even the Old Market on the edge of Fishertown? It was too far from the waterfront to be Fishertown Market itself.

There were people in the streets and courts, but that didn't tell him anything; the people of Hempfield and the people of Newmarket could not be distinguished by their appearance. The market did not look busy, but after all, it was still early; the merchants were still folding out awnings and setting up tables.

Whatever square that was, Sterren was sure it was north of High Street. Apparently Vond was certain enough of his navigation that he didn't need to follow High Street. The corner of High Street and Coronet — that would be in the New City, wouldn't it? Yes, thinking back, Sterren was sure Vond had said Warlock House was in the New City, back when he first mentioned it in the sky above Semma.

They passed the market and Sterren still couldn't identify it, but presumably Vond knew where he was going; after all, from his point of view he had only left the city a year or so ago, and he had probably done some flying here before.

Sunlight glinted from water, and Sterren realized that was a canal, ahead and to the right. There was a tangle of narrow streets and strange buildings that he realized must be the Old City almost directly ahead of them, and beyond that the first structure he actually recognized — the overlord's palace, its rich yellow marble walls gleaming in the morning sun.

That meant that the slope ahead and to the left, with its big stone and brick homes, and its gardens fading with the season from green to brown, was the New City. Warlock House was somewhere in there.

They soared over a corner of the Old City, with its misshapen spires and turrets, then crossed a broad avenue that Sterren guessed must be Arena Street. He looked down at the houses and gardens below, and noticed a pair of gargoyles on one gray stone mansion were watching them, their carved heads turning to follow the two warlocks as they flew past.

Someone had probably paid a lot of money to get those things animated, Sterren thought.

"It should be right..." Vond muttered. "Right about... Yes! Right about there." He pointed.

Sterren didn't bother to look; after all, they would be there in a moment. Sure enough, he hardly even had time to get his feet under him and brace himself before he hit the ground — or rather, the pavement — on what he assumed was High Street.

It hadn't been paved when he last saw it, Sterren was fairly sure, but now it was paved in good red brick, with a broad carriageway in the center, and raised walks on either side, with deep gutters separating the walks from the carriageway. Sterren stumbled as his feet hit the bricks, and he went down on one knee, scraping a hole in his black woolen breeches. His luggage thumped loudly to the street behind him.

The one consolation was that the street was virtually empty, so almost no one had seen his awkward landing. Vond had paid no attention, and the only other potential witnesses were people going about their business on Merchant Street at the end of the block, and a couple strolling High Street two blocks to the east. None of them seemed to take any particular notice of the two warlocks, any more than the guard on the wall had.

When he had gotten himself upright again Sterren turned to find Vond staring at a huge house on the south side of the street. A spiked iron fence and a small dooryard separated it from the street, but it was plainly visible — in fact, it dominated their view. It was immense, four stories high and very wide, with several broad, many-paned windows and a big white door set into an ornate facade of red brick and black stone.

"That's it," Vond said. "Warlock House."

"It's big," Sterren remarked.

"I think that's fitting. After all, I gave up my palace back in Semma to come here; did you think I'd settle for some ordinary little hovel?"

"I had no idea what to expect, your Majesty." He looked at the house — the mansion, really — and allowed himself a frown. This did not look like a place where the present owners would be happy to hand it over to Vond.

But if it belonged to the Council of Warlocks, and there were no other warlocks left...

The gate swung out of Vond's way, but he stopped on the doorstep and knocked, rather than simply walking in. Sterren hurried to catch up to him, leaving his baggage on the street.

They both stood and waited for a long moment, but no one answered. Sterren was uncomfortably aware that they were clearly visible to anyone on High Street or Merchant Street who cared to look. As the wait grew, Sterren remarked, "I'd expect a place like this to have a staff ready for guests at all times."

Vond shook his head. "They don't have any servants," he said. "I'm told they did once, but whenever I was here, everything was done by magic." He glanced up and down the street, then said, "I think we've waited long enough." He gestured, and the door unlocked itself and swung open.

Sterren hesitated, but Vond walked calmly in, and after a glance around at the nearly-deserted street, Sterren followed him.

The entrance hall was quite impressive, with twelve-foot ceilings, white pilasters, and polished wainscoting, but the lamps in the brass sconces were unlit, and there was an indefinable air of neglect. To the left was a grand parlor, to the right a few closed doors, and ahead a majestic staircase led to the upper floors.

And they could hear voices from somewhere upstairs. "We should have knocked louder," Sterren said.

Vond did not bother to reply, but began drifting up the stairs, his feet a few inches above the treads. Sterren hurried to follow, and by the time they were halfway up he started to make out what the voices were saying. They were arguing.

"...*isn't* any Council, Zallin! There aren't any more warlocks, so how can there be a council?"

"We need to stay organized," the other voice insisted. "If we ever hope to get our magic back, we'll need to work together."

"We aren't going to get our magic back," the first voice said, and Sterren could hear disdain in the speaker's every word. "Ithinia said…"

"Ithinia doesn't know everything!" the second voice interrupted. "She has no authority over us. We aren't wizards, we're warlocks!"

"We aren't *anything*, Zallin. We *used* to be warlocks. We aren't now."

"I won't accept that!"

"*Hai*!" Vond called.

The debaters suddenly fell silent, and a moment later a head appeared, leaning over a railing. "May I help you?" The voice was the one that had refused to accept his loss of magic, and Sterren noticed that the man's eyes were different colors. He had never seen that before, and wondered whether one of them might be glass, or whether a spell of some sort had gone wrong.

"I'm looking for the former chairman," Vond replied.

A second head appeared. "Which one?"

Vond smiled. "Whoever the current claimant is."

The two exchanged glances. "Why?" the second man asked.

"Because I believe that *I* am now Chairman of the Council of Warlocks, by default."

"By what right?" the first man demanded. "*I* was chosen to succeed Abdaran."

Vond lifted himself straight up from the stair until he was standing in mid-air, level with the other two, leaving Sterren behind.

"But *I*," he said, "am still a warlock. I do not believe either of you can make that claim."

"Emperor Vond?" the second man asked.

The first man was standing with his jaw hanging open in astonishment; at the other's words he snapped his mouth shut. "Vond?" he said.

"Yes," Vond said. "I am Vond, emperor of Semma, Ksinallion, and Ophkar, lord of the southern lands, and the last warlock in the World. That fellow below me is my chancellor, Sterren of Semma. Who are *you*?"

"My name is Hanner," the second man replied. "I saw you in Aldagmor, though I don't suppose you noticed me in that crowd."

"I'm Zallin, Chairman of the Council of Warlocks," the other said defiantly.

"I think not," Vond said, and Zallin was flung backward, to slam against a wall. Sterren winced at the sound of the impact, and hurried up the stairs.

"That wasn't necessary," Hanner said.

"I was making a point," Vond replied calmly. "A warlock could have resisted."

"You know perfectly well that there are no more warlocks except yourself," Hanner said.

Sterren admired the man's courage — he did not seem the least bit intimidated by Zallin's experience — and wondered how he could be so certain that Vond was the only one of his kind. What did he know about Vond?

"You're sure of that?" Vond asked. He jerked a thumb at Zallin. "*He* apparently wasn't."

"Unless you've made more in the past few days, yes, I'm sure of it," Hanner replied. "I told you, I saw you in Aldagmor — you were the only one of the Called who still had any magic, and everyone I've spoken to since assures me that there are no others, that you're one of a kind."

Vond glanced at Sterren. "Some people," he said, "may be stating their own beliefs as facts. To tell the truth, I don't know whether there are still any other warlocks out there." He gestured to take in the entire World outside the house. "Not *every* warlock was Called, and there may be others with my abilities. But I think it's fairly safe to say I'm by far the most powerful, which is why I have chosen to declare myself Chairman of the Council of Warlocks."

Hanner cocked his head. "Your Majesty, you are already an emperor. Why would you want to be a mere chairman?"

"To amuse myself," Vond answered. "The Small Kingdoms are *boring*, and now that I no longer need to fear the Calling, I came back to Ethshar. My empire has fended for itself for the past fifteen years, and it can do so a little longer. But I'm not going to pretend to just be an ordinary citizen; we all know that I'm much more than that. I don't want to be bothered with running the city, so I have no interest in declaring myself overlord — let Azrad keep the title. But chairman — I think I can claim *that* title, and whatever respect goes with it. Not to mention this house."

"*I'm* the chairman!" Zallin protested. He was back on his feet again, but still looking slightly dazed.

"I'm afraid there's been a misunderstanding," Hanner said. "The Council of Warlocks does not own this house; *I* do. I inherited it from my uncle, Lord Faran, and allowed the council to use it."

Sterren knew he should be following the argument, ready to jump in if tempers started to fray dangerously, but he was distracted by the sudden realization that there was a fifth person in the house. A petite woman with a spectacular head of red hair was standing quietly in a corridor beyond Hanner and Zallin.

"Were you planning to evict the council?" Vond demanded.

Hanner hesitated. "I was not in any hurry to do so," he said.

"Good! Then as the only warlock left, I believe I constitute the entire Council of Warlocks, and I hereby nominate myself as chairman. Any objections?"

"The council is supposed to consist of the twenty most powerful warlocks in the city," Zallin said. "*Twenty*, not one."

The emperor gave him a disdainful glance. "Alas, there *are* no other true warlocks in the city," Vond said. "I am the only one qualified for the council."

"Fine, you're the chairman," Hanner said, turning up a palm. "For whatever that's worth."

"I believe it means I will be living here for the next few sixnights," Vond replied cheerfully. "As your tenant."

"Hanner, *I* am —" Zallin began.

"Oh, shut up," Hanner said. "Do you really want to argue with the warlock who is said to have once bent the edge of the World?" He turned back to Vond. "Welcome to Warlock House, Chairman Vond. Shall I show you to your room? Zallin has been using it, but I'm sure he can have his things out by tonight."

"But I —" Zallin said.

"You'll take the adjoining room, I suppose, so you won't need to carry your belongings more than a few feet," Hanner said, cutting him off. "Rudhira was using it, but she can find another."

"I..." Zallin looked from Hanner to Vond, who was still hanging in the air, his robe swirling gently despite the total lack of any wind in the house. Zallin's shoulders sagged. "I'll move my things at once, your Majesty."

"Thank you," Vond said, with a gracious nod of his head. "Lead the way!"

Sterren started to follow, then remembered his luggage, still sitting on the street out front. "I'll be right up!" he said, as he turned to hurry back out and retrieve it.

Chapter Nineteen

An hour or so after Vond's arrival, Hanner was sitting in the dining room when Vond's chancellor peered in from the hallway. "May I join you?" he said.

"Of course," Hanner said.

The other man entered the room cautiously, looking around at the furnishings and at the big windows looking out on High Street. "This is a nice place," he said.

"My uncle always wanted the best," Hanner replied. He looked the other over.

He was not a big man at all — he was a little below average height, with a slender build. His hair had not been combed recently, but he wore it fairly short, and his beard was neatly trimmed. Hanner guessed him to be in his late thirties. He was wearing a nicely-tailored black silk tunic — expensive, but not ostentatious.

"Your name was Sterren?" Hanner asked.

"That's right. Sterren of Ethshar, originally, but no one's called me that for a long time."

"I noticed that you spoke Ethsharitic like a native."

Sterren nodded. "Grew up in the Old Merchants' Quarter. Then my grandmother's family tracked me down and hauled me off to Semma, and I've been stuck there ever since."

"Vond called you his chancellor?"

Sterren turned up an empty palm. "He can call me anything he wants; I'm not inclined to argue with someone who can kill me with a thought."

Hanner smiled bitterly. "I can understand that. How did you wind up as his chancellor?"

"That's a long story."

"I'm not in any hurry."

Sterren sighed. "Well, here's the short version. My grandmother's brother was the warlord of Semma. He never had any children, so far as anyone knows, so when he died, I was next in line, and they didn't care that I was just a kid earning my living playing dice in taverns. The king of Semma sent a party to drag me back to Semma because he needed his warlord right away; he'd managed to anger the two neighboring kingdoms, Ophkar and Ksinallion, to the point of war." He grimaced. "I didn't know anything about fighting wars, so I did what any Ethsharite would do: I hired magicians to fight it for me. One of them was a warlock who somehow latched onto a source of power besides the one in Aldagmor, then declared himself emperor and started conquering everything in sight. He kept me around more as a translator than anything else, and to have a fellow Ethsharite handy when he got homesick. He gave me a fancy title and left me in charge of all the stuff he didn't want to deal with, and then when he got Called —"

"He *did* get Called?" Hanner interrupted.

"Oh, of course. Yes, he had another source for his magic, but he was drawing on *both* of them without realizing it, so yes, he got Called. By then the empire was established well enough that nobody really wanted to break it back up into separate kingdoms, so the Imperial Council I'd organized kept running it, but they needed a figurehead, so they named me as regent. I've been stuck there ever since — until Vond came back, demoted me back to chancellor, named someone else as regent, and dragged me along to Ethshar."

"It wasn't your idea?"

"Well…" Sterren hesitated. "It wasn't my idea, but I certainly won't say I objected. I didn't mind coming back to Ethshar and getting a look at it."

Hanner nodded. "Where's the emperor now?" he asked.

"He's gone out to reacquaint himself with the city. After all, it's been fifteen years since he saw it. I imagine there have been some changes."

Hanner remembered the walk from Eastgate Market. "I'd say so, yes. But it's still Ethshar."

"I'm sure it is; *I* never flew off to Aldagmor to spend a decade and a half stuck in a protective spell, so if anything *really* drastic had happened I think I'd have heard about it. I did hear about Tabaea, for example."

"Who?"

"Tabaea the Thief? The woman who got hold of a magic dagger and declared herself Empress of Ethshar?"

"*I* never heard of her," Hanner said. "When was that?"

"Oh, almost ten years ago now. Harvest of 5227, I think."

"I was Called in 5219."

"Oh. Well, she did, and the Wizards' Guild had a hard time getting rid of her; they wound up destroying part of the overlord's palace in Ethshar of the Sands in the process."

Hanner shifted in his chair. "I hope they won't need to do anything like that with Vond."

"So do I. He won't say so, but I think one reason he came to Ethshar was because the Guild proclaimed that no warlocks would be permitted in the Vondish Empire, or several neighboring kingdoms."

Hanner frowned. That didn't sound like Vond, from what he had seen and heard of the man. "He accepted that, and went into exile?"

"Not exactly," Sterren answered. "He says that now the Calling is gone, he's free to come home to Ethshar, so here we are. He doesn't admit it had anything to do with the Guild."

"Well, maybe it didn't; maybe it *was* staying in the empire that was his exile, and now he can come home."

"That's what he claims. It might be true."

Hanner considered that quietly for a moment, then asked, "So he's gone out for a walk?"

Sterren smiled wryly. "He doesn't *walk* much, but yes, he's gone out. And that friend of yours — Zallin, was it?"

"Zallin isn't exactly a friend," Hanner said.

"Well, he's gone along as Vond's guide. *He* was never Called, and he's always lived in Ethshar, so he's up to date on the city's status."

Hanner felt uneasy at that. "He's gone with Vond?"

"That's right. I think he's hoping to learn the secret of Vond's magic — why he's still a warlock when no one else is."

A shiver ran down Hanner's spine. "*Is* there a secret?"

Sterren cocked his head. "What if there is? Would you want to know it?"

"*Me*? Blood and death, no! I never asked to be a warlock; I got caught on the Night of Madness. I may be out of a job, but I have family and friends, so I'll be all right. But Zallin would very much like to know Vond's secret."

"He would?"

"Oh, very much so."

"And you wouldn't?"

Hanner hesitated only very briefly before replying, "No."

"There's no Calling to worry about any more, you know. It would be safe."

"Until I angered the Wizards' Guild, or the overlord, or until someone decided that warlocks were too dangerous to allow." There were other, more personal reasons, as well, but he was not about to explain those to this stranger.

"You don't think warlocks would still be accepted?"

"I don't know," Hanner admitted. "But I don't care to make the experiment. And you never answered my question — *is* there a secret? Can Vond teach other people how to be warlocks?"

Sterren gazed thoughtfully at him. "Are you sure you want to know?"

Hanner closed his eyes for a moment, then opened them. "If the answer is no, he can't help anyone become a warlock, I want to know because it would make my life easier."

"It would? How?"

"Do you know who Ithinia of the Isle is?"

"The Guildmaster Ithinia, you mean?" Sterren asked. Hanner nodded. "Yes, I know her. She was the one who delivered the Guild's ultimatum banning warlocks from the empire."

"She's good at that sort of thing," Hanner said with a sigh. "She's asked me to do whatever I can to keep former warlocks from seeking out Emperor Vond in hopes of getting their magic back. It would be a great relief if I could tell her that Vond *can't* give them back their magic."

"Ah," Sterren said. "Ah. Yes. I see your situation. I wish I could help. Unfortunately, I can't, and your friend Zallin —"

"He's *not* my friend!"

"Fine. Your *compatriot* Zallin is out there right now trying to coax Vond into giving him back his magic. I don't *think* Vond will agree — he likes being the only warlock, without any possible rivals. But I can't say for certain he won't change his mind, and as I'm sure you know, the change that makes someone a warlock is irreversible, and that appears to hold true for both kinds."

"He can do it?"

"I'm afraid so."

"How do you know?"

Sterren seemed to hesitate, then said, "Before he was Called, he talked about inviting warlocks to Semma, and teaching them to use the second source, the way he does. He seemed absolutely certain he could do it."

That was not at all what Hanner wanted to hear.

"But he hasn't actually *done* it?"

"He has," Sterren admitted. "Once. Fifteen years ago."

"So there's another warlock out there in the Small Kingdoms?"

"No, not any more. But there was."

"And he could do it again."

"He could, but honestly, Hanner, I don't think he will. Fifteen years ago he thought it was a way of saving his fellow warlocks from the Calling; now he knows that wouldn't work, and the Calling is gone anyway. He brought a bunch of warlocks with him from Aldagmor, and he didn't teach any of them when he had the chance. I think he's decided he doesn't need any competition."

"I hope you're right," Hanner said.

Sterren looked around to make sure no one else was listening, then leaned forward and asked, "Why?"

"What?"

"Why don't you want Vond to make more warlocks? I mean, warlocks aren't monsters. *You* were a warlock. What's the problem?"

Hanner frowned. "Well, in the short term, Ithinia doesn't want any more warlocks, and she's...*requested* me to do what I can to prevent them."

"Why is it any of her business?"

"Because she's the most powerful magician in the city. Or at least, she was until you and Vond showed up. I assume she doesn't want the competition."

"But why does she get to decide?"

Hanner sighed. "You weren't around on the Night of Madness, were you?"

"No. At least, I wasn't paying attention; I was a suckling babe. Why?"

"When warlocks first appeared, no one knew what was happening. A lot of people, including the old overlord, thought we were monsters, that warlocks were responsible for stealing everyone who had vanished. They thought we were possessed by demons, or part of some left-over Northern revenge magic. The general consensus was that we should all be killed, or at least exiled, just to be on the safe side. Several warlocks *were* killed — some of them by other warlocks; Rudhira took down a few other warlocks who were running wild, and killed at least one of them."

"Rudhira? That little redhead who was here earlier?"

"Yes, that Rudhira. Immediately after the Night of Madness, she was the most powerful warlock in Ethshar of the Spices."

Sterren cocked his head thoughtfully. "Where is she, anyway?"

"She borrowed some money from Zallin and went to the market; the pantry here is almost empty."

"She's not a warlock now?"

"Not unless Vond did something to her this morning."

"All right. Go on, then; you were explaining why you care what Ithinia wants."

"Well, back then I was an assistant to Lord Faran, the overlord's chief advisor, and my specialty was magic. I was in charge of keeping Lord Faran up to date on everything that was happening among the city's magicians. On the Night of Madness I went out collecting warlocks, trying to find out what was going on. I didn't know I was one myself right at first; I wasn't very powerful at all. I was a lord, though, so I could invoke the overlord's authority, and I wound up leading a band of warlocks that eventually became the Council of Warlocks, with me as the chairman. We tried to negotiate an agreement with the overlord, but old Azrad was in a panic and wanted nothing to do with us — until Ithinia and the Wizards' Guild came to our aid."

"They came to your aid?"

Hanner nodded. "They did. They had decided it would be better all around if we could negotiate a peace; they didn't want a horde of angry warlocks fighting the overlord's men and flattening half the city." He pointed at the front window. "They showed up in High Street, right out there, between us and the city guard, and delivered an ultimatum acknowledging warlocks as magicians and the council as our governing body."

"I've seen the Guild delivering an ultimatum," Sterren said. "They aren't subtle about it."

"No, they aren't. So the overlord backed down, and warlocks were recognized as respectable magicians, and everything was the way it was when you were growing up, with warlocks living peacefully and earning an honest living with their magic."

"And you believe Ithinia was responsible for that, so you think you owe her a debt?"

"That's part of it, yes. But I'd talked her into helping us, and part of my argument was that the Calling meant warlocks could never be that big a threat. That was right there at the heart of our understanding, right from the first — warlocks were acceptable because the Calling limited us."

"But now the Calling is gone."

"Exactly. Which means that the terms of our agreement have changed. Under our agreement, the Council would punish any warlock who got out of hand. The Guild accepted that, and agreed not to interfere, because Ithinia trusted *me*, personally. She accepted my word that I would keep order among warlocks. And now she's still holding me to that, even though I don't have any magic anymore. Which means the only way I can keep warlocks in line is by making sure there *aren't* any."

"But there's already Vond," Sterren said, eyeing Hanner closely.

"Yes, there's Vond," Hanner acknowledged, "and the Guild agrees that he's not my problem, but making sure there aren't any others — that *is* my problem."

"Because you gave your word thirty years ago?"

"Yes."

"That's very respectable of you."

"I gave my word," Hanner said.

"Thirty years ago, under fundamentally different circumstances."

"I gave my *word*," Hanner repeated.

"Right." Sterren's expression clearly said that he didn't understand this, but wasn't going to argue any further. "You said that was the short term reason?"

"Well, yes. The long-term reason is that Ithinia is right — warlocks who don't have to worry about being Called are really dangerous. I mean, look at your friend Vond — when he thought he was free of the Calling, he built an *empire*, practically overnight. Oh, most warlocks would be peaceful enough, but if just *one* warlock turns out to be a murderous lunatic, think how much damage he could do! And if there were two who got into a fight, it could be catastrophic."

"But if there are a hundred warlocks, and ninety-eight of them are ordinary peace-loving folks, can't they keep the troublemakers in line?"

"I don't know," Hanner replied. "Can they? Warlocks get more powerful every time they use their magic; it wouldn't be hard for a troublemaker to become so strong no one else can match him."

"So you and Ithinia want to make sure that warlockry is gone forever?"

"Except for Vond, yes."

"Except for Vond? Why except for him?"

"Well, he's already *here*, isn't he? We can't undo that."

Sterren glanced at the door, then leaned forward and said quietly, "We can't undo it, but he can be killed. I had assumed the Guild intended to do exactly that."

Hanner hesitated.

"They probably do," he admitted.

Chapter Twenty

Ithinia watched as the air shimmered and then tore open, replacing a section of the plaza in front of the overlord's palace with a patch of mud. She looked through it at the bedraggled crowd beyond. There was an odd feeling of pressure, and a peculiar smell, reminiscent of the ocean before a storm. The wizard's ears ached, though there had been no loud sounds to cause any such discomfort.

You have until sunset tonight, the god's soundless voice announced. *When the light of day departs, the gate will close forever.*

"Thank you," Ithinia said, though she was deliberately vague about whether she was addressing the god Asham the Gate-Keeper, or the four theurgists who had summoned him. She could not see the god, and as she spoke she was less able to feel his presence, as well; he had done what had been asked of him, and now seemed to be fading away, back to wherever the gods went when they weren't in the World. As that sensation of pressure vanished, Ithinia raised a hand and waved.

On the other side of the gate Molvarn waved back, and began calling orders. Oddly, sound did not seem to travel through the opening; Ithinia could not hear a word of what Molvarn said, nor anything else from beyond the aperture.

On her own side, lines of guardsmen in red and yellow were holding back crowds who were watching, fascinated. It wasn't often that magic this showy was performed openly in the streets, and not saved for the Arena or paying customers.

Then the first of the refugee warlocks stepped through, and the air seemed to ripple as he emerged into Ethshar of the Spices. He was a man in late middle age, wearing a black silk tunic belted with black leather; his clothes were much the worse for wear, and his hair desperately needed to be washed and combed. He gave every impression of being exhausted, but when he looked around at the plaza, at the overlord's palace and the familiar houses that lined the other three sides of the square, he broke into a broad grin. The crowd began cheering.

The former warlock turned and gave a cheerful wave to the people beyond the gate, then stepped aside, clearing the way for the next.

That next was an old woman, also dressed in black, as were most of the Called. She was closely followed by two more men, then another woman, and after that it was no longer individuals so much as a steady stream of humanity pouring through the divinely-provided portal. The crowd's enthusiastic applause turned into more specific shouts as people began to recognize lost friends or family members. "Kelder! Over here!"

"Aunt Irith! It's me, Intirin!"

"Oh, gods, it's Shennar! Shen, I thought I'd never see you again!"

"Master Kardig! Master! I'm here!"

"Kelder! No, I mean the other Kelder, Kelder of Hawker Street!"

Ithinia watched for a few minutes, but as the plaza began to fill up she called to one of the soldiers, "Keep them moving! We need to get everyone through before sundown!"

The guardsman nodded, and conferred with his companions; half a dozen men in red kilts and yellow tunics stepped forward and began shouting. "Come on, move it along! Make room for the poor bastards, will you? Keep walking, there's plenty of space up Central Avenue or along Merchant Street. Let them through!" They didn't hesitate to grab shoulders and turn people in the right direction, then give them a shove to help them along.

And that, Ithinia thought, was that. Asham had done what was asked, and then gone away. That before-the-storm smell still lingered, and probably would as long as the gate was open, but the god himself had definitely departed.

With this final portal functioning, and the other spells and operations already in place, fifteen thousand former warlocks were being efficiently distributed to the three Ethshars, to Sardiron of the Waters, and to vacant land suitable for farming in the northeastern corner of the Hegemony — and *not* to anywhere near Lumeth of the Towers. They wouldn't all find places for themselves right away, but the ones who had homes to return to could do so, and the rest would be so scattered they would be no real threat to peace and order.

That was all the Wizards' Guild really cared about, of course — keeping peace and order. Helping out a bunch of people was a pleasant side-effect, and any gratitude they might feel toward wizards would be welcome, but the main thing was to not leave an army of desperate people sitting out there in the cold and mud, ready to cause trouble.

Removing their potential leaders probably hadn't been necessary, but Ithinia was just as glad to have people like Vond and Hanner and Rudhira away from the main group.

Rudhira probably wasn't any threat without her magic, in any case, but Ithinia still remembered the little redhead pulling an entire mountain of water up toward the sky to test her ability. Anyone who had ever tasted that sort of power wanted watching. Most warlocks didn't reach that level before being Called.

Hanner was the natural leader of the group, but even after seventeen years as chairman he didn't seem to realize it. He had always taken his position to be a fluke, never acknowledging how much like his uncle Faran he was. Lord Faran had been the effective ruler of the city for much of the reign of Azrad the Sedentary, and while Hanner hadn't inherited any of the ambition that had made that possible, and he certainly hadn't had Faran's looks or his way with women, he had the same knack for seeing what needed to be done and making sure it *was* done.

Fortunately, what he thought needed to be done usually suited the Guild's own needs nicely. Making him an ally, at least provisionally, was easy.

Vond, though — Vond might be a problem. He was still a warlock because he had learned to use the magic of the Lumeth Towers, as well as the magic radiated by the Warlock Stone, and he *did* have ambition. Unchecked power, ambition — and not, from what Ithinia knew of him, any excess of intelligence. That made him very dangerous indeed. But he had violated the Guild's ban on warlocks in the vicinity of Lumeth, so the Guild had a perfectly legitimate excuse for killing him, and it wouldn't even count as meddling in politics.

Ithinia still hadn't decided whether to kill him directly, or turn the job over to the cult of Demerchan. Either approach could be slanted to make the Guild look good. Demerchan never explained how they decided who to kill, so the Guild could dodge the responsibility entirely, perhaps even blame the assassination on the family of one of the kings Vond had deposed in assembling his empire.

If the Guild killed him directly, they could play the stern-but-fair role. It wasn't as if Vond was particularly loved by his people; he'd been gone for fifteen years, and hadn't yet had time to properly reestablish himself.

She had also decided that if she had to kill him herself, or choose the spell for someone else, she would use a transformation of some sort. She knew that warlocks could be petrified, or turned into animals, and that for some reason it was much, much easier to get such a spell past a warlock's defenses than any more direct sort of attack. Statues or beasts couldn't use warlockry, so once Vond was transformed, he could be killed easily. Also, if a transformation spell failed, it would be less obvious than if Vond survived being struck by a meteor or blasted with supernatural flame.

The trick was choosing exactly the right transformation to make the right impression on any witnesses. Some of the best transformations wouldn't be possible, because so far as Ithinia had been able to determine, nobody knew Vond's true name. It almost certainly wasn't Vond. No one Ithinia had asked admitted to having ever heard of a warlock named Vond prior to his appearance in Semma.

Of course, she might not have asked the right people.

Ordinarily she would have used a divination of some sort to learn his true name, but divinations didn't work on warlocks. That was profoundly annoying.

Eliminating spells that required a true name left about half a dozen possibilities. Haldane's Instantaneous Transformation wasn't practical, though, as that required physically touching the target with the skin of whatever animal he was to become. Llarimuir's Mass Transmogrification was intended for multiple targets, rather than a single individual, but it would work — if Ithinia could find anyone willing to attempt a twelfth-order spell. She didn't care to attempt it herself.

Fendel's Greater Transformation would probably work, but since that normally left the victim with human abilities, such as being able to speak, in addition to the abilities natural to whatever animal or plant he became, Ithinia wasn't *completely* convinced it would stop Vond from using warlockry.

The Greater Spell of Transmutation would do, as would either Bazil's Irreversible Petrifaction or Fendel's Superior Petrifaction. One of those was probably the best choice. The big drawback with all of them was that they required the victim be within sight of the wizard casting the spell. It didn't need to be a direct line of sight, though; a reflected image would do, or the image in a scrying glass or other visual divination. That would be easy to arrange with an ordinary man, but warlocks were naturally resistant to wizardry — it wasn't just finding Vond's true name that was difficult, but *any* sort of divination involving him. Getting a clear enough image in a scrying glass might be difficult.

She hoped that all the Called warlocks he had taken with him to Semma could be removed before any of *them* managed to adapt to the energy of the towers the way Vond had. She knew many had already regretted their decision to accompany him and fled toward the coast, and she was optimistic about getting the rest out of the area once Vond had been dealt with.

Well, now that the main body of the Called had been dissipated harmlessly, she could turn her full attention to the dear little Emperor. She turned away from the divinely-created gate and the steady stream of former warlocks.

"Guildmaster Ithinia?"

Startled, she looked around, and found Rothiel standing a few feet away, waving to be seen above the crowd. "Yes?" she said.

"I have news I think you'll want to hear."

Ithinia felt fairly certain that his news was actually something she needed to hear, but did not *want* to, but she did not bother to argue semantics. "This way," she said, beckoning.

She hadn't bothered to bring any privacy spells, but she reached in the pouch on her belt to see if there was anything that might help. She had the pearl and candle necessary for Fendel's Rune of Privacy, but that would hardly be practical out here in the street, where any casual passerby might disrupt the sphere of silence. No other quick and suitable spells came to mind, and she did not really want to invite Rothiel into her home, where protections were already in place. They would just need to speak cautiously.

The two wizards made their way out of the plaza and up Merchant Street, then onto West Avenue; by the time they reached the corner of West Avenue and Lower Street they were clear of the throngs of warlocks and spectators, who were expanding in other directions than this.

"What is it, Rothiel?" Ithinia demanded, once she thought they would probably not be overheard. She kept walking, in the direction of her own house.

"It's Vond," he said, walking beside her.

Ithinia had feared as much. "What's he done? Has he attacked Lumeth?"

Rothiel waved a hand in denial. "No, no. Nothing like that."

"He isn't invading somewhere? He's still in Semma?"

"Well — no. He's not."

Ithinia frowned. "Not Semma or Lumeth? Then where *is* he?"

"Here. In Ethshar."

"*What?*" She turned to glare at the other wizard.

"In Ethshar. On High Street. At Warlock House. He arrived early this morning."

"What's he doing *there*?"

Rothiel turned up an empty palm. "Right now, I believe he's out for a walk, accompanied by Zallin of the Mismatched Eyes."

"Oh, *blood*," Ithinia growled. Of all the people who might be associating with Vond, Zallin would have been very nearly her last choice. She just hoped Zallin couldn't nag Vond into tinkering with his brain so that he, too, could use the power of Lumeth's towers.

She wished she could be sure whether or not Vond *wanted* other warlocks around. She thought that he would prefer not to have any potential rivals, but she couldn't know that with any certainty.

"Well, at least we won't need to travel to the edge of the World to kill him," she muttered, as they neared her front door.

"If I may, Guildmaster — we may not want to kill him."

"What?" She stopped walking and turned to face her fellow wizard.

"You see, as I understand it," Rothiel explained, "as soon as he was informed of the Guild's edict forbidding warlocks in his empire, he left the empire and came here. He's obeying our ruling; it wouldn't look good to kill him."

"It wouldn't look good to have a warlock running amok in the streets of Ethshar, either."

"He isn't running amok, Guildmaster. He's behaving himself, at least so far. And there's something else."

"What?"

"The overlord's rules. He doesn't allow the killing foreign dignitaries within the city walls — not even by us."

"Foreign dignitaries?"

"I think an emperor qualifies as a foreign dignitary, yes."

"Oh, blood and *death*!" Ithinia had been thinking of Vond purely as a dangerous magician, and had forgotten that he was also an emperor.

At the sound of her outburst one of her gargoyles turned to look down at her; she could hear the grinding of stone on stone, but she ignored it as she considered the situation.

The very fact that Vond was both a warlock and an emperor violated the Guild's rule against allowing anyone to possess both personal magic and political power, and ordinarily that would have been enough to demand his abdication or death, but just how the Guild could enforce this in the present circumstances was unclear. He *was* a foreign official, and therefore under the overlord's protection as long as he was inside the city walls.

Wizards of Ithinia's level certainly had the power to do whatever they pleased, regardless of the overlord's laws or orders, but the Guild had insisted for centuries that its members must obey the local laws wherever practical. Throwing away that long history of cooperation with the triumvirate that ruled the Hegemony of the Three Ethshars was not something to be done lightly, not even to remove the last warlock from the World. Wizards were an accepted part of Ethsharitic society, and everyone liked it that way, but there were limits. Defying Lord Azrad on this might well be a catastrophically bad idea.

Well, maybe Vond wouldn't be staying. Maybe he was only visiting for a few days, and would then go back to the Small Kingdoms, where he could be assassinated with impunity.

"Perhaps it's for the best," Rothiel said. "If he behaves himself, having one last warlock around might even be useful."

"One last warlock, maybe," Ithinia grudgingly admitted. "The Great Vond, self-proclaimed emperor? I doubt that will end well. And that's without mentioning his power source; we don't know what his magic is doing to the towers."

"It probably isn't doing *anything*, Guildmaster."

"Let's hope you're right. While we're at it, let's hope Vond doesn't turn this city into a slaughterhouse."

"If he does, I'm sure the overlord will *ask* us to kill him."

"I'm sure that will be a great comfort to his victims' families."

"Ithinia, he didn't turn Semma into a slaughterhouse; why should he treat his home city any worse?"

"Because we're more crowded here, and less willing to be pushed around. He built his empire by replacing a bunch of kings; those people were *used* to taking orders."

"I don't see how our three overlords are so very different, Guildmaster."

"That's because you've never lived in the Small Kingdoms."

"If you will forgive me for saying so, neither have you. You're from Tintallion, aren't you? And you've been here in Ethshar for centuries."

"Yes, I'm from Tintallion," Ithinia agreed, "and Tintallion has kings, so I know what they're like. The overlords are different."

"If you say so."

"I do. I also say that I will sleep more easily when Vond is dead."

"*I* will sleep more easily if I am not involved in angering the overlord."

"Fine! Then you won't be involved. I'm not going to kill Vond while he's in the city unless the overlord gives permission, or unless I'm acting in self-defense." She smiled. "But that doesn't mean I won't encourage him to go elsewhere."

"I don't think —" Rothiel began.

Ithinia cut him off. "I want to talk to those theurgists again," she said. "And I want to hire some witches."

"I don't…"

"Wizardry doesn't work properly on warlocks, but *witchcraft* does."

"Guildmaster, I…"

"You don't want to be involved? I'm not going to kill him. But that's fine; you don't need to be involved. I'll handle this myself." She turned and strode to her front door, leaving Rothiel standing in the street looking baffled.

Chapter Twenty-One

Hanner was sitting alone in the dim parlor, trying to decide what he wanted to do with the rest of his life, when someone knocked on the big front door.

He had been sitting there for hours, unable to settle on a course of action. Not only had he not developed any long-range plans, he had not even managed to deal with immediate questions, such as whether or not to inform Ithinia of Vond's arrival, or whether to go look up his sisters or his children. He wanted to see Faran, and Arris, and Hala, but did they want to see him? He had abandoned them when he flew off to Aldagmor, and he didn't know whether they would understand that he had had no choice, or would blame him for giving in to the Call.

He knew he probably wouldn't even recognize them — they had been children when he left, and they were adults now, with children of their own. He might have already passed them on the street without knowing it. From his point of view he had seen them barely a sixnight before, but for them it had been seventeen years.

At least he was reasonably certain he would recognize his sisters, Nerra and Alris, but they, too, were seventeen years older. Seeing Mavi had been a shock, even before she chose her new husband over him, and he was not quite ready to see how his siblings had changed, but he knew he could not put it off for long without offending them.

And his children — did they know he was still alive?

He had been letting his mind run in circles, getting nowhere, for much of the afternoon.

He told himself that after his ordeal in Aldagmor, and the stress of the Calling before that, he deserved a little rest, that his family would understand, but he was not at all sure that what he was doing was really rest, rather than paralysis.

The knock broke the spell, at least for a moment. With a sigh, Hanner got to his feet and ambled to the door — there was no one else in the house to answer it. Vond and Zallin were still off on their tour. Rudhira had returned and joined him for lunch, but was now making a second trip to the markets, intent on stocking the kitchens before the weather turned foul enough to make shopping difficult. Sterren had departed immediately after lunch, saying he was going out to look for someone named Emmis of Shiphaven.

Whoever was out there was impatient, and knocked again before Hanner could get to the door. "I'm coming!" he shouted. He hastened his pace a little, and swung the door open, expecting to see Sterren or

Rudhira.on the steps; he doubted Vond or Zallin would bother to knock. If it was Rudhira she might need help with her purchases.

It wasn't Rudhira, nor Sterren. There were half a dozen people standing there, all of them bedraggled and exhausted, several of them shivering, and all but one in nightclothes of one sort or another. It was a safe assumption that all of them were former warlocks; it would seem, Hanner thought, that the wizards had finally started delivering some of the Called back to Ethshar of the Spices.

"Chairman Hanner?" one of them said.

Hanner looked at the speaker; her face was slightly familiar, but he couldn't place it. The rest he did not believe he had ever met. "Yes?" he said.

"May we come in?"

Hanner hesitated. He didn't know these people. He was not particularly in a mood to welcome strangers into his home. Ithinia had told him to be a comforting friend to displaced former warlocks, to encourage them to go on without magic, so he should invite them in and hear them out, but she had also told him to keep former warlocks away from Vond, and Vond was not somewhere a hundred miles away in the Small Kingdoms; he was staying *here*.

"We don't have anywhere else to go," a white-haired old man said, "and it's cold.".

That decided it. "Come in," Hanner said. "All of you, come in." He flung the door wide and stepped back to let them past.

A moment later the seven of them were seated in the parlor. "Now, tell me what's happened," Hanner said. "Who are you all?"

The middle-aged woman who had called him by name said, "I'm Edara of Silk Street, Chairman; we met shortly before I was Called, in 5211."

"I'm afraid I don't remember," Hanner admitted.

"I don't suppose there's any reason you should," she said. "I was just one more frightened warlock hoping to avoid the inevitable."

"Which turned out not to be as dreadful as we thought, didn't it?" Hanner pointed out. "What brings you here?"

Edara blinked, as if fighting back tears. "We didn't know where else to go!" she said. "We came through the gate, and it was wonderful to be back in Ethshar, but when I went to my parents' house on Silk Street it was gone — there was a completely different shop there! No one knew what happened to my parents; hardly anyone even *remembered* them."

"It's been twenty-five years," Hanner said gently.

"But they're just *gone*, everything's gone! The whole neighborhood is different."

"Wasn't there anywhere else you could go?"

She spread her hands. "I was an only child. I never married or had children — I didn't want to leave any orphans when I got Called. Once I realized my home was gone, I came here to ask for your help."

Hanner nodded. "And the rest of you?"

"The Night of Madness," the old man said. "At least, that's what they tell me. I went to bed one night, and had a nightmare, and the next thing I know I'm crawling out of a pit in Aldagmor, surrounded by strangers who tell me it's more than thirty years later. I never *heard* of warlocks or the Night of Madness or any of this until I woke up out there!"

Hanner nodded. "Your name is…?"

"Bardec of Cut Street. I'm a cloth merchant — or I was. When I went home just now there were strangers living in my house, and my warehouse had been split into four different shops, and no one knew who I was. I'd met Edara while we were waiting to come through the gate, and we walked up Merchant Street together, and when we found out…what we found out, she said we should come here for help."

"I see. And the rest of you? Much the same?"

The other four nodded. "I lived on the corner of Embroidery and Velvet," one nightgown-clad woman began.

She was interrupted by a knock on the door. "Excuse me," Hanner said.

This time there were only three unhappy strangers on the steps. Hanner ushered them in.

They had just gotten through the introductions when the next knock sounded. This time Hanner sent one of the others to answer it while he asked, "Several of you mentioned a gate; what gate? Didn't the wizards send you here with a tapestry?"

"No," several voices said.

"It wasn't the wizards who did it," Bardec said. "It was a god."

"Asham the Gate-Keeper," Edara said. "It took four theurgists to summon him."

"It was…it was…" began a woman who had introduced herself as Gita. She groped for words, unable to complete her thought.

"It was a little overwhelming," finished a woman who had given her name as Hinda. "I never saw or heard a god at all until this happened, and now I've heard two, Piskor and Asham."

"Asham was scarier," Gita said.

"He opened a gateway from that wilderness where the wizards found us right into the plaza in front of the overlord's palace," Bardec said. "We just walked through."

"Hundreds of us," Hinda said.

"They made us wait until most of the others had gone," Edara said. "Because we'd been away so long."

"It didn't seem long to *us*," Bardec said. "But it was."

"Thirty-four years," Hinda said.

"For most of us," Gita said, with a glance at Edara.

"It was only half that for me," Hanner said, "but the World does seem to have changed." He remembered Mavi's face. "It's definitely changed."

"We need help," Edara said. "We need…we need a place to stay, and someone to tell us what's happened, and —" She seemed at a loss for words.

"Everything," Gita finished for her. "We need everything."

"I can't give you *everything*," Hanner said, "but I can let you stay here until you can make new lives for yourselves. I'm not going to send you out to the Hundred-Foot Field, or let you be taken by slavers — but this isn't permanent, it's just until you can find your families, or make new places for yourselves. You understand that?"

"Of course, Chairman!" Edara said, relief plain in her voice. "Just until we find our footing."

"And there's a…*complication*," Hanner said. "An important one."

"What is it?" Bardec asked.

"You remember that warlock who called himself Vond, who somehow still had magic? He asked for volunteers, then flew off with them?"

"I remember," Gita said. "How did he *do* that? Why does *he* still have magic?"

"I don't know how he does it," Hanner said. "Apparently he has another source, instead of the one we all used when we were warlocks." He remembered who he was speaking to, and added, "At least, those of us who *were* warlocks, and weren't just snatched away on the Night of Madness."

"There's another source?" Edara glanced around at the others. "Why can't we *all* use it, then?"

"I don't know," Hanner said. "Apparently this one isn't calling for help, and it may be different in other ways, as well. Personally, I don't *want* to use it. I don't trust it."

"Then why did you bring it up?" Hinda asked.

"I didn't," Hanner said. "I brought up Vond."

"All right, why did you bring up Vond?" Bardec asked.

"Because he's living here, in this house. He's declared himself Chairman of the Council of Warlocks, on the grounds that he's the only real warlock left."

The others exchanged looks.

"Where is he?" Gita asked. "Upstairs?"

"No, he's gone out," Hanner replied. "But he could be back at any time, and I don't know how he'll like finding out I've invited you all to stay here."

"If he's chairman now, then how can you invite us at all?" Edara asked.

"Because it's my house," Hanner explained. "My uncle built it. The Council used it with my permission, but never owned it."

"Well, then, what business is it of this Vond's if you have other guests?" Bardec demanded.

"Vond is the last warlock in the World," Hanner said, "and one of the most powerful to ever live. He's also Emperor Vond, absolute ruler of eighteen or nineteen of the Small Kingdoms. He's accustomed to getting his way, regardless of details like law or justice. He has no *legal* say in whether or not I invite you to stay here, but he may not care about such niceties. If you anger him he may smash you against a wall, or stop your heart, or do something else equally unpleasant."

"So we won't anger him" Bardec said.

"We'll *try* not to," Edara said.

"I understand he does have a temper," Hanner said. "If you're willing to risk it, then by all means, stay here. If you think you'd rather face slavers or the Field than a foul-tempered warlock — well, that's a personal judgment."

"Do you think he could tell us how to use this second source?" Hinda asked.

Three or four other voices chimed in, joining in Hinda's inquiry.

"I don't know," Hanner said, raising his hands for quiet. "I really don't. And I'd think long and hard before asking him."

"That's all right for *you*," a man whose name Hanner hadn't gotten yet said. "You have this house, and probably some of your friends and family are still around. Some of us don't have *anything*; our whole world is gone. At least if we had magic again we could earn a living!"

Hanner could not really counter that effectively, but he said, "I'm just asking you not to be too hasty. We don't know how Vond's magic works. Let's give some other possibilities a try before we start harassing the emperor."

"*What* other possibilities?" Edara demanded. "My old life is *gone*!"

"I don't *know* what other possibilities," Hanner said. "But you've hardly *looked*. It's been what, less than a sixnight since we woke up in Aldagmor? Give it some time! Think about it! Some of you have skills from your old lives; maybe you've lost your homes and businesses, but you can start over. Maybe you *do* still have family, and just haven't found them yet. I have three children, and they're all still alive, but none of them live here anymore; they have their own places. Maybe your children, or nieces and nephews, or grandchildren, are still out there, and would be happy to see you if they knew how to find you."

Most of his guests did not look convinced, but some of them appeared to at least be considering his words.

"And I think," Hanner continued, "that other magicians might be willing to give some of you a hand. They've already gotten us all safely back to the city; they might be willing to do more."

"Why would they do that?" Gita asked. "Wizards don't generally do *anything* for free."

"As a favor to their fellow magicians," Hanner said. "The Wizards' Guild and the Council of Warlocks always cooperated with each other. Besides, I wasn't just thinking of wizards; theurgists might help out, as well. You all heard Piskor — the gods *want* us to help one another, and there might be dozens of theurgists who owe her, or some other god, a debt of service. Witches will often help out their neighbors without payment, too."

"Without payment in coin, maybe," Bardec said. "They usually find some way to make it worth their while."

"Well, what's wrong with that? Aren't you willing to earn your keep?"

"What can we *do*, though?" Hinda asked.

"I don't like counting on the generosity of witches," Bardec said.

"Or wizards," someone added.

"Or theurgists," someone else chimed in.

"But you want mine?" Hanner asked, a little annoyed.

"That's different," Edara said. "You're one of us."

"Maybe Vond will help us out. After all, he's a warlock, too."

"Didn't he take those others with him to the Small Kingdoms, and promise them things?"

"Did he really give them important positions?"

"Who knows?"

"But if he's here, he's not *in* the Small Kingdoms."

"If he's here, where are *they*?"

"Maybe they're all in the Small Kingdoms running his empire for him."

"Or maybe he killed them all."

"Or maybe he taught them all to use this second source."

"Where are they, Chairman? Did Vond bring them here with him?"

"No, he didn't," Hanner said. "I don't know what happened to them."

"So they might be warlocks again?"

"Or they might be dead."

"We need to know!"

"Well, we *don't* know," Hanner said loudly. "Vond hasn't said anything about them."

Several people began to speak, but Hanner raised his hands for silence.

"For now," Hanner said, before anyone could argue further, "you can stay here, but I am not responsible for anything that happens if you bother Emperor Vond. That includes anything that happens if you *do* learn to use the Second Source the way he does — just because he hasn't yet heard a new Calling doesn't mean there isn't one, or perhaps there's something different, something worse. For all I know, his new source isn't in the World at all, and could suck him into some other universe at any moment. I know *I'm* not in any hurry to test it out."

"He's been using it for years, hasn't he?" Gita asked.

Hanner shook his head. "Months," he said. "Only a few months. At least, if you don't count the fifteen years he spent in Aldagmor."

Some of the others exchanged thoughtful glances.

"There's no need to rush," someone said.

Hanner held his peace for a moment while the others gradually fell in line; then he said, "Now, let me show you where you can sleep," and beckoned them toward the stairs.

He had assigned rooms to perhaps half the new arrivals when the next group knocked at the door.

A rather bemused Rudhira was with them; she watched as Hanner welcomed them in and ran through more or less the same conversation, listening to them explain how they had nowhere else to go, then telling them that they could stay, but should be careful not to bother Vond. She looked past him, up the stairs at the guests leaning over the rail and listening.

Hanner noticed her gaze, and turned up an empty palm. He also saw that her arms were full of supplies she had brought from the markets. "Let me help Rudhira, then I'll show you to your rooms," he said to the others. Then he took the largest bundle from her arms and headed toward the kitchen.

"How many are there?" Rudhira asked when they were out of earshot.

"There were nine in the first two groups," Hanner said, as he set the bundle on a table and reached for a cabinet door. "How many were there who arrived the same time you did?"

"Five, I think."

"Fourteen in all, then." He frowned thoughtfully. "I don't want to use the upper floors, not until I have a chance to see what's up there, but we can fit fourteen on the second floor. They won't all get individual rooms, but if the furniture is still what it used to be, they can all have their own beds."

"Are you counting Sterren and Zallin?" Rudhira pulled two heads of cabbage from a bag and studied the cabinets, trying to decide where to put them.

"And the two of us, yes. Eighteen. Not counting Vond — I don't think anyone's going to share *his* room."

"Not unless she's pretty."

Hanner grimaced.

"It's not so bad," Rudhira said, pushing the cabbage into a tin-lined bin. "After all, you had thirty or forty people staying here when I was Called."

"Did we? I'd forgotten. That was seventeen years ago for me."

"It was only a few days ago for me."

Hanner had not really thought about that, and was not comfortable with the idea. "I think we can manage, then," he said, sliding a wheel of cheese onto a shelf. "Especially once I make sure the third floor is safe."

"Why wouldn't it be?"

Hanner didn't have a good answer for that. Uncle Faran had kept the top two floors closed off for his own exclusive use, and had stored his magical devices up there, but Hanner had long ago disposed of most of the arcane paraphernalia and moved the remainder to the back rooms on the fourth floor. The third floor, and most of the fourth, should be perfectly suitable for guests.

"No reason," he acknowledged. "We should be able to fit everyone easily."

"For now," Rudhira said. "But what if they keep coming? There were *thousands* who disappeared on the Night of Madness."

"I don't know," Hanner said. "We can't fit *that* many. They'll need to find refuge somewhere else."

"Where?"

That was an excellent question, and for a moment Hanner's mind was completely blank, but then a thought struck him. He blinked. "I…might have an idea," he said. "I'll need to see if I can find a wizard named Arvagan the Gray."

"Who?"

"You wouldn't know him," Hanner said. "I don't think he came to the city until after you were Called. I met him about ten years after you left."

Rudhira cocked her head to one side, sending a wave of red hair rippling across her shoulder. "So you think this Arvagan can do something other wizards can't? If you need a wizard, couldn't you just talk to Ithinia?"

"Well, she might know where he is, but no, I don't want a wizard, exactly. I want something I last saw in Arvagan's shop. I'm assuming he'll know where it is."

"If it still exists, whatever it is."

"If it still exists," Hanner agreed, as he stuffed a final bag of turnips into a bin. "Now, let's go get our guests settled in."

They were crossing back through the dining room when another knock sounded at the front door.

Chapter Twenty-Two

Sterren stepped into Warlock House and found half a dozen strangers sitting in the parlor in their nightclothes. They seemed to be deep in discussion, so he decided not to interrupt them, and instead turned right, into the grand dining room. It was empty, but he could hear noise from the kitchen, so he made his way there and found the little redhead — Rudhira, that was it — shelling peas.

"Hello," he said.

She nodded a silent acknowledgment as she popped open the next pod.

"Who are those people in the parlor?"

She looked up. "Warlocks," she said. "Or former warlocks, anyway."

"Why are they *here*?"

She cocked her head. "You're asking why warlocks would come to Warlock House?"

Sterren felt momentarily foolish. "Well — yes," he said.

She set down the bowl of peas and turned to face him. "Because they have nowhere else to go. Most of them were Called on the Night of Madness, and have no homes or families left after thirty-four years. Some were Called later, but still have no homes. So they came here."

"You let them all in?"

"Hanner did. It's his house. He told them they could stay until they find places."

"*Stay?*"

"He doesn't want them to have to go to the Hundred-Foot Field."

Sterren pursed his lips, then asked, "What does the Great Vond think of this?"

"He isn't back yet."

"I doubt he'll approve."

"You would know better than I."

"What do *you* think of it?"

She turned up a palm. "I am here because I had nowhere else to go, and Hanner took me in. How can I object when he offers others the same?"

"Well, you... Aren't you a friend of his, while they're strangers?"

"We knew each other for a few days, more than thirty years ago. I have no special claim on his affections."

Sterren's eyes narrowed. "I had thought there was rather more than that between you."

"No," she said flatly.

Sterren did not argue, but something about her attitude had him wondering whether perhaps she would have preferred there to be more.

"Where *is* Hanner?" he asked.

"He's out looking for a wizard he knew seventeen years ago, to find something he left in the wizard's shop."

"To find *what*, exactly?"

"He did not see fit to tell me that."

"Did you ask?"

She shook her head.

"Why not?"

She glared at him. "I told you," she said. "I am here on Lord Hanner's sufferance. I am not in a position to make any demands, for information or anything else."

Sterren noticed the glare, and the title. "He *brought* you here, didn't he? Did you beg him to save you, or did he volunteer?"

"That doesn't matter," she said. "I am still a guest."

There was clearly something going on here between Rudhira and Hanner that Sterren didn't entirely understand, but it wasn't any of his business — at least, not unless it upset Vond. Sterren did not pry further.

This did complicate his own plans, though. He had just spent an hour talking to Emmis of Shiphaven, the overlord's customs inspector responsible for overseeing all traffic between the Vondish Empire and Ethshar of the Spices. It was Emmis' specific charge to ensure that no forbidden magic was transported from Ethshar to the empire, and most particularly that no warlocks took passage for any of the empire's eight ports. Sterren had informed Emmis, among other things, that several former warlocks were on their way, and that any who had no family or other accommodations should be sent to Warlock House. Convincing Vond to accept them should not be unreasonably difficult, Sterren had thought, since Vond was the one who had taken them to the empire in the first place.

But that was before Sterren had discovered that Warlock House already *had* several guests he hadn't known about. "How many of them are there?" he asked. "I saw five or six in the parlor just now."

"Oh, it's more than that," Rudhira told him. "Twenty or thirty, I think, and I'd wager more are coming."

"Twenty or thirty? Is there *room* for so many?"

"When I lived here before, we managed about forty," she replied. "But that was crowded."

This was the first Sterren had heard that Rudhira had ever lived here before, but he ignored that for the moment. "There may be others on the way," he said. "The Great Vond brought some with him to the empire when he came back from Aldagmor, and I believe several of them are on their way here, to rejoin the emperor."

"It will be crowded," Rudhira said, reaching for the bowl of peas.

"If it's *too* crowded, Vond may decide to do something about it."

"I suppose he might." She sighed. "The thing Hanner's trying to retrieve from that wizard? I don't know what it is, but it's supposed to help accommodate some of these homeless warlocks somehow."

It was reassuring to hear that Hanner was aware of a potential problem and trying to address it, but Sterren would have been happier if he had some idea just what Hanner had in mind. "Those people in the parlor — they seemed pretty intent on something. Do you know what they're talking about?"

"Last I heard, they were making plans to find a tailor and get some clothes, if they could figure out a way to either pay him or arrange credit."

Sterren looked at Rudhira's own attire; she was wearing an embroidered white tunic and a good green skirt, but both had clearly seen better days. "What about you? Do you have any other clothes?"

"*None* of us do, Sterren," she said, picking up a pea-pod. "We were *Called*, and I have never heard of a Called warlock taking the time to pack." She snapped the pod open, and flicked the peas into the bowl. "I was living here when I was Called, and I've already looked — there's nothing of mine in the closets. I doubt anyone remembers what happened to my clothes after more than thirty years, and I doubt they'd be fit to wear in any case, and really, I wouldn't *want* to wear them."

There was *definitely* some history here he was missing, Sterren thought.

She tugged at her white silk tunic. "*This* isn't really mine," she said. "Hanner's uncle kept clothes here for his women, and I borrowed these. All those clothes are gone, too, or hidden away somewhere; except for Zallin's, the closets and wardrobes are empty. I used money from the Council's treasury to buy this food, so we would all have something to eat tonight, but I didn't take any for myself, for clothes or anything else. That's a matter for another day."

"I see," Sterren said. "You're sure you have no family to help you?"

"I had no family *before* the Night of Madness. I doubt one magically appeared in my thirty-year absence."

"Oh."

Some of these former warlocks probably *did* have family or friends who would help, and just hadn't found them yet, but Rudhira was surely not the only one who was genuinely alone in this new World. The magic Hanner had gone to recover might be something that would locate missing relatives, but that wouldn't take care of everyone.

Vond wasn't going to like this; Sterren was fairly certain of that. What he would *do* about it remained to be seen. He had declared himself Chairman of the Council of Warlocks, so he might feel responsible for helping these people — or he might just dump them all in the Hundred-Foot Field.

Or in the harbor.

"Is there any word from Vond or Zallin?" he asked.

Rudhira shook her head.

Sterren wasn't sure what to make of that. Vond had wanted to look at the city, and see what had or hadn't changed in his absence, but Sterren had expected him to get bored quickly and come back. That clearly hadn't happened. He must have found something interesting.

He could be out there somewhere in the midst of a magical duel with witches or wizards, or tearing apart his old neighborhood looking for mementos of his childhood, or plundering the shops on Extravagance Street.

In fact, he could be *anywhere* — not just anywhere in the city, but anywhere in the World. He might have decided that Zallin made a better aide than Sterren, and flown back to Semma. He might have headed for Tazmor intent on rebuilding the Northern Empire, or out to the edge of the World to take another look at the poisonous yellow mists that lay beyond. Vond could be whimsical, and had the power to do anything he pleased.

This, Sterren thought, might be a good time to disappear into the streets of Ethshar — except that he didn't know where his own family was. Emmis hadn't heard anything from them yet. Lar Samber's son had sent a very brief message, saying he was on his way and would meet with Emmis as soon as he reached the city, but that was the only word Emmis had received from the empire since Vond's return.

Still, Sterren could find himself a place of his own, rather than staying here with these former warlocks. He could keep in touch with Emmis until Shirrin and the children arrived. Vond didn't know anything about Emmis, so he couldn't use that connection to track Sterren down.

In fact, Sterren was beginning to wonder why he had come back here at all. Things were going to get ugly here, one way or another, he was sure. Vond might massacre all these former warlocks, or he might pick a fight with the Wizards' Guild, or with the city guard. If Vond didn't start any trouble, the Guild might, or some other magicians — and then there was the Cult of Demerchan. Sterren strongly suspected that Demerchan would try to assassinate the emperor; he had told Emmis as much, and instructed him to cooperate with Demerchan should the opportunity arise. It wasn't that Sterren especially wanted Vond dead, but he was certain that sooner or later, Vond was either going to kill people or get killed, and Sterren thought it would be better if Vond died without taking anyone else with him. The legends said that Demerchan hardly ever killed or injured anyone other than the intended targets.

"I think I might go out for another walk," he said.

Rudhira glanced at him, but did not bother to reply before returning to shelling peas. She was almost done.

"If his Majesty asks, I'm not sure when I'll be back."

"I doubt the emperor will deign to speak to me," Rudhira said. "If he does, I'll tell him that."

"Thank you," Sterren said. Then he turned and headed upstairs to get his baggage — or some of it, anyway; he couldn't carry the trunk by himself, but he could get the rest.

If anyone asked, he told himself, he could say he was going to take a room at an inn to make more space for warlocks. He hoped no one would ask.

At least none of these people would have magic to tell lies from truth; that was a talent found among witches, not warlocks — though wizards and theurgists also had slower, less direct methods of detecting falsehoods.

He remembered that Hanner had said Ithinia didn't want any more warlocks around, and wondered if she had talked to any witches about it. There were stories about witches being able to partially suppress warlock magic, and even muffle the Calling. In the fifteen years since Vond's departure Sterren had done quite a bit of quiet research into the nature of warlockry, more for his own sake than because he had ever expected Vond to return, and had heard several accounts of witches interfering with warlockry. Some warlocks had reportedly gone as far as hiring witches to block the Calling, but it had never worked for more than a few days; it was exhausting for the witch, and grew steadily harder over time, so that sooner or later the spell would slip and the warlock would be gone.

Sterren had never had to worry about the Calling; he simply wasn't that powerful a warlock. He was barely a warlock at all. He had toyed with the idea of hiring witches to see if they could suppress his own ability completely, perhaps reverse what Vond had done to him, but he had never followed through; there were too many risks.

He knew that no witch had ever managed to undo the transformation that made someone a warlock in the first place. Every so often an apprentice warlock would have second thoughts, especially if his master began having the nightmares that were the first real sign of the Call, and want to back out of becoming a warlock, but it couldn't be done — warlocks couldn't undo the change without killing the apprentice, witches couldn't reverse it, wizards' restorative spells couldn't touch it. Theurgists said the gods couldn't even *see* warlocks, so they couldn't help.

That was all moot now that there were no more warlocks — or it would be, if not for Vond and his second source.

But witches' limited ability to suppress warlockry might be useful somehow in dealing with Vond. Ithinia had probably thought of that.

It wasn't his problem, Sterren reminded himself. He had himself and his family to worry about, and other people could deal with warlocks and witches and empires for now. He slung one bundle on his left shoulder and carried the other in his right hand as he hurried down the stairs and out of Warlock House.

The temperature was dropping, and the sky was gray and threatening; Sterren thought it might rain, or even snow, in another hour or so. He turned west on High Street, heading back toward Emmis' office in Spicetown, but not before taking a quick glance around. He pretended not to notice the gargoyle perched on the house across the street, a gargoyle that had never been there before. He ignored the spriggan that clung to the iron fence and stared at him. He paid no attention to the shimmer in the air above Warlock House, and in fact, he wasn't sure just what sort of magic that might be — sorcery, perhaps?

And he genuinely didn't see the woman who was loitering by the gate. Where it was Sterren's idea to ignore the other signs of magical attention, it was the woman's decision not to be seen. She wasn't actually invisible; rather, she simply made sure that Sterren never quite looked at her. It wasn't a talent witches bragged about, but it was a useful one, and Teneria of Fishertown was good at it.

If Sterren *had* seen her, though, he would have been relieved to know that a witch was there, taking an interest. The more other people concerned themselves, the less responsible he felt he needed to be, and he really did not want the responsibility of dealing with Vond.

Chapter Twenty-Three

Hanner did not want to knock, but he forced himself to raise his fist and rap his knuckles on the door. He hated being back here on Mustard Street. He did not want to see Mavi again — at least, not so soon, and not under these circumstances, when he was still in the same clothes and had done so little to make a new place for himself. The heavy overcast and cold wind that soured his mood did not help.

He had no choice, though, if he wanted to provide a refuge for former warlocks. Arvagan had been very definite — the tapestry had been Hanner's property, and had therefore been delivered to his heirs when he was Called. It had been brought to Mavi at Warlock House, and Arvagan had no idea what happened to it after that. "You'll have to ask your wife," he said.

"Ex-wife," Hanner had answered, and the wizard had turned up an empty hand.

"Ex-wife, then," he said. "I gave it to her, and haven't seen it since."

It could have been worse, Hanner told himself as he waited for an answer to his knock. At least Arvagan had still been operating the same shop, and had remembered the tapestry in question. The tapestry hadn't been destroyed, so far as the wizard knew, nor sold.

And it wasn't raining yet.

The door opened, and Mavi was standing there, but Hanner barely had time to recognize her before he was almost knocked backward by someone else shrieking, "Hanner!" and throwing her arms around him. "You're alive!"

"Ah," he said. "Who?" He looked down at the plump, dark-haired woman embracing him, her face buried in his shoulder. She lifted her head to look up at him, and he exclaimed, "Nerra!" She was heavier than when he last saw her, and her face was showing signs of age, but it was unmistakably his sister.

"Hanner," she said, hugging him again. "We thought you were dead for so *long*, and then there were stories about warlockry not working, and the Called coming back, so I came to ask Mavi if she had seen you, and here you are!"

"Here I am," he agreed, hugging her back. "It's good to see you." He decided not to mention that from *his* point of view, he had seen her — a much *younger* her — scarcely a month ago.

"What's happened?" Nerra asked, raising her head and releasing her hold. "And…you haven't changed! You look so young!"

"I…" He hardly knew where to begin. He looked over his sister's head at Mavi.

"Hello, Hanner," she said. "I wrote them out for you." She reached over to a table by the door and held up a sheet of paper.

"What?"

"The children's addresses. Isn't that what you came back for?"

"Oh — actually, no," Hanner admitted.

"Then what? You didn't know Nerra was here, did you?"

"No, I didn't," Hanner said, looking back to his sister. "That was a pleasant surprise."

"Then what *did* you want?"

Mavi and Nerra were both staring at him in a most distracting manner — Mavi, who he would have expected to be affectionate if not for last night's events, looked downright hostile, while Nerra, who had never been very demonstrative of family feeling, looked almost adoring. Hanner could not get his thoughts sufficiently in order to answer.

"I see you didn't bring your whore with you," Mavi. "Did you think I might reconsider taking you back?"

"She's not my whore," Hanner protested. "She's a fellow Called warlock. And I'm here on behalf of other Called warlocks — I need to know what happened to the tapestry I commissioned."

Mavi's stare changed from hostile to puzzled. "The one that got you Called?" she asked.

He started to argue that the tapestry hadn't been responsible for his Calling, but caught himself before a single word escaped. It *had* gotten him Called, after a fashion, by letting him lower his guard, and besides, that didn't matter anymore. "Yes," he said. "That one."

"We put it in storage with your uncle's old things. *I* didn't want it, and I thought maybe the Council would find a use for it someday. I thought maybe they could figure out what went wrong, why it didn't work the way you expected."

Again he was tempted to argue, since the tapestry *had* worked more or less as he had expected, but he resisted. "In storage? Where?"

"In the house on High Street, of course. Up on the fourth floor."

So it had been right there in Warlock House all along? Or perhaps not — there was no telling what the Council might have done with it in the seventeen years since his Calling. "Where?" he asked again.

"I can show you," Nerra said, before Mavi could reply. "Alris and I helped sort through your belongings after you…after you left."

Startled, Hanner said, "You did? You can?"

"I'd be happy to. It will give us a chance to talk."

"I'd like that," Hanner said. "Thank you." He turned to Mavi. "I'm sorry to have troubled you."

He was caught completely off-guard, as completely as when he had emerged from the tapestry world into the attic of Warlock House and been hit by the renewed Calling, when Mavi burst into tears. He stood, silent and helpless, as she sobbed; he wanted to reach out for her, to comfort her, but she was no longer his wife; it wouldn't be right. He started to reach toward her anyway, before he could stop himself, but she pulled away. He felt a tightness in his own throat, and a stinging in his eyes; he blinked.

Nerra turned to Mavi, and gave Hanner a shove. "Wait outside," she said, stepping back into the house and closing the door.

Hanner waited, trying to regain his calm. He looked up and down Mustard Street, hoping he didn't appear too suspicious or out of place. No one seemed to pay him any particular attention; the street was not very busy, and the people he saw were intent on their own business, walking past without giving him much more than a casual glance.

Then the door opened again — not fully, just enough for Nerra to slip out, a piece of paper in her hand. "Here," she said, handing it to Hanner. "Those addresses."

"Thank you," he said, accepting the list. "I...Is Mavi..."

"Terrin's comforting her. The sooner you get away from here, the better — shall we go?"

He had to blink away tears again. "Yes," he said. He let Nerra take his elbow and turn him away from the door, pointing him toward North Street.

He wanted to turn back, to go back to Mavi, but he knew he shouldn't. He let Nerra guide him.

"Alris will want to see you, too, you know," Nerra said conversationally. "And your children, of course. It'll be very strange for them, seeing you again — not as bad as for Mavi, of course, but...strange."

"Yes," Hanner replied, not trusting himself to say more just yet.

"The whole city is...well, it's a surprise, having all you warlocks come back. No one expected it."

"I know," Hanner said. "Thousands of us."

"None of you can do magic any more, is that right?"

"*Almost* none," Hanner said, without really thinking about what he was saying. "The ones who were witches or theurgists before the Night of Madness got their old magic back. And..."

He stopped himself before mentioning Vond. He wasn't sure whether Ithinia, or Vond himself, wanted it generally known that the emperor was in the city.

"So you spent seventeen years trapped in some cave in Aldagmor?"

"Not a cave," Hanner said, still not paying much attention to the conversation. "A crater."

"I'm surprised most of you didn't go mad from boredom."

"What?" That distracted Hanner from thoughts of Mavi. "No, no. We were all trapped in a preservation spell — we weren't conscious. It was like being asleep, or in a trance. To me, that seventeen years passed in an instant; it feels as if I haven't been gone even seventeen *days*."

"A preservation spell? So that's why you look so young?"

"Exactly." He glanced at her, taking in the lines on her face, the sagging here and there. She had been thirty-five when he last saw her, and now she was...fifty-two? Was that right?

She was older than he was now — how very strange! He had gone from being the oldest of the three siblings to the youngest.

"Tell me all about it," she said. "About the Calling, and your release, and coming back to Ethshar, and all of it. I've heard stories, but they were all third- or fourth-hand; you can tell me what *really* happened."

Hanner took a moment to gather his thoughts, then said, "Well, I'd commissioned a Transporting Tapestry because I hoped to find a place warlocks could hide from the Call..."

By the time he had told her the entire story they were walking up the slope of Coronet Street, scarcely a block from the front door of Warlock House. Telling the tale had distracted him from the emotional turmoil of his encounter with Mavi.

"So the tapestry didn't make the Calling stronger?" Nerra asked. "We assumed it did. You'd been fighting it successfully for sixnights, and then suddenly you were gone — we thought the tapestry had backfired somehow."

"The tapestry worked just as it was supposed to," Hanner said. "It was the shock of coming back *out* that overpowered me."

She nodded. "All right," she said, "I suppose I understand. But then why do you want it now? After all, the Calling is gone, isn't it?"

"It's gone," he agreed.

"Then why do you need the tapestry?"

They were at the corner of High Street by this point, and Hanner waved at the crowd in front of Warlock House. There were a score of people there, some in nightclothes, some in warlock black, all of them dirty, all of them visibly exhausted.

Hanner also noticed one of Ithinia's gargoyles perched on the far side of High Street, watching everything, but he ignored it. "That's why," he said, pointing at the people in the street.

"I don't understand," Nerra said.

"They were warlocks," Hanner told her. "Or they would have been — most of them were Called on the Night of Madness, and never knew what they had become, never learned to use the magic. They were going about their lives, minding their own business, and one night they were drawn away to Aldagmor, and the next thing they knew it was thirty-four years later, and their homes and families and friends were gone. They have no place in the World as it is now. They need somewhere to go, a refuge, somewhere safe they can live, at least for a little while."

"And that's what the tapestry is," she said. "I see."

"Assuming it's still where you left it, and it still works, yes," Hanner said.

"Well, let's see, shall we?" Nerra strode forward, arms raised, calling, "Excuse me! Let me through!"

The little crowd parted, and she and Hanner marched up to the front door. Hanner reached for the handle.

It was locked.

He frowned. "The lock was broken," he said. He released the latch and knocked.

He waited a moment, then raised his hand to knock again just as the door swung open. Zallin looked out at him.

"Hanner! It's you!"

"Zallin! It's you!" Hanner replied. "Stop telling me who I am and let me in."

"Yes, of course," he said, opening the door wide and stepping aside. He threw a glance at the waiting crowd. "I thought it might be one of them."

Hanner looked back over his shoulder, then stopped on the sill. He turned around and called, "Be patient, friends! I hope to have good news for you all very soon!" Then he continued into the house, ushering Nerra in with him.

The instant they were inside Zallin swung the door shut, and clicked the latch into place. "For a moment I was afraid you were going to invite them all in," he said with a nervous smile.

"I might do that later," Hanner said. "There's something else I need to do first."

"But Hanner, where would you *put* them all? You've already filled half the beds. And Vond won't like it…" Zallin's voice trailed off as he noticed Hanner and Nerra both staring at him. It was not a friendly stare.

"Zallin of the Mismatched Eyes," Hanner said, "allow me to introduce my sister, Lady Nerra. Nerra, Zallin was the Chairman of the Council of Warlocks when the Calling ended."

"I'm honored, my lady," Zallin said with a bow.

Nerra didn't say anything, but nodded an acknowledgment.

"The lock was broken," Hanner said, pointing at the door.

"Vond fixed it," Zallin said. "He didn't want those people just walking in."

"Then he's back?"

"Oh, yes. We got home half an hour ago." Zallin shuddered. "He brought a girl with him from Camptown, and I think if she hadn't been here he might have...have... He wasn't happy with those guests of yours, Hanner, or with the people outside. Sterren isn't here, and Vond didn't like that, either. If he hadn't... He didn't want to scare the girl."

Hanner followed this disjointed account well enough to understand the situation. "He's upstairs with her now?"

"Yes."

Hanner nodded. "We'll try not to disturb him." He headed for the stairs, Nerra close behind.

"Wait, Hanner! Where are you going? You just said you weren't going to disturb him."

"We aren't." He turned to look at Zallin. "You seem nervous, Zallin. I take it the Great Vond did not see fit to teach you how to use the second source?"

"No, he didn't," Zallin said. "Not yet, anyway — he said he might someday, if he decides he can trust me."

Hanner did not believe for a moment that Vond would ever trust Zallin that much, but he saw no point in saying so. "What *did* he do?"

"He...he flew everywhere, all the time, but mostly just a few inches off the ground, so he could see everything, and if anyone got in his way he just flung them aside. He didn't even *look* at them. And in Camptown, half of the people he threw aside were guardsmen. If he saw anything he wanted in a shop, he just took it, and ignored anyone who asked for payment. I told them to send the bills here."

Hanner remembered the Night of Madness, when *dozens* of warlocks, not understanding what was happening, had behaved that way. That was why it was called the Night of Madness, rather than the Disappearance Night, or the Birth of Warlockry, or something else. Some of those warlocks had thought they were dreaming, others thought that they had gone mad, and others hadn't cared, they did it simply because they could.

Hanner knew that Vond did it because he could. "That girl he brought back with him," he asked. "Did he give her a choice?"

"Well...she didn't protest. She expects to get paid."

"See that she is," Hanner said.

Just as he said that, Rudhira appeared in the dining room doorway. "Hello, Hanner," she said.

"Hello, Rudhira. Are you all right?"

"I'm fine. The emperor hasn't noticed me."

"This is my sister, Lady Nerra. I don't think you've met."

Rudhira nodded. "Mavi's friend. No, we never met."

"Rudhira?" Nerra said. "The one who...the warlock?"

"The one who was Called just a few days after the Night of Madness," Hanner said. "Rudhira, we need to do something upstairs; I'll be back down in a few moments."

"Take your time," Rudhira said.

Hanner hesitated, staring at the little redhead; he wanted to say something to her, but he didn't know what it was. He wanted to apologize to her for Mavi calling her his whore, but she hadn't been there to hear it, and besides, up until the Night of Madness had changed everything, Rudhira *was* a whore. He groped for words, but then Nerra nudged him, and he started up the stairs again.

This time no one interrupted them, and he and Nerra were able to make their way past the second and third floors, emerging at last on the top floor, where Nerra took charge, leading the way to four rooms at the back of the house.

Hanner remembered these rooms well; they were where he had stored away the remains of his uncle's collection of magical artifacts more than thirty years ago. Now, though, while those mysterious knicknacks were still there, stuffed into drawers and cabinets and stacked on shelves, they were largely hidden by a variety of other things that had been jammed in after Hanner's departure.

Hanner recognized much of this added clutter — hardly surprising, since a significant portion of it was either his or his uncle's. Some of the rest he recognized as belonging to other warlocks he had known; apparently it had all been brought here when they, too, were Called.

This meant, Hanner realized, that he could finally get out of the filthy clothes he had been wearing ever since he went to Arvagan's shop that day. He had aired them out while he slept, but had not had anything else to wear — until now; he could see some of his clothes neatly folded and stacked.

Of course, they had been sitting here for seventeen years. Even if moths hadn't eaten them, they might still fall apart when he tried to put them on.

"I'm fairly sure we put the tapestry in here," Nerra said, interrupting his thoughts as she indicated the room in the southeast corner. "The workmen were very careful handling it, since it was obviously dangerous." She opened the door, raising a cloud of dust, and pointed. "There," she said.

Hanner's gaze followed her finger, and sure enough, there was a thick roll of fabric, shoved between the legs of a dusty table. He stepped forward, bending down for it.

Nerra grabbed his arm. "Wait a minute!" she said. "Won't it... If you touch it, won't...something happen?"

"Not while it's rolled up," Hanner said. "It has to be flat to work."

"You're sure?"

"Positive. It took a year to make this thing after I commissioned it, so I had plenty of time to learn about how it works." He tugged at the roll of fabric, and sneezed as his motion disturbed a decade's accumulation of dust and cobwebs. "Give me a hand?"

Together, the two of them hauled the tapestry out of its resting place and got it hoisted up onto Hanner's shoulder. They carried it out into the central hallway, and had it almost to the head of the stairs when a thought struck him.

"Wait a minute," he said, lowering his burden to the floor.

"What?" Nerra asked.

"I need to check something." He hurried to the stairs — but not to the broad steps going down; instead he opened the door that revealed the steep, narrow stair leading up to the attic, and quickly clambered up them.

"Hanner, what are you doing?" Nerra called after him.

At the head of the stairs he stopped and looked at the attic. It was dim, lit only by a single small window in the north gable and by what light leaked in beneath the unsealed eaves. It was a single room extending the entire length and most of the width of the house, directly under the sloping roof and exposed rafters; headroom ranged from nothing at all at the sides to about twelve feet at the center, though tie-beams ran from side to side just six feet above the bare plank floor.

It looked just as Hanner remembered it; the hole he had smashed in the roof had been repaired, and no one had used it for storage. It was still completely bare and empty.

He had chosen it as the target for his first tapestry, the one that now hung in that other-worldly refuge, exactly because it was empty and unused, and lit from the north, so that the daylight was more or less constant. He had considered using one of the rooms below, and had rejected the idea — it would be too easy for someone to carelessly move a piece of furniture, or leave a stray object, and render the tapestry inert.

He had tested that tapestry before turning it over to Arvagan and his apprentice; he hadn't wanted to be stranded in his refuge. He wished he could test it again, but he could see no way to do that; it was still in that other world.

The attic looked exactly the same to him, but he was relying on mere mortal eyesight, and his own fallible memory. If anything *had* changed, then any trip into the magical refuge might be a one-way journey, with no possibility of return.

But would that really be so terrible? The entire plan, once upon a time, had been for warlocks to live in that other world permanently to avoid the Call. He and Arvagan had designed the image in the tapestry to be as appealing and unthreatening as possible, to be a haven where warlocks could retire in peace and comfort. When he had tested it, a sixnight or seventeen years ago, he had been eager to get back to Ethshar to tell everyone that it had worked, and to be with Mavi and the children again — but Mavi was gone and the children were grown.

He backed down the steep attic stairs.

"Come on," he said to Nerra, as he stooped to retrieve the tapestry. "Let's hang this up somewhere and see if it still works."

Chapter Twenty-Four

The gathering in Ithinia's parlor was more crowded than she liked; if the weather had been warmer, she would have held the meeting in her garden, instead. On a chilly, overcast day like this one, though, that would not work. If the group had all been wizards there were several places they could have met, but they were not; in fact, much of the point of the meeting was to involve the others.

"All right," she said. "What news do we have?" She pointed to a wizard in a mouse-colored robe. "You — Arvagan the Gray, isn't it? Why are you here?"

"I thought you might want to know that the former warlock, Chairman Hanner, came by my shop this afternoon asking after the Transporting Tapestry I sold him," Arvagan replied. "You had asked about tapestries yourself, so I thought you'd be interested."

"That's the one you made him as a refuge where warlocks could avoid the Call?"

"That was the intention, yes, but when he tested it he was immediately Called."

"As I recall, we discussed using it to get some of the refugees back to the city, but we didn't want to route them through another universe."

"And we weren't sure the return tapestry would still work," Arvagan said.

"That's right. So Hanner wanted to know where it is?"

"Yes."

"You told him?"

"I don't *know* where it is, Guildmaster; that was another reason we didn't use it. I returned it to his family after he was Called."

"His family is still in Ethshar?"

"I have no reason to think otherwise."

"So he's trying to acquire the tapestry, to have access to his supposed refuge," Ithinia said thoughtfully.

"But when he tested it, he was Called," Arvagan said.

"But the Calling is gone," Ithinia replied. "That refuge — if Vond entered it, he would presumably lose contact with the towers."

"Until he came back out, yes. There *is* a return tapestry, remember."

"Still, it might prove useful." She nodded, then looked over the faces again, and focused on one she didn't recognize, a man of indeterminate age in a nondescript brown cloak who was sitting quietly in the back. "You," she said, pointing. "Who are you?"

"I am Kelder of Demerchan," he said.

A sudden silence fell over the room.

"Are you indeed?" Ithinia asked.

The man nodded.

"I do not believe I invited you to this gathering."

"You did not, Guildmaster, but we thought it advisable to have a representative here, all the same, to ensure that we would not be working at cross-purposes."

"I see. Will you tell us, then, what interest the Cult of Demerchan has in the current situation?"

"Within limits, yes. Certain persons have asked us to remove the Emperor Vond. We have not yet decided whether to accept this commission."

"By 'remove,' you mean 'assassinate'?"

"The precise means of removal were not specified."

Ithinia considered this. She knew annoyingly little about the Cult of Demerchan. They were an organization of magician-assassins, based somewhere in the Small Kingdoms, that had operated in secrecy for centuries. They made extensive use of tunnels and hidden passages, and used various kinds of magic — apparently including wizardry, though so far as she knew, none of them acknowledged the authority of the Wizards' Guild.

Ordinarily, for anyone outside the Guild to use wizardry the penalty would be immediate execution, but somehow Demerchan had never incurred such consequences. Whether this was an oversight, deliberate neglect, or something else, she did not know; it was not her responsibility. She was the senior Guildmaster of Ethshar of the Spices, and a member of the Guild's Inner Circle, but she was not one of the Hundred; there were levels above her, and the Guild had secrets she did not know. What happened in the Small Kingdoms was usually not her concern. She had intervened a dozen years ago when it appeared that the Empire of Vond might threaten the security of the towers in Lumeth of the Towers, and word had later reached her that her actions met with the approval of her superiors, but she had also been reminded that she was to meddle in the Small Kingdoms only in the most exceptional circumstances.

The existence and behavior of the Cult of Demerchan was therefore none of her business — or it hadn't been until this man showed up in her house.

"If you have not yet decided to accept the commission, then what purposes do you have that we might cross?" she demanded.

"We have our own interests. I am here in part to determine whether your interests align with ours. I am here in person, Guildmaster, and visible to you all, because we prefer not to antagonize the Guild, or the Sisterhood, or the Hierarchies, or the Initiates, unnecessarily; I am to speak up should it seem that a conflict is developing that might be avoided."

That was a reasonable answer, and a believable one. Ithinia had not missed the implication that Demerchan sometimes listened in to the Guild's private deliberations secretly, by means of their own magic, but she decided to ignore that for now — though she might want to reconsider some of her standard wards and protections when this was all done.

"You want to know whether your interests align with ours," she said. "I would say they do. The interests of every living thing in the World are involved."

"Oh?"

Ithinia looked over the crowd of magicians; some of them looked confused, while other faces were alight with anticipation, and still others appeared to be confident they understood the situation. Some of them probably did.

"We are not here because warlockry ended," she said. "The World managed without it for centuries, and will do so again. We are not here because fifteen thousand refugees have suddenly been dumped on our society; the Hegemony dealt with a far worse refugee problem at the end of the Great War, and emerged from it relatively unscathed. We are not even here because of the possible danger posed by a warlock unrestrained by any threat of the Calling, one who has already demonstrated that he is perfectly willing to kill innocent people who get in his way, though that is a matter worthy of our attention. No, we are here because the *source* of that warlock's power is essential to us all, and we do not want Vond, or anyone else, tampering with it."

"Could you be a little more specific, Guildmaster?" asked a white-robed theurgist whose name Ithinia had forgotten.

"You all know that warlocks drew their power from that thing in Aldagmor," Ithinia said. "Well, Vond found a way to draw power from the towers in Lumeth of the Towers, and we fear that this may in time weaken or damage the towers' magic."

"*What* magic?" the theurgist asked.

Somehow, Ithinia had assumed that every powerful magician would know some of the ancient secrets of the Wizards' Guild, but of course there was no reason for that to be the case, and clearly it wasn't. Unless, of course, the theurgist was just testing to see whether the wizardly version of the story matched whatever the priests believed.

"You are all aware, I trust, that the World does not extend indefinitely in every direction, but has edges?" She looked around the room, and saw no one indicating otherwise. "Do you know what lies beyond those edges?"

"No," said Kirris of Slave Street. Trust a witch to be blunt, Ithinia thought. Kirris made no secret of her dislike for wizards, and Ithinia was slightly surprised she had agreed to attend this meeting. Her friend Teneria had probably talked her into it.

"Isn't it all just *sky* beyond the edge?" the theurgist asked.

"No, it's not," Ithinia said. "Beyond the World's edge is a vast cloud of poisonous yellow mist; so far as we know, it goes on forever in every direction except up. No one has ever seen the bottom, or the far side, of the golden mist, though it's possible to fly above it. You can see it in the distance if you go near the edge; most sailors have seen it, and it's visible from much of Vond's empire, and from the western shores of Tintallion's Isle where I grew up. If you've seen it, you must undoubtedly have wondered what holds it back — why hasn't it swept over the World and poisoned us all?"

"Magic?" someone said; Ithinia didn't see who had spoken.

"Magic! Of course. To be exact, the largest sorcerous talismans known to exist — the three towers in Lumeth cast a protective spell over the entire World, holding back the poisons and keeping our air clean and sweet."

"Not the gods?" the theurgist asked.

Ithinia turned up a hand. "The legend passed down in our Guild says that the gods helped build the towers, but that it is the towers alone that now protect us. Our divinations confirm this. *That* is the power that this Vond is meddling with."

"Meddling *how*?" Kirris asked.

"We don't know," Ithinia said. "Warlockry blocks our spells. But we know that's where he's drawing his power from, and we are concerned that he might somehow damage or weaken the towers' magic."

"The warlocks didn't damage the thing in Aldagmor," Teneria of Fishertown said. "There were *thousands* of them drawing on it, and it wasn't affected at all."

"But the towers are different," Ithinia replied. "Ordinary warlocks can't use their power; there's something different about Vond."

"The gods can see him," volunteered old Corinal the Theurgist, from his place in the corner of the room.

"What?" Kirris said, turning.

"The gods can see him," Corinal repeated. "They never could see ordinary warlocks, you know, and until these last few days we could never get a coherent explanation out of them."

"Now you can?" Teneria asked.

"Well — not so very coherent as we might like, even now, but at least we have *an* explanation."

"What is it?" Arvagan asked. "It might be important."

Corinal looked at Ithinia, who nodded. "Well," he said, "the gods do not see the World or anything in it the same way we do. They don't recognize human beings by how we *look* — two arms, two legs, a head, and so on — but by how we *think*. They see our souls, not our physical bodies. They can't usually see demonologists as people because dealing with demons distorts a person's soul, and renders it not quite human enough for the gods to recognize."

"So warlocks don't have human souls?" Kirris asked.

"Oh, of course they do! But they also had something else. They were reflecting, or echoing, that thing in Aldagmor, and that was so *loud*, or so *bright*, or however you want to think of it, that it completely drowned out the warlocks' own souls. That thing wasn't from our reality at all, and the gods only concern themselves with our universe, not with others, so they paid no attention to it — it wasn't part of the World, so it wasn't *real*, as far as the gods could tell. It was like a shadow blocking their vision, or perhaps a roar deafening them, so they could not perceive warlocks or warlockry as anything but a sort of gap in reality. It was only when the Warlock Stone left, and all those human souls reappeared, that the gods understood what had happened clearly enough that they could explain it to us."

"But they can see Vond?" Kirris asked.

"Because the towers are part of our universe," Ithinia said.

"And because the towers aren't trying to communicate," Corinal said. "They aren't drowning out Vond's own thoughts with theirs — they don't *have* any."

"Which is why Vond doesn't need to worry about another Calling," Ithinia said.

For a moment the room was silent as everyone absorbed this explanation, but then Kirris asked, "Does Vond know that?"

"What?"

"Does Vond *know* he won't be Called again?" Kirris asked.

Ithinia blinked, then turned to Teneria. "Does he?" she asked.

Teneria considered the question carefully before replying. "He probably doesn't *know* it," she said. "He *assumes* it, because he senses the energy from the towers as a steady hum, rather than a whispering voice like the Warlock Stone. The Aldagmor source was asking for something, though none of us understood what it wanted, and that's why there was the Calling, and why warlockry was addictive, why warlocks wanted to use their magic even when they didn't need to. The towers aren't asking for anything; they're just doing what they were created to do, so Vond doesn't feel the same urges he did before. But he doesn't *know* anything. He just *assumes* that his new magic is completely safe and harmless."

"I'm not sure I see the significance," Rothiel said.

"It's simple," Kirris said. "If we can convince Vond that he's in danger of another Calling, one just as mysterious and potentially fatal as the one he's already experienced, then he'll limit his use of his magic — perhaps give it up completely."

Ithinia considered this suggestion, and admired its elegance. It might not work, but it did seem worth a try.

"How would we convince him?" demanded the theurgist whose name Ithinia couldn't remember. "I doubt he'll believe us if we simply *tell* him there's another Calling."

"Not until he hears it," Teneria said.

"He won't ever hear it!" the theurgist exclaimed.

Ithinia looked at Teneria, who said quietly, "We can *make* him hear it."

The theurgist turned to look at her. "What? How?"

"Witchcraft," Teneria said.

"I'd be interested in further explanation, my dear," Corinal said. "Just how would that work?"

Teneria looked at their hostess, who said, "Please do explain, Teneria."

Teneria nodded. "Ten years ago," she said, "I was in Aldagmor on an unrelated errand when I encountered a Sardironese warlock named Adar Dagon's son who had just been Called. He was struggling to resist, so without really thinking about it, I helped him."

"Helped him *how*?" the white-robed theurgist asked. "I didn't think anyone *could* help a Called warlock."

"No one else thought so, either," Teneria said. "I discovered, though, that the same sort of calming witches do all the time with frightened children interfered with the Call, and weakened it enough that Adar could resist it for a time. That gave us a little time, and I was able to practice blocking it, but eventually I fell asleep, and...well, I never saw Adar again. I *hope* he's made it safely home to the Passes now, after ten years' rest, but I don't know."

"Why didn't you do it again, though?" the theurgist asked.

"Oh, I did," Teneria said. "Several times, with several different warlocks, working with several other witches, including Kirris here. We kept it secret, though, because if word got out that there was a way for witches to prevent the Calling, or even just delay it — well, the most likely outcome was that witches would all find themselves enslaved by desperate warlocks, forced to devote every waking moment to fending off the

Call. Remember, warlocks were far, *far* more powerful than any witch; even a mere apprentice warlock could stop a witch's heart in an instant. Our magic is more subtle and more varied, but warlocks had more than enough raw power to smash through any defenses we might devise."

"But you saved a few?" Corinal asked. "Or were there further difficulties?"

"Oh, there were very definitely further difficulties," Teneria said. "First off, we had to work in shifts, so that we could sleep — an exhausted witch can't work magic. Further, the Call was so powerful that a witch could only protect one warlock at a time, so it took two or more witches to guard a single warlock. We conducted several trials, using various approaches, but we couldn't find any way to do better than that — two witches taking turns to protect one warlock. We couldn't allow the warlock to go even a few miles closer to Aldagmor, or the Call would strengthen enough that we couldn't fight it, so our movements were limited; one of us had to be near the warlock every instant. Witchcraft only works at close range, you know — it's not like wizards casting spells that take effect a hundred leagues away."

"But it worked?" Corinal asked.

"No, it didn't," Teneria said. "Because even though we were blocking the Call, it grew stronger and stronger, and harder and harder to block — a Called warlock is so receptive to the Call that he doesn't need to use any perceptible magic to become even *more* receptive. It's like a hole in a dike — a dike may hold back the sea indefinitely, but if a hole is made, then the water rushes through it and enlarges it until the entire dike washes away. We tried drawing on the warlocks' own power to strengthen our witchcraft, but then the warlock's susceptibility to the Calling increased even more quickly. We tried adding more witches, and that helped for a time, but...well, that was when we discovered the *real* problem with our efforts."

"And what was that?" Corinal asked.

"*We* started to hear the Call," Teneria said. "Our connection to the warlocks' minds became so strong that the Calling began to draw *us*, as well." She shuddered. "Fortunately, the moment the connection was broken, we could no longer hear it, any more than anyone else could. None of us were drawn all the way to Aldagmor — Called warlocks don't take other people with them, and a witch can't fly that far under her own power — but three or four of us had some very unpleasant experiences."

"So you couldn't save any warlocks?" Corinal asked.

"The longest we ever managed to block the Calling was about a month and a half, and that very nearly killed two witches."

"Why have we never heard about this before?" Arvagan demanded.

"Because it didn't work, and it wasn't any of your business," Teneria said. "We told Ithinia, but we kept it very quiet otherwise. We didn't want hundreds of desperate warlocks coming to us hoping to be saved."

"You all know we magicians are accustomed to keeping secrets from each other," Ithinia said. "Warlocks weren't very inclined to trust any of the rest of us, either; they remembered the Night of Madness and the days immediately after, when half the city wanted them all killed. It wasn't hard to make sure they didn't find out about this. After all, every warlock who was involved in the experiments was in Aldagmor."

Teneria nodded. "Exactly."

"So you know what the Calling felt like," the other theurgist — Samber, that was his name! — said to Teneria. It was not a question.

"Yes." Teneria shuddered again. "It's not something you forget. I still have nightmares sometimes, and I'm sure the others do, too." She glanced at Kirris, who nodded.

"So you can make *Vond* have those nightmares again, can't you?" Ithinia said.

"Yes," Teneria said.

Ithinia saw the witch's expression, and started to say something else, something sympathetic and encouraging, but Arvagan interrupted her. "But you'd need to be very close to do that, wouldn't you? Why don't we wizards use the Lesser Spell of Invaded Dreams to send Vond this false Calling, instead? *We* don't need to be nearby."

"Because it won't work," Ithinia said, annoyed. She had seen this instantly, and was irritated that Arvagan had not. It did not make the Guild look good in front of these outsiders when a wizard made stupid suggestions. "You forget — warlockry blocks some spells, including that one. Besides, we would need to relay the images from Teneria's mind, or the mind of one of the other witches who had been involved, and we'd lose much of the authenticity in the transfer. No, it must be a witch — though we can certainly help her to get close, and provide protective spells while she's there."

"You intend to deceive the emperor?" Samber asked.

"I think it would be our best course," Ithinia said. She smiled. "Unless our uninvited friend kills him." She gestured toward the corner where Demerchan's representative had sat.

All that was there now, though, was an empty chair.

Chapter Twenty-Five

The tapestry rippled slightly as it settled into place, and then stilled, and suddenly it no longer looked like a mere piece of cloth, but like an opening leading out of the fourth-floor bedroom onto a grassy, sunlit slope. Hanner quickly pulled his hands away from the rod he had just set into brackets, and then climbed carefully down from the chair he stood on.

"It's beautiful," Nerra said, staring at the image. "Where is it?"

"Nowhere," Hanner said, kicking aside the dusty old tapestry he had replaced. "It's not in the World at all."

His sister threw him a look. "Really?"

"Really. When I was in there, I couldn't hear the Calling at all, not the faintest, most distant whisper."

"Then why did you go flying off the instant you came out?"

"Because I came out a mile north of where I went in, for one thing, and for another — you know how when you step out of a dark room into the sun, it seems much brighter than when you went in? My mind had adjusted to not hearing the Call, and wasn't ready when it suddenly came back as strong as ever." He shook his head. "I don't remember much after that, but I remember the shock of stepping back through into the attic and being hit by the full force of it."

"We had a lot of theories," Nerra said. "That maybe the Calling was stronger in there, or that the return tapestry focused it somehow. I don't remember whether anyone suggested the truth."

"It doesn't matter," Hanner said. "There isn't any Call anymore."

"Are you going to test it?"

Hanner hesitated. "Is the attic... It *looks* the same..."

"After you smashed your way out," Nerra said, "the other warlocks put it back exactly the way it was, down to the smallest particle of dirt. That was before they decided the tapestry was too dangerous to try again — or before they discovered no one would volunteer to try it, anyway."

"Then the return tapestry *ought* to work."

"Are you going to test it?" Nerra repeated.

"I'm not sure I should," Hanner said. "I mean, if something goes wrong, I might be stuck there, and I don't *want* to be. I haven't even seen how my children turned out yet. I haven't talked to Alris."

"Well, I'm not going to test it," Nerra said. "I have a husband waiting for me, and two children of my own."

Hanner nodded. "Of course," he said, gazing thoughtfully at the tapestry.

"Maybe one of those people from thirty years ago would risk it."

"Maybe," Hanner said quietly. Then a little more forcefully, "Maybe, yes. Come on." He turned, and led the way downstairs.

Rudhira was waiting for them on the second floor. "Did you find what you were looking for?" she asked.

Hanner looked at her for a moment before replying, "Yes, we did."

"That's good. There are more people downstairs who want help."

"They can wait," Hanner said. "Rudhira, do you have anyone to stay with? Anywhere to go?"

"You," she said. "And here."

Hanner blinked. "No one else?"

She glared at him. "Hanner, it's been more than thirty years, and I didn't have much of anything back then, either. I had some regular customers back in Camptown, and some friends among the other girls, and I got along well enough with the guards and the local tradesmen, but none of them were all that close. I didn't have any sisters, the way you do, or brothers. I didn't have a husband, or parents, or children, and except for you and the other warlocks, everyone I knew is thirty-four years older now. They probably don't even *remember* me — and that's the ones who are still alive. Who else could I have? And I never had a home to go to; I was sleeping in soldiers' beds, or on tavern floors, before you found me on the Night of Madness. If you throw me out, it's a hard choice whether to go back to the streets of Camptown, or just head directly to the Hundred-Foot Field, or maybe give up completely and see if I can get a fair deal on Slave Street."

Hanner didn't really see why that would be so hard a choice, since she was still as young and beautiful as she had been before the Night of Madness. Whoring might be a horrible way to make a living, but it surely must be better than begging or slavery.

He didn't say that, though; it wasn't his business. Instead he said, "I wasn't going to throw you out. I was worried that…that you might be missed."

"Anyone who missed me has had thirty years to get over it."

Hanner could not argue with that. Mavi hadn't waited for him, and he had been gone only half as long as Rudhira. "There's something I want to show you, up on the fourth floor," he said.

She eyed him suspiciously, and threw a glance at Nerra.

"We aren't going to hurt you," Nerra told her. "We need a volunteer to test something, though."

"Something magic?" Rudhira asked. "And presumably dangerous, if you're worried about whether anyone will miss me if I don't come back."

"It's magic, yes," Hanner said. "It's not exactly *dangerous*. I mean, it won't kill you. Come upstairs, and I'll explain."

"You don't have to do it if you don't want to," Nerra assured her. "But we'd appreciate it if you at least took a look at it and gave it some thought."

Rudhira essayed a curtsey. "For you, Lady Nerra, I will take a look."

Together, the three marched back up the two flights to the fourth floor, and into the front bedroom where two dormer windows overlooked High Street, and Hanner's Transporting Tapestry hung on the north wall.

Hanner stepped aside as soon as he was through the door, and watched as Rudhira took in the hanging tapestry, its sunny colors so bright they seemed to glow, and the discarded old non-magical tapestry lying heaped on the floor. She glanced at the canopied bed and the twin night-stands badly in need of dusting, at the gold-edged ewer, the unlit oil lamps, and the other furnishings, and Hanner could see her dismissing them as irrelevant and focusing her attention on the magical hanging.

"Is that what it appears to be?" she asked, standing well back and studying the scene from a safe distance.

"It's a Transporting Tapestry, like the ones the wizards brought for the people from the other two Ethshars," Hanner replied. "If you walk up to it and touch it, you'll step through into the place in the picture."

"That's what you want me to test?" Rudhira frowned. "Where's the difficulty? It either works or it doesn't, right? Or is there some way it can go horribly wrong?"

"I don't think it can go horribly wrong," Hanner said. "It worked fine seventeen years ago. But we aren't completely sure you can get *back*."

"I can't just turn around and walk back through it?"

"No," Hanner said. "It's not *there* on the other side. You'll be in an empty field, with no way to come back through this tapestry."

"I see," Rudhira said. She looked over the tapestry, not moving any closer to the fabric. "You say it worked seventeen years ago? Someone went through it?"

"*I* did," Hanner said. "I wanted a place where warlocks would be safe from the Calling." He gestured at the tapestry. "I found one, in there. But then I came back out, and was Called before I could *tell* anyone it was safe."

"So there *is* a way out?"

"There *was*," Hanner said. "We don't know whether it's still there, and still working, or not."

"Ah, and *that's* what you want me to test?"

"Exactly."

"And if it *isn't* still there?"

Hanner and Nerra looked at one another.

"We hadn't really thought that part through yet," Hanner admitted.

"We would find a way to get you back out," Nerra said.

"But it might take awhile," Hanner said. "Possibly a year or more. *Probably* not that long, but it's possible." He hoped they would be able to find some other way to retrieve Rudhira if she became trapped in the tapestry's world, perhaps by buying or borrowing an existing tapestry, but in the worst case, he would commission another new one.

Paying for it might be a challenge, though. He hadn't discussed money with Nerra yet, and while he was sure his family wouldn't let him starve, paying for a new tapestry was something else entirely.

Rudhira considered the blue sky, the golden sunlight, the green grass. Wherever that was, it certainly looked *warmer* than Ethshar was right now. "Tell me about the return magic," she said.

Hanner let his breath out with a sigh of relief; he hadn't realized he was holding it. "You see those houses there?" he said, pointing.

"They're pretty," Rudhira said.

"Yes, they are," Hanner agreed. "Well, in *that* one, on the right, there's another tapestry — or there was, anyway. Arvagan's apprentice hung it there seventeen years ago, and it brought me back to Ethshar. If it's still there, and it works, it will transport you to the attic, right above us."

"Right here in this same house?"

Hanner nodded. "Yes," he said.

"And if it *doesn't* work?"

"If you aren't back in an hour, I'll go talk to a wizard about the best way to get you out," Hanner said. "We'll use the Spell of Invaded Dreams to let you know what I learn."

"And if it *does* work?"

"Then you'll be back safely."

She looked at him with an unreadable expression. "I *mean*," she said, "what are you going to do with this thing? Why is this so important?"

"Oh, I'm sorry," Hanner said, and barely prevented himself from adding, "I thought it was obvious." He smiled. "This is somewhere all the Called warlocks can live. Those houses are empty — or they were seventeen years ago, anyway. It's warm and sunny, there's water from a lovely little stream just over the hill, the sea is over that way — it should be a fine place to live."

"Live?" Rudhira studied the tapestry again, her expression rather different; where before she had appeared to be peering closely, taking in every detail, now she seemed to be leaning back, looking for a general impression.

"You'd be welcome to live there, if you want to," Hanner said. "But please come back and let us know it's possible, first."

"If you don't want to risk it, we can find someone else," Nerra said.

"Oh, no, my lady," Rudhira said. "I'll try it. No need to risk anyone else."

"That's not what —" Hanner began, but before he could finish the sentence Rudhira had stepped forward, hand outstretched. He started forward instinctively, intending to stop her, even though this was exactly what he had wanted her to do.

But then her fingers touched the cloth and she was gone, leaving Hanner and Nerra alone in the unused bedroom.

For a moment, the two of them stared at the tapestry. Then Nerra said, "I like her. Shall we go upstairs and wait?"

Hanner nodded. He was unsure why he had reached out to stop her, and why he felt so uncomfortable that Rudhira had gone through the tapestry; wasn't that what he had wanted? The sight of her disappearance had been almost painful, but he didn't understand why. He tore his gaze away from the tapestry and followed his sister back to the attic stair.

"We need to be careful to stay out of the area that's shown in the other tapestry," Hanner said, as they climbed the steps. "If the reality doesn't exactly match the image, the spell may not work."

Nerra looked back over her shoulder. "Match how?"

"Well, if we were anywhere in the attic that's visible in the image, that could block the magic, because we aren't in the image."

Nerra frowned. "You mean that if we stood in the middle of the floor, she'd be trapped in that other world?"

"Yes," Hanner said. "Or she might be, anyway — there's some variation from one tapestry to another. Quite a *lot* of variation, really. It's one reason these tapestries aren't more widely used — the wizards can't tell in advance just how easily the spell will be to disrupt. They can be very delicate."

"Are the stairs in the image?"

Hanner tried to remember; it had been a few days since his brief sojourn in his magical refuge. "No, I'm pretty sure they aren't," he said. "We designed it to have as few variables as we could, so the window isn't visible, and I'm fairly certain the stairs aren't, either."

"We should stay back, though," Nerra said, stopping a step below the attic floor.

Hanner stopped as well, a few steps lower, and backed down a step so as not to crowd his sister.

His foot hit something, and it was all he could do to keep from tumbling down the stairs when whatever he had stepped on let out a high-pitched squeal and slapped at his ankle.

"What in the World…?" He looked down to see a pointy-eared frog-like green face glaring up at him angrily.

"Hanner? What's going on?" Nerra turned.

"It's one of those…those little green things," Hanner said, pointing. He had forgotten what the creatures were called.

"What little green…oh, it's a spriggan. What are *you* doing here?"

"Wanted to see magic!" it squeaked.

"Well, don't get underfoot, or you'll get stepped on," Nerra told it. The spriggan started to reply, and to climb up the next step, but she cut it off. "And don't go out there in the attic, or the magic won't work."

"Where spriggan go, then?" it protested.

Hanner stared at it, fascinated, as Nerra said, "I don't care where you go, as long as you stay out of the way."

"Here," Hanner said. "Would you like to climb on my shoulder?"

"Oooh! Oooh!" the spriggan replied, jumping up and down. "Yes, yes, yes!"

Hanner held out a hand, intending to lift the little creature, but instead it jumped up, grabbed his wrist, pulled itself up onto his forearm, and scampered up to his shoulder. Then, using his ear as a ladder, it scrambled to the top of his head, where it clung to his hair, swaying unsteadily, its own head missing the rafters by no more than an inch or two.

"That's not what I —" Hanner began.

"Wanna see magic!" it shrieked, drumming its heels on Hanner's temples.

Nerra gave her brother a disgusted look. "Don't *encourage* it," she said.

"Why not?" Hanner said. "It seems friendly enough. Maybe these things could be useful. Maybe we could train them to run errands."

"It's been tried," Nerra assured him. "Yes, they're friendly enough, but they're *stupid*. You can't count on them to remember what they're supposed to be doing. They get into everything, they break things and make messes. Even if you did train one to run your errands, it wouldn't be worth the aggravation."

"Is true," the spriggan said, nodding sadly. "Spriggan very stupid. Make messes everywhere."

Hanner had a suspicion that the spriggan might not be as stupid as it wanted everyone to think it was. Maybe it didn't *want* to be trained to run errands. If that was the case he could hardly blame it; he had never liked running other people's errands, either. "Well, don't make a mess here," he said. "We need this attic to stay exactly as it is, so the magic will work."

"Spriggan try." It started to nod again, but whacked its head on a rafter and stopped, looking up resentfully at the wooden beam it had hit.

Nerra looked at the spriggan, then at her brother's face, then back at the empty attic. "No sign of her."

Hanner turned up an empty palm.

They waited another few minutes in silence. Then Nerra asked, "You went through that tapestry?"

"Yes."

"How long did it take you to come back out?"

"You'd probably know better than I do," Hanner said. "There's no way to tell time in the other world, or at least I didn't notice any, and I don't know what time it was when I emerged because I was Called the instant I was back in Ethshar."

Nerra considered that, frowning. "I don't remember how long you were gone — if I ever actually knew. You hadn't told me what you were doing."

"However long it was, it doesn't mean much. I didn't rush. I enjoyed the sensation of not having the Call muttering at me all the time. Rudhira should be quicker."

"Or maybe she'll take time to enjoy the sunshine, too."

"Maybe," Hanner admitted. "And she does need to walk over the hill and find the right house."

"So we could be here all night."

"I don't think the tapestry will even work after sunset. The image shows the attic in daylight. *Dim* daylight, but daylight."

Nerra considered that. "So if she doesn't reappear soon, she won't until morning?"

Hanner had not noticed how late in the day it was, but now that Nerra mentioned it he could see that the daylight was indeed starting to fade. "Probably," he said.

Nerra turned to face Hanner. "Maybe we should just settle in —"

She was interrupted by a squeal from the spriggan, and there Rudhira was, standing in the middle of the attic. She had arrived facing away from the stairs, but upon hearing the creature's noise she turned.

"It seems to work," she said. She started toward the stairs, then stopped.

Hanner realized she was staring at the spriggan, and he reached up to grab it, whereupon it sprang away, bouncing off the sloping ceiling and tumbling awkwardly to the floor. It did not appear to be hurt by the impact, as it quickly regained its feet and scampered over to embrace Rudhira's ankle. "Pretty hair!" it said.

"Not on my leg," Rudhira retorted, kicking it gently away. She looked at Hanner. "What is *this* thing doing here?"

"It wanted to see magic," Hanner explained.

"How was it on the other side of the tapestry?" Nerra asked.

"Lovely," Rudhira replied. "In fact, I want to go back. I'd have stayed, but I didn't want to worry you."

"You can go back," Hanner told her. "Now that we know it's safe, and that there's a way out."

"All right," Rudhira said. She gave him a look that Hanner couldn't quite interpret. "What about you?"

"Oh, I'll stay here for now," he said. "I need to keep an eye on things. But now we have somewhere to put all those people downstairs."

Rudhira nodded. "It's nice there. At least, the parts I saw. For one thing, it's *warm*."

"And the return tapestry works, so they can come back any time they want," Hanner said.

"They'll still need food," Nerra said. "And other things."

"I know," Hanner said. "Still, it's a start." He turned and headed down the stairs.

Nerra followed closely. Rudhira took a final look around the attic, then came along on Nerra's heels.

Hanner wasn't sure whether he really heard, or merely imagined, Rudhira's voice murmuring, "A start to *what*?"

Chapter Twenty-Six

Kirris of Slave Street watched yet another group of ragged former warlocks make their way through the door into the High Street mansion, and bit her lip. It must be getting crowded in there, she thought. She had seen scores of people admitted, and she had only arrived around sunset.

Going unnoticed in a crowd shouldn't be difficult, and it was clear that these people didn't all know one another, so getting into the house would be easy enough, but if anyone questioned her she was not sure how convincing a story she could tell. Her witchcraft would ordinarily keep people from paying any attention to her, but it didn't actually render her invisible, and if they were systematically interrogating each new arrival, she would almost certainly be included. If they were *looking* for her, they would see her.

Obviously, if questioned she would pretend to be another former warlock, but would it be better to claim she had been Called on the Night of Madness, and therefore knew nothing about being a warlock and using their magic, or to say that she was only recently Called, to explain why she didn't know what Ethshar was like thirty-odd years ago?

Well, why she didn't know *much* about what it was like back then — she had been four on the Night.

Either way, she would be expected to know first-hand what had happened to the Called from the time the Calling ended until Asham opened the portal to Eastgate Market, and of course, she had only second- or third-hand reports.

Still, she couldn't see any reason anyone would ask her too many questions about that, or why they would be suspicious in the first place. She was a witch; she ought to be able to lie convincingly just by reading people's reactions and telling them what they wanted to hear.

Not that witches generally did that, other than when they were comforting the dying, or calming the grieving friends and family of the newly dead. The Sisterhood wanted witches to maintain a reputation for truth-telling — it was supposed to make the lies they *did* tell that much more effective. But it meant Kirris hadn't had much practice in the art of deception.

She really hoped that none of the three warlocks she had tried to help were in there, but she thought her odds were fairly good on that. They had only been Called a few years ago, and had probably found friends or family to take them in, rather than coming here — Warlock House was a last resort. Any of them would probably recognize her instantly if they saw her, despite her being older; she hadn't changed *that* much, and from their point of view, as she understood it, those failed experiments had taken place just a few days ago.

But there were just three of them, which is why she was here, rather than Teneria. Teneria had devoted *years* to meddling with warlocks, and had probably worked with forty or fifty in all, any of whom might be in there. Kirris had much better odds of not being recognized, and of getting in that door without anyone realizing she was a witch.

Once she was inside she would still need to get close to Vond if she was to carry out the scheme that the gathering at Ithinia's house had devised, but that shouldn't be *too* difficult — Warlock House was big, but it wasn't *that* big. It wasn't as if the Emperor had taken over the overlord's palace, the way that horrible Tabaea did in Ethshar of the Sands a decade back.

The last of the Called were being ushered in, and the man who let them in was looking up and down the street for stragglers. Kirris almost moved out of the shadows, but then hesitated. If she went now she would be too noticeable. She would go with the next party.

The man looked up to be sure the lamps on either side of the door had sufficient fuel and were burning well, then stepped inside and closed the door. Kirris let out her breath; she had not realized until that instant that she had been holding it.

There was nothing to be afraid of, she told herself. The Calling was gone. Linking her mind to Vond's would not let that *thing* that had been trapped in Aldagmor back into her thoughts. All these warlocks were free of its influence, and of them all, only Vond still had any magic.

Of course, she was there to meddle in Vond's head, and he might not be pleased about that if he realized it was happening, but he was just a man, not a monster. Ithinia had given her some protective charms to try, just in case — but wizardry was notoriously ineffective against warlocks. Her own witchcraft might be better.

She heard footsteps, and turned to see a girl in a filthy nightgown walking uncertainly up High Street. Behind her was a young man in black, almost invisible in the darkness save for his pale oval face.

Kirris stepped out of the shadowed arch and waited for them.

"*Hai*," the man called. "I…we heard there was a place here where warlocks could go."

"That's it," Kirris said, pointing. "With the lanterns."

"You're sure?" the girl asked. Something about the way she pronounced the words reminded Kirris of her own grandmother.

"I'm sure," Kirris said.

"Thank you," the girl said. She and the man trudged on.

"Wait," Kirris said. "I'll come with you."

Together, the three of them made their way through the gate and up to the door, and stood on the stoop. Kirris waited for a moment, but when neither of the others took action she reached up and knocked. A moment later the door opened, and a petite redhead peered out at them, rather than the pudgy fellow Kirris had seen before. "May I help you?" she asked.

Kirris turned to her companions.

"We heard…we were told that…" the girl began.

"We were Called," the man said.

"I was asleep," the girl said. "And then I was in that pit full of people, and now my master is gone, and my family is gone, and…and someone said…"

The redhead sighed. "Come in," she said. "Welcome to Warlock House. Find a place to sit. Hanner is just starting." She swung the door wide.

"Starting what?" the girl asked.

"Hanner?" the man asked. "*Chairman* Hanner? He's here?"

"In there," the redhead said, pointing.

Kirris followed her finger to a crowded parlor, where the pudgy man was standing in the far corner while the two dozen or so people she had watched enter the house before her were seated, sprawled, or crouched facing him.

"Are there more?" the pudgy man called.

"Just three," the redhead told him.

"Well, send them in. As I was saying, my name is Hanner, once Lord Hanner, once Chairman Hanner, but for the moment, simply Hanner. I own this house, but long ago dedicated it to the use of the Council of Warlocks."

Kirris slipped into the parlor and into a dim corner, while her two companions made their way into the room and found places of their own.

"I know you're probably all tired and confused," Hanner continued. "You woke up out in the freezing wilderness in Aldagmor with no idea what had happened, but then the magicians showed up and brought us to Ethshar. You probably thought that once you got back to the city everything would be fine, and you could go back to your old lives, but instead you found that the World's changed, that you've been gone for twenty, twenty-five, thirty years or more, and you can't find your friends, or your family, or your old homes — or you found them, but your wives have remarried, your homes are occupied by strangers, your friends have forgotten you. You're lost and alone and don't know what to do, or where to go, and you heard that you could come here, and you thought at least it would keep you away from the slavers and out of the Hundred-Foot Field. So here you are." He spread his hands to take in the entire room.

Kirris settled to the floor, her back against the wall.

"You are indeed welcome here, until you can build a new life," Hanner said, "but we don't have any magical solutions. We can't send you back to your old homes; the past is past and gone. Even the most powerful wizards can't travel backward through time. All we can do is give you a place to stay until you can find something better. Some of you will probably find that you *do* still have family, or that you do have friends who haven't forgotten you. If you were snatched away on the Night of Madness, unless you're a child, then presumably you know a trade. Yes, you've lost whatever tools or inventory you had, but you can start anew. If you're a child, even if your parents are gone, you can find an apprenticeship — the World isn't *that* different. I know you've lost a lot; we all have, myself included. Still, you're alive, you're safe, and you can make new lives for yourselves. We'll give you a bed until you're back on your feet, maybe offer some advice — but that's all we can do."

He paused to let that sink in. Kirris looked around at the listeners. Most of them seemed to be accepting Hanner's explanation calmly.

"Now, there are some complications," Hanner said. "First, as I'm sure most of you remember, back in Aldagmor that there was a warlock who called himself Vond who somehow still had his magic, even with the Source gone. How that happened is a mystery, but apparently he found another source that he can use, one that the rest of us are deaf to, and he's as powerful a warlock as ever. Fifteen years ago he fled to the Small Kingdoms to escape the Calling, and when he found his new magic he built himself an empire there. Well, now that the Calling is gone, he decided he'd rather come home to Ethshar than stay out there lording over the barbarians, and he came *here*, to this house. He's declared himself the new Chairman of the Council of Warlocks, and since he's the only warlock left, no one can very well argue with him about that. He's claimed the master's apartment on the second floor. While I own this house, and you are all my guests, you need to realize that the Great Vond is a supremely powerful and very short-tempered magician; do *not* get in his way, or argue with him. He doesn't care that I own the house; he treats it as his, and does whatever he pleases. No one can protect you if he decides he doesn't like you. He throws people around if they annoy him, and at least once, he's killed someone without really meaning to — smashed his head against a wall. He regretted that, I think, but it hasn't made him any more careful, which means *you* need to be careful around him. Does everyone understand that?"

Several of the listeners exchanged worried glances. A woman asked, "How will we know him? What does he look like?"

"He's tall, thin, and pale," Hanner said, "but you'll know him because his feet don't touch the ground."

That elicited murmurs, and Kirris thought there might have been more questions had Hanner not forestalled them by launching into another speech.

"I'm sure you've all noticed that this is a big house," he said. "My Uncle Faran, who built it, wanted a mansion the equal of any in Ethshar. All the same, we have had dozens of you turn up here looking for shelter — *hundreds*, actually, with more arriving all the time. We can't find space for all of you here unless we pack you in so tightly you'd be better off in the Hundred-Foot Field. Fortunately, we have a solution. Seventeen years ago, just before I was Called, I bought a magical tapestry from a wizard, the same kind of tapestry you saw the wizards using to send our fellow Called warlocks home to Ethshar of the Sands and Ethshar of the Rocks and Sardiron of the Waters. This one, though, doesn't go anywhere in the World; instead it goes to a sunny little village in another world. I thought we might be safe from the Calling there, but it wasn't ready in time, and I was Called before I could use it. It works now, though, and I have it hanging upstairs, ready to take you to that village."

"Can we get *back*?" someone called. Kirris did not see who had spoken.

"Yes, you can," Hanner replied. "There's another tapestry in the village that will bring you safely back to the attic of this house."

"Who lives in the village?" someone else asked.

"Nobody," Hanner answered. "Or rather, it was deserted until today. Now dozens of your compatriots are settling in there."

"Is it safe?"

Hanner hesitated slightly; Kirris wasn't sure everyone noticed. "I *think* so," he said. "But we don't really know. It's magic. More specifically, it's wizardry, and I'm sure most of you know that wizardry draws its power from chaos. We can't be *sure* there aren't various hazards in there. I *can* say, though, that I've visited the village and come back safely, and the other people who tried it all came back safely. It *seems* to be safe." He straightened up. "Now, I'm sure most of you are tired and hungry. We've sent some supplies through the tapestry to the magical village, and there are still empty houses there, waiting for you. If you would follow me upstairs, I'll show you the tapestry, and you can see what you think."

Kirris was not eager to draw attention to herself, but stepping through a Transporting Tapestry into some miniature universe was not part of her plans. She joined the crowd, but as they climbed the stairs she maneuvered herself close to Hanner and murmured in his ear, "I don't know about this tapestry thing. I don't trust wizardry. Could I stay here in the house?"

Hanner glanced at her. "I can't promise you a bed," he said. "I won't throw you out on the street, but Vond might."

"I'll risk it, if you don't mind."

"Please yourself, then, but do come take a look at the tapestry first. You might change your mind."

Kirris didn't argue, but let herself gradually fall behind the others as they made their way up three flights to the dusty bedroom where the magical tapestry hung. By the time they reached the room she was at the rear of the group, and stood in the doorway, not entering the chamber, as Hanner presented the tapestry.

Kirris had to admit the scene it depicted was beautiful — blue sky, green grass, bright sun. She was not tempted, though; she preferred the real world to some wizard's fantasy. She listened as Hanner explained how each person had to step aside to make way for the next, because the spell probably wouldn't work if the reality no longer matched the image, and watched as the first former warlock timidly reached out, touched the fabric, and vanished.

Then she slipped back out into the hallway, and hurried down the stairs, back to the second floor and to the carved door at the top of the grand staircase.

The door was closed, but she was a witch; ordinary physical barriers did not stop her. This room was supposed to be where Vond slept; she reached out, trying to sense him, to feel his thoughts.

It wasn't hard. He was there, all right, and he was definitely not sleeping. His thoughts were clear, and focused on what he was doing.

Kirris had never really given much thought to the erotic possibilities in warlockry, but Vond obviously had. Magic that provided unlimited stamina, and allowed its wielder to move anything, exert pressure anywhere, heat or cool surfaces — Kirris wondered why she had never before heard stories about the amorous prowess of warlocks. Now that she observed it in action, it seemed obvious. She knew that some witches used sexual magic, she had dabbled in it herself a few times, but she had never heard of it in connection with warlocks.

Maybe the Calling had distracted normal warlocks, or concerns about being Called had kept them from experimenting freely. Vond, however, had no such concerns. The woman with him was happily exhausted, barely able to stay awake; they had clearly been at it for quite some time.

Kirris looked around. She could hear voices from downstairs — more homeless warlocks, perhaps? She could not just stay here at the door; sooner or later someone would see her and want to know what she was doing there. She would be too busy using her witchcraft elsewhere to maintain the spell that kept people from noticing her.

Ideally, she would slip into Vond's bedchamber and hide in a wardrobe or closet, but she could not see how to manage that with the couple awake in there — they weren't *that* intent on their activity, and if the door opened, they would notice. Or at least Vond would; that girl might not stay conscious much longer.

She might be able to hide her entrance with magic, but she was unsure how effective witchcraft would be against Vond. She preferred not to risk it. But the bed was against the west wall, and one of the guest bedrooms adjoined it. She crossed to that room's door and tested the latch. The door swung open.

There were signs of recent occupancy, including several bundles of clothing and a stack of books on the floor by the bed, but no one was in the room. Kirris slipped in, and closed the door behind her. Kirris looked at the wall that separated this chamber from Vond's, and was pleased to see a closet door. She quickly crossed the room.

The closet was empty, which was a little surprising at first, especially given the bundles by the bed, but then she remembered that most of the house was inhabited by refugees who had no clothing except what they had been wearing when they were Called. This room's occupant had apparently acquired some garments somewhere, but probably hadn't had time yet to put them in the closet.

She stepped into the closet and pulled the door shut behind her, then settled to the floor in the darkness, her back against the wall. She could have made a light, but it might show; instead she left the closet dark, and closed her eyes, using her magic to sense what lay beyond the wall behind her.

Vond was finally done, not because he was tired, but because his companion was unable to stay awake any longer. He slid off her, and started to get out of bed.

That was not what Kirris wanted. She reached out, and cast a whisper into the warlock's mind. "A little sleep might be nice," she thought. "Not needed, of course, but nice. Enjoy this lovely bed, and wake up next to this girl."

She could feel him hesitate. She felt him turn and look at the sleeping woman.

"There's no hurry," she thought at him. "There's all the time in the World. Everyone else is going to bed now; why shouldn't you?"

She knew that her messages were reaching him, but she was not certain they were coming across as his own thoughts. She did not sense any real barrier from his own magic, but he was always wary — she could see that, could see that it was part of his nature.

She knew he had stopped, and was looking at his sleeping companion. Then he glanced around the room, at the burning lamps, at the marble statue of a woman and the little bronze on the bedside table, and at the white-and-gold bed-curtains.

Kirris waited, holding her breath. Then Vond lay back, let out a sigh, and closed his eyes. A moment later he was sound asleep.

Kirris still waited, crouching in the closet with her eyes closed, watching as the warlock — the *last* warlock — settled into a sound slumber. When she was certain that he was not going to awaken for at least a few minutes, she felt his mind, felt the shape of it. She could sense the structure in the brain that resonated with the magic that permeated the World.

She had studied that structure before, and she could tell immediately that Vond's was slightly different. It was…bigger here, smaller there, shaped a little differently. It was sensitive not just to the magic that had formerly poured out of Aldagmor, but to the very different power that came from somewhere to the southeast — from the towers in Lumeth, presumably.

Kirris knew that normal warlocks could not be turned back into ordinary humans; once the brain had become attuned to it, it could not close out the Aldagmor source and continue to function. This other power, though, might be different. She might be able to shut down Vond's magic, reducing him to just one more former warlock. She reached out…

And hit a barrier. She could magically *see* the inside of Vond's head, but she could not *touch* it. It wasn't that the structural changes couldn't be reversed and the power shut out without destroying his mind, as was the case with an ordinary warlock, but that he had erected a protective barrier that somehow stayed in place even while he slept. She could not tell whether it was a permanent structure of some sort, or whether he had trained himself to maintain it even when unconscious, but it blocked her witchcraft quite effectively.

That was not really a surprise. She had not known such a thing was possible, but given that it *was* possible, Vond was exactly the sort of person who would have made such an arrangement. He had probably done it long ago, before he was Called, when he thought the kings he had deposed in creating his empire were plotting against him.

She couldn't take his magic away. Her own private plan was not going to work.

She had feared that might be the case. It would have been too easy if she could simply turn off his power supply, or block it somehow. She had not even bothered to tell Ithinia and the others she intended to try.

That protective spell meant she would have to try the plan that she *had* discussed with Ithinia. She let out a soundless sigh, gathered her reserves of energy, and dug down into her own memory of those long-ago experiments she and Teneria had conducted.

The images were still there, burned indelibly into her mind when she had shared the experience of the Call. She gathered and shaped them.

This was taking a lot of energy, she knew. To all appearances she was sitting quietly in a closet, but in fact she was using more witchcraft in this hour or so than she would normally use in a sixnight. She was going to be tired, hungry, and shaky when this was done — but it had to be done, and the sooner the better.

She could feel herself trembling, and she forced herself to stop, to focus on the magic, the memories, the images, the sensations, and the feel of Vond's sleeping mind on the far side of the bedroom wall. She reached out, and began to filter the remembered images into his thoughts as a dream — a dream of falling, and burning, of ferocious inhuman *need*, of a demand and a direction, of being buried deep in ash and mud, smothered and trapped.

And then Vond was awake, awake and screaming as he tore upward from his bed, through the canopy and the ceiling above, as shredded fabric and shards of plaster spattered down across his companion, startled from her own exhausted slumber.

Chapter Twenty-Seven

Hanner had ushered the last of the new arrivals through the tapestry, and was walking down the stairs from the fourth floor to the third, a candle in his hand, when the entire house suddenly shook, and unearthly screams sounded somewhere nearby, accompanied by crashing. He picked up his pace, and when he reached the third floor he ran in the direction of the sound.

He could hear a dozen voices now as various people called questions, trying to understand what was happening. He ignored them all as he dashed toward the back of the house. He could see an orange glow under one of the bedroom doors; he snatched at the knob and flung that door open.

As he had expected, Vond was hanging in mid-air in the room beyond, glowing orange, hair drifting out in a nimbus around his head. As Hanner had *not* expected, the emperor was stark naked, his skin pale and slick with sweat. Two women were cowering in beds on either side of the room, sheets pulled up — they were probably naked, as well.

The floor between the two beds had been smashed upward, leaving a hole about six feet across directly below the hovering warlock. Bits of wood and plaster were scattered on all sides.

Vond had stopped screaming, and as Hanner stepped in, his gaze focused on Hanner's face.

"You," he said. "Did *you* do that?" Vond did not look frightened, even though he had been screaming in terror a moment before. He looked angry.

"Do what, your Majesty?" Hanner asked. "What happened?"

Vond did not answer. Instead he looked first to one side, then the other, then demanded, "Who are you?"

"Anra the Warl...Anra of Southwark, your Majesty," one of the terrified women replied.

"My...my name is...is Pirra," the other stammered.

"They're my guests," Hanner said. "They were Called warlocks with nowhere else to go."

The warlock looked down, past his own feet, and called, "Leth! Are you there?"

"Yes, your Majesty," a woman's voice called from below.

"Are you all right?"

"I think so. I'm...sore, though."

"Hanner," Vond said, looking up again. "Where's Zallin? And Sterren?"

"Zallin was downstairs with a bottle of *oushka* last I saw," Hanner replied. "Sterren's gone; no one's seen him since early this afternoon, and most of his luggage is gone."

"Gone? Still? Gone where?"

"I have no idea."

"He should have…his *luggage* is gone?"

"Yes."

"That sneaky little traitor — *he* must be behind this. Wants my empire for himself, probably."

"Behind *what*, your Majesty?"

"I had…I dreamed…" He looked baffled and furious. "Someone put a *spell* on me, Hanner."

"What kind of a spell?"

"A dream. A Calling nightmare."

Hanner blinked. "Why do you think that's a *spell*?"

Vond had been looking around the room; now he turned to glare at Hanner. "Because the Calling is *gone*, idiot."

"How do you —"

"You think it's another Calling? That my power has its own Call?" He shook his head. "I went and took a good close look at the source of my magic, Hanner. I flew right up to it, and all around it. There's a powerful protective spell, so I didn't actually touch it — maybe I could have gotten through that spell if I wanted to, but why should I? I might damage something. I might have destroyed my own magic. So I didn't force it, and I didn't *need* to — I was right there, less than fifty feet from the source. I could feel it all through me. I could see its power all around me. I saw and heard everything there was to see and hear, and I know that there wasn't any Calling. It wasn't alive. It didn't have any more consciousness than a rock — and I don't mean some wizard's gargoyles, I mean an ordinary rock. There was *no Calling*. None. And if I couldn't hear any right there, fifty feet away, I don't believe for an instant that I could be hearing it now, on the far side of the Gulf of the East."

This was interesting. Hanner hadn't realized that Vond knew exactly where his power came from, let alone that he had visited the source. "Maybe it was asleep when you were there, and now it's woken up?"

"It wasn't asleep. It was *dead*. It was never alive, any more than the Tower of Flame is alive. It's a construction, a device, a big magical device, and it isn't Calling anyone."

"Then maybe your dream was just an ordinary nightmare, dredging up your memories of the Calling."

That stopped the warlock for a moment; he cocked his head in thought. His lips thinned.

Then he shook his head. "I don't think so," he said. "I think it was a wizard trying to trick me. Isn't there some spell they use to send dreams?"

"The Spell of Invaded Dreams," Anra volunteered. Hanner glanced at her, startled; her face looked strange in the orange light.

"There, you see?" Vond said triumphantly.

"That a wizard *could* have sent the dream doesn't mean one *did*," Hanner replied.

"Well, it certainly doesn't mean one *didn't*."

"Why would a wizard send you a Calling dream?"

"To frighten me, of course! To make me afraid of using my power."

Hanner had to admit to himself that Vond's theory was not completely absurd, but he was not about to say it aloud. "How realistic was it? The dream, I mean. Was it like a real Calling nightmare?"

"It was *exactly* like a real one! That's another reason I know it wasn't from my new source — it was too much like the messages from Aldagmor, and the one in Lumeth is completely different."

"Maybe you're somehow still hearing the thing from Aldagmor, then."

Vond sneered. "You know better than that."

"I know *I* can't hear it anymore, and none of the other Called warlocks, but we don't have any magic anymore. Maybe your new power makes you more sensitive."

"You know it *stopped*," Vond said. "You were there. You felt it stop. We all did. It Called, and it was answered, and it stopped calling."

"It could have started again," Hanner said, knowing even as the words left his lips how weak that sounded.

"Why would it? It was rescued. Its…its friend came and got it, and they flew away together. It doesn't need to call for help anymore."

"Maybe it's another one of those things, trapped somewhere else — out beyond the Great Eastern Desert, perhaps. Maybe it's been there all along, but no one's ever been sensitive enough to hear it until now. You *are* the most powerful warlock in history."

"Yes, I am, but still, that doesn't fit. I don't hear any whispering, I don't feel the slightest tug when I'm awake, but the minute I'm soundly asleep I have a full-sized Calling dream? You know it doesn't work like that; we don't reach the nightmare threshold until long after we've heard the whispers and felt the urges, and the early dreams aren't anywhere near as detailed and powerful as this one was."

"Your mind is accustomed to the nightmares, Vond — you were already Called once."

He shook his head. "I don't think so. I don't hear any whispers, Hanner. I don't hear anything but pure, clean power from the source in Lumeth."

Hanner wondered what that felt like. He had been a warlock for seventeen years, but his magic had always had a certain mysteriousness to it, a dark edge, a slightly unclean feeling, even before he began to consciously feel any urge to head toward Aldagmor. What would it be like to have a warlock's power without that taint?

For a moment he was tempted to see if Vond would teach him to draw on the Lumeth source, but the urge passed. He didn't need to be a warlock. His previous experience of that magic had cost him his uncle, his title, and in the end, his marriage and seventeen years. This other source might be different, but it might have its own hazards, and it very definitely worried the Wizards' Guild. Hanner had no desire to annoy the Guild, especially when he had already agreed to accept their money to talk others out of precisely the temptation he was now facing.

"It could still be your own memory playing tricks on you," he said.

"Maybe," Vond admitted. "But I think a wizard's spell is more likely."

"Can you be sure it was a wizard?" Anra suggested from her bed. "Other magicians can use dreams, too."

"Can they?" Vond asked, turning to her.

"Demons can send dreams," Hanner said, thinking back to the years he had spent researching magic for his uncle. "I'm not sure, but I think some gods might, as well."

"And witches," Anra offered. "They use dreams to soothe sick children."

"And…and…" Pirra murmured.

Hanner had almost forgotten she was there. Startled, the other three all turned to look at her.

Intimidated by their gaze, she pulled her blanket up to her chin. "Dancers," she said over the satin-wrapped hem. "Ritual dancers say they can make happy dreams. My mother told me that."

"I don't think that's real," Hanner said. "Dancers make a lot of claims they can't prove."

"Why would any of them *want* to?" Vond demanded. "Either Sterren hired someone, and he'd probably go to a wizard, or the wizards are angry with me for creating my empire — they banned warlocks from the whole area, you know. This could be part of their campaign."

"What campaign?" Hanner asked.

"To keep anyone from using the source in Lumeth! Sterren knew about that — they warned him a dozen years ago, he said. Maybe he didn't have to hire anyone, maybe it wasn't his idea at all, but they could have warned him again, and that's why he left, so he wouldn't be involved. That must be it — it's the Wizards' Guild that's behind it. If Sterren had wanted the empire he wouldn't have come here with me in the first place."

Hanner found it interesting to hear Vond thinking this through out loud. The nightmare, or spell, or whatever it was had clearly shaken him — he had reacted instinctively at first, smashing his way up through the ceiling, and then had realized that, just as he had explained, the dream couldn't be a genuine Call. The mere fact that he had gone straight up, and not headed for either Aldagmor or Lumeth, demonstrated that there was some deception involved. He was still getting his thoughts straight, working out what had happened.

He might even be right. Ithinia had said that the Guild didn't expect Hanner to deal with Vond all by himself, which rather implied they had other plans for dealing with him. This mysterious dream might be part of those plans.

"It must have been a convincing dream, to scare…to *startle* you out of your sleep so violently," Hanner said.

"Oh, it was perfect," Vond said. "It was *exactly* like the real thing — didn't I say that was one way I knew it was a fraud?"

"Maybe you did. My experience of the Spell of Invaded Dreams hasn't been so impressive — perhaps it wasn't the Guild, but some other magicians."

Vond waved a hand dismissively. "I haven't done anything to antagonize anyone else," he said. "It must be the Guild."

Hanner remembered Zallin's description of Vond's behavior during their tour of the city, which could easily have antagonized any number of people, but decided not to mention it. "What do you intend to do about it?" he asked.

Vond's eyes narrowed. "That's a good question," he said. "I'm not sure yet." He looked down. "Right now, I think I should put on some clothes, and I have some repairs to make."

"I'd appreciate the repairs," Hanner said.

"I suppose you would, since you claim to own this house."

"I *do* own this house," Hanner replied angrily.

"Hanner, you were Called. Called warlocks are considered dead. You may have owned this house before you were Called, but it's not so clear as all that whether you *still* own it."

"I…I don't…" Hanner let his voice trail off. He had not really given the matter much thought. Like every warlock, he had written a will when he began to feel the Call, and he had left the house to his children, to be held for them by the Council of Warlocks until such time as they claimed it; had they ever claimed it? They weren't living here, which implied that they had not, and Hanner had returned, and the Council had been disbanded...

This was complicated. It might require a magistrate to sort it out.

"You invited these two to stay here?" Vond said, interrupting Hanner's thoughts. He gestured toward the two beds.

"Yes," Hanner said. "They didn't have anywhere else to go."

"You have other guests, as well?"

"Yes."

"All former warlocks?"

"Yes."

"How many?"

"I'm not...why do you ask?"

Hanner felt himself rise off the floor. "Answer the question!" Vond demanded.

"I don't know!" Hanner said, as he hung helplessly in mid-air. "I haven't kept count."

"You haven't... Really? Give me an estimate, then. Twenty? Thirty?"

There was no particular reason to hide the truth, and there were others who would tell him if Hanner refused. "Dozens," Hanner said. "A hundred or more."

"A...a hundred? Seriously?"

Hanner noticed that the warlock's clothing was rising up from the room below, slipping through the hole in the floor. "Yes, your Majesty," he said.

"I don't see that many."

"They...they aren't all in the house itself," Hanner said.

Vond raised his arms to allow his robe to slide on. "Where are they, then?"

"That's a little difficult to explain. There's magic involved."

The robe fell into place, and Vond's belt wrapped itself around his waist. "I'm not in a great hurry," he said.

Hanner did not want to explain. He was afraid that Vond would see the tapestry as a threat, since after all, it was a gateway to a place where his magic wouldn't work. He feared that the emperor might destroy it. But he couldn't really see any way to avoid an explanation.

"I bought a spell," he said. "Before I was Called. I wanted a refuge where warlocks could go to escape the Call, and I hired a wizard to create one for me. It's a magical tapestry that will transport anyone who touches it into another world, one where the Source couldn't be heard."

Vond's clothing stopped arranging itself. "You had this *before* you were Called?" he demanded.

"Yes, but only by an hour or so," Hanner said. "I was Called immediately after testing it, before I could tell anyone it worked, so my family thought it must have made the Calling worse."

"So there's a way back out of this other world?"

"Yes, of course!"

"You've been sending your guests into the other world?"

"Yes."

"Huh. Interesting. And warlockry doesn't work there?"

"That's right."

"That sounds as if it might be very useful, under the right circumstances."

"Well, it's certainly kept this house from getting impossibly crowded."

Vond nodded. He glanced down, then looked back at Hanner. "I'm going back downstairs," he said. "I want to fix the damage, and talk to Leth, and take care of a few other things, but then I want you to show me this magical tapestry of yours. Meet me on the second-floor landing in half an hour, and bring Zallin. And Sterren, if you can find him."

"Your Majesty, I don't —"

"Half an hour," Vond said, as he sank slowly and gracefully down through the hole in the floor. A cloud of debris swirled up from around the edges and began to arrange itself over the opening as the warlock vanished from sight.

Hanner watched him go, then looked at the two women. "I'm very sorry for the disturbance," he said. "If you would prefer to find somewhere else to sleep tonight, something can probably be arranged."

"Please," Pirra said. "Let me get dressed, and then please find me somewhere else."

Anra looked at the floorboards reassembling themselves, then at Hanner. "He could reach me anywhere," she said. "I'll stay here, thank you."

"As you please," Hanner said. "Pirra, I'll be waiting out here." Then he stepped back, closed the door, and turned to find Rudhira standing there. He started.

"How long have *you* been there?" he asked.

"I heard you tell him Sterren's luggage was gone," she said. "Hanner, it's not really my business, but are you sure it was wise to tell him about the tapestries?"

"No," Hanner replied. "I'm not sure at all. I didn't see a good way to avoid it, though — I didn't have a set of lies ready, and I've never been good at making them up on the spot."

"I know," she said. "It's not in your nature to lie. But tonight I almost wish it was."

Hanner did not know what to say to that, and instead said, "Can you find another place for Pirra? I need to go find Zallin, and drag him to Vond's door."

"He's probably passed out drunk."

"That would make the dragging a little more difficult, yes."

Rudhira grimaced. "Go ahead, then. I'll take care of this Pirra. Maybe she can demonstrate the tapestry for the emperor."

"That might be useful," Hanner said. "If she's willing."

"I'll ask her."

"Thank you, Rudhira," Hanner said, as he hurried past her and headed for the stairs. "I don't know what I would do without you!"

Chapter Twenty-Eight

Kirris crouched in the closet, alone in the dark, trying to stop trembling. She was terrified. This was not what was supposed to happen.

Vond had been fooled by her remembered dream, but only for a moment. He had figured out the truth with frightening speed. That did not fit Kirris' expectations; she had been given the impression that the emperor was a rather stupid man. He did not seem stupid now.

At least he had not guessed *all* the details. He had accepted the idea that he had been the target of the Spell of Invaded Dreams. That meant he had not assumed the magician responsible for his nightmare was nearby, since wizardry could work at great distances, and he had not gone looking for the perpetrator. If he had realized the dream came from a witch, he could have easily found Kirris — found her, and killed her.

Her first reaction had been to think that she had to get out, and get away, but then she had caught herself. If she was seen fleeing, that would be highly suspicious. Vond had no reason to suspect her presence, and if she stayed here, in the mansion, she could spy on him, and perhaps do some good.

Staying in the closet would be suspicious, too, of course. She had to slip out and find somewhere else — an empty bed, perhaps. Unfortunately, she could not get out as easily as she had gotten in; other people had been awakened by the racket when Vond awoke and smashed his way through the ceiling, and were standing outside the bedroom door, talking quietly. Getting past them unnoticed would be difficult; they would be alert, and her usual distraction spell would not be reliable.

Kirris listened as Vond talked to Hanner, and she read the emotions of the woman in Vond's bed — Leth, he had called her. Kirris could not hear Leth's thoughts through the closet wall, and through the haze of magical energy Vond was creating by levitating himself, but she could sense what the other woman was feeling. She was oddly calm. Part of that was sleepiness and the happy relaxation that followed hours of passion, but even so, she seemed surprisingly unsurprised. Maybe she had had previous experience with powerful warlocks.

Leth did not really matter, though, so far as Kirris was concerned; it was Vond who was the problem. He was talking to Hanner, and Hanner was answering his questions, and then Hanner was going off on some errand, and Vond had descended back into his bedchamber. He told Leth to get dressed and go, and Kirris could sense Leth debating, as she retrieved her tunic and skirt, whether or not to demand her money now. Vond was paying her no attention at all, but reassembling the ceiling he had smashed.

The ease with which he restored broken beams, torn fabric, and shattered plaster to its former undamaged state was frightening; Kirris did not remember any of the other warlocks she had known having that much power and control.

She could not stay in the closet; Vond might notice her as he checked for damage to repair. She quickly opened the closet and headed for the bedroom door. She had belatedly realized that the former warlocks would find nothing suspicious about her presence; to them, she would be one more house-guest curious about all the racket. She tried to project her customary don't-notice-me magic, but she knew her effort was shaky.

She stepped out into the lamp-lit corridor just as Leth emerged from Vond's chamber. Kirris met the other woman's gaze, and realized she had been so intent on not being seen by Vond or noticed by the other guests that she had done nothing at all to avoid Leth's attention.

There were a dozen other people standing in the hall or on the stairs, drawn by the shaking and noise, and several of them glanced at Kirris — her witchcraft was not effective in her agitated state. Others stared at Leth, in her red skirt and low-cut tunic, as she ambled toward the grand staircase.

Then Hanner came trotting down the stairs at the other end of the passage, a candle in his hand, and it didn't matter whether Kirris had been noticed or not, as the former chairman's presence distracted everyone. Kirris was able to reshape her spell, reinforcing it so that no one would see her unless they actively looked. As she did, several voices called out.

"Hanner!"

"Chairman!"

"My lord!"

"I'm sorry, I can't talk right now," Hanner said, as he hurried past and headed for the grand staircase down to the ground floor. He called back over his shoulder, "Don't bother the emperor! He was disturbed, and didn't appreciate it!"

Leth turned at the sound of Hanner's voice and stepped to one side, letting him pass; he paused as he did, and murmured something to her that Kirris did not catch.

She grimaced. She had still had her attention and her magic focused elsewhere. Still, she doubted whatever Hanner had said to the street-walker was important. Kirris watched Hanner go, and Leth follow him down the steps at a far more leisurely pace. The witch tried to decide what she should do next. The whole false-Calling scheme was obviously a complete failure. Vond had seen through it almost immediately. He was not going to be frightened out of using his magic as easily as Ithinia and the others had hoped. He was still dangerous, and still drawing power from those towers in Lumeth that Ithinia said were essential to the World's existence.

Kirris wondered whether it might have been possible to talk Vond out of using his magic by simply *telling* him how much was at risk, how much harm he would do if he damaged the towers. If it ever had been — and she had doubts about that — it probably was not possible any more, now that he had been antagonized by that dream.

Killing him would be the simplest solution. Ithinia could turn him to stone, or maybe Demerchan would remove him in some mysterious fashion. But Ithinia had hoped to avoid that, as she did not want to anger Lord Azrad, or risk open warfare with Vond, with the chance of massive damage to his surroundings.

And there was the chance that killing him might cause some sort of backlash, and damage the towers. Since the nature of his link to them was completely unknown, so were its effects. It seemed very unlikely that killing him would do any real harm to his power source, but they couldn't be completely sure.

In any case, *Kirris* wasn't going to kill him. She doubted she could. Witchcraft was too similar to warlockry to bypass his defenses undetected, and his magic was a hundred times more powerful than hers. He could easily block any direct attack she might make.

She couldn't kill him. She couldn't remove his ability to work magic. She couldn't fool him into giving it up.

There was that magical tapestry upstairs, leading into a world where warlockry could not reach; if she could trick him into touching the tapestry, and somehow block the return, that would render the Great Vond completely harmless — but how could she do that? Vond wasn't that stupid. If he had seen through the dream so quickly, he would know better than to go near the tapestry.

Maybe Ithinia or Teneria could think of a way to get Vond into that tapestry, but Kirris couldn't. Instead, she would stay in Warlock House for the night, since leaving at this hour would draw attention, and she would do nothing drastic. She would watch and see what Vond was up to, but in the morning, she thought, her best course of action would be to go back to Ithinia and report what had happened, and leave it up to the Guild, or the cult of Demerchan, or someone else, to decide what must be done. She had given the dream idea a good try, and it had failed; she had done her part and could now leave with her head held high and let others handle the problem.

She paused to take one final look at what Vond was doing behind the carved door of his bedchamber, but before she could bring her magic to bear that door opened again, and the emperor himself emerged, floating several inches off the ground and glowing eerily orange. Kirris wondered how a black robe could glow orange, but somehow it did.

The warlock paused, hovering at the top of the stair, and looked over the dozen or so people watching him. "My comrades," he said. "You *were* all Called, I take it? You shared that experience with me?"

Several of the observers exchanged uneasy glances. About half of them made low noises of agreement. Kirris said nothing, and kept her gaze fixed firmly on Vond.

"A wizard has just tried to frighten me with a lying dream," Vond announced, his voice unnaturally loud. "I believe the Wizards' Guild is trying to intimidate me, and I don't intend to allow it. I am about to go express my displeasure to their Guildmaster, Ithinia of the Isle, and to Lord Azrad, the overlord of this city. If you don't want to be involved, this would be a good time to leave and never come back — leave not just this house, but the city. If you want to stand with me, and support me in my defiance of the Guild, then stay — I may be able to use your help. And if you serve me well, I *do* know how to turn you back into warlocks — not using your old source, that's gone, but using the same source *I* have. Show me you're loyal, show me I can trust you, and you can join me as *new* warlocks, unfettered by any Calling. If not — go now, while you can."

"But the wizards *helped* us —" a woman standing by the stair rail began.

She was interrupted by a sudden movement as she was snatched upward, flung upward until her back pressed against the ceiling.

"They didn't help *me*," Vond roared. "If you think they care about you, then go to them. They just tried to scare me out of using my magic! They're *afraid* of me, and I'm going to show them they have good reason to be."

Kirris heard a door slam open somewhere downstairs, and Vond rose from the landing until he was face to face with his terrified captive.

"Are you with me?" he demanded. "Or are you with *them*? This is the confrontation between wizards and warlocks we've all been expecting ever since the Night of Madness, and it's time for you to choose sides. Choose *now*, woman!"

"I don't...I don't want any trouble!" the woman said, trembling.

"Then you're in the wrong place!" Vond bellowed, and his prisoner suddenly plummeted down the stairwell, swooping out of Kirris' line of sight — not falling, though, but flying, and Kirris did not hear a thump or crash, only a scream that faded with distance.

Then the door she had heard open a moment before slammed shut, cutting off the woman's cry of fear.

When the screaming stopped, Vond turned his attention to the others. "Choose now," he said. "Anyone who is still in this house when I get back is *mine*. Loyalty will be rewarded, and disobedience — well, I don't have time to be bothered with pleas and forgiveness and second chances, or enforcing a lot of different rules and handing out different punishments. It's going to be absolutely simple: Disobey me, and you'll die."

"You can really make us warlocks again?" a man asked.

"Yes," Vond said. "Yes, I can. I've done it once."

Kirris watched as some of the others looked about nervously. They obviously wanted proof that Vond could do what he claimed, but no one dared ask for it. She wondered whether he really *had* already done it once, and if so, to whom? Where was this other new warlock? She was sure several other people were thinking exactly the same questions, but no one had the nerve to speak them aloud.

And if it was true, if he really *could* create more warlocks, would he?

If he did, if there were a *hundred* warlocks drawing on the power of whatever it was in Lumeth that gave him his magic, what would that do to the towers that Ithinia had been worried about? Quite aside from that, how much damage would they do? If two of them fought, with no Calling to limit them, they could lay waste to an entire city. If the stories about Vond were true, if he really had once bent the edge of the World, a hundred such warlocks could destroy *everything*.

Kirris could not allow that. She had been thinking her part in this was done, but now she knew she had more to do. She could not defeat Vond, but perhaps she could prevent the creation of more warlocks.

"You think about it," Vond said. "You think about it, and decide — are you with me, or not? You have until I get back." Then he dropped away from the ceiling, and like his victim of a moment before, swooped down the stairs and out of sight.

For a moment there was only stunned silence, but then the people in the corridor began to mutter to one another. Several of them cast worried glances down the stairs.

"I don't trust him," Kirris said, reversing her spell so that instead of going unnoticed, she would be the center of attention. "You heard how power-mad he is; do you really think he'd ever let any of us share in that? He's never going to make any of us warlocks again. I don't think he even *can*. He'll just lead us on with promises, use us as slaves, and probably get us all killed. I mean, yes, he's powerful, but he wants to fight the entire Wizards' Guild! That's *insane*! I say we should all get out of here while we still can."

"She's right," a young man said.

"But I want my magic back!" someone protested.

"He's not going to give it to you!" Kirris insisted, using her magic to make her words more persuasive. "If he really did make someone else into this new kind of warlock, where *is* he? Why not *show* us? It's all lies. He's trying to trick us; he can't do it."

Several voices spoke at once. "I don't know…"

"What if he…"

"Maybe we should…"

But then they all fell silent, and every eye turned to stare at the stairs as Vond reappeared, rising up from below, his robe flapping in a nonexistent wind.

"Oh, I can do it," he said, his gaze fixed on Kirris. "My former apprentice lived in Semma, in the Small Kingdoms; I transformed him fifteen years ago. He wasn't Called."

"Why should we believe you?" Kirris demanded, her heart pounding as she tried to hide her fear. "Where is this apprentice now?"

"I don't know where he is," Vond said. "I was Called, just like the rest of you, remember? I don't know what happened to everyone I knew before."

"But why haven't we heard of him? A powerful warlock in the Small Kingdoms — wouldn't we have heard?"

"Do you hear about every strong warlock? I don't think so," Vond replied.

"But in the Small Kingdoms? Warlocks are scarce there. The Wizards' Guild doesn't even *allow* warlocks in some of them!"

Vond cocked his head. "How did you know that?" he asked. "When were you Called? If it was after the ban, why are you here? Didn't you have anywhere else to go?"

Kirris felt sweat break out on her forehead. "I…I was talking to someone…"

"No," Vond said. "You're lying. Your heart's pounding, and you're sweating."

"I'm not lying. I'm terrified!" Kirris said. "Of *you!*"

"I suppose you… Wait."

Kirris felt her skin crawl, though she did not know why. "Wait for what?"

"*You* aren't a warlock," Vond said accusingly. "You never were. You don't have the thing in your head."

"I don't know what you're talking about —"

"You're a *witch!*" Vond said. "What's a witch doing here?"

"I… Some witches were Called on the Night of Madness, you know that," she said desperately.

"You were *never* a warlock," Vond said. "Did you think we can't tell? How could we ever make apprentices if we couldn't tell the difference? You weren't a warlock!"

"All right, I wasn't," Kirris admitted, "but I heard... I didn't have anywhere else to go, and I heard about this house, and —"

Vond shook his head, and Kirris felt her spells stripped away, wiped from her by Vond's own magic, like a cloth wiping away dust. "You're a witch, a *strong* witch, and you've been using a *lot* of magic, I can feel it. I can't tell what you did with it, but I can see that you've been using energy, and that your muscles haven't been working hard, so you've been working magic. You've been *spying* on us, haven't you?"

"I wasn't... I don't..." Kirris was suddenly shoved back against the wall, pressed flat against the wallpaper, arms spread, palms out, head up.

"Or maybe...maybe you did *more* than watch," Vond said. "Maybe *you* sent that dream. Maybe it wasn't the wizards at all."

Kirris tried to turn her head, to see what the others in the corridor were doing, but she could not move. Her eyes were fixed on Vond's face, whether she wanted them to be or not. "I don't know what you're talking about," she said.

"Why did you do it?" Vond asked. "Is the Sisterhood trying to make me stop using magic? Did someone hire you?"

"I didn't," Kirris said.

"You wouldn't have done it by yourself," Vond said. "I don't know you; you'd have no reason to do that to me. You must be here representing *somebody*."

"I didn't mean any harm," Kirris said.

The invisible force holding her against the wall suddenly pressed harder; she felt plaster crack under her shoulder blades, and something broke in her left hand, sending shooting pain up her arm. "Any *harm*?" Vond bellowed. "You sent me a nightmare! You sent me the *Call*!"

"I didn't want to," Kirris said. She was beginning to have trouble breathing. "I tried to help."

"Help *who*? Not *me*, certainly! Who were you helping? Who sent you?"

"No one!"

"You know you're going to die if you don't tell me the truth, don't you?" Vond told her. "Was it the Sisterhood? I never thought they had any problem with warlocks, but you're a witch, so perhaps I just missed it."

"It... Not the Sisterhood," Kirris said, struggling for breath.

"Then why a witch? Why did they send *you*, whoever they are?"

"I knew what the Calling felt like," Kirris admitted. "I shared minds with a Called warlock, long ago."

Vond's eyes widened. "Did you? No *wonder* it felt so real! But who sent you? The overlord? Or..." His eyes widened further as a thought struck him. "Was it Sterren?"

"Who?"

Vond's eyes narrowed again. "Not Sterren," he said. "You aren't that good a liar, not with your magic blocked. It wasn't Sterren, then. Lord Azrad?"

"No." Vond's eyes seemed to be drilling into her head. Kirris knew that warlocks could not hear thoughts the way witches could, but they could see things, sense things inside the body, that let them tell truth from falsehood with considerable accuracy.

"Not the overlord. Who, then? A wizard would just use one of his own spells..."

Kirris tried not to react, not to give the warlock the slightest hint, but she knew she had failed. She saw his eyes widen again.

"A wizard?" he said. "Which one? Ithinia of the Isle?"

Kirris did not answer in words, but she did not need to. Vond could read the truth in her response to the name.

She felt her heart pounding, felt the sheen of sweat on her brow, felt the pain of her broken hand, the pressure on her back where she was shoved against and into the wall.

She felt her heart stop, and a sudden jolt of pain flash through her chest.

And then she felt nothing at all, ever again.

Chapter Twenty-Nine

Zallin was leaning heavily on Hanner's shoulder, but he was on his feet, not being dragged, as they emerged from the dim dining room into the brightly-lit entry hall. Hanner was focused on keeping his drunken companion moving, and if Zallin had not said, "Who's that?" Hanner might not have even noticed the woman standing by the front door, waiting for them.

Hanner turned to see who Zallin was talking about, and saw the red-skirted woman. "Oh," he said.

"I haven't been paid," she said, as Vond shouted something upstairs.

"I know," Hanner said, glancing up the stairs. "This really isn't a good time, though."

"I can see that," the streetwalker replied. "He sent a woman flying out the door a moment ago, and I can hear him yelling. Still, someone owes me five rounds."

"*Five* rounds?"

"That's what he promised me."

Hanner looked at Zallin, but the other man offered no comment. He was too busy staring down the woman's tunic. Hanner sighed. "What was your name?" he asked.

"Leth of Pawnbroker Lane."

"Leth. Yes. This is *really* not a good time. If you could come back tomorrow, I'll see to it you're paid."

She hesitated, glancing up the stairs, then said, "I'm not at all sure this place will still be standing tomorrow. He just announced that he's going to go tell the overlord and the Wizards' Guild that he's angry with them."

"He did?" Hanner looked up the stairs; Vond was shouting, but he could not make out the words.

"He said anyone who's still in this house when he gets back is his property."

Hanner closed his eyes for a moment, then opened them again. "Then you really don't want to be here, do you?" he said. "Listen, I *promise* you'll be paid, but this drunken idiot here is the one with the money, and he's in no condition to deal with it right now. If you won't come back here tomorrow, go to the overlord's palace and tell the guards on the bridge that you need to see Lady Alris — the Lady of the Household. Tell her that her brother Hanner owes you five rounds."

Leth stared at him. "The palace? And you think she'll *believe* me?"

"Yes," Hanner said. "I do. Tell her the whole story, if you need to. Now, I really need to get this man upstairs and talk to the emperor. Excuse me."

He turned away, and had scarcely gotten Zallin up the first step when he heard the front door close. A quick glance assured him that Leth was indeed gone.

He boosted Zallin up one more step, and then was suddenly slammed against the wall, Zallin beside him. The front door burst open again, and Vond came swooping down the stairs, his black robe flapping, a second dark figure trailing in his wake. He paused in mid-air when he spotted Hanner.

At least, Hanner thought, he was decently dressed this time, and not glowing.

"Ah, it's you!" Vond said. "You might want to know, it was a witch who sent me that dream." He gestured toward the thing following him, and with a shock Hanner realized it was a woman's body; the arms and head dangled limply. From her misshapen appearance Hanner concluded that she had been crushed, "She's dead," Vond said, unnecessarily. "I'm going to return her to the wizard who sent her."

Getting a look at her face, Hanner belatedly recognized the dead woman as one of that evening's arrivals, the one who had said she didn't trust the tapestry. He swallowed, and tried not to let his horror show. "How do you know who sent her?" he asked.

"She told me before she died," Vond said. "It was Ithinia of the Isle."

"Guildmaster Ithinia? She's the most powerful wizard in the city; why would she send a witch?"

"Because this witch had shared the Calling with a warlock," Vond replied. "So she came to share it with me, and now I'm going to share the results with Ithinia."

"Your Majesty, do you —"

"I don't intend to discuss it with you," Vond interrupted. "She may be the most powerful wizard in the city, but I'm the most powerful warlock who ever lived. I am going to explain to her that she should not antagonize me."

"Of course, your Majesty," Hanner said, managing as much of a bow as he could without letting Zallin fall.

"And I'm claiming this house as my own, Hanner. You can stay on as one of my retainers, or not, as you please. If you decide to leave, though, I'll want you to show me this magical tapestry of yours before you go."

"That woman Leth said something…"

"I've told everyone to choose sides. Anyone who stays in this house will be loyal to me, and me alone. I can be very good to those who help me. Those who defy me will die. Anyone who won't accept that had better be out of this house by the time I get back."

"I see," Hanner said. He glanced at Zallin, who seemed to have sobered up considerably listening to this. He also looked up the stairs, and saw several faces peering over the railing, Rudhira's among them. He was reassured to see that she was still alive and well.

"He stays," Vond said, pointing at Zallin. "I like him. I'm going to keep him."

Zallin's mouth fell open, and he made a dull, strangled noise.

"As your Majesty says," Hanner said quickly, to cover any other reaction Zallin might have made.

Then Vond flew out the open door, arcing up out of sight, the witch's corpse following a few feet behind. He did not bother to close the door after himself.

Hanner stared out the open door at the dark street for a moment, then turned to look at Zallin.

"Oh, Hanner," Zallin said. "I don't want this. What I saw when he was touring the city — I was hoping the *oushka* would let me forget. That woman..." He shuddered, and his shoulders heaved as if he was trying not to vomit.

"Did he kill anyone else when you were out?" Hanner asked.

"I don't...I don't think so," Zallin said. "But he hurt people. Threw them around. And he wants me to stay? What, as his *pet*?"

Hanner looked up the stairs. "Did he hurt anyone else up there?" he called.

There were murmurs he could not make out, and then Rudhira called down, "Not that we know of."

"Did he say exactly what he was planning to do?"

Rudhira glanced around at the others, then replied, "No."

Hanner bit his lip, looking up at Rudhira, then at the open door. He guided Zallin into a sitting position on the stairs, and released him. "I think I'd better go see what he's up to," Hanner called. Then he turned and trotted out the door. Unlike Vond, he did close it behind him, cutting off Rudhira's cry of protest.

Once outside the gate on High Street Hanner looked up and down the street, and although the street lamps and the lit windows of neighboring houses provided adequate light, he saw no sign of Vond. He remembered to look up, as well, but saw only clouds, with a few stars and the lesser moon peeping through gaps between them.

Vond had said he was going to confront Ithinia, who lived on Lower Street, a few blocks to the east. Hanner turned east, then rounded the corner onto Coronet Street to get the one block north to Lower. He hurried down the hill, wishing he could fly — this was almost the first time he had really missed his magic.

Coronet did not quite reach Lower Street; the corner was cut off by a short stretch of Merchant Street. Hanner turned right, then fifty yards later he turned right again, onto Lower. He looked down Lower Street — and then up.

Vond was there, hanging in the sky a hundred feet up, glowing brightly. A gargoyle was also hanging in the air, about halfway between the warlock and the street; it was not moving, and appeared to be bound somehow.

The few pedestrians who were out at this hour of the night had all stopped in their tracks to stare up at this apparition. Hanner did not stop; he broke into a run, east on Lower Street.

"*Ithinia!*" Vond roared, his voice magically amplified to the level of thunder. It rolled through the streets and echoed from the rooftops. "*I've brought back your witch!*"

Hanner did not see the witch's body anywhere at first, but as he hurried toward Ithinia's house he could make out a dark lump on her doorstep.

"*This gargoyle that was watching my house — that's yours too, isn't it?*"

The gargoyle suddenly plummeted to the ground, landing in the street with an earth-shaking thud. Hanner struggled to move faster as he ran down the street, though he really had no very clear idea what he intended to do when he got there.

"*You think this city is yours, and you can do what you please here?*" Vond bellowed. "*I say it's mine now. And I'm about to show you why!*"

With that, the warlock turned and flew away to the north.

Hanner slowed to a stop, baffled. What was Vond up to now? The warlock himself had vanished from Hanner's view, behind the rooftops, but the orange glow was still there — he had not gone very far. Hanner took a few more paces, to the corner of Center Avenue, and looked north down the slope, along the broad avenue, past Second Street and Short Street to the plaza at the end of the street, and to the overlord's palace on the north side of the plaza.

Vond was flying directly over the palace, rising higher and higher. Hanner felt a chill of foreboding.

For any citizen of Ethshar of the Spices, the palace was a symbol of the city's power, the heart of the government, the overlord's residence, but for Hanner it was also his childhood home. He had grown up in that place, behind those yellow marble walls. He had played in those stone corridors, dropped pebbles in the surrounding canals, run shouting across the red brick plaza.

And he had family in the palace. His sister Alris was in there, and according to Mavi, his daughter Hala. After seventeen years he didn't know who else might still be living there, but Alris and Hala — Hala who was now a grown woman, who he had last seen as a little girl, who he had not yet taken time to visit — were inside those walls, beneath that roof. Hanner watched in dread as Vond hung glowing in the sky above the familiar structure.

The warlock stopped rising, a mere glowing dot against the night sky, and although it was hard to be certain at such a distance, Hanner thought he looked down.

Then the ground shook, and Hanner heard the loudest sound of his life, an immense roar as the entire palace shivered, shook, then tore free of its surroundings and began to rise. The shattered remnants of the bridge that crossed the canal from the plaza to the palace door fell, rattling and splashing, as the palace ripped loose. The guards who had stood at the outer end of the bridge ran, arms over their heads, to escape the flying debris, and Hanner stared in open-mouthed horror as the entire palace ascended into the night sky — not merely the three stories above ground, but the huge underlying block of dark, rough stone that Hanner realized must contain the cellars.

The guards at the *inner* end of the demolished bridge were now perched on a narrow ledge, where they had flattened themselves against the tightly-closed doors to keep from falling to their deaths. Hanner could see that one had dropped his spear, while the other had not.

As the initial indescribable noise faded to the rumble of settling wreckage, Hanner registered that people were screaming all around him, and had been for several seconds; the roar of the palace tearing out of the ground had drowned them out.

He didn't blame them for screaming. He had never seen anything so frightening — not on the Night of Madness, nor any time since, not even when he first awoke in Aldagmor to see that inexplicable *thing* in the sky above him, and the other thing in the ground beneath. The very alienness of the Source and the Response had made them less terrifying than this horrible distortion of the World as he knew it.

He had known Vond was powerful. He had heard the stories about how Vond once bent the edge of the World itself, how he built a gigantic palace of his own overnight, magically cutting the walls from bedrock. Hanner had thought he comprehended what a powerful warlock could do; he had seen Rudhira, long ago, pull a literal *mountain* of water out of the city's harbor.

None of that had prepared him for this, and he stood frozen to the spot, staring with his mouth open, as the overlord's palace rose to a height of a few hundred feet, then moved majestically southward, across the plaza and over the mansions of the New City.

It did not come *directly* south, up Center Avenue, though; it was veering to the east, toward Arena Street. Hanner watched as it glided through the night sky, dark against the darkness, until it came to rest centered two blocks east and a hundred yards up from where he stood.

That put the western end perhaps a hundred feet east of his position — as he had been taught as a child, the palace measured eight hundred and four feet from one end of the southern facade to the other, and the blocks on Lower Street were scarcely three hundred feet. Hanner could look up and see the western windows.

He could see the terrified faces of servants and courtiers staring out those windows, looking down at him and the others in the streets below, and his heart clenched in his chest as he realized his sister and daughter might be among those at the windows. They probably had no idea what was happening, he realized; they could not possibly see Vond from where they were, and had probably not heard his shouting through the palace's thick stone walls.

Then a movement caught Hanner's eye, and he watched as Vond came swooping down around the palace, and descended to the street in front of Ithinia's house.

Hanner started forward again. He did not know what Vond had planned, or how Ithinia would react, but he knew them both, and he wanted to be there, to provide a voice of calm reason, a neutral voice, in the inevitable confrontation.

Only then did he notice that save for Vond, the gargoyle, and himself, the street below the palace was empty; the few pedestrians who had been on Lower Street had fled, eager to get out from beneath the palace. The gargoyle was back on its feet, and seemed unhurt by its fall and whatever else Vond had done to it, but it was backing away, clearly unwilling to confront the warlock as Vond floated toward Ithinia's door.

The body of the dead witch was still there, as well; Vond kicked it aside as he arrived on the wizard's front step. "Open up, wizard!" Vond bellowed, his voice still unnaturally loud, but well short of the thunderous volume he had used earlier.

Hanner was still half a block away when the door swung open, and a man's gentle voice said, "Would you care to come in, your Majesty?" Hanner clearly heard the thump as the man, presumably Ithinia's servant Obdur, was flung back against a wall to make way for the enraged warlock. Hanner watched Vond sail through the door into the warmly-lit interior.

"Wait!" he called, breaking into a desperate run. "Wait, I should be there, too!"

No one replied. Vond did not re-emerge. For a moment nothing changed, and Hanner heard nothing but his own panting, the pounding of his own feet, and distant shouting as the city reacted to the theft of the palace and its inhabitants. The oblong of lamplight that was Ithinia's open door drew nearer, and for a moment Hanner thought he was going to make it, that no one was going to close the door.

But then the door swung shut after all, and the latch fell into place with a distinct click.

Hanner slowed. He took a deep breath of the cold night air, letting its chill fill his lungs, and then looked up.

The palace was hanging above him; its vast dark mass blocked out the sky, and the glow of the streetlights did little to illuminate the gray stone of its underside. It was hovering motionlessly above the city — above the three blocks of Lower Street between Center Avenue and Arena Street. It was as unmoving as a ceiling, despite being supported by nothing more than a hundred yards of air and Vond's invisible, inexplicable magic.

If anything happened to Vond, the palace would fall. Everyone in it would die, including Alris, Hala, and the overlord. Everyone beneath it would be crushed.

If the Wizards' Guild had intended to kill Vond, it would seem they had missed their chance. Even an organization as ruthless as the Guild was rumored to be would not deliberately allow that thing to drop onto the city.

But surely, even Vond couldn't keep it up there forever. He would need to sleep eventually, wouldn't he? Warlockry could provide all the physical energy he would need, but even warlocks needed to sleep to stay sane.

Of course, Vond might not be particularly concerned with sanity. Hanner looked down at the pitiful remains of the dead witch, lying on the hard-packed dirt, limbs and clothing askew, cast aside by the Great Vond as beneath his notice.

He had never even learned her name, Hanner thought. This woman had died in his house, and he had no idea who she really was. She might have family, friends, perhaps an apprentice, expecting her to return home at any moment.

He looked up again at the palace, then at the surrounding houses, their windows a patchwork of lamplight and darkness. Ithinia's front windows were bright, while others varied. Hanner knew that Vond and

Ithinia were meeting behind those windows, probably exchanging ulti-matums. He had wanted to be in there with them, trying to keep them calm. If he knocked on the door, Obdur might let him in — but would his presence really help? He might just infuriate the others. He might say the wrong thing and bring the palace crashing down.

He looked at the surrounding houses again. There might be people sleeping in those houses, completely unaware of what was happening. Yes, uprooting the palace had been impossibly loud, and had shaken much of the city, but some people slept soundly, or might have dismissed it as thunder, or an earthquake, and gone back to sleep.

He should rouse them, Hanner thought, and get them clear. Or per-haps he should go to the Wizards' Quarter and see if magicians could get up to the palace and rescue the hundreds of people trapped in it. He could probably do more good that way, getting innocents out of harm's way, than by thrusting himself between the two sides in this magicians' quarrel.

He looked up and down the street to see if there was anyone he could recruit. No pedestrians were in sight; everyone had fled that looming impossibility overhead.

Everyone *human*, at any rate. That gargoyle was still there, crouched so motionlessly that Hanner had somehow briefly overlooked its pres-ence.

"*Hai!*" Hanner called. "Gargoyle! We need to get people out of here!"

The thing straightened and turned. "Do we?" it asked in its deep, rasping voice.

"Yes, we do." Hanner waved at the houses on the south side of the street. "We need to make sure there's no one home! If that thing comes down, we want to keep the carnage to a minimum."

The gargoyle craned its neck back with a hideous grinding sound and looked up at the palace.

"I will inform my mistress' household," it said.

"If you can get word to any wizards, can you ask about getting people down from the palace? With flying carpets, or levitation spells?"

It nodded slowly.

"Good!" Hanner said. "You do that, and I'll start knocking on doors."

The gargoyle spread great stone wings, and took to the air.

Hanner spared only a second to watch it before he turned and ran toward the door of the house across the street from Ithinia's.

Chapter Thirty

Vond's arrival was not a surprise. Ithinia had been in her garden, watching the overlord's palace move into position over her house, and when it stopped, she knew what was coming next. The warlock had made his announcement, and now he would want to deliver his terms. She did not hurry, but turned and went back inside.

She found Obdur waiting in the hallway and told him, "We're expecting company. When the warlock arrives, I will see him in the parlor. Address him as befits an emperor — there's no need to antagonize him over trifles."

"Yes, mistress," Obdur said with a bow. He turned and headed toward the front of the house.

Ithinia made her way to the parlor, picking up a few small items on the way. The other magicians who had attended her little gathering had all gone about their own business afterward, but she thought it was likely some of them might want to talk to her when they saw the flying palace, and she did not think Vond would look kindly on any interruptions, so she drew a quick rune of warning and invoked a simple protective spell of her own invention. She had never bothered to name it, since she had never shown it to anyone else; maybe, she thought, she should pass it on to one of her former apprentices. Call it Ithinia's Distraction, perhaps — she did not yet have her name officially attached to any spells, but it might be time to forgo false modesty and change that. Whatever one called it, it would divert visitors, cause them to make wrong turns, or be unable to open doors, or find other things to do; only the most determined would be able to reach her while the spell was in effect.

Of course, the warlock was very determined indeed. Ithinia heard Vond shout, "Open up, wizard!" as she stepped into the parlor. She tried to remember the etiquette for addressing royalty — she had learned it long ago in Tintallion, but Ethshar did not bother with such formalities. She could not sit until he did, or until he invited her to, and she must never turn her back on him — was there anything else?"

She heard Obdur open the front door and invite Vond in, heard the warlock shove Obdur against the wall, and then he was there, floating into her home about six inches off the floor.

"Your Imperial Majesty," she said with a bow.

"Wizard," he said.

"May I ask what brings you here? You referred to a witch?"

"You sent a witch to invade my mind," Vond said. "You sent her to shove her memories of the Calling into my head while I slept."

Ithinia considered denying it, but decided against it for two reasons — first, both she and Vond knew the charge was true, so that acknowledging it would let them get down to business more quickly, and second, it might also throw Vond off balance a little — he would probably *expect* her to deny it.

"I suggested it, yes," Ithinia said. "I take it poor Kirris failed to convince your Majesty that you still need to fear a Call?"

"I know better than that," the warlock replied. "It disturbed my sleep, though, and that cost the witch her life. I hope you're proud of that."

Ithinia thought that if anyone deserved blame for Kirris' death it was the man who killed her, but she knew better than to argue the point. "I very much regret you found it necessary to kill her, your Majesty."

"I'm sure you do." He did not quite sneer, but it was close.

"May I ask why you're here?" Ithinia said. "Since we both now see that the idea of a fraudulent Calling was a mistake, I can assure you I won't encourage any further such attempts."

"I want to know why you encouraged *that* one! I haven't done anything to you or the other wizards, Guildmaster; why are you persecuting me? You and Chairman Hanner made a truce between wizards and warlocks back in 5202; why are you breaking it?"

Ithinia marveled that he would think a pact between two entire schools of magic was relevant here. "I'm sure you will admit, your Majesty, that the situation is rather different now. Our agreement with Chairman Hanner was based on the understanding that warlocks would police themselves, and that any warlock who broke the law would be held accountable by his fellow warlocks. You *have* no fellow warlocks, your Majesty. You have no Calling to worry you. You have no check on your power at all. We merely hoped to create one, to discourage you from using your magic too freely and endangering innocents."

Vond glared at her. "Didn't work out very well, did it?"

"No, it didn't. Still, your Majesty, had we truly meant you ill, we might have killed you in your sleep, rather than just sending an unpleasant dream."

"You might have *tried*," Vond retorted.

Ithinia sighed. "Really, your Majesty — do you think you're completely indestructible? We have undetectable poisons, we have subtle potions, we have a thousand ways to get at you. There are spells that are quite effective against warlocks. We turned Chairman Hanner's uncle to stone, after all. If we had really wanted you dead, you would be."

If Vond was shaken by this, he did not show it. "So you didn't try to kill me — yet. Maybe you thought you could turn me into your puppet, instead, and now that that hasn't worked, maybe you *would* try to kill me — except that now you don't dare. You've seen where the overlord's palace is, haven't you?"

"Yes," Ithinia admitted.

"Well, I'm the only thing holding it up there. I can hold it there forever — regardless of which source we use, we Calling-level warlocks don't tire. But if I die, ten thousand tons of stone will fall out of the sky onto this house. I don't even need to die, really — if you turn me into a frog, down it comes. If you do anything that breaks my concentration badly enough, it falls. The overlord and his family will die, your neighbors will die — *you* might not, since I'm sure you have a dozen protective spells on this place, but I think the damage would be extensive enough to deter you."

"You're going to *keep* it up there? Indefinitely?"

"Unless you can convince me I don't need to, yes."

"But the overlord! The city's government!"

He smiled crookedly. "They will need to deal with a few inconveniences, won't they?" The smile vanished. "If you think you can find some way around this, some way to make it so it won't matter if I drop the palace, I suggest you reconsider, because I can pick up something much larger than the palace if I need to. I can lift the entire *city*, and leave it hanging over the Gulf of the East — or I can lift a piece of the Gulf and hang it over the city, ready to crash down and drown you all."

"That won't be necessary, your Majesty."

"You're acknowledging my authority, then? You'll accept me as the ruler of Ethshar?"

That caught Ithinia off guard, as few things had over the past century or two. "I don't...I'm not in a position to decide that."

"Aren't you?"

"I cannot speak for Lord Azrad, your Majesty."

"I didn't ask about Lord Azrad. I asked whether *you* acknowledged my authority."

Irritated, Ithinia said, "I acknowledge that you are in a position to dictate terms to me, your Majesty. Isn't that enough?"

Vond smiled unpleasantly. "Why, yes, I think it is."

"Then what do you want of me?"

"I want your oath that you will make no further attempt to harm me, to deceive me, or to interfere with my actions."

"I certainly won't try to hurt you while you're the only thing keeping the palace from crashing down!"

Vond laughed. "Of course not."

"Do you seriously intend to hold it up there forever?"

"Oh, probably not. It would get tiresome. I'm sure I'll want to take a nap now and then, and I don't know whether I can keep it steady in my sleep. That's why I want your oath. And before you start thinking about whether or not killing me in my sleep might be worth forswearing yourself, consider this — you don't really *know* that I'm the only warlock left, do you? I have dozens of other Called warlocks at my house on High Street, and can you be sure I haven't given any of them the ability to use the magic I do?"

Ithinia knew better than to say anything about *that*. She was fairly certain that Vond was not the sort who would be willing to share his power; he *liked* being the only one of his kind, she was sure. Saying that, though, was exactly the kind of thing that might prompt him to actually carry out the implied threat.

"If you're thinking you can handle one or two, remember there might be dozens, and they wouldn't all sleep at once. They would avenge me — not because they love me so much, but so no one would do the same to *them*. You'll never catch *all* of us asleep."

"I understand," Ithinia said. She understood that Vond was bluffing — which meant he knew he was vulnerable. It was, she thought, a very good thing that warlockry was a purely physical magic, and that Vond could not hear her thoughts as a witch might. He could probably sense the signs that would mean an ordinary person was lying, but Ithinia was not an ordinary person; a few centuries of practice had given her the ability to lie so well that even witches could not always detect it.

"Then swear you won't try to harm me or deceive me."

Ithinia decided it was time to calm her foe. She put a hand on the hilt of her athame. "I swear by my life and my blade that I will not attempt to harm you, and that I will not again use magic to deceive you, nor advise others to do so."

Vond glared at her for a moment, then nodded. "That will do. I'm tempted to demand that you swear loyalty to me, but I suppose that would conflict with some Guild oath you've taken."

"Yes, it would," Ithinia answered. It might even be true, she thought.

"Then I'll do without it." He turned to go. "You might want to warn the other magicians not to get in my way," he called back over his shoulder.

"Your Majesty?" Ithinia said.

He paused. "What?"

"May I ask what your plans are? What is it you intend to *do* with your power?"

Vond seemed puzzled by the question. "Whatever I please," he said.

"Yes, but what pleases you?"

Again, he seemed confused. "Good food. Beautiful women. Sunny days. A comfortable home. The same things that please anyone."

"So you have no plans to usurp the overlord's position?"

Vond waved a hand dismissively. "I can't be bothered to run a government. I tried that in Semma — it's tiresome. I will happily let others deal with the necessity of keeping order, so long as they do so in a way that pleases me and does not interfere with my own actions."

"You have no schemes for expanding your existing empire to include Ethshar?"

He snorted. "Wizard, the entire World is *already* mine — it's just that some people don't realize it yet." He turned again.

This time Ithinia let him go. She did not send Obdur to see him out; she did not want to risk Vond killing her servant simply because he was there.

She waited for the sound of the front door closing, but it didn't come. After a moment she went to look, and found that Vond had left the door standing open, allowing the cold air of a winter's night to pour in.

"Inconsiderate fool," Ithinia muttered, as she shut the door. A moment later, though, she opened it again and stepped out.

The street was empty, but she heard voices. She looked around. Her gargoyles were fluttering clumsily about the neighbors' rooftops, calling to one another, and she realized they were guiding people out through the courtyards and alleys between Lower and High Street, out from under the hovering palace. She could hear human voices in the distance, as well, shouting instructions.

And the air above the houses was full of flying carpets, and those newfangled flying carriages that had come into fashion a few years ago, and levitating wizards, fetching people and papers down from the palace. Clearly, several people had not waited for her to take the lead in dealing with the situation.

That was good. It was a relief to see people showing some initiative — but at the same time, she fervently hoped they were being careful about it. Vond could be irrationally touchy; he might take almost anything as a personal affront.

She had sworn not to harm him, so she would not, but she certainly wasn't going to stop anyone else from harming him. She wondered whether the Cult of Demerchan had decided yet whether they would kill him.

If they *did* kill him, someone had better be ready to bring that palace down safely, and she only knew one spell she would trust to do the job — the structure was too big for the usual restoratives and stasis spells. She glanced around, looking for the orange glow of the greater moon

— Varrin's Greater Propulsion could only be completed when both moons were full, and while the lesser moon ran through its cycle in less than a day, the greater moon would only be in the correct phase once a month. She hoped that Demerchan would not be hasty, as she thought the necessary occasion was still a sixnight or so away.

She would also need seven pure white stones, iron that had fallen from the sky, a peacock plume, a thick black candle, a blue glass bottle, a dagger carved from rock crystal and sharpened with a feather, and of course several pounds of seawater-scented incense, with a silver censer to burn it in. Her set of stones was in her workshop drawer, and there was a suitable bottle holding a few flowers in the southwest guest room, but she was not sure exactly where the other components were; she might need to buy or borrow some of them. She had a vague recollection of selling her crystal knife to one of her former apprentices a century or so back.

She wondered whether the overlord might want to keep his palace airborne for awhile once this was all over. Flying castles, never common, had been considered quite prestigious during the Great War. That assumed, of course, that it would someday *be* all over, and that Lord Azrad, or at least one of his heirs, would survive that long.

At least Vond wasn't actively malevolent, just greedy and stupid — and at that, she didn't think he was as stupid as that silly thief Tabaea, who had declared herself an empress in Ethshar of the Sands a decade back.

Ithinia grimaced at the memory of how badly Telurinon and the others had handled the problems Tabaea created. She liked to think she would have done far better. But then she looked up at the overlord's palace, hanging in the air three hundred feet above her head, and decided she had nothing to brag about, either.

Chapter Thirty-One

Hanner tried to be modest, but he really thought he had been rather clever in telling the former warlocks who chose to leave Warlock House, rather than serve Vond, that they should claim to have fled homes on Lower Street, or in the surrounding neighborhood. The overlord had ordered the city guard to find space for all such refugees in the city's defenses — in the towers by the various gates, in the barracks in Camptown, or in the wall itself. There was no way for the guards to know who really lived in the threatened houses, and who had spent the last twenty years frozen in Aldagmor, so Hanner had passed the word among the Called to go to the guards and claim to have been displaced from the houses beneath the palace.

Of course, that only applied to the Called who had been using the guest rooms; the ones who had vanished into the tapestry had stayed where they were. That other-worldly village was probably the safest place anyone could be, as far as any threat Vond might pose was concerned; his magic could not reach it at all, and Vond himself, Hanner assumed, would never dare set foot there.

Or at least so Hanner thought, as he wearily climbed the stairs. Vond could be unpredictable.

Hanner had finally done everything useful he could think of, and he was exhausted, eager to get some sleep. He had worked the night through, directing the evacuation of Lower Street, helping get people and possessions safely down from the palace, and making sure that all his guests in Warlock House understood the situation and knew they were volunteering themselves for Vond's service if they stayed.

About three-fourths of them had left, but a dozen or so seemed to like the idea of becoming underlings to the apparent ruler of the World. Hanner had told them he didn't think Vond would ever carry through on making anyone else back into a warlock, but some of them didn't believe him, and others didn't seem to care — they preferred the security of Vond's service to the uncertainty of the streets.

Hanner was almost to the second floor, lifting a foot toward the landing, when the door of Vond's chamber opened and the warlock drifted out.

"Oh, *there* you are!" he said. "I've been waiting."

Hanner lowered his foot and blinked stupidly at Vond from the top step. "What?"

"You were going to show me that tapestry," Vond said impatiently. "You should have been back here hours ago!"

Hanner glanced back down the stairs, and along the corridor, hoping to find someone else who might distract the emperor, but no one else was in sight. "My apologies, your Majesty," he said. "I'm afraid I was so distracted by your…your demonstration that I completely forgot."

"Demonstration? Oh, you mean the overlord's palace?" Vond grinned happily. "Isn't it magnificent? I'm holding it up right now, and it's no more trouble than wearing a hat."

Hanner stared dumbly at the warlock, trying to comprehend what it would be like to possess that level of magical power.

"I told you to bring Zallin," Vond said, the grin vanishing.

"I…I did try to, but then I went out…"

Vond waved a hand. "Don't worry about it. I talked to him earlier. He claims to know nothing about your magical picture, but he agreed to serve as my aide."

"He…he never saw the tapestry, your Majesty. It was my own project, not anything the Council did."

"That's fine. Show me."

Hanner wanted nothing more than to fall into bed and sleep for a day or two, but he could think of no way to safely refuse the emperor. Perhaps if he were not so muddled by exhaustion, he thought, he might have managed to talk his way out of it, but as it was he simply said, "Yes, your Majesty. This way."

His legs did not want to carry him up the two additional flights, but he managed it, with Vond sailing happily along at his heels, until the two of them stood in the fourth-floor bedroom, looking at the tapestry.

"How does it work?" Vond asked. "Is there some ritual, or a magic word?"

For a moment Hanner considered lying, and luring the warlock into touching the tapestry. Then he could run up to the attic and do something to block the exit, trapping Vond in the other world, and putting an end to the threat he posed.

But if he did that, the palace would fall out of the sky and smash several blocks of the New City. People might die, and even if everyone had been safely evacuated, which Hanner did not believe to be the case, the property damage would be immense.

It might be worth it. It *might* be. But Hanner did not feel he had the right to decide that, and in his current bone-weary state he did not trust himself to make so important a choice. Perhaps later there would be a time when tricking Vond into the golden village would be a good idea, but right now — no.

"No," Hanner said. "The spell is active — if you touch it, you'll instantly be transported to the place in the picture. And if you do that, your

Majesty, the overlord's palace will fall, so please be very careful to stay well clear."

"Ah," Vond said. He nodded, and moved back a few inches. "So anyone can just step through into that place?"

"Yes, your Majesty. I've sent fifty or sixty people there."

Vond turned. "You mean they're in there *now*?"

Startled, Hanner stepped back, blinking. "Yes, of course, your Majesty. That's why it's here."

"And they can come back out whenever they want?"

"Ah…yes, your Majesty." Hanner did not see any reason to explain the existence and nature of the return tapestry.

"Here in *my house*?" Vond demanded.

Hanner swallowed his resentment at Vond's casual appropriation of the house Uncle Faran had built. "Yes, your Majesty."

Vond turned to stare at the tapestry. "If I tore this thing to shreds, would the people in there still be able to get out?"

"Yes, your Majesty — but no one else could get in. Please don't do that. The spell was very expensive."

"So *anyone* who gets into that pretty little world of yours can just reappear here in my home, whenever they want?"

"More or less, yes, your Majesty," Hanner answered wearily.

"Is there any other way to get there, other than touching this hanging?"

Hanner blinked. "I…I don't know, your Majesty. I don't think so."

"But you don't *know*?"

"No, your Majesty. I suppose some wizard might have made another tapestry just like this one, that would go to the same place."

"And if someone went through *that* tapestry, could they still come out *here*?"

"In this house? Yes, your Majesty."

Vond shook his head. "That won't do. People could just pop in here undetected?"

"Well, yes, I suppose so."

"I can't allow that," Vond said. "That's completely unacceptable. We need to get everyone out of there and seal it off somehow — destroy the tapestry, or get it out of the house."

"If it troubles you to have it here, we could move it to my sister Nerra's house, your Majesty," Hanner said. "Or simply roll it up and put it away; it won't work if it isn't spread flat."

"What would happen to the people inside, if we moved it or rolled it up?"

"Nothing, your Majesty."

"Could they still come out in *this* house, even if the tapestry was somewhere else, or not working at all?"

Hanner hesitated. He was unsure exactly where this was going, but he was becoming more and more certain that he did not want Vond to understand how the tapestries really worked. "That would depend, your Majesty," he said. "The magic involved is complicated."

"Depend on *what*?" the warlock demanded.

"Well, there is a second part to the spell, your Majesty, in *there*," Hanner said, pointing to the tapestry. "That determines where users return to our world."

"So if someone changed that, people could use this to come out *anywhere*?"

Hanner blinked again. He had not really thought about this himself. If someone brought other tapestries into the village, then his refuge could have more exits, coming out anywhere the tapestries depicted. "Yes, I suppose so," he said.

"That could be valuable," Vond said. "You could send armies right inside an enemy's walls. You could send spies into your enemy's home. I wonder why no one's done that? Or maybe they have, and we just don't know about it."

"I don't know, your Majesty," Hanner said.

"That could be useful," Vond said, stroking his chin thoughtfully. "But no, it's too dangerous. Is there some way to ensure that no one can get into this house through that magical village?"

"I don't know what wizardry can and can't do, your Majesty," Hanner said. "I'm not sure anyone does." He hesitated, then said, "Perhaps you should move elsewhere, if this concerns you so."

Vond waved the idea away. "No, no. This is Warlock House, and I am the last warlock. The symbolism is important. Besides, I mustn't look weak. I am staying here, and that tapestry cannot be allowed to remain as it is. The spell as it is now, the way you bought it — can it be changed so that no one can emerge in this house?"

"I don't know," Hanner said, hoping that Vond would not notice any of the physical indications that this was his first outright lie. Up until now he had managed with misleading answers and half-truths, but he knew perfectly well that the return tapestry could easily be blocked or even destroyed.

"But right now, there are fifty or sixty people in there who could walk back out into this house at any moment?"

"Yes, your Majesty."

"If we got them all out, and then rolled this tapestry of yours up, would there be any way anyone *else* could use this village as a path into my home?"

"Not with any magic *I* know, your Majesty," Hanner said.

"Then I want you to get in there and get them all out, Hanner."

"I'm sure that we —"

"*Now.*"

"What?"

Vond pointed at the tapestry. "I want you to go through that thing *right now*, and get all those people out of there. I will not tolerate having them in my house, in a place I cannot go."

"But your Majesty, I don't —"

"*Now.*"

"Of course, your Majesty," Hanner said, taking a step toward the tapestry, "but you understand, it may take awhile. I don't know how big that...that place is; I was only in there very briefly. They may have spread out. There may be hiding places."

"*Get in there and get them out!*"

Hanner bowed. "Yes, your Majesty!" He turned, took a deep breath, and stepped through the tapestry.

Warlock House vanished, and he was standing on a grassy slope, looking down at the golden village. The air was sweet with the scent of flowers and the sea, and he heard happy voices somewhere in the distance.

Then someone exclaimed, "By all the gods and the stars! It's *Hanner*!"

Hanner turned to look back the way he had just come, but instead of the tapestry and the dusty bedroom he saw half a dozen people sitting cross-legged in a circle on the grass, surrounded by half-finished baskets and crude tools. They were all wearing either worn nightclothes or warlock black, but most appeared to have washed out the worst of the grime they had accumulated on the journey back from Aldagmor.

They were staring at him. He recognized them as people he had sent through the tapestry, but could not remember any of their names. He was not sure he had ever learned any.

"Hanner the Generous!" a woman said.

"Welcome to the Refuge, Hanner!"

"Go tell Rudhira." The woman who said that nudged the girl next to her, who sprang up and dashed past Hanner, down the slope toward the village.

"Rudhira's here?" Hanner asked, startled.

"She has been for hours," said the young man who had welcomed him. He got to his feet, brushing bits of something from his tunic.

"Maybe days," called the woman who had sent the girl running.

The young man grinned. "Maybe days," he agreed. "We can't tell time here."

Hanner blinked, and looked up at the sky, and at the sun that hung there.

"It doesn't move," the woman said, following his gaze. "At all. It's always exactly where it is now."

"There's no night," an older man said.

"At least, there hasn't been one yet," the young man said. "How long have we been here?"

Hanner tried to think. So much had happened, and he had been so busy and gotten so little sleep...

"A day or two," he said. "I think."

The others exchanged glances. "That sounds about right," the older man said.

"I thought it was more," another man said.

"Time may not pass at the same rate here," an older woman suggested.

"It doesn't matter," the young man said. "Hanner, why are you here? *You* don't need somewhere to stay, do you?"

"Vond sent me," Hanner said. "It wasn't *my* idea. I just wanted to get some sleep."

A woman laughed. "Well, you can sleep here," she said.

Hanner started to protest, to say that he couldn't spare the time, that Vond was in a hurry, but then he stopped. Why should he care what Vond wanted? He was in the one place he knew of where Vond was absolutely powerless to harm him, and he could stay here as long as he chose. He had told Vond it might take awhile to evict his guests; why should he rush?

"That sounds wonderful," he said. "Where should I go?"

This time all of the other smiled, and two or three laughed. "Wherever you want," the woman said. "Right here on the grass, if you like, or in one of the houses."

"We don't think we need to worry much about shelter," the young man told him. "The sun hasn't moved, the temperature hasn't changed, and we haven't seen a cloud since we got here. The breeze does rise and fall a little, but not enough to matter."

"Oh," Hanner said. He started to say something else, but then a familiar voice knocked the words out of his head.

"Hanner!" Rudhira called. She was trotting up the slope from the village.

"Rudhira!" Hanner called back, smiling broadly. "I didn't know you had come here."

"I thought it was the best way to stay out of Vond's path," Rudhira said. "I had put Pirra in the room across the hall, and I didn't see any reason *not* to come here and get warm. It's lovely here, isn't it?"

Hanner looked around again, and admitted, "Yes, it is."

He had designed it to be, of course, when he commissioned the tapestry. He had expected to spend the rest of his life here, and had tried to ensure that it would be as pleasant as possible — though Arvagan had warned him that wizardry had no guarantees.

"We've been working on fishing nets," Rudhira said. "And we've been planting seeds from the fruit you sent, and those trees over there — I don't know what kind of nuts those are, but they taste good and haven't made anyone sick yet."

"The water is good?"

"Oh, the water is lovely! Cool and clean. We could use more pitchers, though, if you're planning to send more supplies."

Hanner remembered why he was there. He shook his head. "There won't be any more supplies," he said. "Vond wants us all out of here."

That triggered a storm of protests. "What business is it of his?"

"Why does he care?"

"Why should we care what *he* wants?"

Hanner raised his hands. "Please, please!" he said. "I'll explain it all. But…but I need to rest a little, first. I was up all night. Let me take a little nap, and then I'll tell you all about it."

Rudhira and the basket-makers exchanged glances, and then Rudhira and two of the others hurried to escort Hanner.

"This way," Rudhira said. "There's a bed waiting."

She led him to the village, and into one of the houses, where a pile of old clothes had been made up into a crude bed. Hanner sank down onto it gratefully. He lay back and closed his eyes.

"Are we really going to wait until he wakes up to find out what's happening?" someone whispered; Hanner barely heard it. The speaker probably thought he was already asleep, Hanner told himself.

"We don't have to," someone else replied. "We can go look for ourselves."

"Hush!" Rudhira said. "Let him sleep!"

Then they left him alone, and Hanner was finally able to drift into deep, peaceful slumber.

Chapter Thirty-Two

Edara of Silk Street crept down the attic stairs as stealthily as she could, but she knew she was no spy or thief, no expert at moving silently. She expected at any moment to find herself facing a guard of some sort, or even worse, Vond himself. She opened the door at the foot of the steps and crept out into the fourth-floor corridor.

No one was there. Sunlight spilled in from the window above the stairs at the southern end of the hall; she was slightly surprised to realize that it was early morning here. She hesitated, then hurried across and peeked in the door of a bedroom on the other side of the hall.

The tapestry was still there, hanging undisturbed and unguarded. She was tempted to go touch it, and pop back into what the inhabitants were calling Hanner's Refuge, but she steeled her nerve and closed the door again. She took a deep breath, told herself that no one had any reason to hurt her, and started cautiously down the stairs.

The third floor was as deserted as the fourth, and that didn't seem right. Where Hanner had kept the fourth floor vacant, there had been people staying in the rooms on this floor. Had they all gone out for the day? If so, where? The whole reason they were here in the first place was that they didn't have anywhere to go!

Maybe they had all gathered downstairs for some reason. She frowned, and started down the next flight.

On the second floor she once again saw nobody, but now she could hear voices from below, so she knew the house was not entirely abandoned. She leaned over the rail to listen.

"…need some trustworthy men," a man's voice was saying. "I can't be *everywhere*."

"If you let us use your magic, *we* could do it," someone replied.

"You have not yet convinced me you are *that* trustworthy, Zallin. If I let you use the remaining source, you will instantly be as powerful as you were before the Aldagmor source departed, and that might make you strong enough to defy me."

"Your Majesty, I was never Called! I would be well below your own astonishing level."

"A little practice would take care of that, wouldn't it? Your turn will come, Zallin, I promise you that, but only when I *know* I can trust you. It's been less than a sixnight; give me a month or two to get to know you."

"A month or two?"

"Is that so very long? You have your whole life ahead of you! You served at least three years as an apprentice, didn't you?"

"But I was given my magic on the third day!"

"Have I *known* you for three days?"

"Well…almost."

"At any rate, I'm not looking for more warlocks. I want some men who can fight *without* magic."

"Why?" This was a new voice, one Edara did not recognize at all.

"Because there may be times and places I can't use my magic! You know the wizards are trying to stop us from resuming our rightful place in the World; what if they find a way to block my source of magic? What if they destroy it outright?"

"If they destroy it, then we're all done," a fourth voice said. "That's the end of it, and we can all go back to being nobody."

"I won't!" Zallin protested. "I don't care *what* the wizards want — I'm a warlock!"

"You don't have any magic," the third voice said.

"Nonetheless, I *am* a warlock!"

"You're a fool," someone muttered — Edara could just barely make out the mumbled words, and could not be sure whether this was a new voice, or one she had already heard.

"Your Majesty," the fourth voice said, "if the wizards cut off your magic, then the palace falls out of the sky. They won't allow that. You're worrying needlessly."

Edara wondered what that meant, about a palace falling out of the sky.

"Wizards can be ruthless when they think it necessary," the first voice — Emperor Vond, Edara assumed — said. "Oh, I don't think they'll do it, I don't even know whether they actually *can*, but I want to be prepared. If I'm going to run things the way I want here in Ethshar, I'm going to need a staff, and I'm going to need guards. The overlord has his soldiers, Ithinia has her gargoyles, and *I* need some trustworthy men. Now, I know most of you were thrown into the future just the way I was, but you, Zallin, you were never in Aldagmor. You know people. You know how the city works. I want you to go out and hire those men for me."

"You want them to be loyal," Zallin said. "How can I guarantee that?"

"Well, for one thing, we're going to pay them very, very well," Vond said. "Money won't be a problem for us."

"How do I convince them of that?"

Vond gave a bark of laughter. "You're joking! Just show them what's hanging in the air over Lower Street."

Edara was puzzled; what was hanging there? She would have to go take a look, if she could figure out how to get out of the house undetected.

This whole discussion about Vond wanting to hire himself a small private army was interesting, but Edara could not see what it had to do with Hanner the Generous turning up in the Refuge in an advanced state of exhaustion, or with the absence of anyone in the upper stories of Warlock House.

"Why can't *we* do it?" the third voice asked.

"Do what?" Zallin said.

"Why can't we be your guards?"

"Because you were warlocks," Vond said. "What do *you* know about using a sword or a spear?"

No one spoke for a moment, then Vond clapped his hands and said, "Well, then! Zallin, go find some recruits — men who *do* know how to use swords — and fetch them back here. I'll want a couple of dozen, at the very least. As for the rest of you, you'll be my staff. I'll need a purser, and at least one secretary, and an envoy — maybe *several* envoys. Why don't you think it over? Discuss among yourselves, and when I come back down you can tell me who's chosen which role."

"Where are you going?" the fourth voice asked.

"Upstairs," Vond said. "I want to change my clothes — ah, Zallin, you might also see about finding a tailor or two, while you're at it! My wardrobe here is hopelessly inadequate."

"Yes, your Majesty," Zallin said sullenly.

"Off with you, then!"

Then Edara heard footsteps, and a moment later the front door slammed. She leaned over a little further, to peer down into the entryway, and found herself looking the Great Vond in the eye. She froze.

"*Hai*," the warlock said. "Who are *you*?"

Edara's mouth opened, but no sound came out. She closed it again.

"I won't hurt you," Vond said gently. "You're a former warlock, aren't you? I can see you are."

"Yes, my lord," she said, drawing back over the railing.

"It's 'your Majesty,'" Vond said. "Where did you come from? I thought I'd gone through the whole house."

Edara tried to think of some clever answer, some foolproof lie, but nothing came, and as Vond's eyes began to harden at how long she was taking to answer, she lost her nerve and blurted out the truth.

"I was in Hanner's Refuge, your Majesty!"

"Hanner's…you mean that magical tapestry thing?"

"Yes, my lo…your Majesty."

"And he chased you out, as I ordered?" Vond looked past her. "Where are the others?"

"No, he…I came back on my own, your Majesty. No one chased me out."

"Hanner didn't tell you I wanted everyone out of there?"

"No, your Majesty. I haven't seen Hanner since I touched the tapestry." She carefully didn't specify *which* tapestry.

"But I saw him step into it!"

"I…well, time is different in the other world, your Majesty. I didn't see him."

"Time is…Is it?" Vond's eyes lit up. "Really?"

"Yes, your Majesty. I was quite surprised to see that it was morning here; it was mid-afternoon in the Refuge." She didn't mention that it was *always* mid-afternoon there, if the term had any meaning, and if the direction she thought of as "west" was really west, and not east or south.

"How interesting! Why did you emerge, then, if Hanner had not yet informed you that I wanted you all evicted?"

"I…I just wanted to see what was happening, your Majesty."

Vond turned and called down to someone below, out of Edara's line of sight, "*That*, my friends, is why I want the place cleared out, and one reason I want some guards around here. This woman simply popped out of nowhere right here inside our stronghold, and we didn't know a thing about it! It's intolerable."

"I don't understand," Edara said. "What's going on?"

"What's going *on*," Vond said, "is that the lying scoundrel who calls herself the head of the Wizards' Guild in Ethshar of the Spices, Ithinia of the Isle, tried to trick me into abandoning my magic so that she could continue to play the power behind the throne here. In my own defense I had to make some changes, and that included claiming this house for my own, and removing all those guests Hanner had allowed to clutter up the place. A few have stayed on as my sworn supporters; the rest I sent away. Now, my dear, you have the same choice to make that all the others made — will you swear eternal loyalty to me and to the cause of restoring warlockry to a position of supreme power in Ethshar, or will you be cast out into the street to make your own way?"

Edara met Vond's eyes for a moment as she considered that. The emperor almost made it sound tempting, but she had no interest in swearing loyalty to *anyone*. Besides, she wanted to know what was happening in the rest of the city before making any irrevocable decisions. She could probably come back if she decided following Vond was her best option. "I…I guess I'll just go," she said.

"Fine!" Vond drew himself up to his full height — or rather more than his full height, actually, since he rose upward into the air of the stairwell. "Go, then!" He pointed toward the door.

Edara went. She wanted to find out what was hanging over Lower Street, and to see where Zallin was going, but most of all, she wanted to get away from this flying madman. Perhaps she could also stop in to talk to this Ithinia of the Isle, whoever she was.

She hurried down the stairs, dodging quickly around Vond's dangling boots, and then out the front door, across the dooryard and through the gate onto High Street. Then she stopped and looked around.

The gargoyle that had perched on the house across the street was gone; that was odd. The street was neither deserted nor crowded, but everyone in sight seemed to be in a hurry, trotting or running rather than walking. The one coach she saw was moving west at bone-rattling speed.

Lower Street, Vond had said. She rounded the corner onto Coronet Street and jogged quickly down the hill, then around the angle onto Merchant Street, which seemed a little more crowded than usual, and thence to Lower.

Then she stopped dead in her tracks and stared eastward, not believing what she saw.

There was a *palace* hanging in the sky. The top half of it was golden marble, like the overlord's palace, shining in the sun; the lower half was rough dark gray stone she did not recognize.

She took a few steps back, out onto Merchant Street, and looked down the hill toward the plaza. The street was still there, and the plaza was still there, crowded with people, but the part of the palace that should have been visible beyond the plaza was gone; there was a gap, and then in the distance a cluster of strange, crooked little buildings that she recognized as the Old City — which should have been hidden behind the overlord's palace.

She looked at the thing in the sky over Lower Street again, then down Merchant Street, then above Lower Street.

Yes, that *was* the overlord's palace up there. It had been ripped up out of the ground, taking thirty or forty feet of stone foundation with it.

Edara had been a warlock; she knew how the magic worked. Since waking up in Aldagmor she had heard plenty of stories about the Great Vond, supposedly the most powerful warlock who ever lived. She knew immediately who and what was holding that thing up. She just didn't know *why*. She lowered her gaze, thinking that there might be some indication on the street below.

Much of Lower Street was closed. A line of half a dozen guardsmen in the familiar red kilts and yellow tunics — at least *those* hadn't changed in her twenty-five year absence! — stretched across it three blocks east of where she stood, turning aside anyone who tried to enter the portion of the street beneath that hanging horror. They might not know anything beyond their orders, but on the other hand, there was no harm in asking. Edara trotted the three blocks quickly, then waited politely until one of the soldiers was standing quietly, not talking to anyone else.

"*Hai*," she said. "What's going on?" She pointed at the structure blocking out the sky.

"Warlock," the guard said. "Feuding with a wizard who lives up the street." He pointed a thumb toward a house on the north side of the street.

"Didn't the warlocks all lose their magic?"

The guard turned up an empty palm. "Most of them," he said. "Not this one."

"What did the wizard *do*?"

The empty hand came up again. "Don't know." He glanced up over his shoulder. "Whatever it was, I wish she hadn't. I have friends up there."

"Oh," Edara said, startled. "*Oh*. There are people in it?"

The soldier nodded. "Lots of them. They did get most of them down earlier this morning, with flying carpets and the like, but there are still at least a dozen guardsmen, and some other people, too. In fact, the wizard who started all this is up there, trying some spell to keep it from falling if the warlock drops it."

Well, Edara thought, so much for talking to Ithinia of the Isle. Edara had no way of getting up there; if Ithinia was in the floating palace, then they weren't going to have any discussions any time soon.

She might be able to find Zallin, though. He had been sent to recruit fighters, and in her day, twenty-five years ago, there had been two parts of the city where she would have gone if she was looking for hired swords. If she wanted simple thugs, men who would do anything for a round of silver, and she didn't care that some of them wouldn't be much smarter than the average rat, she would go to Westwark, or maybe a few blocks up into Crookwall.

If she wanted men who knew what to do with a weapon, and who could be trusted to handle something more complicated than a street brawl, she would go to the south side of Camptown, past Superstition Street, and on into Eastwark. That was where one could find retired guardsmen who might be bored of the quiet life and eager to enhance their pensions...

But no, that was what *she* would do. It wasn't what *Zallin* would do. He would want something faster and simpler. Her method would involve asking around, knocking on doors, talking to people — he wouldn't want to spend that much time and effort on it, not when Vond might be getting impatient. Zallin would go where recruiters always went to find gullible young idiots seeking adventure, or simply people with no resources who were looking for work — Shiphaven Market.

She thanked the guard, then turned and headed west along Lower Street, across Merchant Street into the Old Merchants' Quarter, but then stopped.

Zallin had spent his adult life as a warlock; he might be more familiar with the notice-boards and recruiting at the Arena, up near the Wizards' Quarter, than with Shiphaven Market. He was also supposed to find a tailor, and Shiphaven wasn't the best place for that. Neither was Arena.

Edara realized she didn't need to find Zallin, in any case. Wherever he went to hire his guardsmen and tailor, he would be bringing them back to the house on High Street. She turned back, and headed back toward Warlock House.

Simply standing in the middle of High Street did not seem wise; she did not want to attract Vond's attention. Instead she walked up and down, trying to blend in with the normal traffic, but always turning back just before she got out of sight of the iron gate and white door.

The sun crept across the sky, as the one in Hanner's Refuge had not, and Edara's feet grew sore. She was tired, hungry, and thirsty, all sensations that were still not entirely familiar after her recently-ended years as a warlock. She wondered whether there was really any point in waiting, but she didn't know what else to do, or where else to go. She would happily have gone back through the tapestry into the refuge if she could have found a way to get safely into the house and up to the fourth floor, but she could not see how that might be accomplished.

At last she spotted Zallin marching up High Street from the west, with perhaps a score of men at his heels. She saw no sign of a tailor; these all looked very much like the fighters Vond had wanted. She hurried toward them, trying to think what she would say.

Nothing came; she stopped at the corner of the fence and gripped the iron railing, trying to come up with *something* to tell or ask Zallin.

He glanced at her as he led his troops through the gate, but showed no sign of recognition. He crossed the dooryard, then turned on the doorstep and announced, "Wait here, while I inform his Majesty of your arrival."

His followers stopped, about half in the dooryard, the other half still on the street outside the gate. Then Zallin turned, opened the door, and strode inside.

Edara studied the men, trying not to draw their attention. They were mostly young, and all looked reasonably strong and formidable. None of them had any visible weapons beyond the belt-knives that almost every Ethsharite carried, and Edara wondered about that; she had the distinct impression Vond had wanted swordsmen.

Then the front door opened again, and Zallin emerged. He stepped down into the dooryard as his men made way for him. Seconds later

Vond emerged, flying, as always. He rose up and hovered over the men, who stared up at him with varying degrees of surprise. He looked down appraisingly, then spoke.

"Welcome!" he said. "I trust Zallin had made clear why I am hiring you?"

"Not entirely," one of then men said.

"Your Majesty," another quickly added, with a bow.

"I intend you to be my honor guard," Vond proclaimed. "You will stand ready to defend me from any threat that I do not see, or any danger from which my magic cannot protect me. You will be treated with honor and respect. You will be housed here, in Warlock House, and fed at my table. You will be paid generously — has my aide Zallin named an amount?"

"Four rounds a day," someone called.

"Done! Excellent! And a bonus will be paid for every incident in which you serve me well. Now, I do not see any weapons — are you armed?"

Several of the men exchanged glances. "No," one replied.

"Zallin said you would provide weapons," another said.

"Then so I shall! Go inside, and let Zallin assign you your rooms, and see that you're fed; I will be back shortly with your arms and armor."

"Wait, your Majesty," Zallin protested. "Where are you going?"

Vond turned. "I am going to Camptown to get what these fine men need. Then you and I, Zallin, are going to direct my troops in evicting a bunch of trespassers from my home."

"Trespassers?"

"Yes, trespassers! Including that Hanner who used to own it. I told him to send out all the squatters he invited in, but have they emerged? No, they have not! Apparently I can't trust anyone else to handle this, so I will see to it myself."

"You mean the tapestry?"

"*Yes*, I mean the tapestry! I wonder whether Ithinia somehow arranged for Hanner to have it. However it got here, though, I can't have it in my home with all those people on the other side — Hanner tells me that they could emerge into my home at any time, and probably murder me in my sleep, if I don't do something about it. Certainly, that one woman popped out of nowhere, just as Hanner had predicted. Simply destroying the tapestry apparently won't solve the problem; I need to get all those people out first. So that's what we're going to do, and *then* I'll destroy the damned thing."

"I understand, your Majesty," Zallin said with a bow. "Then we'll await your return."

"Do that," Vond said. Then he shot upward, and vanished into the eastern sky.

Edara watched him go, then turned to see Zallin herding his new recruits into the house. She bit her lip, trying to think what she should do. She needed to warn Hanner and Rudhira and the others, but how could she get past all those men to get back to the tapestry? She could see no way to do it.

But maybe she could get a message to them, even if she couldn't get there herself. If she could find a wizard and talk him into doing a spell on credit, and if Hanner was still asleep, there might be a way. She turned east, as Vond had, but instead of flying she simply ran up High Street, headed for the Wizards' Quarter.

Chapter Thirty-Three

Hanner opened his eyes to see a completely unfamiliar ceiling overhead, and bright midday sun outside the room's only window. He blinked, and sat up. Only then did he remember where he was. He was in the refuge, the village beyond the tapestry, and Vond had sent him here to chase everyone out.

"Feeling better?" Rudhira asked.

His head snapped around. She was sitting quietly on the floor in one corner. "I didn't know you were here," he said.

"Where else would I be?" she asked. "You're in my bed."

"I am?" He looked down at the collection of rags that had served as his mattress, and realized they were all either nightclothes or warlock black.

"When I brought people new clothes, I took the old ones," Rudhira said. "Some of them might be wearable again, with a little care, but why bother? They're all thirty years out of style. So I brought them in here and used them as bedding."

Hanner nodded. "Sensible," he said.

"So why are you here? I didn't really expect you to come through the tapestry. In fact, I came here myself partly to get out of your way."

"Vond sent me," Hanner told her. "He wants everyone cleared out. He's claimed my house, and he doesn't like the idea of having dozens of people who could get into the attic without his knowledge."

"It would be easy enough to block the exit, wouldn't it?"

Hanner frowned at her. "It probably would, yes," he said, "but I wasn't about to tell *him* that! Then you'd all be trapped here."

"That wouldn't really be so dreadful," Rudhira said. "I mean, look around — it's pleasant here. Warm and sunny, and there are nuts and fish, and the water's good."

"Fine, but I wanted to make it *your* choice, not Vond's."

She smiled. "Generous as always," she said. The smile vanished. "I'll go tell everyone you're awake, and when you're ready you can come tell us all about it. We'll meet in the village square."

"There's a village square?"

"Well, there's an open area we *call* the village square, though I guess it's really more of an irregular hexagon. You'll see."

"Thank you. Could you please try to get *everyone*?"

"I'll try." With that she clambered to her feet, and ambled out of the room, leaving Hanner alone.

He watched her go, then yawned, stretched, and stood up. He ran his fingers through his hair, straightened his clothes, and otherwise did his best to make himself presentable and ready to face the day — or the next few hours; he supposed "day" wasn't really the right word in this place where the sun never moved.

He realized he was ravenously hungry, but he did not see any handy food, and decided he could wait a little longer. Poking around the place seemed rude; it was Rudhira's home, not his, even though in a way it was inside his own place.

He made his way out of the house, and found half a dozen people waiting for him. He recognized their faces, but could only put a name to one of them, Bardec of Cut Street. "Hello," he said.

"Hello, Lord Hanner," Bardec replied.

"I'm not a lord anymore," Hanner protested. "I had to give up my title when I became a warlock."

"Well, you aren't a warlock any more, are you?" Bardec said. "Seems to me you should get your title back."

"Maybe I will someday, but that's up to the overlord, and it hasn't happened yet. So it's just Hanner."

Bardec turned up a palm. "If you insist. Whoever you are, Rudhira and some of the others are out gathering everyone they can find, to hear what you have to tell us."

"Good," Hanner said. "How long will that take?"

"Who knows?" Bardec pointed at the sky. "They'll be back before the sun's moved an inch." He grinned.

Hanner was in no mood to grin back. "Vond must be getting impatient by now. We need to get started before he loses his temper."

One of the other men, who had been leaning against a wall, straightened up. "Correct me if I'm wrong, no-longer-a-lord Hanner, but isn't this the one place in Ethshar where the emperor can't hurt us?"

"Well, he can't touch us here directly, but he can make things difficult. We won't be able to bring in any more food or clothing, or tools."

The people exchanged glances. "That could be inconvenient," a woman admitted.

"We could manage," the man who had been leaning on the wall said.

"Could you?" Hanner said.

"Oh, I think so. We've already brought in copper and iron cook-pots, and there's clay to make pottery once we can build a kiln. Of course some of us have knives, so we can probably get by without any more tools. We have wood and reeds and grass — you must have seen the basket-makers when you first arrived."

"I did," Hanner admitted.

"They're up there as much to watch for new arrivals as to make baskets, but they *are* making baskets. We can make fish traps, too. We can manage."

"I hope you're right — and I must ask, whoever you are, if you're so eager for self-sufficiency, why didn't you settle on that land up near Aldagmor?"

"Out on the edge of the wilderness, with mizagars in the woods, and snow likely to fall any minute?" He shook his head. "It's warm and sunny here, and these houses were already built, and if there's anything dangerous around, we haven't seen it yet."

Hanner had to admit that the man had a point.

"Besides," Bardec said, "we're just a few steps from the city here, rather than dozens of leagues."

"When the magic is working and the emperor allows it," Hanner said.

"Why *wouldn't* he allow it?" Bardec asked.

"Well, that's what I came to tell you," Hanner said. "He wants everyone out of here."

As he said that another handful of people came around the corner of a neighboring house. "Who wants us out of here?" one of them asked.

"Emperor Vond," answered one of the women in the original group.

"Why?"

"I'll explain that when everyone's here," Hanner called.

"Rudhira said to gather in the square," someone said.

"Where is that?" Hanner asked.

Several fingers pointed, and several voices said, "Over there," or "That way."

Hanner walked in the direction indicated, and found the vaguely-hexagonal space that Rudhira had mentioned, a pleasant area surrounding a stretch of stream, shaded by four large trees and equipped with some boulders of suitable size and shape to serve as crude benches. Hanner settled on one of the rocks to wait, and chatted idly with some of the others, asking questions about the refuge.

There was, he learned, much more to it than the grassy slope and the village. There was a broad beach below the village, where a fairly calm sea extended to the horizon. At the top of the slope, on the far side of where the tapestry delivered new arrivals, there was a fair-sized meadow, and beyond that was a forest of unknown size — as yet, no one had ventured more than a mile or so into its interior. One boy had climbed the highest tree he could find, and reported that he could see mountains in the distance — two peaks for certain, and possibly a third. There were several groves of nut-bearing trees; as yet the only variety anyone had gathered in any quantity appeared to be walnuts of a tasty but unfamiliar sort, but people were optimistic about others that had been seen in passing.

As yet no fruit had been found, but there were trees in blossom that looked as if they would bear fruit in time. No one knew whether this place had any seasons, let alone which season it was at present, so they could only guess when that might happen.

The largest animal anyone had yet seen on land was something the size of a large cat or a small dog, with gray and black fur, that lived in the woods; none of the three people who had caught a glimpse of it could identify it as any known species.

There were various birds, but no one had yet managed to catch any, and there was some disagreement about just what varieties had been spotted.

The streams and the sea both held plenty of fish of various sizes, and half a dozen people thought they had seen something much bigger than any familiar fish break the surface of the sea a couple of hundred yards from shore, but all they could agree on was that it was big, smooth-skinned, and dark gray or black, moving very swiftly indeed.

In short, this refuge was not merely a village, as Hanner had thought, but an entire world in its own right, though probably much smaller than the World.

As yet, no one had done much serious exploration; no one saw any need to rush. They were still settling in, and the village was large enough to fit everyone comfortably. The supplies Hanner and Rudhira had sent had been divided up and stored away safely, so that they had plenty to eat for a few days, and the hope was that by the time the delivered food ran out, they would be producing their own, in the form of fish, nuts, and possibly game. Growing grain would take awhile, but that, too, might come in time.

Hanner had assumed when he allowed these people to use the tapestry that this place would be no more than a temporary shelter, but at least half the people he spoke to seemed to think they wanted to stay permanently. That made what he had come to do even more unpleasant, but it also changed what he intended to say.

More and more people arrived in the square as he talked, more than Hanner remembered actually sending through the tapestry; he wondered whether Rudhira or Zallin might have sent along more when he himself was otherwise occupied. Finally, though, Rudhira brought up the rear of a final group, then crossed to where Hanner sat and said, "I think that's everyone. There might be one or two out in the hills somewhere."

"Thank you," Hanner said. He stood, then climbed up to stand on the boulder and announced, "My friends! I have important news!"

The murmur of conversation died.

"The Great Vond, self-proclaimed emperor, has now proclaimed himself master of Warlock House," Hanner said. "He wants no one inside its walls but those who have sworn total loyalty to him. As far as he is concerned, everything we see around us, the entire world on this side of the tapestry, is inside those walls. He finds the idea that someone can pop out of this village into his attic uninvited to be unacceptable. He has sent me to get all of you out. Those of you willing to swear fealty to Vond will be allowed to stay in Warlock House — maybe here, maybe back in the World — while the rest of us will be cast out to fend for ourselves on the streets of Ethshar."

A surge of muttering began to rise, but Hanner raised his hands for silence.

"The situation has become complicated," he said. "A group of magicians led by the wizard Ithinia of the Isle attempted to trick Vond into thinking that his new magic was accompanied by a new Calling, but the ruse failed, and made Vond very, very angry — so angry that he picked up the overlord's palace, the *entire palace*, and is holding it suspended a hundred feet over Ithinia's house. If Vond is harmed, or his magic is blocked, the palace will fall and crush a significant portion of the New City. The overlord's guards have evacuated the inhabitants of that part of the city, and found them places to stay, for now, in various garrisons and defensive structures. Those of you who leave here can probably join these refugees, rather than being forced to sleep in the Hundred-Foot Field — but still, you will be living in a city where the most powerful warlock in history is feuding with pretty much everyone else. Right now, Ethshar of the Spices is not a safe place."

"It never was!" someone called.

"True enough," Hanner acknowledged. "Still, right now it's worse than usual. So, that's the situation. I've been ordered to get everyone out of here — but Vond doesn't know how many people are in here, and since he can't come here himself without losing his magic and dropping the palace, he won't be able to check. So if *some* of you leave, we can tell Vond that it's everyone, and the rest can stay here undisturbed. You probably won't be getting any more people or supplies coming in unless and until someone finds a way to remove Vond, and anyone who goes back through the tapestry into the attic of Warlock House after we tell Vond everyone's out will be doing so at the risk of his own life, but other than that —"

He never finished the sentence. He was interrupted by a woman's startled scream. Like everyone else, Hanner turned to see who was screaming, and why.

It was an old woman, who was pointing up a street that led out of the village and up the slope toward the arrival point. "Soldiers!" she said.

Everyone turned to look, and there were more screams and shouts. Hanner jumped down from his rock and ran to see for himself. He had to push his way through the crowd, but after a moment's effort he had a clear view.

Half a dozen men were marching down the slope toward the village, swords bare in their hands. They were not wearing the yellow and red of the city guards, though; instead they wore black tunics, black kilts, and black boots, as well as gray metal breastplates and helmets. For a moment Hanner wondered whether these might be the natives of this world, come to reclaim their village from the invading Ethsharites. But then he looked up at the top of the hill and saw another one appear out of thin air, followed by another. They were definitely coming through the tapestry from Warlock House, then.

But who were they? They weren't the overlord's guards, not in those colors. They weren't any military Hanner had ever seen before — soldiers didn't wear black!

More appeared, and the nearest had stopped advancing. A dozen or so were spread across the slope now.

"*Hai*!" Hanner called. "Who are you? What are you doing here?"

"The emperor sent us," one of the nearest replied. "We're here to get you all out of here, and back to Ethshar."

"I was just telling them —" Hanner began.

"You're Hanner?" one of the swordsmen interrupted.

"Yes," Hanner said, a trifle warily.

"His Majesty is not pleased with you, Hanner. You should have had all these people out of here hours ago."

"I've been doing my best, whoever you are! There's a lot more to this place than just the village, and it took me awhile to find everyone."

The swordsman looked past Hanner at the crowd, then called to his own men, "Keep them all in the village. If anyone tries to leave, kill him."

"Yes, sir," three or four of the other swordsmen replied, more or less in unison.

"Wait a minute," Hanner said. "Who *are* you? What gives you any right to give orders?"

"My name's Gerath Gror's son," the swordsman replied, "and his Imperial Majesty the Great Vond appointed me commander of this cohort. He wants everyone out of here."

"Why should we care what he wants?" Hanner demanded. "This isn't his property, it's mine! I paid good money for that tapestry."

"It's in the emperor's house, and he doesn't want all of you people trespassing."

"It's *my* house, not his!"

Gerath looked both amused and annoyed. "Hanner, if that's who you are, do you *really* want to argue with him?"

"Why not? You do know his magic doesn't work here, don't you?"

For the first time, Gerath's confidence faltered. "It doesn't?"

"No, it doesn't. That's what this is all *for* — a place warlocks could go that the Calling couldn't reach. He can't touch us in here."

Gerath considered that, turned up his empty hand, and raised his sword. "Well, even if he can't, *we* can, and we have our orders. Everyone out!"

Hanner stared at him, groping for some response. He instinctively resisted simply doing as he was told — this was *his* place, no matter what Vond might say. The people of the refuge outnumbered the swordsmen four or five to one; they could resist, refuse to go...

But many of the refugees were women, children, and men too old to fight, and they were unarmed, while those swordsmen looked like they knew their trade. The refugees were completely unprepared, with no leaders or organization. If it came to an actual fight several people would be hurt, maybe killed, and it was not at all clear who would win.

For that matter, maybe some of the refugees wouldn't *want* to fight; they might be happy to go back to Ethshar. That would further weaken any opposition the emperor's swordsmen might face.

Immediate open resistance was not the way to go, then.

"You, Hanner," Gerath called. "How do people get out of here and back to Warlock House?"

"Ah?" Hanner blinked. "Oh, yes. Of course. This way." He turned toward the house where the tapestry hung.

"Wait a minute!" Gerath said. "Where are you taking us? Don't we need to go back up the hill, where we arrived?"

Hanner glanced up the slope to where two men were guarding the hilltop. "No, no," he said. "That tapestry only works in one direction. Come this way, and I'll show you the way out."

"Hanner, are you sure...?" someone muttered by his ear.

"They'd find out soon enough. If we try to trick them, someone will get hurt," Hanner murmured in reply.

"It's not a spell?" Gerath called.

"Of course it's a spell!" Hanner shouted back. "And it's over there." He pointed.

Gerath muttered some instructions to his companions, but Hanner could not make them out. Then Gerath and three others came marching into the village, following Hanner, while the other swordsmen remained on the open ground of the grassy hillside.

It occurred to Hanner that he had seen more of these soldiers appear while several were on that slope, and that some of them would have been in the area shown in the tapestry image. There were no swordsmen in the picture, but there had been swordsmen in the place depicted; weren't such things supposed to block a tapestry from functioning? Didn't the recent arrivals need to move out of the way before more could come through?

Arvagan had said that tapestries varied in how they behaved; apparently the one that led to this world wasn't as finicky as some. In fact, it didn't seem finicky at all. That was interesting. Hanner wondered how picky the one leading to the attic really was.

He looked around at the crowd of refugees, and realized that it was smaller than it had been, and that he was by no means the only one heading for the house where the Transporting Tapestry hung. It would seem that some people were not waiting to be forced to return to Ethshar.

Then he was at the door of the house. He stepped inside, from bright sunlight into pleasant shade, and stopped for a moment to let his eyes adjust. As he did, he saw a woman vanish — he had barely registered her presence when she touched the tapestry and disappeared.

Yes, some people were cooperating. Hanner grimaced.

Gerath and his three companions arrived close behind him; Hanner stepped aside to let them into the house, where they could see the enchanted hanging.

Gerath stopped and stared at it. "Another tapestry," he said.

"That's right," Hanner replied.

"I should have guessed."

Hanner turned up a palm.

Gerath frowned. "Well, that's simple enough, then," he said. He stepped backed out into the street and called, "All right, all of you, go through it. Starting now."

Hanner could not see the crowd's reaction, but he leaned over and called out the door, "If you have any belongings, fetch them. I don't think you'll have a chance to come back."

"Sidor," Gerath said, addressing one of the three who had accompanied him to the house, "Go tell the others to get everyone into this house at once. Tesra, grab someone and throw him at the tapestry — let's get this started."

Sidor raised his sword in salute, then marched back out of the house, while Tesra grabbed the arm of a girl who had gotten too close, and dragged her into the room where the tapestry waited. She struggled in his grip, trying to dig her heels into the tile floor, but Tesra was too strong for her; he flung her at the tapestry. She instinctively reached out to catch herself, and was gone.

Hanner watched, horrified. He knew she probably wasn't hurt, but the swordsman's crude violence was appalling.

Then Tesra grabbed someone else and shoved him toward the tapestry.

"No need," the man said. "I'll go quietly." He pulled away from the swordsman and marched into the room, head high.

As he approached the tapestry he turned and grinned at Hanner. "I'll be right back," he whispered.

Hanner had not thought of that, but in fact there was nothing he knew of to stop any of these people from simply stepping back through the tapestry on the fourth floor. He glanced at Tesra, who was looking for a third victim, and at Gerath, who was standing just outside the open door on the village street.

If everyone waited on the fourth floor, and then rushed back through the tapestry as soon as Vond emerged from the attic, he might never know it had happened; he would assume that they had simply left Warlock House, as instructed.

But there would be no way to maintain contact between Ethshar and the refuge, with Vond occupying Warlock House. In fact, Vond might well destroy the tapestry.

If Hanner were to take the tapestry down and take it somewhere else — Nerra's house, perhaps, since the palace was displaced and he was not welcome in Mavi's home — then it would no longer be any of Vond's business...

Except that the return tapestry came out in the attic of Warlock House. Hanner frowned. There had to be some way to keep the refuge functioning, despite Vond's soldiers. It seemed more urgent than ever not just to have someplace former warlocks could go, but to have somewhere Vond and his hirelings *couldn't*.

Hanner stepped aside, trying to think what he could do, as the soldiers began marching refugees through the tapestry into the attic.

Chapter Thirty-Four

Kolar the Large hung back in the hallway, and did not follow the others into the fourth-floor bedroom. He did not trust that magical wall hanging. Yes, the warlock *said* it would transport them safely into another world, and that there was an easy way back, but even if Kolar entirely trusted the warlock — which he did not — how did the warlock know? By his own admission, *he* had never been through there.

This whole mercenary-soldier business was beginning to look like a bad idea, and Kolar wished he had stuck to working the docks. It had sounded good when that fellow with the strange eyes had talked about it in Shiphaven Market, but no one had said anything about walking through enchanted tapestries. Standing around with a sword looking dangerous was no problem; Kolar was big enough that he often looked dangerous whether he wanted to or not. Getting involved with magicians, though, really *was* dangerous, whether it looked it or not, and this Great Vond character was obviously even more dangerous than most. Hanging the overlord's palace up in the sky that way — that was *crazy*.

Now the crazy warlock had marched about half his men through the tapestry, and *none had come back*. That was not what Kolar had thought he was being hired to do.

The warlock seemed to be thoroughly focused on the tapestry, so he might not notice if Kolar slipped away — but then again, he might. Magicians didn't necessarily need to use their eyes to see things. Vond did not seem like the sort who would take desertion lightly, either. True, Kolar had not signed anything, or sworn an oath, or even been paid, but he had been given the nice uniform and the good sword, and had made no protest when Vond announced what he wanted.

If they had been on the ground floor Kolar might have tried to slip away, but they were on the fourth floor; the front door was a long way away. Kolar glanced about, wondering if there might be some other exit.

That was how he happened to be looking directly at the attic door when it opened and a girl peered timidly out. She spotted him immediately, and froze.

Kolar quickly raised his hands, fingers spread, to show he meant her no harm. He smiled at her, then threw a quick glance into the bedchamber. The warlock was getting the next man ready to touch the tapestry, and paying no attention to anything outside the room.

Kolar made his decision, and trotted quickly and quietly over to the attic door. "*Hai,*" he said, keeping his voice low. "Who are you?"

"Détha," the girl said. "Détha of Newgate."

Kolar took in her worn clothing and said, "You aren't one of the maids, are you? What are you doing here?"

"I...I was Chairman Hanner's guest," Détha said. "But that soldier threw me out."

Kolar cocked his head. "What soldier?"

"The one in charge called him Tesra. He wore the same uniform you do."

Kolar knew who Tesra was; they had chatted a bit on the way from Shiphaven. He had been one of the first to disappear into the tapestry. "You were on the other side of that magic tapestry?"

She nodded.

"Is that where this door goes?" He tapped the wooden panel.

"Ah...sort of." She looked up at him, then past him at the corridor. "Where am I supposed to go? No one told me."

"No one told me, either," Kolar admitted. "I know the warlock wanted you out of his house, though."

Before Détha could reply, a third voice called from behind her, "Who are you talking to?"

Kolar frowned and pulled open the door, peering over the girl's head. He saw stairs going up, and at least a dozen people standing on those stairs, looking down at him.

"More of you," he said.

"They're throwing all of us out," Détha said.

"Some of us didn't wait to be thrown," one of the men on the stairs said. "But they didn't say where we should go."

This looked like an excellent opportunity to make himself useful without going through any magical portals. "Wait here," Kolar said. "I'll go ask." Then he turned and trotted back across the passage and leaned into the room where the warlock and perhaps a dozen of his other mercenaries were waiting. "Your Majesty?" he said.

The warlock turned. "What is it?"

"There are people appearing. They say they were on the other side of the tapestry, and our men have been sending them back here."

"Appearing? Appearing *where*? Why aren't they appearing *here*?"

"They're...well, I found them on a stairway on the other side of the hallway. I'm not sure if that's where they're appearing — is there a fifth floor?"

"Show me," Vond demanded.

Kolar bowed. "Of course, your Majesty. This way." He stepped aside to allow Vond out of the room, and when the warlock had floated out into the hallway Kolar pointed to the open attic door. Détha was standing framed in the doorway, watching apprehensively.

Vond swept across the hall and hovered over the girl, then spoke, inhumanly loud. "You are one of Hanner's guests?"

"Yes, your Majesty," Détha said, making an awkward attempt at a curtsey.

"You went through the wizard's tapestry?"

Détha glanced back over her shoulder at the others. "Yes, your Majesty. We all did."

"Why are you coming back *here*, instead of where the tapestry is?"

"Because…because the return magic comes out in the attic, your Majesty."

"It does?" Vond peered past her at the unlit stairs.

"Yes, your Majesty."

"I didn't even know there *was* an attic!"

Détha had no reply for that.

"It can't come out anywhere else?"

The girl looked confused. "No, your Majesty. Just in the attic."

"Hanner didn't tell me that."

Again, Détha had nothing to say.

"Where *is* Hanner? Has he come back yet?"

Détha glanced back up the stairs. "He was there…"

"He was off to one side," someone called from farther up. "He hasn't come through yet."

"Your Majesty?" someone else called. "Could we come down, please? It's getting crowded here."

"Of course! Kolar, get them out of there." Most of the other swordsmen who had not yet touched the tapestry had followed Vond out into the corridor, and now the warlock turned to them and ordered, "Escort these people out of the building. Station yourselves with one at the top and bottom of each stair, and see that they all leave."

Kolar stepped forward and put a hand on Détha's shoulder, guiding her out of the attic stairwell and directing her toward the stairs down to the third floor. One of the other mercenaries, a man whose name Kolar had not caught, positioned himself at the top of those stairs, while others trotted down to take up their posts further down.

Détha was followed by a string of others, and Kolar set about making sure each of them made an orderly exit from the attic, and was headed the right direction. Vond hovered nearby, watching, as person after person emerged from the attic and crossed to the stairs going down.

As he herded an old man out of the attic, Kolar was startled by a shout. He turned.

One of the refugees had tried to duck aside, back into the room with the tapestry, and the guard at the top of the main stair had moved to head him off. The steady downward flow had been interrupted as the other exiles turned to see what was happening.

Then the man was suddenly flung across the hall, slamming into the opposite wall.

"You will *not* go back there!" Vond roared, his voice magically amplified. "You will leave this house *now*!"

Shaken, the man got to his feet, gave Vond a single terrified glance, then stumbled down the stairs. The instant his head disappeared around the corner of the landing, the rest of the procession began moving again, and in a matter of seconds it was as if the incident had never occurred. It was about that point that Kolar noticed the daylight was fading. Vond had apparently noticed, as well; he waved a hand, and the lamps on the walls all blazed to life.

After several more minutes and several dozen people there was a break in the steady stream descending the attic stairs, and as Kolar leaned through the door to see whether more were coming, Vond asked, "How many is that?"

"I don't know, your Majesty," Kolar said. "I wasn't counting."

"I didn't see Hanner."

"I wouldn't know, your Majesty. I've never met him."

Vond frowned. He glided through the door and up the stairs, glowing gently.

Kolar made no attempt to follow his employer, but instead waited at his post by the attic door. A moment later Vond called down, "There's nothing up here."

Kolar could not think of a useful reply, so he did not respond.

"There's no portal that I can see," Vond continued. "I don't feel any magic at all. It's just an empty attic."

Kolar waited, and a few seconds later the warlock swooped back down the stairs and out into the corridor. "Do you think they could be appearing somewhere else now?" he asked.

Kolar turned up an empty hand. "I couldn't say, your Majesty. I don't know anything about magic."

Vond frowned. "I don't sense anyone new."

"Maybe that's all of them, then."

Vond shook his head. "I didn't see Hanner, and even if that's all the trespassers, what about Gerath and the others? Why haven't *they* come back?"

"I don't know, your Majesty."

"About how many *did* we get out?"

Kolar had no idea, but he did not think the warlock wanted to hear that, so he made a guess. "Fifty, perhaps?"

"Well, that's *most* of them," Vond said, more to himself than to Kolar. He peered back up into the attic, then glanced across the hall to the room where the tapestry hung. Then he called to the man at the head of the stairs, "Is everyone out of the house?"

"I can't see anyone from here, your Majesty."

"Well, *ask*, stupid!"

The man opened his mouth to say something, then caught himself, turned, and shouted down the stairs, "Are they all out down there?"

Kolar could hear the question being relayed; a moment later the answer came back. "The man at the front door says the last ones are in the dooryard, your Majesty."

"Good," Vond said, looking around thoughtfully. He considered for a long moment. Then he turned to Kolar. "You're coming with me. Don't be frightened; I'll keep you safe."

"Coming where? Your Majesty, I..." Kolar began. Then as his feet left the floor he let his protest trail off; it obviously wasn't going to do any good. He closed his eyes and swallowed hard.

When he opened them again the wall ahead of him was melting, or dissolving, or doing *something* that walls don't normally do; the plaster was flowing like molasses, and the wooden lath beneath was curling like ribbons as a hole appeared and grew.

Then he, and Vond, and the man who had been stationed at the top of the stairs, were flying out through the hole into the twilight sky. They had been on the fourth floor, so they were thirty feet up to begin with, and immediately swooped dizzyingly upward. Kolar gulped, and decided not to look down.

They were flying northeast, he realized, toward the overlord's palace, where it hung motionless a hundred yards above Lower Street, gleaming orange in the light of the greater moon and blocking out the stars.

"Your Majesty, what are we doing?" the other mercenary asked, shouting to be heard over the wind of their passage.

"We're putting my toys away," Vond replied.

Kolar's eyes widened. Was the warlock going to put the palace back where it belonged? But wouldn't that leave him open to attack? Kolar didn't know the entire story, but it was his understanding that the whole point of stealing the palace in the first place was that as long as it hung above the city, no one would dare harm Vond. If he put it back, wouldn't that provide a perfect opportunity for the wizards and witches to kill him?

But the palace was unmistakably starting to move; it was eerily silent, but Kolar could tell from the way the moonlight shifted that it was moving. He glanced down, trying to orient himself. If the palace was going back where it belonged, it should be heading a little west of due north. Kolar tried to make out the grid of streets below to confirm that it was indeed going that direction.

It wasn't. It was heading *east* of north.

"Where are you taking it?" he asked.

"Out to the sandbars off Newmarket," Vond replied. He hesitated, then added, "You might want to cover your ears."

Kolar did not need a second warning; he didn't know just what to expect, but he immediately clamped his hands over his ears, ducking his head down and hunching his shoulders.

"*People of Ethshar!*" Vond's voice roared out, so loud that not just his ears, but Kolar's entire skull seemed to ring. His teeth bit down so tightly they hurt as he tried to shut out the deafening sound. "*I am going to be taking a short break, but rest assured, I'm not done. I will return momentarily, and when I do I will restore the palace to its position above the New City. Any attempt to harm me during my nap will be* most *unfortunate for anyone involved.*"

The sound rolled out across the city and the sky, and Kolar squeezed his eyes shut as the echoes died away. His head hurt, and he knew that this headache was going to last for awhile.

When he finally opened his eyes again they were flying over the waterfront somewhere; the water below was black and empty, but white lines of surf gleamed as they moved across that darkness. The city was mostly behind them, though he could see docks below, dark gray against the black water.

The palace hung in the sky ahead of them, and for the first time Kolar noticed that some of its windows were lit. Not as many as usual, certainly; most of it appeared dark and deserted. Still, there were at least half a dozen lamps burning. There were people in there. Kolar had seen the carpets and contraptions ferrying people out earlier, and he had assumed they got *everyone* out, but evidently that was not the case.

But then the palace was descending, sinking gently down through the night air, and Kolar could see where those white lines of surf were breaking on the elongated ovals of the sandbars of the Newmarket Shoals.

This was beginning to make sense. Vond was going to do something about those people who had not returned from the tapestry world, and he didn't want to worry about keeping the palace airborne while he did it, so he was setting the palace down here — someplace safe but inconvenient, so that the overlord would be that much less tempted to try assassinating the emperor while the palace was on the ground.

But why was *he*, Kolar, here? And that other man?

The palace settled heavily onto the sandbar, tilting slightly to the north; Kolar imagined that most of the furniture would be falling over or sliding to the lower side of whatever room it was in. He hoped the damage wouldn't be too extensive.

Then it was down, and Vond whipped around, dragging the two mercenaries in his wake as he headed back toward Warlock House at breathtaking speed.

"You have your swords?" Vond asked.

Kolar put a hand on the hilt of his fine new weapon. "Right here, your Majesty," he said.

"I trust you know how to use it?"

Kolar swallowed. "Of course, your Majesty."

He was lying. He had never wielded a sword in his life; he was a longshoreman, not a soldier. He glanced the other man. "My blade is at your service."

"Where we're going, my magic may not work," Vond explained. "Old warlockry didn't. My power is different, but perhaps not *that* different. If I *am* rendered powerless, cut off from my magic, it will be up to the two of you, and your blades, to defend me, and to enforce my orders. This is why I hired you, to protect me when my magic can't."

"Yes, your Majesty," Kolar said unhappily. He did not like this. He was fairly certain that the warlock intended to go through that tapestry and take Kolar and the other man along as his bodyguards, and Kolar did not want to go exploring a strange world. He was not happy about the possibility that people had stopped appearing in the attic because the magic that brought them there had stopped working; the three of them might wind up stranded in that other place. He was tempted to say something, but the warlock surely must have thought of that, and he knew far more about magic than Kolar did.

"Serve me well tonight, and you'll each have a round of gold," Vond added.

Kolar's mood brightened considerably at that. A round of gold was more money than he had ever seen in one place in his entire life.

Then they were flying back through the hole in the wall of Warlock House, into the lamplit corridor. Behind them the lath and frame were bending themselves back into place, and the plaster was flowing back to heal the wall. Kolar's boots thumped down onto the floor.

"This way," the warlock said, beckoning. As Kolar had thought, they were heading for the tapestry. "Your Majesty, do you really think this is wise?" he asked.

"Maybe not," Vond said, "but I think it's necessary. My men have defied me, and stopped sending out those trespassers."

"Maybe they *can't*," Kolar suggested. "What if we get trapped there?"

Vond shook his head. "I sent Hanner through there to chase people out, and he didn't, and I thought maybe he couldn't. Then when I sent Gerath and the others, they started chasing people out with no problem, so the magic is working fine, whatever it is. But then they stopped, so there must be something over there making people disobey me. Maybe there's some strange magic involved, or maybe something's just persuaded them to ignore my instructions, but whatever it is, I can't allow it. I can't tolerate disobedience, whether I'm present or not. If I can't trust anyone else to clear them out, I'll do it myself."

"How do you know what's happening there, though?"

"I don't. That's why I'm going, and why you're coming with me." He smiled. "Besides, I want to see this other world. I admit it, I'm as curious as anyone, and it might be useful. Even if I don't have any magic there, I have you and Gerath and the rest."

"But what if something's happened to them?"

"Then I need to know about it!"

"Couldn't you hire a wizard to find out?"

Vond turned to glare at him. "*No*, I can't hire a wizard! The wizards are my enemies; I need to do this myself. I need to prove I'm not afraid, that even without my magic I can still control the situation."

"But your Majesty, what if you *can't*?"

"I *can*," Vond insisted. "You and the other swordsmen will obey me because you know I'll pay you when we get back, and some of the former warlocks will obey me because they want their magic back. That should be enough. Now, unless you want me to smash you, come on!"

Kolar still wasn't convinced, but he did not dare argue with the warlock any further. Reluctantly, he trudged toward the tapestry.

Chapter Thirty-Five

Hanner watched as person after person vanished into the attic tapestry — men, women, and children snatched back to the World. Some went willingly; some had to be dragged, screaming or crying, and flung at the hanging. So far, none of the soldiers had tried to push *him* through, but he supposed that they would get to him eventually. There weren't very many of the former warlocks left. Most of the soldiers were out looking for stragglers, to make sure they had not missed anyone; about a dozen refugees were clustered in or near the house.

Hanner had noticed that Rudhira was not among them, but he was not about to mention that to anyone. If she preferred to remain here, Hanner had no objection. There might be others missing, as well, but since he had never kept track of who was in the refuge to begin with, Rudhira was the only one he was sure of. Everyone else he knew had been there was accounted for.

He had also noticed that no one seemed to be reappearing. Apparently the other tapestry was being guarded, or had been rolled up, or destroyed, so that the exiles sent through to the attic were not able to return. Hanner winced inwardly at the thought that Vond might have vaporized that very expensive hanging.

Then two of the swordsmen gave one woman a shove, her hand touched the cloth — and nothing happened. She stood there, hand on the tapestry, hair awry, blinking in surprise.

"*Hai*!" Tesra called, raising a hand of his own. "Something's wrong."

The three other swordsmen in the house stopped and turned to see what was happening, while the woman stood where she had been shoved, running her hands over the fabric. She spread her fingers wide and pressed both palms on the tapestry.

"What's going on?" asked one of the swordsmen whose name Hanner had not learned. "Why is she still here?"

"Maybe she's under some kind of spell," Tesra said. "*You* try it, and if it works, you can tell the emperor we may have a problem."

"Seems to me we have a problem if it *doesn't* work," the other said.

"Yes, I know," Tesra agreed, "but you won't be in a position to tell him that, will you?"

"We'd be *stuck* here!"

"Well, try it, and see if we are," Tesra said, pointing at the tapestry.

The other man frowned and said, "Pass me another warlock first, and we'll see if *he* goes through."

While this conversation was taking place Hanner had moved in for a closer look, while most of the other refugees in or near the house had retreated; therefore it was Hanner's arm that Tesra grabbed, while the other swordsman pulled the woman away. "Here, you," Tesra said to Hanner. "Put your hand on that thing."

Hanner obeyed, not sure what to expect. He could think of a few reasons the tapestry might have stopped working; in fact, he was surprised that there had not been any previous interruptions. He would have expected delays after each transition, while the most recently transported person got out of the area depicted on the tapestry, but until now that had not happened — apparently this tapestry was not as particular about that as were most of the others Hanner had heard of.

Arvagan had always said they varied. Nervously, Hanner put his hand on the fabric.

Nothing happened. The material under his fingers felt like ordinary silk. It was wonderfully smooth, but silk usually was.

"So it's not just her," Tesra said.

The other swordsman, seeing that no harm had befallen Hanner or the woman, also reached out to stroke the cloth. Again, nothing happened; there was no sign of any magic.

"What's happening?" a new voice asked. Hanner turned to find Gerath standing in the doorway, looking annoyed.

"The tapestry stopped working," Tesra said.

"It *what?*" His head snapped around to stare at the tapestry. "Blood and death, are you serious?"

"Yes, sir," Tesra said, stepping aside.

Gerath strode to the tapestry and put his hand on it, between Hanner's and the other swordsman's. He, too, failed to disappear. "Damn!" he muttered. Then he recognized Hanner. "Do you know what's gone wrong?"

"I don't *know*," Hanner said. He was stalling, trying to decide what he wanted to tell these people.

"You have a theory?" Gerath demanded. "This tapestry was yours originally, wasn't it?"

"Yes, it's mine," Hanner said.

"So what's wrong with it?"

"Nothing, so far as I know," Hanner said. "It's more likely something's changed on the other side, so that the image doesn't match the reality closely enough. When that happens, the tapestry won't work."

"Changed? What could have changed?"

Hanner stepped back, and gestured at the tapestry. "Several things," he said. "You see that the image shows an empty attic; if there's something in the real attic now that isn't in the picture, that would explain it."

"But it didn't stop working when we sent people through," Tesra said. "Wouldn't *they* have been there?"

"Yes, they would," Hanner said, impressed, despite himself, with how quickly Tesra had figured this out. "With some tapestries, you have to wait until the first person moves out of the way before you can send another. Apparently *this* one isn't that picky."

"Or it wasn't," Gerath said. "Maybe it wore out a little, and *got* picky."

"Maybe," Hanner conceded. "Or...well, when I first tested this tapestry, a couple of sixnights...I mean, seventeen years ago, when I was still a warlock, I smashed a hole in the attic roof. I think that must have stopped the tapestry from working until the damage was fixed. If Vond, or some wizard he's angered, broke something — snapped one of those beams, or tore open the roof — then the tapestry won't work until the damage is repaired."

"That could be bad," Tesra said.

"It could," Hanner agreed.

"Why would Vond smash anything?" one of the other soldiers asked, but everyone else ignored him.

"Any other possibilities?" Gerath asked.

"Well, yes," Hanner said. "I don't think either of those is the most likely, actually. If you take a look at the image, I think you'll see what I mean."

"I don't," Tesra replied, annoyed.

"It's *daylight* in the picture," Hanner explained.

"So? It's daylight here, too," Gerath said.

"It's *always* daylight here," Hanner said. "The sun doesn't move; hadn't you noticed?"

Gerath frowned. "I've been busy," he said, a bit defensively. "So it doesn't necessarily match what's happening in the real World?"

"It *doesn't* match," Hanner said. "None of the people here had any way of telling time, because it's always midday."

"But it's after dark in Ethshar," Tesra said. "It was late afternoon there when we came through the tapestry — it must be night by now."

"This tapestry doesn't work at night?" Gerath demanded.

"That's my theory, yes," Hanner said.

"So we just need to wait until morning?"

"That's my theory," Hanner repeated.

"We're stuck here all night?" Tesra asked. "There's no way to speed it up?"

"Well, *I* don't know of any," Hanner said. "I've heard of tapestries where if the time of day or some other detail doesn't match, you can still step into them, but you don't come out on the other side until the conditions are right. *This* one doesn't seem to do that, so yes, I think we have to wait for daylight."

"Is there any way to get a message to the emperor, and let him know what's happening?" Gerath asked.

"Not that I know of," Hanner said, turning up a palm.

"Then we wait," Tesra said.

"Since we can't tell what time it is in Ethshar, we'll keep testing it every few minutes," Gerath said, pointing at the woman who had first failed to go through. "With her."

"Yes, sir," one of the swordsmen said, catching her arm.

"Hanner, is there any *other* way out of here?" Gerath asked.

Hanner shook his head. "No," he said.

"You're sure of that?"

"No," Hanner repeated. "Nobody really knows much about this place. I know *I* didn't provide any other way out, but I suppose there might be a natural one somehow."

Gerath considered that, then ordered Hanner, "Out. You're coming with me."

Hanner had no objection, and followed Gerath out into the street, where half a dozen swordsmen and the last dozen or so refugees were standing idly, awaiting word on their situation.

"You know everyone who was here, don't you?" Gerath asked, jerking a thumb toward the former warlocks.

"Not really," Hanner said.

Gerath glared at him. "You've been watching people go through the tapestry, and you see everyone we have left here. Is anyone missing? Is there anyone you know was here who's unaccounted for?"

Hanner looked over the cluster of the Called, then shook his head and lied. "No," he said.

The only one missing, so far as he knew, was Rudhira, but she was definitely missing. He wondered how and when she had slipped away. He also wondered whether there really were any others. He had no way to tell; half a dozen people might have escaped to the woods.

Gerath beckoned to Sidor, and the two of them marched off to one side to converse quietly. Hanner could not make out what they were saying, and the other swordsmen made it clear he would be unwise to try too hard. He and the other refugees, except for the one woman still in the house, were kept gathered in a circle in the street.

Hanner looked the others over, trying to judge their spirits and health. None of them looked happy, but none seemed on the verge of collapse, either. "*Hai,*" he called to the swordsmen. "It's going to be hours; couldn't we all get something to eat, and maybe get some sleep?"

Gerath looked up, considered for a moment, then called, "Yes, go ahead. You men, each of you take one or two of them, and see they're fed."

"But *you* don't sleep," Sidor added. "We don't want anyone deciding to play hiding games."

"There's food?" one of the swordsmen asked.

"I'll show you," a refugee said. "My place is just up the street."

With that, the little group quickly dispersed, until only Hanner, Gerath, and Sidor were left standing in the street. Tesra and two other soldiers were still in the house, periodically testing the tapestry's magic, while everyone else had scattered in pursuit of food and rest.

Hanner wondered if there might be some way to arrange a rebellion, now that Vond's hirelings were separated and off-guard, but he could not see how to organize it. The soldiers were still armed, and instead of being outnumbered five or six to one, as they had been at first, the numbers were now more or less even.

Hanner also wondered where Vond had gotten his little army on such short notice. They gave every appearance of being trained and formidable — though thinking about it, Hanner now wondered whether that was really the case. He had not seen any of them actually *use* their swords to do anything but threaten.

But then, none of the refugees were trained warriors, either; they had been magicians, not fighters. What's more, they didn't have any swords, which made a difference even in untrained hands.

After what seemed a surprisingly long discussion, Gerath and Sidor finally looked at Hanner. "You're still here?" Sidor demanded.

Hanner turned up a hand. "Everyone seemed to think I was your responsibility," he said.

"That's probably just as well," Gerath said. "We're going back up the hill to see if maybe the tapestries are working in the other direction now. Tesra and Thellesh and Kelder will let us know if someone comes through the attic one, so we're going to check the other. You're coming with us."

Hanner started to say something, to point out that the tapestries *never* reversed direction or worked both ways, that the idea was ridiculous, but he caught himself. He had no reason to tell these men anything. "All right," he said.

Gerath took the lead, with Hanner following, and Sidor in the rear, his sword drawn and pointed at Hanner's back, as they made their way up out of the village and across the grass. They were about halfway up when another swordsman abruptly appeared atop the slope.

Gerath stopped dead, and drew his own blade. "What...?"

"It's Kolar," Sidor said. "I remember him from Shiphaven."

Before Gerath could reply, a second man appeared, a tall, thin man in black, holding a sword awkwardly, but with no breastplate or helmet. But where the first man, the one Sidor called Kolar, had been steady on his feet, and was now looking around at his surroundings with interest, this new arrival stumbled, dropped his sword, then fell to his knees, gasping.

Kolar immediately turned to help him, and Gerath broke into a run, bounding up the hill. Sidor stayed where he was, but Hanner felt the tip of his sword press against his tunic. They all knew who this latest visitor was. Even at this distance, there could be no mistaking him.

It was Vond. Even though it had meant giving up his magic, the emperor had come through the tapestry. Hanner stared in wordless astonishment.

If Vond was here, what had happened to the overlord's palace? Vond's magic clearly did not function here; had the palace plummeted to earth? Hanner desperately wanted to ask, but did not dare — knowing the answer would not change anything.

The loss of his magic had obviously hit Vond hard, probably much harder than he had expected. Hanner remembered his own first visit to this place, when the change had been almost overwhelming. It was probably even worse for Vond.

A third man appeared, another of the uniformed soldiers, who also rushed to Vond's aid.

A moment later the warlock was back on his feet, unsteady but brushing aside the three swordsmen. "I'm fine," he said — Hanner could just barely hear him. "I was caught by surprise, that's all." He looked around, and spotted Hanner and Sidor. He started stumbling slowly down the slope, moving like someone who had forgotten how to walk.

"*Hai!*" Vond called, his voice oddly weak. Hanner realized he must have used his magic to amplify his voice so often that he had trouble speaking loudly without it. "Hanner! Is that you?"

Hanner called back, "Yes, your Majesty!"

"Why are you still here? I told you to get everyone out of here!"

"And *I* told *you*, your Majesty, that it might take awhile! I had only just gotten everyone gathered when your hired bullies arrived." He saw no need to mention that he had slept for several hours.

"Really? What *took* you so long?" Vond demanded.

"I am not sure how long it was; time may be different here. And there is much more to this place than just the village, your Majesty!"

Vond looked from side to side, as if only now noticing the truth of Hanner's words. "Ah," he said. Then he turned to the hirelings walking down the hill with him. "Gerath, why did you stop sending people back?"

"The magic stopped working, your Majesty," Gerath replied. "Hanner thinks it's because it doesn't work at night."

Vond blinked up at the bright midday sun. "It's not night here," he said.

"It never is," Hanner called. "But it is in Ethshar, isn't it?" He tried to think what he should do about Vond's unexpected appearance, and obvious lack of magic. This was surely an opportunity to be seized. Vond was powerless here — magically, at least. He still commanded his soldiers, and with the latest arrivals the swordsmen probably outnumbered the remaining people of the refuge. Still, this might be the best chance they would ever have to dispose of Vond before he killed anyone else, or further disrupted the peace of the World.

But at least half the remaining handful of refugees were women, or men too old to fight, and they were scattered, completely unprepared, with no leaders or organization, and unarmed. If it came to open battle several people would be hurt, maybe killed, and Vond's men would probably win. Immediate open resistance was not the way to go, then; instead Hanner resolved to watch how the situation developed, and see whether he could find a better resolution.

"What kind of magic is it?" Vond asked. "Why wouldn't it work at night?"

"It's another tapestry," Gerath said. "It shows the attic of your house in Ethshar."

"The attic in daylight," Hanner added.

"Another tapestry? Oh, for..." He turned to glare at Hanner. "You might have *told* me that when you first told me about this place."

"Didn't I?" Hanner asked, feigning innocent surprise.

One of the soldiers sucked in his breath at that.

"No, you did not."

Hanner dropped the pretense. "You didn't ask."

"I shouldn't have had to!"

"Forgive me, your Majesty, but I am not one of your subjects. You stole my house and now you're stealing the tapestries I spent my fortune on. Why would I help you any more than circumstances force me to?"

"Because you want to *live*, idiot!" Vond shouted, his voice still thin and weak. "Serve me faithfully and you'll thrive under my rule, but this sort of pointless resistance could get you killed."

Hanner did not bother to answer that; he closed his mouth firmly. He suspected that if this conversation had taken place back in Ethshar, he would have been smashed against a wall by now.

"Show me the tapestry," Vond ordered.

A few minutes later all of them were standing in front of the tapestry, where Tesra and the refugee woman demonstrated several times that it was not working.

"You didn't change anything in the attic?" Hanner asked.

"No," Vond said. "It looked just like that when last I saw it." Then he corrected himself. "Or rather, the last time I saw it by daylight. You're right — it stopped working when dusk faded."

"Then it should be fine once the sun rises again," Hanner said.

"And if it isn't?"

"Then we're all trapped here."

Vond looked at him thoughtfully. "You don't seem very upset by that idea."

Hanner turned up an empty hand. "I have been in worse places," he said. "It's sunny and warm here, and we have food, water, and shelter."

"Is that all you want? Don't you have a family in Ethshar?"

"I do," Hanner said. "But for years they all thought I was long dead, and accepted it."

Vond shook his head. "But they know now that you're alive. No, I think you know another way out. You're hoping to strand *me* in here, where I won't trouble the Wizards' Guild any further, but *you* have another way out."

"No," Hanner said. "I really don't."

The emperor studied Hanner's face for a moment, then nodded. "Maybe you don't. But you think there *will* be another way out eventually, don't you?" Vond raised his sword and rested the point on Hanner's chest. "Will it still happen if I kill you?"

The other people in the room all tensed, but none of them spoke, and no other blades were raised.

"Probably not," Hanner said, trying to keep his voice perfectly steady. "Honestly, your Majesty, I don't know of another way out, but I *do* know that there are people in Ethshar who care about me, and as you say, they know I'm alive. When they realize I'm missing, they'll try to reach me — they'll hire a magician, most likely a wizard or a theurgist, and they'll find me, and arrange for a way out. Perhaps they'll bring another tapestry here, or open a portal. Will anyone do that for you? I rather doubt it. As for these other people, the ones *I* brought here are here in the first place because no one cares about them, and the men *you* hired — does anyone know where they are, or even who hired them? Will anyone miss them?" He shook his head. "I'm the only one here who is certain to be missed, when my sisters don't hear from me."

Vond straightened up and lowered the sword. "Interesting logic," he said. "And quite possibly true. Oh, I think there are people who care for me — Zallin and the others who stayed in Warlock House want me to give them back their magic, and I think I pleased Leth — but I concede they aren't likely to hire a wizard to find me. I told Zallin where I was going, and that if he ever wanted to be a warlock again he would want to make sure I got back safely, but that doesn't mean he'll do anything. Even if someone did hire a wizard and the Guild allowed that wizard to try to find me, given that they don't know my true name, perhaps they couldn't. So you may be right."

"Ithinia certainly wouldn't be in any hurry to get you out of here."

"Very true," Vond said. "She swore not to harm me, but I don't trust her. She may well be conjuring up some assassin this very minute, hoping to kill me in my sleep before I can hoist the palace into the sky again."

"I doubt an assassin could find you here," Hanner said.

"You think not?" Vond cocked his head to one side. "You might be right about that, too." He looked over his shoulder out the open door, at the bright, steady sunlight. "This place could be useful." He looked back at Hanner. "These tapestries — you bought them?"

Hanner nodded.

"They were made to your specifications?"

"Yes."

"So I could buy more, couldn't I?" He snorted, then laughed. "Buy, or steal. I could bring them all here, and be able to appear anywhere in the World just by walking into the right one."

"Well, not *anywhere*," Hanner said. "There are limitations. But I don't see any reason you couldn't have several here. I believe the higher ups in the Wizards' Guild have an arrangement along those lines somewhere."

"But of course, this all assumes we get back to Ethshar," Vond said.

"I think we will," Hanner said. "Once the sun is above the city walls." He glanced up. "The *real* sun."

"If Ithinia hasn't laid a dozen traps for us," Vond said. "Or smashed the attic, so there's nothing to match the image."

"If that, yes," Hanner agreed. "But you're assuming she knows where we are."

"She's a wizard," Vond said. "You have to assume she knows everything she might want to."

"There is that," Hanner acknowledged. He looked around at the swordsmen and the remaining refugees. "It must still be hours until dawn. Maybe we should all get some sleep."

"Maybe," Vond agreed. He looked at Tesra and the woman who had been testing the tapestry. "I want at least two men awake and watching the tapestry at all times — Gerath, you work out the roster, and whoever isn't doing that should get some rest." He smiled a very unpleasant smile.

"If our friend Hanner is correct, the tapestry may start working again at dawn — or it may not, in which case we will have to wait until his family arranges to rescue us. Either way, we may find some excitement waiting for us, if and when we get back to Ethshar."

Gerath nodded, and began giving orders.

Chapter Thirty-Six

Ithinia knelt before the low table where she was making preliminary preparations for Varrin's Greater Propulsion. She could not complete the spell for another four days — well, three and a fraction — but the early steps could be done at any time, and she wanted them out of the way. She kept her hands moving in the necessary gestures, her eyes focused on the elements of her spell, as she said, "How long has it been?"

"Two or three hours, Guildmaster," Rothiel replied, standing well back from the table.

They were in a guard-room to one side of the overlord's grand audience chamber; it was not as centrally located as Ithinia might have hoped, but it did have several large casements that gave a good view and would aid in navigating the palace when the spell was complete.

Right now, the view from those windows showed her the night-lanterns of Crooked Pier and the lights of the Newmarket waterfront. She had thought the spell would be needed to keep the palace from falling when Vond eventually let it go, but it was no longer airborne; instead it stood on a sandbar a hundred yards out from the beach. The spell would still be necessary to set the palace back in its proper place, of course, and at any rate, once she had begun it was not *safe* to stop until she reached one of the spell's natural breaks.

"Do we know what happened?" she asked.

"That's why I'm here, Guildmaster. We have received reliable reports that Vond did indeed follow Hanner and the rest through the tapestry Arvagan made."

Ithinia considered that silently for a moment, swaying back and forth gently as her hands circled over the seven stones.

"Hanner had that tapestry made as a refuge from the Calling, I believe?" she said at last. She was not really asking Rothiel as much as reminding herself what Arvagan had told her.

"That is my understanding, Guildmaster."

"But when he tested it, he was Called immediately."

"So I was told, yes."

"Warlockry should not reach through a Transporting Tapestry." She frowned. "But I don't think Vond would want to give up his magic even for a moment, and Hanner's refuge apparently did not protect him seventeen years ago. Perhaps there is yet *another* source of magic on the other side, one that increased Hanner's susceptibility to the Call."

"We have no way of knowing, Guildmaster."

"Don't be an idiot, Rothiel. Dozens of Called warlocks went through that tapestry, and were then chased back to Ethshar by Vond's hirelings

— *they* would know whether there is a third source on the other side. We can ask them."

"Oh," Rothiel said. "Of course." Ithinia glanced up from her work long enough to see that the man was actually blushing.

"Everyone misses the obvious on occasion," she said. "Now that your oversight has been pointed out, perhaps you will make up for it by talking to some of these refugees and learning as much as you can about Hanner's other world. What does Vond want there? Why hasn't he returned yet? When *will* he return?" She paused. "You might want to talk to Arvagan about what return mechanism he provided when Hanner first purchased the tapestry. Talk to the refugees first, though. I'm sure you can think of the questions we want to ask."

"Yes, Guildmaster."

"Was there anything else I needed to know before you attend to interviewing the refugees?"

"Not about the general situation, but Lady Alris wishes to speak to you."

"Then by all means, send her in."

Rothiel bowed, then turned and left the room.

A moment later Lady Alris entered.

Ithinia did not know the Lady of the Household well; Alris' duties generally kept her in the palace, while Ithinia had preferred to stay out of the seat of government. Still, they had met before, in passing.

"You will forgive me, my lady, if I do not bow," Ithinia said. "As you can see, I am in the midst of a spell I hope will restore the palace to its proper place."

Alris nodded. "Of course, Ithinia."

For a moment neither woman spoke; then Ithinia asked, "Are you here on behalf of Lord Azrad?"

"I am here as his representative, yes," Alris replied, "but I am also here on my own behalf."

"Are you?" Ithinia's tone was polite, but uninterested.

"Yes. But first, the overlord wishes to know what he might expect from you and this demented warlock."

Ithinia nodded. "Please extend to Lord Azrad my apologies for allowing this situation to arise. I regret to say I am not entirely sure what he should expect. Emperor Vond has disappeared. He may return at any time, and when he does I expect he will lift the palace off this sandbar and once again suspend it over the city."

"Lord Azrad has been given to understand that the emperor has done this because you attempted to deceive him in some fashion."

Ithinia sighed. "Yes, we did. We had hoped to discourage him from using his magic recklessly."

"Who is 'we'?"

"Myself and certain other magicians, most particularly a witch named Kirris of Slave Street. I very much regret to say that Kirris is dead now; Vond killed her." Ithinia allowed herself a sigh. "We meant no harm."

"Yet here we are, in a palace that has been yanked out of the ground like a weed, dangled over the city for hours, and then flung aside."

"I am aware —" Ithinia began.

"Lord Azrad is not interested in what you may be aware of," Alris interrupted. "He has sent me here to express his very great displeasure at being caught in the middle of a feud between two magicians."

Ithinia was startled; she was not accustomed to being interrupted. She said, "I —"

"Furthermore," Alris continued, cutting her off, "he wishes me to convey to you his intense annoyance at the apparent hypocrisy involved. We all know your Guild forbids the overlord to interfere with magical business, yet you and the warlock seem to have had no compunction about interfering with the overlord."

"On the contrary, I am appalled that Vond —"

"Heretofore," Alris went on relentlessly, "Lord Azrad and his predecessors have allowed wizards a great deal of leeway, as have the other overlords. He would remind you that it was you and your fellow wizards who convinced his father to allow warlocks to live in this city in the first place. He would also remind you that while he knows wizards and warlocks are very powerful, there are other powerful magicians who would be happy to see your position in Ethshar reduced."

"Yes," Ithinia said. "I know."

Alris glared silently at her.

"Are you done?" Ithinia asked.

"I have delivered the overlord's message," Alris replied.

"Good. Tell Lord Azrad that he has every right to be upset, and I can assure him that I will be more careful in the future. The spell I am working on, once completed, will allow us to keep the palace airborne for a month, even if Vond releases it. It will not, I regret to say, prevent him from smashing the palace in some other way, but at least if he drops it — if, perhaps, he were to die suddenly while the palace is aloft — it won't fall, but can instead be lowered gently back into its place. Furthermore, I am doing what I can to make peace with Emperor Vond; I have sworn not to harm him, and I hope that once his temper has cooled we'll be able to reach some sort of agreement to leave each other alone. I apologize for all this."

Alris listened, then asked, "You've sworn not to harm him?"

"Yes." Ithinia saw no need to explain any further, or offer any greater assurances than a simple statement.

"Does *he* know that?" Alris demanded.

"He heard me say it."

"And yet the palace is still on a sandbar."

Ithinia grimaced. "Obviously, his temper has not yet cooled. I would also guess that he is not necessarily sure my word is good, or that my friends and allies won't take action against him without me."

Alris nodded. "I see. I will tell Lord Azrad what you've said."

"Thank you." Ithinia frowned as she completed a tricky pass, then looked up from the table and asked, "Was there anything else?"

"Not from the overlord. For myself, though — have you seen my brother Hanner? Do you know whether he's all right? He was staying in our uncle's...at Warlock House, and that's where Vond is now."

"It's where Vond *was*, certainly," Ithinia said. "My friends and I aren't entirely sure just where he is now."

"Do you know where *Hanner* is?"

Reluctantly, Ithinia admitted, "I'm not sure. We think he went through that tapestry he commissioned before he was Called, but we don't know for certain whether he's still over there. You might consult another magician, though; I've been rather busy with other concerns."

"I haven't seen him since he was Called," Alris said. "Nerra did — Lady Nerra, our sister — and he visited Mavi, who used to be his wife, but *I* haven't seen him, and neither have any of his children. *You* did, didn't you?"

"Yes, I did," Ithinia said. "He seemed fine."

"Did he?" Her tone made it clear that Alris was genuinely concerned for her brother's welfare.

"Very much so," Ithinia said. "Like all the Called warlocks, he didn't age while he was in Aldagmor, so he isn't any older than he was sixteen years ago —"

"Seventeen," Alris interrupted.

"Seventeen, then. He looked a little tired and worn after his hardships in the wilderness, but he seemed to be healthy and in good spirits."

"Tired?"

"Yes," Ithinia said. She knew that since Hanner had been a warlock, Alris had not seen her brother tired in decades. "Tired. He's free of the Calling, and no longer a warlock. But he's fine."

"Then why didn't he come to *see* me?" Alris asked plaintively.

"He's been busy," Ithinia said, suddenly sympathetic. "And remember, for you it's been seventeen years, but for him it's only been a few days."

"You don't think he's been avoiding me?"

"I'm afraid I really have no idea," Ithinia said. "I've known him for decades, but we've never been close; I won't pretend to know his thoughts. I think he's found it somewhat unsettling to see how much things have changed in his absence; perhaps he doesn't want to see how much you've aged."

Alris stared at Ithinia for a moment, then shook her head. "That's silly," she said. "He's my brother, not my lover."

"You're now a decade older than he is."

"No, I'm younger…oh. Well, yes, but…" She hesitated as she thought it over, then shook her head again. "That's not it," she said. She frowned. "But that's…you know, sometimes I really *hate* magic."

Ithinia grimaced as she completed the elaborate pattern of gestures, and lowered her hands. "I'll need to continue the spell when the lesser moon rises, but for now I can rest." She looked up at Alris. "I love magic. Yes, it can do strange and unexpected things, but I love it. It gives the World flavor. I think I would love it even if I couldn't work a single spell."

"You can have it," Alris said. "Magic killed my uncle, and snatched my brother away, and now it's dumped my home out here, where I need the longest ladder we have just to get down from the front door, and I'd need to wade fifty yards to reach the Newmarket beaches. It makes everything dangerous and unpredictable — sooner or later it might kill us all just because some wizard mispronounced a word, or a demonologist said the wrong thing. Yes, it's wonderful when it works, but it's not worth it." She turned away. "I'll tell Lord Azrad what you said." She headed toward the door.

"Please make it clear that I do apologize," Ithinia called after her.

Alris didn't reply.

Then Ithinia was alone in the room, the makings of her spell spread out before her.

Poor Alris, she thought. Poor Azrad. Poor Hanner. They were all caught up in this mess through no fault of their own. But that was the way of the World; as Alris had said, magic was dangerous. It had consequences and complications, and not just for its practitioners.

Ithinia certainly hoped it would have serious consequences for Vond. That damned fool was endangering *everyone* by meddling with those towers. Maybe she should have just *told* him that in the first place, and asked him to be careful, but she had feared he might not believe her, or worse, that he might consider it an opportunity for massive blackmail — let him do whatever he pleased, or he might smash the towers. But she hadn't told him, and it was obviously too late now. He was in no mood to trust her ever again. She had sworn not to harm him, and she hoped that would be enough to prevent any further open conflict, but she knew better than to think she could talk him into anything.

Of course, she had sworn that *she* would not harm him — but she was not about to stop anyone else who tried to harm him, and she thought that his spectacular display of petulance, pulling the palace out of the ground, would probably attract others who would do it for her.

Just as she thought that, someone cleared his throat. She looked up, and there was the man in the brown robe who had been in her parlor. "Demerchan," she said.

"Just Kelder," he replied. "I am hardly the entirety of the cult."

"Is Kelder your true name, then?"

"You don't think I'm stupid enough to give a wizard my true name." It was a statement, not a question.

"I suppose not. What brings you here, then?"

"A courtesy," he said. "Nothing more."

"Oh? And what courtesy would that be?"

"I thought you would want to know. The cult has decided not to remove His Imperial Majesty, the Great Vond. We would prefer to see the Wizards' Guild make peace with him, as well."

Ithinia had lived for centuries, and was not easily surprised by the foolishness of others, but this startled her. "Why?" she demanded. "He's a threat to us all!"

"We do not believe he poses as great a threat as you assume."

"But he's interfering with the towers in Lumeth!"

Kelder shook his head. "We think you misjudge his situation."

"He could make a thousand new unCallable warlocks!"

Kelder smiled wryly. "Do you think he *will*?"

"No," Ithinia admitted. "But why risk it?"

"The cult has its own reasons."

"As does the Guild."

"Of course. Let me remind you, Guildmaster, that you swore not to harm him."

"I am not likely to forget it."

"Let me remind you also that wizards who break oaths die. If the Guild does not see to it, the Cult of Demerchan will."

"You're threatening me?"

"I am reminding you of the stakes."

"I don't need your reminder."

"Nonetheless, I have given it. Here's another reminder — the lesser moon will be rising in less than an hour. You should get something to eat."

"I know that!" Ithinia snapped. "If you weren't here with your nonsensical reminders, I would be on my way to the kitchens."

"I won't keep you, then." He bowed, wrapping his brown cloak around himself, and vanished.

"We wizards aren't the only ones he's annoyed, you know!" Ithinia called at the empty air. "Sooner or later, someone's going to cut his throat."

There was no reply, and after a moment she turned and hurried toward the door. She really did want something to eat before beginning the next part of the spell.

Chapter Thirty-Seven

Hanner wondered idly where Rudhira was hiding, and whether she had a specific plan in mind, or just didn't want to cooperate with Vond. He had not seen her in hours. While it was possible she had slipped away into the woods, or somewhere else well away from the village, Hanner thought it was more likely she was still close at hand, watching and listening. She had been in the refuge for some time before Hanner himself arrived, and probably knew her way around better than anyone else; if there were safe hiding places to be found, she might well have found them.

He glanced at the sleeping figures lying all around, soldiers and refugees alike, taking up almost all the floor space in the three rooms of the house where the tapestry hung. There were enough of them that Hanner thought he could feel their accumulated body heat, and he knew he could smell them. None of them seemed to have noticed that the redhead was missing; probably most of them had either never realized she was there at all, or thought she had already gone back through the tapestry to the attic of Warlock House.

Hanner had hoped that some of the refugees who had been sent back to Ethshar would return to the refuge, but none had. A guard named Balrad, the second of the pair who had accompanied Vond himself, had explained, before he went to sleep, that the emperor had assigned some of his hirelings to stand guard, making sure that no one else used that tapestry until Vond returned. Hanner had feared that might be the case, and would have liked more details, but Balrad had not been willing to provide them. Like most of the others, he had been tired and eager to rest.

Hanner almost wished *he* could sleep, but after staying up the entire night before, and then sleeping away most of the day here in the village, he was wide awake. The unmoving sun here did not provide any of the visual cues that might have helped him to get back on a normal schedule; quite the contrary, in fact. Combine that with the stress of his situation, and sleep was not a possibility, and after awhile he gave up any attempt to doze. He asked the waking guards a few questions every so often, but for the most part he sat quietly, watching, listening, and thinking.

Ever since he woke up in Aldagmor he had been reacting to events, doing what seemed to need doing, and never really stopping to think. He had led the Called warlocks as best he could, trying to guide them to safety, but then he had been snatched back to Ethshar by the wizards. Ithinia had hired him, more or less, to keep the former warlocks in line — he had not done very much in that regard, really, but why had he agreed to do it at all? It had been expedient, but was it really the right thing to do? The wizards had helped him, so he had been inclined to help them in return, but why should he side with the Wizards' Guild against other warlocks? Ithinia said they were dangerous, and they probably *were* potentially dangerous — certainly Vond was a real threat. But would Vond have been so very dangerous if Ithinia and her coterie hadn't attacked him? Sending a false Calling nightmare had only made Vond *more* dangerous, by making him angry.

Perhaps reasons no longer mattered; however it had happened, Vond was now *extremely* dangerous — at least, when he was in Ethshar. Pulling the overlord's palace out of the ground and holding it over the city — that was *insane*.

At least if that man Kolar was to be believed, Vond had put the palace down safely before stepping through the tapestry, rather than letting it fall; Hanner had eventually gotten up the nerve to ask about that. True, the emperor had put it down on a sandbar, and not back where it belonged, but it was better than dropping it on the New City.

Vond had only intended to be gone for a few minutes, not an entire night, and he planned to pick the palace up again as soon as he had his magic back. Hanner knew Vond intended to continue his feud with Ithinia. Whether he hoped to kill her eventually, or to force some other sort of capitulation, Hanner was unsure; he did not think Vond himself had any clear idea how the conflict might be resolved. Killing Ithinia would put him at war with the entire Wizards' Guild, and he couldn't hope to defeat *all* of them, but how could he trust any lesser sort of surrender Ithinia might offer?

For that matter, would Ithinia and the rest of the Guild accept anything less than Vond's death? Any assassination would need to catch the emperor off-guard; if Vond had even a second to retaliate, he might be unable to save himself, but he could kill everyone nearby — or perhaps worse, from the Guild's point of view, he might be able to turn anyone in sight into a warlock. Depending on who that might be, the result could be even worse than the present situation. Vond was a short-tempered egotist, but he was not actively malicious, nor was he subtle. A more vicious warlock could do far more damage in the short term, and a smarter warlock could do more given time.

Hanner did not think Vond would ever give anyone else access to his new Source while he lived; he was not the sort who would want to share power, nor would he trust an ally for very long. If he was about to die, though, he would almost certainly want to carry out a final act of revenge.

Right now, while Vond was in this magical refuge and cut off from his own power, there was a sort of unintentional enforced truce. Vond had no magic, and Ithinia could not easily reach him here, if she even knew where he was. This *should* be an opportunity to end the whole stupid conflict peacefully, Hanner thought. If he could find a way to keep Vond here, and powerless, that should be enough to satisfy Ithinia. If he only had some way to communicate with her, perhaps he could arrange something.

His time was limited, though. He glanced at the tapestry. When the sun rose in Ethshar it would start working again, Vond would leave, and this chance would be lost forever. Hanner doubted Vond would ever again risk coming here, and giving up his magic; it was astonishing that he had done it even this once.

Before falling asleep Vond had said he had been driven largely by curiosity in coming here, and now his curiosity was satisfied. He had also wanted to demonstrate that he was not afraid to come here, and he had done that. With those motives gone, he would not be back. He and his swordsmen would drive everyone out. Then he might destroy the tapestry and seal this place off from Ethshar forever — or he might carry through on the idea of bringing in several more tapestries and using it as a sort of mystic junction to reach various spots around the World more quickly than he could fly. Either way, he wouldn't allow anyone but himself and his loyal followers to visit this place.

If only someone in Ethshar knew what was happening, and could block the attic tapestry somehow to keep Vond isolated until matters could be worked out — but the only chance for communication Hanner could think of was if someone was attempting to reach him with the Spell of Invaded Dreams, and that would only work if he could sleep.

He couldn't. Even if he could, there was no guarantee that anyone *was* trying to reach him; after all, it was the middle of the night in Ethshar, and Hanner had no reason to think anyone there was aware of the situation. Sleeping might merely mean giving away any chance at a resolution that he had.

He could not rely on outside help for a solution. He needed to take action himself if he wanted to end this. If someone were to kill Vond here and now, that would be an end of all this trouble, but Hanner could not do that. He was not a killer by nature — and more importantly, Vond was guarded by a dozen men, and not all of them were asleep. At the moment the two on duty were Kolar and Marl; they were awake and ready to defend their employer, as well as the attic tapestry that they hoped would take them home.

A thought struck Hanner, and he looked at the tapestry. *Would* the two soldiers defend it? If the tapestry was ruined, Vond would be stuck here, and powerless. This stupid war between wizards and warlock would be over.

Of course, the rest of them would be stuck here, as well. That was a fairly major drawback. He and Rudhira, wherever she was, and the other refugees would be stranded here with a furious Vond and his soldiers. They might well be killed.

Or perhaps not — as Hanner had said, if he died, Vond might *never* get back to Ethshar. Zallin could not be trusted, and even if he tried to obey, the wizards and their allied witches and other magicians might stop him. If Hanner lived, though, there was always a chance someone would eventually come for *him*. His sisters would miss him, or Ithinia might contact him on her own to find out what had become of Vond. He, Hanner, would be the one in a position of power, able to dictate terms, because he was the one more likely to eventually provide a way home. He could bargain for the lives of the refugees, and for his own — assuming he lived long enough.

It was a risk, certainly, but wouldn't it be worth it to ensure that Vond and Ithinia stopped trying to destroy each other, and that no one else would be caught in the middle and killed, as that poor witch had been? Even if Hanner died, wouldn't it be worth it? He had already lost his old life, and had not yet had time to build a new one. His death would mean that Mavi would be free of any lingering guilt or second thoughts. His sisters and children could get on with their lives — they had thought he was dead for years, and a second death would surely not be so very painful. He didn't *want* that to happen, but it would not be so very terrible. Hanner got to his feet.

Kolar saw that movement, and turned to watch. He said nothing, but stared directly at Hanner.

"Mind if I test the tapestry?" Hanner asked quietly.

Kolar glanced over at his sleeping employer, and all the other unconscious forms on the floor, the woman who had previously tested the magic curled up among them. He turned up a palm. "Why not?" he said.

Hanner smiled, and walked across the room, trying to look completely calm and casual. He let his hand fall to the hilt of his belt-knife, and pretended not to notice when Kolar responded by dropping his own hand to the hilt of his sword.

Marl, who had been dozing on his feet, started and straightened up. "Test?" he said.

"This fellow's going to try the tapestry," Kolar said.

"Oh," Marl said. He glanced at Vond, then looked back at Hanner. "All right," he said. "Go ahead."

"Thank you," Hanner said, bobbing his head in acknowledgment. His right hand closed on his knife, while his left reached out toward the tapestry. Kolar stepped back to give him room.

This would mean he would be trapped here, Hanner reminded himself. He might not see his children for months, if he ever saw them again at all. He might be killed. He might be tortured. But it would put an end to Vond's reckless displays of power, his murders and thefts and arrogance. Lives would almost certainly be saved, even if Hanner's wasn't among them. He grabbed the fabric of the tapestry in his left hand, then drew his knife and slashed.

"*Hai!*" Kolar shouted. "*Hai,* what are you doing? Are you crazy?" His sword flashed as he snatched it up.

Marl's blade was out, as well; the tip was at Hanner's throat as he said, "Drop the knife!"

Hanner dropped the knife and raised his empty hands.

The commotion had awakened several of the others; now a babble of voices arose as they saw what was happening.

Then silence fell as Vond got awkwardly to his feet and advanced toward Hanner. He stopped and stared at the tapestry, at the long diagonal gash in the cloth that cut a jagged slice out of the attic's sloping ceiling and rough tie-beams. Then he turned to face Hanner.

"You've *ruined* it!" he said.

"Yes, I have," Hanner said.

"The magic won't work any more, will it?"

"No, it won't," Hanner said. "It will take a wizard months of work to repair it, if it can be done at all."

"So we're all stranded here? Is that what you wanted?"

"Someone will contact us eventually, I'm sure," Hanner said, trying to keep his voice steady as Marl's sword-point pressed against a point an inch below the corner of his jaw. Hanner was not sure, but he thought that was roughly the location of his jugular vein.

Vond strode forward and snatched the sword from Marl's hand, but kept it pressed against Hanner's neck. He pushed a little harder, drawing a drop of blood. "You did this to keep me from getting my magic back, didn't you?" he said. "You think you're in charge now, as the one who someone in Ethshar will contact. You don't believe Zallin will do anything; you think *you're* the one someone will rescue. You think you can leave me here, powerless, or maybe that I'll agree to whatever terms the wizards set to get them to help me."

Hanner tried to raise his jaw higher, to pull away from the sword's point. He did not answer.

"You think I won't kill you?" Vond shouted, his voice rising in pitch.

Hanner tried to move to one side, to get away from the blade pressing into his throat, but Vond turned to follow. Kolar stepped back to make room.

The pressure on Hanner's throat increased, and he could feel blood running down his neck and under the collar of his tunic. He would have swallowed, but that would only make the sword cut deeper.

Hanner realized he was going to die. Vond had already demonstrated that he didn't mind killing people who annoyed him, and Hanner had just done far worse to him than anyone else ever had — well, anyone except perhaps that poor witch who had sent him the Calling nightmare.

A motion above and behind Vond's head caught Hanner's eye, and he looked upward for an instant. A panel had opened in the ceiling, and he could see a dark space there. He caught a glimpse of red hair. No one else seemed to notice; they were all facing the other way, staring at Hanner and the ruined tapestry.

Then Vond flicked the sword slightly, drawing a stinging scratch across his skin, and Hanner's attention returned to the warlock.

"They'll come for me eventually," Vond said. "Zallin or one of the others. I'm the one who can bring warlockry back into the World, Hanner. Maybe *you* don't want your magic back, but plenty of people do. Maybe *you* don't want power, but *someone* will, and he'll come here to find me. I don't need you, and I can't trust you. You'll have to die. I'm sorry about that — you were almost a legend, you know. You founded the Council and saved warlocks from extermination, but now you've turned against us, and I can't allow a traitor to live. You understand that, don't you?" The blade cut a little more deeply, and Hanner felt the stream of warm blood running down his neck thicken. He could feel it trickling down his chest.

He was going to die.

He had faced an inevitable doom before, when he heard the Call, but this was more immediate, more personal. He could feel his entire body tensing; his hands were trembling. He wanted to close his eyes, to not see the killing blow, to not see the hatred in Vond's expression, but he kept them open; he did not want to give the warlock the satisfaction of seeing how scared he was.

Hanner stared defiantly at the warlock, his heart pounding. Vond drew his hand back to strike.

And Rudhira plummeted from the opening in the ceiling, an iron cooking pot in one hand and her belt-knife in the other. She landed on the warlock's shoulders, then slammed the heavy pot down onto Vond's head with ferocious force. Hanner heard bone crunch.

Vond collapsed, with Rudhira riding him to the floor; the sword fell from his hand, and Rudhira's knife reached around and slashed his throat from ear to ear.

Someone screamed. The crowded room was thrown into complete chaos as anyone who had still been asleep awoke, while some people were trying to escape the violence and others were trying to get a better look.

Blood spurted from Vond's opened throat as he struggled on the floor, trying to speak, trying to get his limbs under him; his eyes were wide with terror and pain.

Rudhira had not waited to make sure Vond was dead, or to see how the others would react; once she had finished her attack she dropped the iron pot, sprang to her feet, and ran for the door, her bloody knife still in her hand. Two of Vond's men reached for her, but not in time. The two or three people directly in her path stepped aside; no one wanted to touch the woman who had just appeared out of nowhere and cut a man's throat. She vanished out the door into the sunlit street.

For an instant Hanner, Marl, and Kolar didn't move; then Hanner and Marl simultaneously dove for the dropped sword. Hanner did not worry about reaching the hilt, so his hand got there first, closing around the blade. He felt the edge cut into his fingers, but he didn't care; he snatched the weapon up and stepped back. He was just reaching his other hand toward the hilt when Kolar's blade pressed against his chest.

He froze, but did not release the sword. He nodded toward Vond. "He's not dead yet," he said.

Kolar did not allow himself to be distracted, but others, jarred from immobility by Hanner's words, moved to roll Vond over. Someone had a piece of cloth, perhaps from a tunic, that he was using as a makeshift bandage to stanch the flow of blood, but it wasn't enough; the pool of blood was spreading, and Vond's movements were weakening. His eyes were wide and staring. He was still choking, but more weakly.

"What did you do?" Kolar demanded.

"I ruined the tapestry," Hanner said.

"You killed Vond!" Marl shouted.

"I most certainly did not!" Hanner shouted back. "If I had meant to kill him, why would I have cut the tapestry and trapped *all* of us here?"

"Kill him, Kolar!" Marl yelled.

Kolar kept his sword in position, but did not advance. Instead he eyed Hanner thoughtfully. "Was Vond right? What he said about you thinking you can get us out of here?"

"More or less," Hanner said. "I think my sisters will look for me, and find some way to get us all back to Ethshar."

"Who *was* that?" Kolar asked. "The woman who attacked Vond?"

"Her name is Rudhira of Camptown," Hanner said. "She's another of the Called."

"Why did she do it?"

"You'll have to ask her. I don't know."

"I should kill you for what you did."

"Maybe," Hanner said, "but if you do, you'll be hurting your chances of ever getting home. And Vond won't be paying you now — he doesn't have any allies to make good on his debts once he's dead."

Hanner had managed to keep his voice steady as he spoke, though he was not sure how he had done it — perhaps he had been so certain that Vond was about to kill him that Kolar's threat carried little weight by comparison. Now he met Kolar's gaze, looking him directly in the eye, just as he had Vond. If he *was* about to die after all, at least he could still do so with dignity.

"*You* won't make good his debts?"

The question caught Hanner by surprise. His eyes flicked very briefly to the rest of the room, to see how the other swordsmen were taking this, then back to Kolar. "How much did he promise you?" he asked. "I don't have much money of my own, but my sisters are wealthy; we might be able to work out a partial payment of some sort."

Kolar was still considering when someone called, "That sounds good enough to me!"

"He ruined the tapestry that would have gotten us all home!" a new voice protested.

"It wasn't working," another voice retorted. "We don't know if it *ever* would have worked again."

At that the whole room seemed to break out in argument.

As swordsmen and refugees debated Hanner's fate, the Great Vond, emperor of Semma and the Vondish Empire, died there on the floor. The crude attempts to help him had been too little, too late — though in fact, it was unlikely anything but powerful magic could have saved him. Even if something had stopped the bleeding, the blow to the head had cracked his skull and might have been fatal on its own.

For several moments it appeared Hanner might follow him, but in the end, no one really wanted Hanner dead. If he had been run through immediately it would probably have been accepted as a reasonable response, but no one had the heart to kill him in cold blood long after the tapestry was ruined and Vond was dead.

If Rudhira had been present, providing a more appropriate target, matters might have been different, but by the time anyone thought to attempt pursuit she had vanished completely. Hanner hoped that she was all right, wherever she might be.

And while he did not care to admit any approval of her methods, he knew she had probably saved the World a great deal of trouble.

Chapter Thirty-Eight

Zallin stared at the tapestry in the fourth-floor bedroom, but kept his distance. He did not understand exactly how the spell worked, and had no intention of getting close enough to risk suddenly learning more.

Vond had vanished through that thing, and had left Zallin in charge in his absence — but he hadn't given Zallin any magic, and how was he supposed to be in charge without magic? He wasn't a lord, with a family history of authority. He wasn't a guardsman, with weapons and training in giving orders. Zallin had only ever had the ability to command anything when he was a warlock. If Vond had made him a warlock again...

But Vond hadn't given *anyone* access to his new kind of warlockry. He had claimed that he would, in time, but he hadn't yet. He had gone adventuring off through the tapestry without giving anyone the means to keep order in his absence.

In fact, Zallin was beginning think Vond would *never* teach anyone else to use the Lumeth source. He would keep dangling it just out of reach.

Zallin was also beginning to wonder whether he really even *wanted* his magic back, if it was conditional on being Vond's underling. He wanted to be a warlock again, yes, very much, but he wanted to be the kind of warlock he had always been — a respected magician, a normal part of Ethshar's society, someone people hired to do things that could not be done without magic. He didn't want to be a servant to a madman who was terrorizing the city, feuding with witches and wizards and antagonizing the overlord.

Most of all, he didn't want to hurt anybody.

He had seen Vond throwing people around. He had seen the palace hanging in the air above the city. Vond didn't care who he hurt, or what damage he did. Zallin did not consider himself a soft-hearted weakling — when he happened to observe a thief's flogging, he had applauded justice being done, and he didn't regret seeing murderers hanged. That was all part of the way the World worked. The sort of casual violence that Vond displayed, though, was not justice, it was brutality. Claiming Warlock House for his own, ordering everyone out — it wasn't right.

Zallin had stayed on, putting up with Vond's behavior, tolerating his...his evil, in hopes of getting his own warlockry back, but now that he had had time to do some serious thinking about this, and some serious drinking to try to make it work out, he was reluctantly coming to the conclusion that if serving Vond was required to be a warlock again, it wasn't worth it. Not even if the *oushka* held out, which didn't look likely.

Right now Vond was on the other side of that tapestry, but he might reappear at any time and start ordering Zallin to run his errands again, and Zallin did not *want* to run the emperor's errands.

Sterren had not wanted to serve Vond anymore, so he had simply disappeared. He had taken his luggage and vanished into the city streets. Vond had complained and called Sterren a traitor, but he had not *done* anything about it. He had not gone looking for Sterren, or demanded his return. Several of the other former warlocks who had initially pledged to obey Vond had also quietly slipped away. No one had wanted to be purser or envoy for the emperor; they had wanted to be warlocks. When it began to look as if, despite his promises, Vond wasn't ever going to permit that, they had left.

If Zallin disappeared in the same fashion, would Vond do anything more? Zallin could not see why he would. Vond didn't care about him; Vond didn't care about anyone but himself. He wanted a few people around to run his errands, but he didn't care whether it was Sterren, or Hanner, or Zallin, or Gerath who ran them, just so long as *someone* did.

In fact, now that he had his band of sword-wielding hirelings, Vond would probably find Zallin more of a nuisance than a help, and anyone Vond considered a nuisance was likely to wind up injured or dead. Zallin thought bitterly that Vond's chief bully-boy Gerath was more likely to become a new warlock than he was.

The time had come, Zallin decided, to get out, while he had the chance. He turned and headed for the stairs.

A few moments later he was in the room he had been using since Vond usurped the master's chamber, where he was gathering his belongings into bags and bundles. The entire time he was packing he was listening nervously for sounds from upstairs, for any hint that Vond had returned. He was ready to make a run for it without his baggage, if necessary.

But it wasn't necessary. He was able to get everything vital stowed into two bags, a large one he slung over his shoulder, and a small one he carried in his other hand. The rest he shoved into the empty closet, in case he ever had a chance to retrieve it. Half an hour after reaching his decision to leave he was in the front hall, wrapped in his winter coat and with a broad-brimmed hat pulled down to his ears, reaching for the door.

That was when someone knocked, startling him so badly he dropped his bags. He stood frozen, staring at the white-painted wood.

When nothing more happened he glanced into the parlor, then peered into the dining room, and saw no one. He knew most of Hanner's guests had fled, and Vond's hirelings were all upstairs, but he was still somewhat startled to see no one else around. Uncertainly, he reached out and opened the door.

A young woman was standing on the front step, and while Zallin knew immediately that he had seen her before, it took a moment to place her. Eventually, though, he realized that this was the whore Vond had brought back from Camptown. She was wearing a long cloak that was entirely appropriate for the weather, but which hid her bright clothing and made identification more difficult. "Yes?" Zallin said.

"Hanner told me to come back for my pay," she said. "Well, actually, he told me to go find his sister at the overlord's palace, but I'm not about to swim out to that sandbar and try climbing up the stone. So I'm here, and I want my money."

"Hanner isn't here," Zallin said. "At least, I don't think he is."

"Hanner isn't the one who owes me," she said. "That skinny warlock who calls himself an emperor is."

"He's not here, either," Zallin began.

"*You* are," she snapped. "And you were with him in Camptown, too. I saw you. You started to talk to me."

"Yes, I remember," Zallin said.

"So you can pay me."

Zallin closed his eyes. He did not need this right now. He wanted to get out of Warlock House and away from High Street before Vond reappeared. He opened his eyes again and said, "*I* wasn't the one who hired you."

"You work for him."

"But I don't —"

She cut him off. "You know what? I don't care who you are, or what you do. You're here in the warlock's house. You can pay me, or you can find someone who'll pay me, or I can start screaming for the city guard — and in case you hadn't noticed, there are at least a dozen guardsmen in the street out front. Which will it be?"

"Fine," Zallin said, reaching for his smaller bag. He had packed up a good bit of the Council's treasury — not all of it, because he did not want Vond labeling him a thief and finding additional motive to look for him, but more than half, since after all, no one other than himself knew how much money had been there to begin with. It wouldn't be missed, as long as he left a believable sum. "How much?"

"Five rounds."

Zallin closed his eyes again, and sighed. He did not bother to doubt her; Vond had almost certainly agreed to her price, no matter how outrageous it was. After all, he didn't intend to actually *earn* his money; he would simply take it, since no one could stop him.

"I'm waiting," the woman said.

"Yes," Zallin said, opening his bag and digging for a purse. A moment later he counted forty bits into the woman's waiting hand. He had to stop after twenty, though, so she could transfer the money to a purse of her own, somewhere under that heavy brown cloak; forty was more than she could hold in both palms.

When he had finished he tucked the purse away, and when he looked up again the whore was grinning at him. "Thank you," she said. "I was beginning to wonder whether I'd ever really get it."

"Well, you did," Zallin said, picking up his baggage. "I wouldn't suggest coming back for another night, though. I'm leaving, and I think Hanner's already gone, and no one else around here is likely to keep his Imperial Majesty honest."

"I wasn't planning to come back," she said. "Oh, it was quite an experience, I don't think I'll ever forget it, but he's crazy and he's dangerous."

Zallin nodded. "Yes, he is."

"He smashed right through the ceiling when I was here, and hung naked in the air. It was amazing."

"So I heard."

She looked at his bags. "You're leaving? Where are you going?"

Zallin opened his mouth to answer, then closed it again. He frowned. "I don't really know," he admitted.

"I know a cheap inn in Eastgate. I can show you."

"That sounds as good a place as any. Thanks." He slung the larger bag over his shoulder, and together the two of them marched out the door onto High Street.

As they walked eastward they chatted idly, their breath visible in the chilly air. Zallin finally managed to remember the woman's name, Leth of Pawnbroker Lane. He had been drunk when he heard it before, but it came back eventually.

"When Vond and I were in Camptown," Zallin remarked, "most people were avoiding us — with good reason. Why didn't you?"

"There was money to be made," she said. She hefted the fat purse under her cloak to emphasize her point. "Throwing people around reduced the competition."

"Weren't you worried it would reduce your lifespan, as well?"

She turned up an empty palm. "Not really," she said. "I knew he wouldn't kill me."

"How?"

She gave him a sideways glance, then said, "Do you really want to know?"

Zallin hesitated, but curiosity triumphed. "Yes, I do," he said.

Leth nodded. "All right, then. About ten years ago, when I was a little girl, I got sick — seriously sick, to the point my mother expected me to die. She hired a wizard named Orzavar the Seer to advise her — in fact, she sold our house on Pawnbroker Lane to pay him, and to pay the healer he sent her to. I hope she thought it was worth it — she said she did, but you know how parents are."

"Of course," Zallin lied. He knew *his* parents wouldn't have sold their house to pay a magician to help him. "But I don't see the connection."

"Well, since she was already giving up everything to pay the seer and the healer, she wanted to be sure it would work, and she asked a few other questions. Orzavar informed her that I was going to die peacefully in my sleep at the age of eighty-one. He swore it, by several gods and by his magic — he wasn't just trying to comfort her. So I don't worry about getting killed."

"Oh," Zallin said.

"I can still get hurt, of course," Leth said conversationally. "But Vond didn't look interested in hurting people just for the sake of hurting them — I've known men like that, and he didn't seem to be one of them. If he did throw me around — well, I knew I'd survive."

They walked on in silence for a moment as Zallin absorbed this, and then he asked, "What happened to your mother?"

"She was murdered a sixnight later," Leth said. "With the house gone, we were sleeping in the Hundred-Foot Field, and she didn't hide what was left of her money well enough. That's why I've been walking the streets in Camptown."

That matter-of-fact little biography horrified Zallin. He remembered his own mother, who was still alive — or at least, she had been a month ago.

"What about your father?" he asked.

"I have no idea who he is. My mother never said. Well, when I was very little she said he was a sailor by the name of Kelder who was lost at sea, and maybe he really was, but I don't know."

"No other family?"

"No other family. What about you?"

"I grew up in Westwark, with three older brothers," Zallin said. "Everyone thought I was magical because of my eyes, so I decided I might as well *be* magical, and apprenticed myself to old Feregris the Warlock. I haven't seen my family much since, and after Feregris was Called..." He stopped in mid-sentence, blinking.

"Feregris was Called?" Leth prompted, after they had gone another half-dozen paces in silence. "You were saying?"

"He must be back now," Zallin said. "Feregris, I mean. It's been almost twenty years, but he must be back. *All* the Called came back."

"You think so?" Leth asked.

Zallin stopped walking. They were in the short block of High Street between Arena Street and Fishertown Street, just across the line from the New City into Allston, and the tall houses on either side gleamed golden in the early morning sun. "We're going the wrong way," he said.

"Not if we're headed to Eastgate," Leth said.

"I'm going to Crookwall," Zallin said. "I want to see if Feregris is back."

"He lived in Crookwall? Not the Wizards' Quarter?"

"In Crookwall," Zallin said. "On Incidental Street. When I was twelve I didn't dare go as far as the Wizards' Quarter, and Feregris was the only magician in Crookwall or Westwark."

"You said it's been twenty years," Leth pointed out. "Would he still have a place there?"

"He had a daughter."

Leth nodded. "If she's still there it's worth asking her, anyway."

"If Feregris is there — he was good to me. I want to be sure he's all right."

"That's kind of you."

Zallin blinked. No one had called him "kind" for as long as he could remember. No one had been kind *to* him, either, that he could recall.

But then, he hadn't done much to deserve kindness. Ever since he lost his magic he had been so focused on getting it back that he had not given much thought to anything else. He had followed Vond around, begging for his magic like a puppy hoping for a treat. He had ignored or argued with Hanner, who had merely tried to talk sense to him. He had treated all the other Called warlocks as a nuisance, something to be pushed aside as much as possible.

He remembered Feregris smiling patiently at him, surprising him with candies every so often, showing him clever little things a warlock could do, ways to accomplish his goals with a minimum of power, so as not to hasten the Calling. Those tricks hadn't been enough to save his master, though. By the time Zallin completed his apprenticeship, Feregris was having nightmares almost every night, and had a tendency to turn his face northward whenever he wasn't paying attention. Two months later he was gone.

That had hurt, losing his master. Feregris' daughter Virris had wanted no reminders of her father's magic, and had asked Zallin to stop visiting, and he had complied. He did not particularly want to be reminded of his loss, either; he had stopped visiting *anywhere* in Westwark or Crookwall.

Then he had set out to be the best warlock he could be, to prove himself worthy of his master's memory, and he had worked his way up until he became Chairman of the Council of Warlocks. He had used Feregris' old tricks to avoid using too much magic, so he had never been Called.

But then he had lost his magic, and he had tried to find a *new* master, in the form of the Great Vond.

Zallin mentally compared Feregris with Vond, and then his own behavior with both. He did not think he fared well against Feregris at all, but at least he wasn't as bad as Vond.

Not *quite* as bad as Vond, anyway.

His magic was gone; he had finally accepted that. Now he had to think about what he was going to do without it — not just how he might earn a living, but who he was going to be.

Being more like Feregris would be a good start, and finding Feregris, offering to help him, was the first step of that start. He looked at Leth, and held out a hand. "It was a pleasure talking to you," he said, "but I'm going the other direction."

"Oh, I don't have any business in Eastgate if you aren't going there," Leth said. "I'll come along, if you don't mind."

Zallin was startled. "You don't want to get home to Camptown?"

"Not particularly. Meeting this Feregris and your family sounds much more interesting."

"I wasn't...I mean, I didn't say anything about my family."

"If you're going to Crookwall, Westwark's just a few blocks farther."

Zallin hesitated, looking down at the bright red skirt showing beneath her coat that indicated Leth's occupation. Then he smiled.

Being more like his old master didn't mean he had to be the obedient little boy his mother and brother had tried to make him be. "You'll like my mother," he said.

"I will?"

"Oh, yes. Everyone does. But she'll *hate* you."

Leth grinned. "Sounds like fun," she said. "Let's go."

They turned and walked west.

Chapter Thirty-Nine

Hanner had been expecting the dream, so when he found himself in Ithinia's parlor, facing Rothiel of Wizard Street, rather than on his makeshift mattress in the village beyond the tapestry, he was not surprised.

"What's going on, Hanner?" Rothiel demanded. "Where are you?"

"Hello, Rothiel," Hanner said. "I'm in the refuge beyond the tapestry."

"You are? Is Vond... We had reports that he followed you through the tapestry, but since he'd be powerless there, we don't...Is he there? Where *is* Vond? Do you know?"

"I do," Hanner said. "He did come here after me."

"He's *there*? But he doesn't have his magic there, does he?"

"He doesn't have anything," Hanner replied. "Vond is dead. The return tapestry was ruined, and we were all stranded here, and someone cut his throat."

"Dead?" Rothiel looked shocked. "You're sure he's really dead?"

"Oh, yes," Hanner said. "His body has been burned. He's unquestionably dead."

"Then it's over?" Rothiel asked. "It's really *over*? There are no more warlocks?"

"Well, *I* don't know of any more," Hanner replied, nettled at the wizard's attitude. Rothiel seemed to have forgotten that he was speaking to a former warlock.

"Ithinia will be pleased."

"Ithinia?" Hanner's temper got the better of him. "This... This... Ithinia *caused* this! If she had left Vond alone, he might never have caused any real trouble! If she didn't want him using his magic, she could have *talked* to him, made a deal of some kind!"

The wizard stepped back, startled by Hanner's outburst, then shook his head. "He couldn't be trusted, Hanner," Rothiel said soothingly. "How many times did you see him break promises? How many people did you see him hurt, simply because they were in his way? Yes, we tried to trick him into giving up his magic, but did *he* try to talk to *us* when he found out? No, he killed our agent, and made threats and demands, putting hundreds of innocent lives in danger — lives that included your own sister and her family, I believe! Sooner or later, he would have done something catastrophic. He had to be stopped."

Hanner did not really want to defend Vond, but he could not resist saying, "So *he* couldn't be trusted with such powerful magic, but Ithinia *can*?"

"Ithinia has had her magic for centuries, and I don't see any disasters she's caused," Rothiel replied. "Besides, the Guild disciplines its own members, while no one could discipline Vond."

"The Guild disciplines its own?" Hanner said sarcastically, his hands on his hips. "Really? Who has the power to keep *Ithinia* from doing whatever she pleases?"

Rothiel's expression changed. He cast a furtive glance over his shoulder.

"Don't ask that, Hanner," he said. "You really don't want to know."

Startled out of his anger, Hanner blinked and did not answer for a moment. Then he said, "Can you get me back to Ethshar, even though the tapestry is ruined?"

"I'm fairly certain we can arrange something," Rothiel said. He hesitated, then asked, "Are you alone? No, you said you *all* were stranded. Who else is there, besides yourself?"

"About a dozen former warlocks, and a dozen or so mercenary swordsmen Vond hired."

"Mercenaries? Do you mean professionals from the Small Kingdoms?"

"No, I mean recruits from Shiphaven Market."

"Was it one of them who killed Vond, then? Lost his temper over the ruined tapestry, perhaps?"

"No. It was…someone else."

Rothiel considered that for a moment, obviously considering possible reasons Hanner had not named the killer, then turned up a hand. "Well, we'll see about getting you all out, and I don't think anyone is going to bring any charges about any of this — after all, I would think that place is outside the overlord's jurisdiction. I trust you can hold out for a few more days?"

"Yes, I think so."

"Good. I hope to see you in the waking world soon."

And with that, the dream was over.

When he awoke, Hanner told the others about the dream. He had the very definite impression that not everyone believed him, but there was nothing to be gained by arguing about it. It didn't really matter what anyone thought; they had all come to terms with their situation, and accepted the reality that there was nothing they could do to aid their rescue or hurry their return to Ethshar. All they could do was wait, and make the best of their situation while they waited. They gathered nuts, caught fish, and made do, Vond's mercenaries and the former warlocks working side by side.

The unchanging sun gave the refuge a timeless feel and made it impossible to judge just how long it really was before a wizard's apprentice appeared at the top of the slope, a heavy tapestry across his shoulders. Hanner and the others had slept twice more, so two or three days seemed like a reasonable guess.

Rudhira had not been seen during that time; in fact, no one had seen her since she fled after cutting Vond's throat. Hanner hoped she was safe. There had been vague suggestions that she should be hunted down and imprisoned, to be brought before a magistrate if and when they were able to return to Ethshar, but no one seemed eager to pursue the matter. Certainly, no one had done anything about her by the time the apprentice was spotted.

The new arrival was greeted with shouts of joy, but Hanner noticed that not everyone joined in — and it wasn't just the Called who appeared unenthusiastic. A couple of Vond's hirelings did not cheer. Marl, for one, looked more pensive than excited.

"Do you think it's a trick?" Hanner asked him.

Startled, Marl turned to look at him. "No," he said. "I just don't have much to go back to."

"Neither do I," said Sidor, who had overheard, "but I don't want to stay *here*. It's creepy, the way it's always early afternoon — it doesn't feel real. Those houses are all a bit strange, too — and who built them, anyway?"

"I'm not sure anyone did," Hanner said. "They may have been created by magic."

"Well, I don't like them."

"You could build your own, if you wanted to stay."

Sidor shook his head. "I don't. I'm going back to Ethshar."

Hanner nodded, and argued no further. Together, they joined the crowd following the apprentice down the hill. When they reached the village, the boy turned and said, "Which of you is Hanner the Generous?"

Hanner blinked; he had heard someone call him that before, but had not realized it was becoming his accepted name.

"He is," Marl said, pointing.

"Where would you like it, sir?" the apprentice asked Hanner.

Hanner chose a building more or less at random, and a moment later he watched as the apprentice secured the tapestry's support rod to the exposed rafters of one of the village houses, and then unrolled the hanging.

Hanner noticed that the rod had curious orange crystals at either end, and that two more crystals weighted the tapestry's lower corners. Those drew his attention so that he did not even register the tapestry's image at first. When he did finally look at the picture, he was startled to realize he recognized it; in fact, he was fairly certain he had been through this very tapestry once, long ago. It showed a sunlit little room with whitewashed walls and wicker furniture, though the image had been carefully arranged to hide the sun's angle. Hanner knew that room; it was in Ithinia's house on Lower Street, overlooking her garden.

If this tapestry did still work, that meant her house was still standing, which was good news — the overlord's palace really had not been dropped on it. It also meant that Ithinia was making an effort to be helpful; she had not offered this tapestry to bring the thousands of warlocks home from Aldagmor, presumably because she did not want a horde that size traipsing through her home, but she was willing to use it now to get Hanner and the others back to Ethshar.

But there were still some things about the tapestry that puzzled him. "What are those orange things?" he asked the apprentice. He did not recall anything of the sort being attached when he had been sent through this tapestry all those years ago.

"Hm?" The apprentice glanced at the support rod. "Oh, the Returning Crystals? Yes, well, you see, sir, this tapestry cannot *stay* here; the Guildmaster needs it back. She's put a very complex spell on it, combining Pallum's Returning Crystal, the Spell of Reversal, and the Spell of the Obedient Object. Precisely thirty-five hours after she placed the enchantment, this tapestry will vanish and return to its rightful owner. It took some time for me to bring it here, so I would estimate you have about thirty-two hours remaining."

"So anyone who isn't out of here by then will be stranded again?"

The apprentice nodded vigorously. "Yes, sir. That's exactly right." He glanced around. "I would suggest that you waste no time. Any delay increases the chances that something will go wrong."

Hanner decided not to ask what could go wrong.

"Now, if you'll excuse me, sir," the apprentice continued, "I will be returning to Ethshar myself. We leave it to you to make sure everyone is out; we will not be sending any further aid. The Guild does not consider anyone who is stranded here after the tapestry vanishes to be our responsibility. Further, if the tapestry is impaired or damaged in any way, that, too, is on your own heads. These things are *expensive*, and we will not risk another one."

"I understand," Hanner said.

The apprentice nodded once more, reached out to touch the tapestry, and was gone. Hanner realized as the youth vanished that he had never even caught the lad's name.

"Who's next?" Gerath called, before Hanner could react.

"Where does it go?" someone called.

"What does it matter?" Gerath demanded. "You know it's safe, or that kid wouldn't have used it."

That didn't necessarily follow, since they had no way of being certain the apprentice had been what he seemed, and that it had been the tapestry, and not some other spell, that made him vanish, but Hanner was not about to say that. Instead he said, "It comes out in a wizard's house on Lower Street. I've seen it before."

That caused a murmur, but then Gerath repeated, "Who's next?"

"I am," Sidor said. He pushed past one of his comrades, stretched out a hand, and disappeared.

That started a rush, but Hanner and Gerath joined efforts to enforce some order, to make sure the tapestry and its appurtenances — like those crystals — were not damaged, and that each traveler had time to step aside, once in Ithinia's house, before the next approached.

One by one, with varying degrees of enthusiasm, Vond's hirelings and the former warlocks vanished through the tapestry.

"Where will we go, in Ethshar?" one of the Called asked, standing unmoving before the tapestry.

"We'll find somewhere for you," Hanner assured her. "My family is rich and powerful, and I'll see to it that something is arranged."

"Go on," Gerath said, pushing her forward. She still did not reach out, but another shove sent her close enough that one hand brushed the fabric, and she was gone.

"We *could* let some of them stay," Hanner said.

Gerath shook his head. "I was sent here to get everyone out, and I'm getting everyone out. If some of them slip back in, that's not my problem. For now, though, everyone goes."

"What about Rudhira?" the last of the Called, a middle-aged man Hanner thought might be named Elner, asked.

Gerath frowned. "I'll make an exception for her. *I* don't want to go searching for a crazed throat-cutting murderer; do you?"

"No," Elner, if that was his name, agreed. He stepped forward, and vanished.

Hanner stared at the tapestry, and the empty patch of floor where Elner had stood, and then turned to look at Gerath.

Crazed throat-cutting murderer?

Technically, Hanner had to admit the description was fairly accurate, but since her attack on Vond had probably saved his life, and quite possibly the lives of hundreds of other people, he did not think of it as "crazed."

There were enough people back in Ethshar who might look on it that way, though, that perhaps Rudhira would be safer stranded here in the refuge. Rothiel had said no one was planning to charge her with murder, but still, there were the mercenaries, and the various Called warlocks who had hoped Vond might restore their magic; she might find a very unfriendly reception on the other side of the tapestry.

But Hanner thought it should be *her* choice, not his.

There were only three men left in the village now — Hanner, Gerath, and Marl. Gerath was starting to look impatient; Marl looked uncertain. "Gerath," Marl said, "I was wondering if…"

"No," Gerath said, grabbing Marl by the arm. "Go."

Marl gave Hanner a look, but Hanner did not meet his gaze. Marl shook off Gerath's grip, then said, "I'm going." He turned, stepped up to the hanging, and disappeared.

"You're next," Gerath said.

Hanner frowned. "Why?" he said.

"Because I said so," Gerath said.

"I wanted to get the other tapestry and take it back with me, to see if it can be repaired," Hanner protested.

"So go get it," Gerath said. "Then get back here."

"You don't need to wait," Hanner said.

"I want to be sure everyone is out of here," Gerath said.

Hanner started to ask why, what concern it was of his, then thought better of it. "All right," he said, "but you can do that just as easily from the other side. If I'm not there in a few minutes, you can go back to Warlock House and come back and get me."

"Or I can wait here."

"If you want," Hanner said. "If you aren't worried about Rudhira popping out of hiding and cutting your throat. She didn't much like you."

Gerath stared at him for a moment, then turned up a palm. "Please yourself," he said. "But if you aren't there in half an hour, I *will* come back for you."

"Of course. I'll just go get the tapestry, then."

"Whatever you like." Gerath watched as Hanner headed for the door, but had marched into the tapestry before Hanner had gone a single step past the threshold.

Out in the street Hanner paused. He looked around, then called, "Rudhira?"

No one answered. Hanner shook his head in disappointment, then ambled across to the house where the ruined tapestry hung.

He brushed it, just to be sure, before taking it down, but it did not transport him anywhere; it was mere lifeless fabric, with a long gash in it.

He had it rolled up and slung on his shoulder, and was halfway back to the other house, when Rudhira stepped around a corner.

"Hello, Hanner," she said.

He stopped in his tracks, and smiled. "Rudhira," he said. "It's good to see you! I was a little worried."

"You shouldn't have been," she said. "I can take care of myself."

"I know, I know, but I'm a worrier." He hesitated, then said, "Thank you. You probably saved my life."

"That was the idea," she answered. "I couldn't let him hurt you."

"You didn't have to —" Hanner began.

"Yes, I did!" Rudhira interrupted. "I had to! I couldn't let him hurt you, Hanner. You're too good a person for that. You...I care too much for you to let that happen! When I saw that sword at your throat, I *had* to."

"You..." Hanner blinked, overwhelmed by her words. At last he managed, "Thank you."

"You're welcome."

"I suppose you couldn't just wound him..." He let his sentence trail off unfinished; he knew the answer even before Rudhira spoke.

"If I left him alive, he would have sent his men after both of us," she said.

"I know," Hanner admitted.

"It's not as if I had never killed a man before."

"I know that, too."

For a moment they stared silently at one another. Then Rudhira said, "So you are going back?"

For a few seconds Hanner hesitated; then he nodded. "I want to see my children," he said. "They haven't seen me for seventeen years, and I want to see how they've grown up, and be sure they're happy. I want to see my sisters. I want to make sure the tapestry that brings people here is somewhere safe. I want to help clean up Vond's mess."

"It isn't *your* mess."

"Still, I want to help. I take it you intend to stay here? The wizards tell me no one's planning to charge you with anything, that the overlord's laws don't apply here, so you *could* come back with me."

She shook her head. "I'm better off here. I like it here."

Hanner looked up at the unmoving sun. "I like it here, too. I think I might eventually miss the moons and stars, though."

"You don't have to come back. You certainly don't have to stay."

"If I come back, I *do* have to stay — that new tapestry is going to disappear soon."

"Is it?"

Hanner nodded. "It's not too late to change your mind," he said. "If you stay here, you'll be trapped."

The little redhead looked around thoughtfully at the deserted village, then nodded. "That's fine," she said.

Hanner had hoped she would reconsider; he did not want to leave her here. It was not, he realized, that he was concerned for her safety; it was that he would miss her. Her outburst proclaiming her concern for him had caught him by surprise, but now that it had sunk in he found himself warmed by the thought. She cared for him, and he cared for her.

He hefted the damaged tapestry. "I'm going to see about getting this thing fixed," he said. "Or maybe commission another one, if I can ever afford it. I'll bring it back here. Then you can come and go as you please."

"So can you," Rudhira pointed out.

"That's true."

There was another moment of silent contemplation; then Hanner said, "I'll come back, whether I have it fixed or not. Eventually. I do want to see my family, all of it, and make sure everything is as right as I can make it. It may be months, maybe even a year or two, but I'll be back."

She looked up at him. "I'll be waiting," she said. Then she smiled, and he dropped the tapestry so he could lean down to kiss her.

A few minutes later, uncomfortably aware that Gerath was probably getting impatient, Hanner pulled away from her. He smiled at her, then hoisted the damaged tapestry back to his shoulder, and trudged into the room where the new, functioning tapestry waited. He reached out toward the image of that sunny, whitewashed room. Just before his fingers touched it, he repeated, "I'll come back."

"I'll be waiting," Rudhira answered again, from the open door.

In the end it was eight months before he could return, but return he did.

And she was waiting.

Chapter Forty

Sterren looked thoughtfully out at the harbor, at the masts swaying slightly as ships rocked at their moorings. The air was cold, but the afternoon sun on his back kept off the worst of the chill.

He glanced up at the overlord's palace, hovering above the Fishertown docks to the east. The workmen were supposed to have its old site prepared for its return any time now, if they didn't already, but rumors said Lord Azrad was in no hurry to give up his newfound mobility. For most of Azrad VII's reign there had been no consensus on just what cognomen should be attached to his name, but now, after more than a decade of being labeled Azrad the Hard to Classify or Azrad the Ambiguous, more and more he was called Azrad the Airborne. He had already taken one aerial cruise along the coast as far as the mouth of the Great River, and had not seemed to be in any hurry to return.

But the spell only lasted a month, and Sterren knew Ithinia had no intention of renewing it, so Azrad would be earthbound again in another few days.

Well, let the overlord enjoy his flying palace while he could. Sterren had had his fill of flying, and he hadn't had a palace around him while he did it. Right now, he had his own concerns.

He had thought, when he escaped from Vond, and then when Vond's death was reported, and when his wife and children had finally reached Ethshar safely and rejoined him, that his worries were over. He had thought he could take his savings from his fifteen years as regent, invest them, and live off the earnings — or if necessary, if the investments failed, then he could live by cheating at dice, as he had when he was a boy. He was, after all, the only warlock left in the World, and almost no one else knew there were *any*. No one would ever suspect him of using warlockry to win. He had thought he would settle here in Ethshar, in his home city, and live happily ever after.

But it seemed that wasn't going to work.

He had thought that the Imperial Council might want him back, and that that might be a problem, but so far there was no hint that they cared one way or another whether he returned to Semma. No messages, magical or mundane, had reached him. From what little Sterren had heard, Lady Kalira seemed to be doing just fine as the new regent.

He had thought some of Vond's victims and enemies might hold a grudge for his service to the late emperor, but again, no one seemed to care.

No, his big problem was one he had never expected at all, and he felt foolish that he had not foreseen it. It was really quite simple, and he should have considered it.

Shirrin didn't like it here.

In fact, that was seriously understating the case. His wife *hated* Ethshar of the Spices. She hated the crowds, the smell, the size of the city. She hated how closed in it felt. She hated not being recognized as a princess and the regent's wife. She said it was dirty and dangerous and decadent, and she wanted to go *home*.

The children weren't quite as emphatic, but they didn't care for Ethshar, either. They, too, wanted to go back to Semma — or at least, to *somewhere* in the Small Kingdoms, somewhere other than this vast, intimidating city.

Sterren, however, did not particularly want to go back to the Vondish Empire. He was not at all certain that he could reclaim his title of regent from Lady Kalira, and if he retired instead, what would he *do* with himself? But he didn't want to make his family miserable.

"May I join you?"

Startled, Sterren looked up to see a man of medium height wrapped in a worn brown cloak. "Of course," he said, sliding over to make room on the bench.

The man sat down, and for a moment the two of them sat silently side by side, looking out at the harbor. A cold breeze brought the odors of fish and salt water to Sterren's nose, and he shivered slightly.

Then the brown-clad man said, "You are Lord Sterren of Semma, I believe? Late of His Imperial Majesty's service?"

Sterren threw the man an uneasy glance. "And if I am? Who are you?"

The man held out a hand. "I am called Kelder of Demerchan," he said.

Sterren had started to stretch out his own hand in response, but at the name "Demerchan" he froze, staring.

Kelder smiled. "Don't worry," he said. "If you were our target, you would already be dead."

"That assumes that *all* you wanted was my death," Sterren replied.

"That's true," Kelder acknowledged. "Let me rephrase it, then, and simply say that we mean you no harm." He lowered his hand, which Sterren's own had never reached.

There was no point in arguing about that; if they *did* mean him harm, there was little he could do to prevent it. "Then what can I do for you, Kelder?" he asked, in the tone he had learned, during his years as regent, to use when speaking with troublesome petitioners.

Kelder's smile broadened. "I'll answer that eventually, my lord, but I would like to discuss a few things first."

"I am at your service," Sterren said, with a bob of his head.

"You indeed do not, I notice, seem to be heavily burdened with other duties at the present time."

"I'm not," Sterren said, pulling his elbows in against his sides.

"I would think a man of your experience would be in great demand."

Irritated, Sterren said, "I doubt you sought me out to discuss my career options."

"On the contrary, my lord, that is precisely why I am here."

Sterren blinked. "What?"

Kelder smiled at him. "You recognized the name Demerchan."

Sterren snorted. "I was Regent of the Vondish Empire for fifteen years. Yes, I have heard the name."

"Of course."

"What does that have to do with anything, Kelder of Demerchan? Why are you talking to me?"

"Bear with me, my lord. Let me begin, then, by saying that despite requests from you, the Imperial Council, and the Wizards' Guild, we had no part in the death of the Great Vond."

"I had wondered," Sterren remarked.

"Many people wondered, and we have no objection if people want to credit us with his removal, but in fact, we were not involved. We had come to the conclusion that the late emperor was worth more to us alive than dead."

Sterren cocked his head. "Why?" he asked bluntly. "He wasn't going to hire any assassins; he was perfectly capable of carrying out his own killings."

Kelder grimaced. "Yes, he was. But the Cult of Demerchan is not merely a company of assassins, and we wanted him alive."

"Why?" Sterren repeated.

"The Cult of Demerchan is dedicated to gathering and preserving knowledge, my lord."

This was the first time Sterren had ever heard anything of the sort. "It is?" he asked. "I thought you were assassins."

"We are. Among other things. The name 'Demerchan' does come from an old word meaning 'hired killer,' but that is not *all* we are. We collect information, as well, and in fact we consider *that* our primary purpose. We protect secrets — we ensure that they are not lost, but also that they do not fall into the wrong hands. Yes, half our name says we are assassins, but do not forget the other half — we are not a guild, or brotherhood, or company, but a *cult*. We have a hidden purpose, and that is the gathering of secrets."

That made a certain amount of sense, and would explain why they had wanted the late emperor alive. "You wanted the secret of Vond's new form of warlockry?"

Kelder nodded.

"What a shame, then, that it died with him," Sterren said.

Kelder smiled again. "We both know it did not," he said.

"Do we?" Sterren said, suddenly very uncomfortable indeed. He glanced over his shoulder to be sure no one else was in earshot — though of course, nowhere was safe from scrying spells.

"We dedicate our entire existence to collecting secrets, my lord," Kelder said. "Did you think we had missed yours, after fifteen years?"

"Well, I had hoped so," Sterren said. He did not see much point in further denials.

"Then I regret to say your hopes have been disappointed. We know that you are a warlock, albeit a weak one, and that Vond attuned you to the power of the towers in Lumeth of the Towers."

"That's very unfortunate," Sterren said. "That you know that."

"Perhaps not. We mean you no harm, my lord, as I said before. Indeed, I am here to offer you a position."

"A position?" he asked warily. "What *sort* of position?"

"As an acolyte in the Cult of Demerchan."

Sterren's jaw dropped. Then he snapped it shut, and said, "I would think I'm a little old to be an acolyte."

"Your age is of no concern, my lord."

"It is to me. I'm not interested in joining a cult. I'm too old for that sort of idiocy."

"I don't think you understand the situation, my lord."

Sterren turned to stare out to sea again. "I understand that you want me because I'm the last warlock in the World, and you want that secret for yourselves."

"Well, yes. That's true. But we did not approach Vond, because we knew he was unfit for the cult, while *you* seem very suitable."

"I do?" He could not resist giving Kelder another glance. "What do you know about it?"

"We have been observing you for fifteen years, my lord, ever since you first went to Semma."

"Oh, *that's* endearing!" Sterren grimaced. "Knowing you've been spying on me just makes me *so* eager to join up!"

"You were the warlord of Semma, and then the Regent of the Vondish Empire," Kelder said. "Of *course* you were watched."

Sterren could hardly deny that it had been reasonable to keep an eye on him, but that still did not make the idea appealing. That was not the important issue here, though. "I'm not interested in joining a cult of assassins so that you can have a warlock at your beck and call," he said.

"Yet I suspect you know almost nothing of the cult's origins and purpose," Kelder said.

"*No one* outside the cult knows its origins and purpose."

"That is not literally true," Kelder assured him. "There are exceptions. And *you*, my lord, are about to be, at least partially and briefly, one of those rare exceptions."

Sterren did not at all like the sound of "briefly," but he ignored that and said, "Go on."

"You are aware, of course, that the Small Kingdoms were once a single nation?"

"Old Ethshar. Of course."

"Yes, the Holy Kingdom of Ethshar. Which went to war, centuries ago, with the Northern Empire."

"Yes."

"You know that the Hegemony of the Three Ethshars was created after the war by the military of Old Ethshar."

"Yes."

"You know that the founders of the Hegemony, Azrad, Anaran, and Gor, made no attempt to reunite the fragments of Old Ethshar."

"Yes, I know that," Sterren said, baffled as to where this was leading.

"They were unable to decide which of the hundreds of squabbling governments in the Small Kingdoms was the legitimate heir to the old national government, so they stayed out of the old homeland. They had had enough fighting and bloodshed, and did not want to intervene in any internal disputes."

"Yes. What does this have to do with Demerchan?"

"Patience, my lord. Now, think back to when you first came to Semma and were thrust into the role of Ninth Warlord, and ordered to defend the kingdom against its neighbors. What resources did you have for your war?"

"Resources?" Sterren was puzzled. "I had a miserable, under-sized, half-trained army."

"What else?"

Baffled, Sterren said, "I had a reasonably defensible castle, and the king let me have some money to hire Ethsharitic magicians."

"What else? Or perhaps I should say, who else?"

Sterren tried to think back. He had been a boy in his teens, dragged from Ethshar at sword-point. Lady Kalira, then the king's trade expert, had been sent to fetch him, accompanied by a couple of the kingdom's biggest soldiers, and had brought him back to Semma Castle, where he had been given his great-uncle's rooms and dressed in his great-uncle's clothes. He had met his officers, and...

And Lar Samber's son. "My spies," he said. "My intelligence service."

"Ah! Yes," Kelder said. "Now, you know that Old Ethshar's armies became Ethshar of the Sands and Ethshar of the Rocks, and Old Ethshar's navy became Ethshar of the Spices, and Old Ethshar's hired magicians became the Wizards' Guild and the Sisterhood and the various schools of magic. But of course Old Ethshar had an intelligence service, too."

"Devoted to collecting secrets, and making sure only the right people knew them," Sterren said. He nodded. "I see. You're claiming that the intelligence service became the Cult of Demerchan."

"Oh, I not only claim it, we can document it. We still operate out of some of the same hidden bases our ancestors used in the Great War. We have tunnels and secret passages and hidden rooms all over the Small Kingdoms. We have ancient magic that has been lost everywhere else."

"Do you?"

Kelder nodded silently.

"Yet the cult of Demerchan let Old Ethshar disintegrate?"

Kelder spread empty hands. "When the government broke apart, like the generals and Admiral Azrad, we didn't know which faction to back. We did know that *we* should stay united, and fight only the Northerners, not one another, so we stayed neutral. We thought that in time the rifts would heal, but instead everything just kept splintering. Eventually we did begin to intervene — it was the cult that first introduced and enforced the rule that no magic is used in wars in the Small Kingdoms, and over the centuries we did remove various individuals who threatened to make matters even worse. I'm sure you've heard that we were available for hire, and we have indeed been happy to accept payment for our actions, but in truth, we always chose our own targets in accord with our own goals."

"I always heard that you refused commissions if you considered the intended target to be morally superior to your client."

"That was a handy explanation, but in fact we removed those we considered dangers to the well-being of the Small Kingdoms as a whole, whether we were hired to do so or not. We tried to find them before they did any real damage. You were one of our failures, Lord Sterren — we had our limited resources elsewhere and did not notice when you brought your little band of third-rate magicians to Semma's aid. The far south had never been an area of great interest for us, as it was poor in magic and the other resources we cared about, so your arrival was not seen as anything of immediate importance. Then, when Vond began his conquests, we did not react quickly — partly because we did not understand where he got his power, but also partly because we did not see the removal of King Phenvel as a bad thing, and Vond's relatively bloodless unification of the southernmost Small Kingdoms seemed like quite a *good* idea to us. In fact, we *still* think the Empire is an improvement on what was there before, so we did nothing to interfere with it."

"Well, thank you for that," Sterren said. "I suppose that any interference would have involved my assassination."

"Probably," Kelder agreed cheerfully.

"But you knew I was a warlock all along?"

"Oh, not *all* along, but we did figure it out after a year or two."

"But you didn't do anything about a warlock ruling the Empire? A magician holding political power?"

"We aren't the Wizards' Guild, my lord, and we don't enforce their rules. We don't even *obey* their rules. We have our own. We are much older than the Guild, my lord."

Sterren stared at the other man.

The only other person he had ever heard speak of the Guild so dismissively had been Vond, and Vond was dead — but the Cult of Demerchan had indeed been around for a long time. Perhaps not as long as this Kelder claimed, but a long time, all the same.

Seeing that Sterren was not going to reply, Kelder continued, "Demerchan failed to preserve Old Ethshar's unity, my lord, but we have preserved most of its secrets, and we have deliberately kept them out of the hands of the kings and councils of the Small Kingdoms, so that they will not be misused, or turned against other heirs of Old Ethshar. In particular, we have preserved as much as we could of the Holy Kingdom's magic. The Wizards' Guild has surpassed us in their own field, and to some extent a witch's abilities depend on the individual rather than anything we can teach, but in sorcery, science, demonology, and theurgy we are the greatest magicians in the World today. It was the cult that kept warlockry severely limited in the Small Kingdoms, but we had our own warlocks, hidden away, until the Calling ended. We have every sort of magic we could discover, and we use that magic to keep the peace, as much as we can."

"That can't be much, then," Sterren said. "There are always wars being fought in the Small Kingdoms."

"Small ones, with relatively little bloodshed. We don't want to interfere too much, or make ourselves obvious, so we do not suppress every little squabble between kings. We *do* keep them from getting out of hand."

Sterren could think of several questions and arguments he could make in response to this claim, but none of them seemed very important just now. He was more concerned with his own situation. "You don't have any other warlocks left?" he asked. "You're based in the Small Kingdoms — no one else ever learned to use the power in Lumeth?"

Kelder shook his head. "No. We've tried. We've particularly been watching the warlocks who came back from Aldagmor with Vond, and none of them have managed it. They just get headaches; they never make the transition Vond did. We've tried to help them, but we couldn't make it happen. Vond must have been a fluke, a freak of nature, one of a kind. We've given up trying to duplicate his experience; there's no point in torturing those poor people. Apparently the headaches are agonizing."

"They did appear to be painful," Sterren said.

"And useless." He shook his head. "No, we haven't found another Vond, another person who could spontaneously attune himself to the Lumeth source. And Vond didn't create any others. You're the only warlock left."

Sterren nodded. "So I'm the only one. So you want to control the remaining warlock, to ensure I don't start any wars or go sending palaces flying?"

"Oh, we aren't worried about you starting any wars or smashing any cities," Kelder said with a wave. "We watched you administer Vond's empire for fifteen years; we know you aren't going to do anything stupid or destructive. No, we want to *protect* you, to preserve the secret of warlockry. You can live almost anywhere in the Small Kingdoms you please, and do what you want, so long as you allow us to keep watch over you, and permit us to study your abilities, so that we can ensure that you don't do anything that would drastically impair our own activities. Perhaps, in time, you might take an apprentice, and should that happen, we would want to be closely involved in selecting a trustworthy candidate."

"That's all?" Sterren waved a hand. "You said you wanted me to be an acolyte; I won't need to wear a robe and live under guard in a temple somewhere?"

"No robes or temples. Unless you want them. And your guards will stay out of sight and let you go wherever you want."

"But I'll have guards?"

"I told you, we want to protect you."

"From what?"

"From the Wizards' Guild."

Sterren blinked. "What?"

"Hadn't you figured that out? The Guild doesn't want *anyone* using the magic of the towers, for anything. They're afraid it might interfere with the towers' actual purpose."

That did indeed fit with what Sterren knew of the Guild's edicts and actions, but he asked, "*What* purpose?"

"Perhaps I'll explain that later. For now, though, I'll just point out that you, my lord, are the only person in the World who *can* use the magic of the towers. The Cult of Demerchan believes that sooner or later, the Guild will decide to remove that potential problem, and the secret will be lost forever. We want to ensure that doesn't happen. We *preserve* secrets, we don't allow them to be destroyed. Which is why I'm here, offering you a position as a ward of the cult. We'll conceal you — and your family, of course — from the Guild. We're very good at that; we've been hiding things from them for centuries."

Sterren looked at Kelder, then back over his shoulder at the crowded streets of Shiphaven, then up at the palace hanging in mid-air — a palace no longer supported by Vond's warlockry, but by a wizard's spell.

"*Anywhere* in the Small Kingdoms?"

"Almost."

"My family will accompany me?"

"If you choose, of course."

"Will you tell them who you are?"

"A convenient fiction can be arranged, if you would prefer not to acknowledge accepting a position among assassins."

"Is this a *paying* position?"

"Of course, my lord! And in addition to a generous allowance, when you complete your acolyte's training you will have access to the cult's magic. All of it."

That was a fascinating detail, and Sterren thought it very interesting that Kelder had left it until last. "I'll want to discuss it with my wife," he said, "but I think we have a deal."

Kelder smiled, and held out a hand. Sterren hesitated only briefly before shaking it.

Two months later, when certain wizards decided that the World would be better off without any functioning warlocks, no matter how feeble those warlocks might be, they could find no trace of Lord Sterren, former Regent of the Vondish Empire. Divinations failed to locate him, or determine what had become of him. It was eventually concluded that Vond must have killed him at some point before the emperor's own death; several witnesses attested to Vond's anger at his missing aide.

And that, so far as the Wizards' Guild was concerned, was the end of warlockry, once and for all.

Epilogue

In the end, it proved surprisingly easy for the Hegemony of the Three Ethshars, the Baronies of Sardiron, and the Small Kingdoms to absorb tens of thousands of former warlocks. Many of the Called returned to trades and positions they had held before the Night of Madness; others became farmers, or joined the overlords' guards, or found other employment that did not require formal apprenticeship. The significant financial assets of the Council of Warlocks in all the various cities were devoted to assisting former warlocks, Called or not, in establishing new businesses; many became locksmiths, tinkers, or artisans of one sort or another, applying the knowledge of materials and structures that they had acquired as warlocks.

Sensella of Morningside returned to her family safely, and became a seamstress. She was not particularly successful at it, but managed to get by.

Edara of Silk Street did not accomplish anything useful for Hanner in her hurried trip to the Wizards' Quarter, but that began a series of curious events that culminated in her employment as a procurer of wizards' ingredients.

Zallin of the Mismatched Eyes, Leth of Pawnbroker Lane, and Feregris of Crookwall became partners in a confectionery shop on Sugar Lane in the New Merchants' Quarter.

Kolar the Large was called upon to testify before assorted magistrates and officials in various hearings, and presented himself well enough to wind up as the personal bodyguard to Lord Augris, the treasurer of Ethshar of the Spices.

Gerath Gror's son decided he was no longer welcome in Ethshar of the Spices, and hired on as a sailor on a Tintallionese trading vessel; his subsequent misadventures eventually led him to become a pirate captain operating out of Shan on the Sea.

Hanner the Generous and his second wife, Rudhira of the Refuge, became the landlords and proprietors of Hanner's Refuge, providing lodging for some three hundred tenants and exporting lumber, seafood, and exotic nuts.

And to Lord Azrad's regret, his palace was safely restored to its original position and never flew again.

11109773R00208

Made in the USA
Charleston, SC
30 January 2012